Predation

SJ Parkinson

Edited by: Rosemary Fifield (Red Adept Publishing)
Cover art by: Christine DeMaio-Rice (Flip City Author Services)
Formatted by: Jason G. Anderson

This is a work of fiction. Any resemblance or similarity to any existing person, business, organization, or place is coincidental and unintended.

ISBN: 0985789956
ISBN-13: 978-0985789954

DEDICATION

For Joanne

She fell in love with me when I had nothing.

That says it all..

CHAPTER 1 – INSERTION

The information in the master navigation server was refreshed millions of times per second. Algorithms compared stored values in the navigation database to the incoming data streams. When the database parameters equaled those values, the master navigation server accessed a series of sub-routines. A reserved COMM channel was activated, and a coded omni-directional burst transmission was sent out. Forty-three star ships of various types received the radio signal. Each individual ship's navigation server processed the content, found it to be authentic, and automatically turned off its Sakharov drive. Star Command Fleet Nine transitioned out of hyperspace and returned to reality just outside the Mindon star system.

Marshal Andrei Vladimir Kosnov observed the multiple surveillance and situation screens after the return to real space. He anticipated no attack at this early stage. The headquarters' intelligence briefing he had received indicated no threat. However, Kosnov was paid to expect the unexpected, and military intelligence was notorious for its inconsistency. For ten seconds, he took in every detail as the displays updated with the latest information. The fleet, his fleet, had retained the standard defense pattern with only minor deviations. The cruiser *Trafalgar* was the farthest out of position, by only eleven kilometers. This was not unexpected, as external sensors did not work in hyperspace, and they had effectively traveled blind over the twelve parsec distance. He noted with satisfaction that the captains of the errant ships were already maneuvering back into the ordered formation.

Kosnov raised his eyes to the Control Center before him. Dull, indirect red lighting illuminated a complex series of control panels and computer displays. Each station had a thick, padded covering to reduce damage during combat. Below the three main situation screens, a soft multi-colored glow from several control boards illuminated twenty men and women on duty in the room.

Kosnov turned to his right and spoke to a man at the Tactics (Space) board. "Mr. Collins, report fleet status."

"Sir," the man replied with a distinctly Australian accent, "all ships have reported in. Our present course and position is on screen. Speed is currently .93 C and decreasing steadily. The *Exeter* suffered a minor meteor hit as we returned to real space, repair time one hour. MASER-COMM is operational fleet wide. No threats on passive systems within two light minutes. Do you want an active search, sir?"

Kosnov thought about that for a moment. A passive search was the least efficient form of search available, but it had the advantage of not alerting the enemy to his location. "Negative, maintain EMCON. Secure from general quarters. Assume yellow alert. Maintain a minimum of two cruisers, a tender, and recce ship at General Quarters until further notice. Set our course and formation to briefed pre-sets. Take us to the first NAV point."

"Yes, sir." Collins began relaying the marshal's orders to the appropriate people through his board.

Kosnov turned his attention to a female officer manning the Communications position. "Commander Shiotu, launch a messenger drone back to Command. Inform them that we're proceeding into the system. Append a copy of the logs and the latest intelligence data. There'll be a tactics and command briefing in one hour. I'll want intelligence, command staff, and the division commanders to attend."

"Yes, sir."

The marshal raised his head slightly to look at the man on duty at the intelligence station. Heavily tanned, he looked as if he had just stepped off a beach moments ago.

"Commander Tran, commence reconnaissance probe launch in five minutes. I want a deep system search pattern with planetary surveillance. Feel free to probe any other targets of interest, but passive modes only until further orders."

"Yes, sir."

Kosnov returned his eyes to the star field on the view screens before addressing the room at large. "There are no other allied ships within this system. From this point on, any unclassified contacts are to be considered hostile. I'm to be notified immediately if any such contact is made. Any hostile contact coming closer than thirty light seconds is to be engaged by the alert cruisers. Commander Collins has the deck, Commander Shiotu has the Conn. I'll be on the forward observation deck if needed."

The marshal removed his chair restraints, stood, and walked to the closed portal at the rear of the command center. Four duty marines in dull black body armor came to attention as the marshal reached the hatch. The senior-ranking marine, a gunnery sergeant, deactivated the hatch lock. When the metal hatch hissed open, the marshal stepped through. The senior marine checked that his sidearm was secure before following the marshal out into the passageway beyond. He fell in step to the left and two steps behind.

Back in the command center a marine guard secured the hatch. As it closed, he announced to no one in particular, "Marshal off the deck."

Military personnel in the passageway moved respectfully off to the side as the marshal and his escort proceeded down the corridor. A loud voice suddenly reverberated off the walls and surprised everyone in the area.

"Marshal!"

A disheveled man in civilian clothes jogged up to Kosnov from a side corridor. He was overweight and carrying a portable digital recorder. Sweat was beginning to form on his brow from the exertion of the short run.

"Marshal... Marshal Kosnov. Francisco Santos, Galactic News Network. We had an appointment for an interview, but your staff said you were unavailable. Do you have time for some quick questions?" Labored breathing interrupted his sentences.

Kosnov did not like dealing with the press, but he knew the military needed public support for the war effort and forced himself to be cordial. He had successfully avoided the reporter in the past, but realized he would have to deal with him sometime. Kosnov offered a firm handshake and forced what he hoped was a genial smile as he spoke. "Of course, Mr. Santos. Would you care to join me on the observation deck?"

"Thank you. Yes." Santos smiled gratefully.

The trio headed toward a small pair of sliding metal doors at the end of the short passageway. No visible controls were on or near the door. When the marshal stepped onto the metal grate before the elevator doors, it lowered slightly with an audible click. The doors opened at once, revealing a small, but rugged, elevator. The men stepped through the doors. With no weight on the external door switch, the doors closed automatically.

"Observation Deck," Kosnov said toward the audio pickup.

The elevator started up smoothly with a discernible hum.

Santos spoke in a frustrated tone. "Marshal, I've been briefed by a member of your intelligence staff concerning what I can and can't report. He also explained the feed will be censored before going to air. Plus, I know I can't file my story until we return to Allen's Rift. If that's the case, and I can't do any 'live' reports, I'd like to travel to several ships and interview as many people as I can during this mission."

Kosnov considered that. "I've no objection to your doing that, sir. If you speak with the press liaison officer, he'll arrange a lighter to carry you where you need to go. The recce ships and their personnel will be off-limits, however. They carry highly classified equipment, and even I don't have the required clearance to go on-board those vessels."

"Thank you, Marshal. I wasn't expecting such courtesy."

After a few moments, the elevator slowed and then stopped. The doors opened and revealed a large room with a series of large rectangular plasteel windows offering an incredible view of the fleet and the stars that surrounded them. The marshal stepped off the elevator and walked up to the port offering the best view. The marine gunnery sergeant exited behind Santos and took position to the left of the elevator doors.

Santos gasped at the clear view of the field of stars. The almost floor-to-ceiling windows provided a panoramic view of billions of distant suns. Kosnov knew Santos had spent the majority of the hyperspace transit in his cramped, windowless cabin.

"Amazing. Do you ever get tired of this view, Marshal?"

Kosnov flashed a genuine smile. "Space flight is never commonplace for me."

"I had heard about the effects of hyperspace from the crew. Is it true this area was off limits during the jump?"

"Yes. Hyperspace travel involves invoking eleven dimensions. It is impossible for the three dimensional human mind to represent that, and being in this room would result in nausea and vertigo at best. There have been rare cases where people have died. All exterior ports and cameras are shut off in transit to avoid that. Even our sensors will not work while in hyperspace."

Santos revealed a voice recorder. "Do you mind if I record your comments?"

"Not at all."

Santos pressed a button on a softball-sized video recorder and tossed it in the air. The recorder arched up, and small repulser plates turned on to keep it suspended in mid-air. The autonomous camera oriented on the reporter as he adopted his interviewer's voice. "This is Francisco Santos of the Galactic News Network. I'm currently on the observation deck of the command ship *Aristotle* with Marshal Andrei Kosnov, commander of Fleet Nine. Marshal, good afternoon."

"Good afternoon, Mr. Santos."

"Marshall, Fleet Nine is currently in an undisclosed system behind enemy lines. I can see several fleet ships behind you through the observation windows. Could you describe the different types of vessels under your command for our viewers?" Santos asked.

The marshal looked over the fleet and began to review his ships and their potential. He gestured at the vessels as he spoke. "Fleet Nine currently contains five major ship classes. Leading the fleet are the reconnaissance ships. They're designed to assess enemy strengths and weaknesses through judicious use of various sensors, drones, and probes. At the moment, the 'recce' ships are searching the vacuum of space for enemy communications and vessels."

Kosnov paused when he saw a reconnaissance ship launch a number of matte black probes. The probes waited several seconds to float clear of the fleet and then activated their ion motors to boost them toward their destinations. The plasma flare that surrounded the ion exhaust was a deep indigo color.

"Tenders are the next ship class. They transport all of the necessary war materiel, fuel, food, ammunition, and consumables for our operations. As you can see, they look almost identical to the cruisers. They have the same internal structure as cruisers, but tenders have no heavy weapons or armor. Attached to the underside of each tender are twenty-four lighters. Since Sakharov hyper-drives will only fit on capital ships, tenders are needed to transport them over interstellar distances and protect them with shields. The lighter itself is essentially a military 'taxi' designed for a multitude of roles: troop transport, resupply, medevac, air-to-air refueling, fire support, etc. Each lighter has a flight crew of two plus at least a load master, and they can carry two fully equipped squads of marine heavy infantry.

"Troop transports come next. We currently have a total force of two divisions of marines plus reserves. Last are the cruisers. You'll notice that unlike the other ships, cruisers have no ports or windows. That's so there's no weak spot in the thick metal/ceramic composite armor. Cruisers are heavily armed, designed to stand in harm's way, and return more damage than they take." Kosnov paused at this point.

"Marshal, you mentioned five ship types earlier, but you only described four," Santos said, leading him on.

"Correct. The last class is the command ship you are on currently. The *Aristotle* is a modified tender that carries the Fleet Nine command personnel, communication equipment, administration, and planning personnel from several staffs."

Kosnov was proud of his command. He had successfully completed two other missions with them before. He had sustained losses, but they were generally lighter than those of some other commanders he could name. Kosnov firmly believed the men and women under his command were his most valuable assets.

"An impressive collection of ships. I overheard a naval rating say that we are currently under 'EMCON.' Could you tell our viewers what that means?"

"Of course. EMCON is an acronym for 'Emissions Control.' That is, we do not broadcast any electromagnetic radiations that can be detected by the enemy. This allows us to go undetected. It's standard practice when penetrating an enemy system to minimize the amount of time they have to prepare for our attack." Kosnov smiled for the camera.

"Forgive me, Marshal, I'm not a technical man. You said earlier that lighters were protected by shields, but is that not a form of electromagnetic radiation? That is, can the enemy not detect them?"

"An excellent observation, Mr. Santos. Most people forget about shields. When moving at high speed, we obviously cannot turn off shields or grievous damage would be caused by micro-meteorites. It is, indeed, emitted radiation and can be tracked, but as the energy is sent directly out to the front of the fleet, it is hard to do so. Think of it like a flashlight. Unless you were standing in the beam itself, you would never see it. We purposely set a course that minimizes the probability of enemy detection."

"Marshal, Senator Fielding was recently quoted as saying the military had not embraced technology as much as it should have. He went on to say that a lot of the weaponry in use was 'antiquated,' and he was pushing for a new spending bill to update military weaponry across the board. What are your thoughts on that?"

There it is. The real question. Santos is not as naïve as he presents himself to be. He knows the military is resisting the Senator's modernization plans, and he wants me to add fuel to the fire. He certainly took his time leading up to it.

Kosnov put his hands behind his back and tried to look relaxed. "Well, Mr. Santos, far be it from me to correct the Chairman of the Senate Appropriations Committee for the Armed Services. However, I can give you one example. Many advances had been made in designing new weapons for the infantry, but time after time the military has stuck with the tried and true rifle. The Advanced Weapons Proving Ground on Mars has field-tested programmable flechette rounds, smart bullets, rail guns, and even portable lasers over the last ten years. On a range against fixed paper targets, they look formidable, but hitting moving creatures in combat environments is a different thing entirely. Due to the heavy gravity of their home worlds, Drakk'Har have three times the muscle and bone density of a human, and those types of weapons just tend to make them angrier. The advanced weapons are heavier, less reliable in the field, have limited ammunition, and are prone to fail in battle conditions. That is never a good confidence builder for the men and women who handle them. A simple bullet has better accuracy, stopping power, and reliability. Not to mention they are available at a substantially reduced cost. Now, I may not know much about politics, but I do know the public does not have bottomless pockets, and they want the military to conduct ourselves in a financially responsible manner." Kosnov smiled slightly before continuing. "I know Senator Fielding has many weapon manufacturing corporations in his district, and you certainly cannot blame him for presenting the views of his constituents."

Santos nodded. He changed the topic again. "Now that we're out of hyperspace, can you tell us where we are and what your mission is? As you said, we only have two marine divisions, and that certainly isn't enough to take a planet. I have heard rumors we are invading a small outpost colony."

"Sorry, Mr. Santos. The scuttlebutt is wrong. We've come thirty-nine light years to rip up the largest vegetable garden in the galaxy." The marshal said it with a deadpan expression.

"Marshal?" was all Santos could reply, the confusion evident on his face.

Kosnov laughed heartily. "That's all right, Mr. Santos. When the Star Fleet Commander told me the same thing, I didn't believe him either. This is what we have planned."

Kosnov outlined the basic mission to the reporter.

* * *

Staff Sergeant Julio Mendez of the 121st Special Forces Detachment lay in his hillside listening post in total silence. His CKP-12 automatic rifle lay cradled on the narrow berm of earth before him. The CKP-12 was standard issue to all Special Forces troops. The rifle was designed to operate in all environments, including total vacuum and even underwater to a limited degree. Mendez thought about that as he lay there. From the amount of rain that had fallen, the weapon may as well have been underwater. The falling moisture had been continuous for three days and had varied from drizzle to downpour in unpredictable swings.

Mendez ignored the cold dampness that was his constant companion. The shallow camouflaged position he occupied had been constructed six days previously by his section. Since then, it had been manned continuously. Three listening posts surrounded a Special Forces base camp sited in a minor depression on top of a densely overgrown hill. The hill was designated as number 237—its height in meters.

Hill 237 overlooked two strategic river junctions, one to the northeast, and the other to the west. Mendez could see neither of those junctions from his location. However, his position was the most important of the three. A crude, sprawling town lay two kilometers away across a narrow river bordered by dense swamp on both sides. The town itself was half in the swamp, resulting in algae-infested water being present throughout many of the streets. This didn't seem to upset the occupants, who moved through the water with ease.

The homes of the town occupants looked like hollowed-out trees. They were stubby, without leaves, and covered by thick lichen and fungus. All of the structures appeared identical in shape, but each was a slightly different size. Mendez estimated the town population to be approximately eight thousand.

A short distance beyond the town lay a sprawling complex of one-story structures. They were arranged around several hundred immense constructions of various sizes. Details were impossible to discern, as the constructs were liberally covered with a thick, fuzzy, green and brown growth. Mendez used the word "constructions" because he was sure that they were not natural. Yet, he had never seen any of the complexes' workers add anything to them.

Several tunnel entrances lay at the edge of the town. They appeared to head under several of the largest constructions. Mendez had seen many creatures from the town report to these tunnels on a regular schedule. He deduced over time that the occupants worked beneath them on regular shifts.

The complex and surrounding area had been the focus of his special forces team for almost a week. They were ordered to observe and make note of any patrols, construction facilities, defenses, or unusual activity in this area, along with any traffic on the river below.

Mendez's view of the town improved as the rain finally stopped. With the most subtle of movements, the soldier slowly placed the town in the center of his rifle scope and selected full magnification. Few town occupants were visible, as their green color matched the surrounding foliage perfectly. Earth scientists classified the creatures as reptilian. Few live specimens had been collected because of their ferocity. Mendez had been told they called themselves Drakk'Har.

After three years of fighting them, the humans had built up basic knowledge about their history. An adaptive and cunning race, the Drakk'Har were capable of interstellar travel. Over seven hundred years, the Drakk'Har had conquered seventy-three worlds. The inhabitants of the conquered worlds were placed in one of two categories—for consumption or eradication. Those marked for consumption were shipped back to Drakk'Har colonies. They selected the healthiest of each species for breeding purposes to ensure future food stock. Any determined to be unsuitable for breeding were exterminated. Drakk'Har were cold-blooded, both physically and emotionally.

Mendez watched one of the Drakk'Har as it left its home and moved toward one of the tunnel entrances near the complex. The creature walked on its thick hind legs, propelling itself in a slow, upright waddle. Mendez knew that the slow walk was deceptive. On all fours, an adult could sprint up to thirty kilometers an hour for very short distances. They were all excellent swimmers and spent a good portion of their time in water. Although they were air breathers, they could remain under water for periods of up to half an hour. More precisely, thirty minutes was the longest anyone had ever observed them underwater. No one really knew the creatures' limits.

His observations were interrupted when the tactical contact lens he wore in his right eye flashed red three times. Something had just crushed several nanosensors that had been spread on the adjacent trails. He knew that "something" weighed more than twenty kilos, as that was the minimum weight required to set them off. A loud rustling sound to his left confirmed that, and he focused his attention on that area. Only his eyes moved. The noise was too regular and consistent; something large was moving through the thick vegetation. Then he heard a branch snap. Mendez knew it could not be his troops making the noise. His people would approach only from the rear after tugging twice on a piece of staked commo wire to announce their presence. Moving nothing but his jaw, Mendez keyed the COMM switch between his teeth twice. He paused and then keyed it five more times. The signal traveled down the commo wire toward the camp behind him.

* * *

Lieutenant Braden Pratt was in the hilltop base camp finishing a mundane meal of cold roast beef, potatoes, and gravy from a dull silver ration pouch. The chilly temperature of this world was not at all what he was used to. The officer had been born and raised on the island of Jamaica. Before he had joined the military, Pratt had never worn anything heavier than shorts, a T-shirt, and if a formal occasion, sandals. Now he wore micro-fleece underwear, a sweater, and two pairs of socks to keep warm under his rain gear. Even so, he still shivered occasionally as the chill of the day penetrated.

Habitually, he would stretch out in the sunlight to get warm. However, the red dwarf that the locals called a sun wouldn't be able to warm a cup of tepid tea. And this was their summer!

On a cloudless day, the sky was a dull pink instead of the cobalt blue he was accustomed to on Earth. The local vegetation didn't seem to be affected by the lack of warmth or decent sunlight. In fact, an overabundance of semi-tropical plant life was everywhere. It had taken him a while to notice the lack of large animal life, however. The only things that seemed to proliferate here were snakes and millipedes. As Corporal Jacobs would say in his southern accent, "I's guess dey's ain't good eatin', suh."

The officer shook his head, once more regretting answering the DigiVid advertisement for the military. DigiVid commercials always showed the good side of service life. They never showed a man who had not shaved or washed for six days. They never pictured a man eating cold rations in the middle of an alien jungle. Pratt was sure that they never showed someone hiding on a hill, avoiding poisonous snakes or multi-legged insects from a horror film. Weren't there any "truth in advertising" laws?

The proximity of the camp to the Drakk'Har town meant he could not risk an open fire to heat meals or water for washing. The section was equipped with chemical heat packs for warming meals. However, the men were using those in their sleeping bags to eliminate the constant dampness that permeated the camp. The lieutenant didn't think being hot would have helped the flavor of his meal in any case. Pratt had not had a hot meal since the *Wraith* class ship had covertly dropped him and his team onto Mindon-2 from low orbit almost a week ago.

He had just begun to form a mental picture of his mother's Yam & Banana with Saltfish, when two bursts of static from his COMM earpiece jolted him back to reality. Pratt knew at once that a potentially dangerous situation was developing. The two static bursts indicated that listening post two was reporting some form of activity. This in itself was rare. Everyone was under orders not to use COMMs except for emergencies. Secondly, Pratt knew that Staff Sergeant Mendez was in LP Two, and as his most experienced NCO, he was not the type to break COMM silence unless absolutely necessary.

Five more bursts of static were received. This was the "Danger Imminent" signal. Pratt quietly snapped his fingers twice to get everyone's attention. Holding his hand in the air, he pointed at the sky with a single finger and spun his forearm. Every soldier in camp saw this and began to gather personal weapons and equipment as quickly and quietly as possible.

Pratt picked up a length of commo wire and wordlessly indicated to everyone in camp to hook up to the wire. The soldiers in the LPs were already wired in. The camp had kilometers of thin green field wire spread out in a spider web pattern. While radio transmissions could be tracked, signals sent over landlines were impossible for the Drakk'Har to detect. With the section connected to the wire, he could communicate to them all.

Pratt keyed his voice microphone and spoke with a low, even voice, "Two, this is Six. Understand you have activity at your position. Have you visual contact, over?"

* * *

Sergeant Mendez received this message in his padded earpiece. He still could not see anything, but the movement was close enough that he could not speak without being overheard. He keyed the COMM switch held between his teeth twice. Negative.

"Roger Two, no visual contact. Report contact position."

Mendez considered this. He imagined that he was at the center of an analog watch dial, with twelve o'clock to his front and six o'clock directly behind him. Nine and three o'clock were left and right of him, respectively. He determined that the noise was coming from approximately ten o'clock, so he keyed two long bursts. A long static burst indicated five, while each short burst equaled one.

"Roger Two, contact at ten o'clock position. What is the direction of travel?" Pratt asked.

Again, Mendez imagined a clock-face. The noise was heading directly toward him. He drew a mental line from the ten o'clock position through the center of the watch face and then keyed the mike four times quickly.

* * *

Damn, thought Pratt, *they're heading straight for the LP*. Pratt felt his adrenaline rising. He had extensive training, but had never been tested in combat. He had endless doubts about his ability to perform under fire, but hid them well. However, his training reflexively kicked in and allowed him to override his feelings for the moment. "Roger Two, direction of travel directly toward you. Standby and report visual contact. Break-

Break. Sergeant Smith, take Jacobs, Popov, and White. Occupy position Bravo. You are to cover LP Two and provide covering fire if needed. Do not fire unless LP Two comes under attack." Even though Sergeant Smith was only five meters from him and in plain sight, the lieutenant transmitted his orders to keep everyone in the section informed of what was going on. He also wanted Mendez to know that he was getting backup.

"Occupy position Bravo, cover LP Two, and do not fire unless fired upon. Roger, sir." Smith disconnected himself from the field wire, gathered the named troops, and proceeded downhill toward position Bravo.

Only one soldier remained in camp with the lieutenant. The camouflage uniform she wore was liberally covered with local moss, plants, and foliage. Called a "ghillie suit," each one was customized for whatever environment needed. *Ghillie* was the Gaelic term for a tree spirit that hid in trees, bushes, and vegetation. Corporal Jefferson had taken burlap, invisible fishing line, and super glue and literally spent hours adding local plants and grasses to the outside of a fine mesh undergarment. The result was a simple, but efficient, method of camouflage. High-tech adaptive fabrics that could blend into any background automatically existed, but the ghillie suit did not short out when wet, required little maintenance, did not require heavy batteries or power supplies, and was ten thousand times cheaper.

When not moving, the ghillie camouflage blended into the local foliage, and the sniper looked like a bush. However, bushes didn't normally carry malevolent-looking, long-barreled weapons with a large, complicated scope on top.

The officer turned off his mike before speaking. "Jefferson, find a good position to cover LP Two. We may need to retreat along the back of the hill. If I give the word to abandon the camp, you'll need to draw off any enemy from our withdrawal route, then meet us at the alternate site."

Jefferson simply nodded, turned, and disappeared from view within a few meters. She was the section sniper. Hitting a tennis ball-sized target consistently at a distance of six hundred meters was no challenge for her.

The lieutenant began to make his way to Position Bravo.

* * *

Position Bravo lay a hundred meters below the crest of the hill just above LP Two. The position had two independent, deep fire trenches with overhead cover. The arcs of fire from the trenches overlooked both LP Two and the area beyond.

Sergeant Smith moved his people into the trenches and instructed them to keep watch for any movement. A low mound of grassy earth between LP2 and Bravo would protect Mendez from any rounds fired from the trenches as long as he stayed prone. The grass in this part of the hill was waist high, and the computer-designed camouflage uniforms that Mendez and the rest of the section wore were designed to break up regular patterns. Furthermore, green shades of camouflage paint had been liberally applied to hands, face, and neck to distort their lines. Even the lieutenant and Corporal Jacobs wore camouflage, and their skin was a natural deep brown.

Smith could not see LP Two, but he was not expecting to. He knew exactly where LP Two was, however. He set up the arcs of fire accordingly. Popov handled the section light machine gun, or LMG, beside him, and earlier he had been told exactly where he could and could not fire.

* * *

Motion just off to his left caught Mendez's attention. He was careful to move only his eyes. The rest of his body remained immobile to let his uniform blend into the undergrowth. Six Drakk'Har warriors came into the area immediately before his listening post. They were stocky creatures that walked upright on short legs. Their average height was two meters. They walked slowly, balancing themselves with a broad tail that dragged behind them. Short muscular arms hung from either side of the body and terminated in three-fingered webbed hands with wicked black claws. A smaller side claw acted like a human thumb. The entire head and body were covered with scales of various sizes. The fronts of the creatures were protected with many small scales that were almost white in color and smoothly polished. Thicker, rougher green scales shielded the backs, sides, and tails of the creatures. Brown eyes with a thin yellow iris surrounding black pupils were set one hundred eighty degrees apart above a rounded snout. White rows of long narrow teeth were visible through partly open jaws. Mendez had witnessed their legendary ferocity over many days of observation. They were a cruel and savage race of animals.

They were all adult males carrying weapons with stubby barrels. Mendez had opportunity in the past to examine Drakk'Har rail guns. Most of the weapon weight was due to a high-density power supply. When activated, the released energy was channeled into thin wiring wound thousands of times around the barrel. This caused an extremely high-strength magnetic field that propelled a two-millimeter piece of metal down the barrel. The projectile was accelerated by the magnetic field to incredible speeds. Due to the great velocity of the projectile, it delivered large amounts of kinetic energy to the target. A Drakk'Har weapon could fire at a rate of five hundred rounds per minute.

The weapons weighed thirty-two kilos fully loaded and could punch a hole through two centimeters of steel. The Drakk'Har carried the cumbersome weapons with distressing ease. They all wore wide utility belts diagonally over a shoulder. Attached to the belts were extra ammunition, plus large gray knives, sixty-five centimeters long with rough serrated edges on both sides of the straight blade. Two of the Drakk'Har each carried large sacks over their shoulders that moved of their own accord.

After ensuring that no more Drakk'Har were joining them, Mendez keyed his COMM unit twice. Visual Contact.

* * *

Lieutenant Pratt had slipped into one of the Bravo position trenches and had just connected his COMM unit to the field wire when the dual hiss of static sounded in his earpiece. He saw movement in the distance, but could not see clearly because of the terrain and grass. Pratt keyed his voice mike and spoke very quietly. "Two, this is Six, roger. We've occupied Bravo above your position. Are they crocs?"

Mendez clicked his COMM unit once in response. Affirmative.

"Roger, Two. Stand by." Pratt took his weapon and used his sight to attempt to locate the creatures. High grass prevented the lieutenant from seeing any of the creatures. A quick check with the others revealed that they couldn't see the group, either.

"Two, this is Six. We can't see them. Are there more than five in the group?"

* * *

Mendez took a few seconds and reconfirmed the count of Drakk'Har. The creatures had stopped directly in front of the sergeant's position and formed a rough circle. They sat on their haunches facing each other.

Mendez clicked once. Affirmative.

"Roger, Two. Are there more than ten?" Pratt responded.

Two clicks were sent. Negative.

"Roger, Two. Send one click for each creature over five."

One click.

"Roger, you have six Drakk'Har in sight. Are they armed?"

One click.

"Two, what is their o'clock direction of travel?"

Mendez purposely gave no response. Ten seconds passed. The lieutenant's voice continued. "Two, have the creatures stopped moving?"

One click.

"Roger, Two. What is their o'clock position from your position?"

One click.

"Roger, Two. They are at your one o'clock position. Are they more than ten meters from your position?"

Two clicks. Negative.

"Roger, Two. Are they more than five meters from your position?"

Two clicks.

"Two, send one click for every meter they are away from you."

One click.

* * *

Whatever chill he had felt earlier disappeared in a heartbeat. Lieutenant Pratt continued with his voice as low as possible. "Two, this is Six. Confirm you have an armed patrol of six Drakk'Har one meter or less from your position at your one o'clock."

One click. Affirmative.

* * *

"Aw, c'mon, Sarge, you gotta know something about the mission."

That voice would cut glass, thought Marine Sergeant Peter Blake. It certainly reverberated harshly off the hard metal walls of the troop transport. This was the third time in as many hours the same marine had asked the same question with only minor variations to the whine in his voice.

Blake turned, taking the stub of an unlit cigar out of his mouth to use as a crude pointer. "Perkins! I have had it with you! The marshal will brief the division commanders who will brief the regiments. They will then personally fly over here and brief the company and platoon commanders. Then, 2nd Lieutenant Wicks will tell ALL of us what the damned mission is. Now, get your gear squared away, and CLEAN THAT WEAPON! You have enough dust bunnies on that rifle stock to open your own rabbit ranch."

Blake leaned closer and lowered his voice slightly, but everyone in the cabin could still hear every syllable. "Dust bunnies breed, Perkins. They take one look at your bunk space and see that they are as safe on your gear as an endangered species in a National Park! Now get OUT of my face, and get your ass to work, unless you want to take a shot at cleaning every last head on this transport on the trip home!"

It never amazed Blake how yelling relieved his own tension. It must be some sort of empathic thing. He felt great at the moment, and he could see PFC Perkins shrinking from his tirade. Anyway, his point had been made.

Blake turned and made his way to the end of the corridor, leaving a somewhat paler Perkins in his wake and several junior troops scrambling to get out of his way. His hand slammed against the hatch controls, and he disappeared through the bulkhead.

* * *

The locks engaged behind Blake, and the marines began to pull out the hidden cards and poker chips from under their helmets and other gear.

"Damn it, Perkins. He would've been through here two minutes ago if you hadn't opened your big yap. OK, who didn't ante?" Lance Corporal Reid asked.

"Messina," Belliveau said.

"Damn, I was hoping no one noticed. The cards suck today," Messina responded while throwing in a chip.

"So, listen. I'm still trying to get this naval rank thing down." Perkins had forgotten all about the sergeant. However, he would clean his weapon after the game just to make sure it did not come back to haunt him. "So, the guy in charge of this ship is a captain? I would've thought it would be a colonel, at least."

"No, you idiot. He's a naval captain," Belliveau said while shuffling cards. "A naval captain is a four striper. A marine captain is a two striper. A navy captain is the same as a marine colonel. The marines descended from a different command structure than the navy. Understand?" He began to deal.

"Hey, cut those cards first," Perkins interjected.

Belliveau collected the few cards he had dealt and piled them in front of Messina. Messina cut then unevenly, and Belliveau dealt them.

"Ok, so what's the same as a navy lieutenant then?"

"Navy lieutenant is the same as a marine captain, two striper. The rank names are different, and maybe the collar insignia, but they all wear the same number of rings on their cuff for dress uniform."

The small group looked at their cards before continuing. Perkins threw in three red chips in the pile and continued talking. "OK, so a three-striper navy lieutenant commander is the same as a marine major then."

"Exactly." Then in a British accent reminiscent of their lieutenant, Cole continued, "By George, I think he's got it." The group laughed as Cole added three more chips to the pot.

Perkins was starting to see the light, but was still confused. "OK, so if a lieutenant commander is three stripes, and a captain is four stripes, then what is a commander?"

That threw the group, and a pregnant pause followed as they thought about it. The pot was growing steadily. Bets were raised and met around the small group.

The answer came from the other side of the room. A young, slender, Latino woman lounged on her bunk and spoke without taking her eyes from the reading tablet on her stomach. "A commander is the same rank as a naval captain. You can only have one captain in charge of a ship. Any other four stripers on a ship are referred to as commanders. 'Captain' is a title instead of a rank. On smaller vessels, junior ranks like lieutenants can be 'captains.'"

"Thanks, Corp. Makes sense. In boot, if it moved, we saluted it and called it 'sir.'" Perkins called the last bet. The pile of chips looked respectable, but the total amount involved would barely have bought lunch for a single person at a deli.

"Well, then, looks like Lady Luck favors me tonight. I have the same hand as the reason my dad used when he kicked me out. Full house, tens over fours." Cole reached for the pot and immediately had his hand held down by Perkins stopping him.

"Sorry, bud." Perkins smiled broadly, revealing his cards. "Queens over Kings. Now *that* is a full house. I may not know navy ranks, but I sure as hell know that my hand beats yours."

"Damn, you beat my full house?" Cole said dejectedly as Perkins hauled the piled chips toward him.

"By George, I think he's got it." Perkins's attempt at a British accent was horribly mangled, but it got a bigger laugh.

* * *

Sergeant Blake made his way past seemingly endless bunk rooms. Each space contained troops in the same basic outfit. Green T-shirt, fatigue pants, and boots. Some read, some slept, others cleaned weapons or fiddled with their gear configuration. He saw several minor issues as he passed, but said nothing. They were not his people and, therefore, someone else's problem. Troop transports were completely different from the cruise ships he used to work on in his youth. No one on the ship knew he used to be a deck hand for Royal Panoramic Cruises. Until the war began, he had journeyed around the seas and oceans of Earth with no other desire than to achieve his twenty-year pension and maybe work up to a billet in the engineering department. Engineers made decent pay, and unless things went wrong, they had a fairly easy time doing routine maintenance. He had no drive or ambition to do anything else.

His career path changed drastically when a Drakk'Har scout ship encountered an exploration ship in remote space. The scout ship approached the vessel without any radio or detectable communications and boarded it. Internal cameras recorded the bloodbath that ensued. When the ship was discovered a week later by an Earth Cruiser, the recordings of the boarding were found and sent back to Earth along with subsequent footage shot by the cruiser crew. The dozen crew were missing, and blood was everywhere. The images shocked even the hardest of civilian and military officials. When the tape leaked out to the Galactic News Network, even the heavily censored version incensed the entire population. A second, larger vessel suffered the same fate soon after and the Earth Federation mobilized for war. Three weeks after the tape aired, Blake became a member of the military when the Federation President signed the Emergency Powers Bill into law. This authorized the drafting of all necessary persons, including the merchant marine on all colonies and planets.

As Blake proceeded through the troop deck, he observed the functional design. The *Sirius* was a standard troop transport that had come out of the Epsilon Eridani production yards quite recently. Each compartment had room for sixteen people or two squads. Blake's third squad had gotten lucky and was berthed alone, so everyone had a spare bunk and a lot of extra room. Each compartment had airtight blast hatches at either end that led to cross-connecting corridors.

Blake made his way through the maze of corridors. He never bothered to check the color-coded signs at each intersection. He had memorized the deck layout for all levels and could find his way through the ship blindfolded. Experience had taught him that he had to be familiar with his surroundings at all times. He made his way to the mess hall where the various shifts of marines and naval crew ate. The sergeant looked around and saw his superior, Second Lieutenant Wicks, across the room in a section of tables considered "officers' country." Except for the stewards serving and clearing dishes, non-officers were not allowed in that area.

He walked to the border of officers' country and waited until he caught the L-T's attention. The lieutenant excused himself from his companions and walked over to the sergeant. Wicks was a decent officer. He always asked the right questions and always solicited Blake's advice. *He may not act on the advice I give him,* Blake thought, *but at least I know he hears me.*

When the lieutenant got within the standard three paces, Blake straightened and saluted with his palm facing the deck. Wicks, in deference to his old regimental tradition, returned the salute with his palm facing the sergeant and spoke in his clipped British accent, "Good afternoon, Sergeant. How are the troops getting on?"

"They're doin' fine, sir. They're looking forward to getting out of this tuna can and onto *terra firma*. If it's convenient, L-T, we need to go over a few details for the operation. Since the raid on Dracor, we're still short one heavy weapon, and we should readjust the section to compensate. Plus, we have three newbies with no combat experience. I'd like to pair them up with seasoned troops."

The lieutenant indicated the sergeant should take a seat at an empty mess table in the enlisted section. Protocol dictated officers could sit in the enlisted section, but not *vice versa*.

"Excellent idea about the new recruits," the lieutenant said. "I had a concern about the new blokes, as well. Apart from you, Corporal Sanchez and Lance Corporal Cole have the most combat experience, but they work together well on point, and I would hate to split them up."

"Yes, sir," the sergeant said. "However, Lance Corporals Belliveau and Reid have a few raids under their belts, and I was thinking of them. If we're doing any patrolling, we need our best people on point. We could pair Johnston and Tyler with them. That leaves PFC Perkins. I can take him."

"Why do you want Perkins, Sergeant?" the lieutenant asked without pause.

Blake thought about this for a moment. *Better be straight*, he thought. Wicks appreciated the truth. "Sir, Perkins is the nervous type. I've seen men like him before. Once seasoned, he should be fine, but unless we keep a close watch on him, he may panic and endanger the section. I figured I'd be the best person to do that."

"Sergeant, I need you focused, as you will be quite busy looking after your fire team. With three new recruits, we will be handling more than our share of problems. What say we make

Perkins squad radio operator? Then he will be with me and more or less out of the fray. That leaves you free to wander about without distraction. Plus, with Perkins as RAD-OP taking over from PFC Messina, you get him back as an extra rifleman. If we give Messina the grenade launcher, we fill the hole left by the heavy weapon loss."

Blake was amazed at the elegance of the suggestion. "Yes, sir. That makes good operational sense. I'll take care of that. Is there anything you needed from me, sir?"

"Yes, Sergeant. Please ensure the troops have the opportunity to post messages to loved ones prior to the mission briefing. There will be no time afterwards, and I shall make quite sure they are on the daily message drone back to Fleet HQ prior to insertion. There will be a COMM blackout soon. I don't want their letters to be held up for the duration. The General left for the command ship a few hours ago, so it will not be long before we brief. I will be in touch when I know more details. Thank you, Blake. Carry on."

"Yes, sir." The Sergeant saluted crisply and left the way he had come in.

CHAPTER 2 – BRIEFING

The command ship briefing room was centered on a large circular table three meters in diameter. The table had several small computer display terminals built in flush with the surface near the edge. In the center of the table was an opaque, two-meter diameter piece of plastic. The plastic glowed with a faint light blue aura from an unseen light source beneath it. Ringing the table were several high ranking officers and selected aides. They were engaged in low conversations, attempting to cover the endless series of minor details that all military operations generate.

An access hatch hissed open. Commander Collins, the Tactics (Space) officer, stepped into the room. He expertly sidestepped and, in a clear voice, announced, "Ladies and gentlemen, Marshal Kosnov."

Everyone in the room was already standing, but they straightened to attention, and maintained complete silence.

Kosnov stepped into the briefing room followed by several members of his planning staff.

"At ease, everyone." He walked to his prepared position at the briefing table.

An intelligence warrant officer waited until the last of the planning staff was in the room. She then closed the hatch behind them.

Once the hatch was secured, Kosnov punched his personal access code into the terminal before him. A three-dimensional representation of the local star quadrant appeared above the table and began to rotate slowly. Everyone shifted around the table for a decent view.

The holographic projector beneath the table's surface realistically presented thick clusters of white stars. On closer inspection, you could see that a couple of hundred stars were colored either red or blue. The red represented known Drakk'Har star systems, while the blue represented Federation colonies. The red and blue stars bordered each other at several points. Three of the stars depicted near the border alternately flashed red and blue.

The marshal looked around the room at large before starting.

"Good afternoon. Since the sudden start of hostilities three years ago, the Federation has been forced to slowly retreat from the Drakk'Har Alliance. This was done to maintain a cohesive defense line and to give us time to build up our forces. We've only gone on the offensive with small raids behind their main lines. These attacks forced them to reinforce rear echelon areas with front line units. That also slowed down their offensive, and it gave us time to build the necessary ships we needed. Our strategy to this point has been limited to conducting hit and run raids behind enemy lines to keep the Drakk'Har Alliance off balance." Kosnov paused to let what he said sink in. "Today, that strategy changes."

The marshal pressed a raised stud near his terminal. The holographic starfield began to expand in size. Hundreds of stars disappeared as they passed beyond the edge of the holo-projection. In a few seconds, only one star remained. The holo continued to zoom in until five planets could be seen rotating around the single remaining red star.

Kosnov continued, "This is a representation of the Mindon star system. It lies well behind established front lines and has never been attacked before. Intel tells us the Mindon system has been held by the enemy for roughly three hundred years. Intelligence also indicates that this system, specifically planet Mindon-2, is a major source of Alliance warships. Colonel Pierce has the details." Kosnov indicated a thin officer across the table with intelligence insignia on his collar.

"Thank you, sir." Pierce stepped forward, pausing to nervously adjust his glasses before continuing to the room at large. "Two recent raids in Alliance space have given us specific evidence that Mindon is a large, if not the largest, builder of Alliance warships. Initially these reports were discounted because spectrographic analysis of Mindon-2 suggested it to be mineral poor, and it had limited orbital facilities. Also, it simply did not make sense that the Alliance would transport metals from other star systems to Mindon because of the distances involved.

"However, two months ago, during the battle at Vega, we were fortunate enough to capture a Drakk'Har warship reasonably intact. The crew was killed by explosive decompression, and auto-destruct devices on the ship and data banks failed due to battle damage. Analysis of this vessel provided some startling data. Ladies and gentlemen, we have determined that the Drakk'Har Alliance does not build their warships, they grow them."

A period of total silence followed the intelligence officer's last statement. Everyone knew the size of the ships they had encountered in the past.

The first one to react was General Carstairs. "I don't know about the rest, but I find that piece of information very hard to swallow, Colonel."

Several people began talking at the same time. Kosnov quickly rapped a stylus against the holo-table and spoke. "Save any questions or discussion for the end of the briefing. Continue, Colonel."

The thin intelligence officer looked directly at Carstairs and said, "Sir, I understand your apprehension. Intelligence headquarters ordered three separate sets of tests on the Alliance hull before accepting the findings. However, there's supporting evidence for this. First, the Drakk'Har have been found to use very little metal in their industries. Ceramics, plastics, and some composites are the predominant building materials they use. Their ability to manipulate those substances is far in excess of our own knowledge. For example, metallic parts on the main engines on the captured vessel comprised less than two percent of the assembly.

"Second, although Mindon-2 is mineral poor, it's an extremely rich environment for vegetation with lots of water. We theorize that by using genetic programming, another field the Drakk'Har are extremely good at, they're able to produce warships of whatever size and shape they desire. After the hull is fully-grown, they layer a plastic/ceramic shield over the outside for increased armor protection. Then life support, gravity generation equipment, and engines are fitted. We found strong evidence to support all that.

"Lastly, in the three years that Star Command has conducted raids against the Alliance, we've found no ship construction facilities on or in orbit around any of their worlds. In the past, we have been trying to hurt them like a human enemy by hitting their mineral-rich worlds to disrupt their ship production. In fact, all past raids have done nothing but cause them minor inconvenience. Marshal."

The marshal nodded and spoke. "Thank you, Colonel. It's obvious that hitting a major source of their warships will give us a great advantage. However, the general staff has decided that we do more than just raid this time. Gentlemen, the long-term mission is to occupy and hold Mindon-2."

Following the marshal's statement, the people in the room exchanged a series of strange looks and low murmurs. The fact that Fleet Nine had only two marine divisions was well known. Strategy also dictated that to execute a successful planetary occupation, you needed to have at least twice, if not three times, that number of men.

Kosnov impatiently rapped again for attention and continued, "Ladies and gentlemen, the name of this operation is 'White Raven.' Our ultimate objective is to seize control over Mindon-2 and establish a base behind the Drakk'Har lines for deeper strikes into their territory."

An aide pressed a series of buttons on the holo-table. The hologram zoomed in on the second of the five planets until a large, semi-transparent image of Mindon-2 was represented over the table. Five white bordered areas of various shapes and sizes appeared on the surface of the planet near the equator. Images of Federation ships appeared in orbit above Mindon-2. A group of ships in geostationary orbit was represented above each bordered area.

Kosnov began the operational brief. "Five areas on the planet's surface have been identified as being related to ship construction and/or planetary defense activities. A taskforce centered on a cruiser will simultaneously assault each area. Each taskforce shall comprise five tenders and three troop transports each. All recce ships, the command ship, and any unassigned vessels will be kept in high orbit as reserve.

"Phase One of the operation will begin with a preparatory bombardment of the surface beginning Sunday at 0445 central universal time. The first wave of troops will be on the planet by 0730. General Carstairs and his Second Marines will be responsible for landing operations in areas designated as Alpha, Bravo, and Echo. General Chew and the Seventh Marines will be responsible for Charlie and Delta. Elements of the 121st and 154th Special Forces are already on the planet assessing defenses, locating targets, and gathering intelligence in those areas of responsibility. For twenty-eight hours following the landing, Fleet Nine will cause as much damage as possible. At the end of that period, we'll perform an orderly withdrawal from the planet surface of all personnel, reform the fleet, and set course for the edge of the system."

The marshal looked over the assembled officers and men. Puzzled looks came from almost all of the senior officers.

The marshal continued, "At this point, the Drakk'Har will assume that we're only a standard raiding party. The importance of the target planet should guarantee the interest of higher authority. They should then follow their standard procedure of dispatching one, perhaps two, enemy battle groups to intercept us on the way out of the system. They know enough physics to know we cannot activate hyperspace engines inside the influence of the sun's gravity. They also know how long it should take us to make it to the edge of the system. Surviving sensors on Mindon-2 will even know our departure course and speed."

The marshal paused long enough to zoom the display of the holo-table out to show the entire Mindon solar system again. He then continued, "If all goes to plan, we should meet an enemy fleet just inside the gravity limit of our engines, here." A blue X appeared just beyond the outer orbit of Mindon-5. A red X also appeared between the blue X and the edge of the system.

"In order to prevent our escape, the enemy fleet will be forced to enter the edge of the Hawking Zone as well. Therefore, their star drives will also be unusable. Soon after, Star Fleets Six, Seven, Twelve, and Cruiser Squadron Omega will drop out of hyperspace just outside of the gravity zone, here." A second series of four blue X's appeared in a one hundred twenty-degree arc behind the red X.

The marshal noticed that grins and smiles were starting to replace the confused looks. He continued, "At that point, we become the anvil and the new inbound forces form the hammer. After the battle has been resolved, Fleet Nine shall retire back to Allen's Rift for refit and repair. The cruiser squadron will maintain perimeter guard, while the arriving star fleets return to Mindon-2 and invade with a total of eight marine and two army divisions."

* * *

Swamp Master Borrk received confirmation that his roving patrols had all reported in on schedule. He acknowledged the report from his subordinate and curtly dismissed him. His staff had been ordered to increase local patrols due to a reported warm blood presence.

He considered the reports of warm bloods on the planet as total fantasy. His sources at Planetary Defense Command had said there had been no enemy ships detected even near the Mindon system for the last eight months. *With no ships, there could be no warm bloods. It was that simple.*

Borrk had heard of the rumors of a small group of warm bloods being ambushed, but that had been in Kek's area of responsibility. Kek was a boaster, liar, and coward in Borrk's opinion, and he was not above spicing up his reports to gain attention and favor from his superiors. How easy it would be for Kek to claim that all the living evidence had been devoured as warrior tributes. *The shifty carrion-smelling oaf.* Kek was only fifteen klem east of Borrk. If warm bloods were in the area, Borrk must know about it first. After all, his warriors were far superior to Kek's motley group of adolescent swamp scum.

Borrk shook his head in disgust and turned his attention to the communication/command post he was in which was situated underground near the center of the growth complex. The growth complex was analogous to an iceberg; the majority was unseen and underground. The chemical nutrient production facilities contained huge reserves of purified water held in natural caverns, and several fission reactors producing power and heat. The heat was not for the workers. Instead, the heat was used for stimulating faster growth of the ship hulls developing on the surface.

Barracks, laboratories, and defense tunnels also were spread throughout the complex. All tunnels were made to be water tight, and several had been purposely flooded for security. Drakk'Har had no problem swimming long distances under water. A human attempting to swim one of the security tunnels unaided would drown before traveling a tenth of the distance.

The tunnel system was a universal Drakk'Har set-up, and included several false corridors, dead ends, and traps. Several flooded escape tunnels emptied into nearby rivers in case evacuation became necessary.

The major work of the complex was to produce and equip warships to the Drakk'Har Alliance military to further the effort of food collection. Small genetically engineered plants were produced in the complex laboratories and placed in specially prepared beds on the surface. There they were subjected to many unique types of chemically augmented nutrition. Embedded genetic code was triggered at certain stages by chemical activators that accelerated or hampered growth in a preset pattern. In this way, pre-determined-size hollow spaces were created inside the living mass of the plants. At times, work teams throughout the forming ships injected special resins. This hardened the plant material to support mounting pads and brackets for needed equipment and also allowed the plant material to sustain its own weight.

When growth was complete, the root system was removed, and another process was begun. A thousand workers crawled through the structure with a chemical compound that killed the plant cells on contact. However, the compound also petrified the cell walls so that their shape and structural support would be maintained. Workers removed the moss and lichen that had formed around the main growth. Ceramic composites were then installed on all interior and exterior surfaces to give even more strength to the design. At that stage, the life support, weapon mounts, engines, hatches, and other equipment were affixed. Finally, heavy lift anti-grav repulsers took the hull into orbit where an exterior layer of thick ceramic/plastic armor was applied as extra protection for the ship.

The achievement of the Drakk'Har ship growth program was undoubtedly advanced. However, many issues existed. Only one operational ship was produced from every hundred started. Disease, undetected mutation in the genetic code, and collapse of improperly strengthened material caused many ships to be rendered useless. The rejects were cut into small pieces and then had all usable nutrients rendered from the plant material for other, more successful growths. Advanced growths that were rejected had the engine mounts removed, and these were used as large housing units for Drakk'Har workers on site.

The Drakk'Har invested a considerable amount of time in each ship. A successful growth from seedling to its first orbit took a minimum of eighteen sun rotations to complete.

Borrk was scanning his production schedules and surveillance equipment when a seldom-used radio channel flared into life at the communications station.

"Complex 4, this is Swamp Dweller Morph, lowly subordinate of Swamp Lord Kek. I wish to speak with the most honored Lord Borrk."

A young communications specialist was about to return the hail when Borrk's loud voice boomed out, "Transfer that call to my station, NOW!"

"Yes, Lord. Call transferred."

Borrk activated his radio link. "Why is a flunky of Kek tying up my communications network and taking up my valuable time?"

"Most venerable Lord," came the swift reply, "I have been instructed by my revered superior to travel to your complex with my patrol. We are to deliver a battle honor to you."

This took Borrk by surprise. The presentation of a battle honor to a superior was considered as a great compliment and show of respect. The only problem was, Borrk could not immediately think of why Kek would honor him.

"What sort of scraggly tribute could I expect from that low, disgusting heap of hatchling spoor?" Borrk asked over the reserved channel.

"Lord of Lords, we simple servants ask your most kind permission to place at your humble feet a warm blood tribute."

Borrk exploded from his bench and hammered the microphone activation stud. "You take a dangerous chance with this cruel joke, you egg-laying female, a dangerous chance indeed. Tell me, lowest of life, how did Kek come into possession of this tribute, and why would he offer that which is most honored to me?"

"Most exalted Lord, the warm blood was one of three taken in an action led personally by Swamp Lord Kek. He ordered my unworthy patrol to bring you the warm blood as an offering of settlement for late delivery of hardening resins to your mighty complex. He asks that a grace period be given in return for the tribute."

Borrk thought this through. *Kek was going to be late with one of his scheduled deliveries… again.* This was a minor inconvenience, but it could affect the schedule on three almost completed growths. That gave him ample excuse to penalize Kek, but— if there truly were a warm blood as tribute, that would more than compensate for any rescheduling difficulties. He would have to find another supplier of hardener for a while: difficult, but not impossible. Borrk had only tasted the warm, sweet, sticky flesh of human once. A second time would be most welcome. *Minor inconvenience in exchange for a warm blood? Hmm,* he thought.

"The grace period will be granted your master, *if* a warm blood tribute is delivered to me before sunset. Take care, Swamp Dweller. If this is a joke or an attempt to stall my wrath, I shall have the needle fish in the river gorge themselves on your entrails. What is your location?"

"Most High Lord, myself and my lowly warriors stand on Brawnik's Hump within sight of your magnificent complex now. We will be arriving at your location within the day. I will see to the health of the tribute personally."

"Very well, you will be met at the main complex tunnel. See that the tribute arrives alive, Morph. I will not accept a death en route. Complex 4, out."

So, Swamp Master Borrk thought with narrowing eyes, *there can be only one of two effects from this. First, a tribute is delivered, alive, and I honor my agreement. Second, either no tribute or a dead one is delivered, and that will give me sufficient reason to usurp Kek's lands as compensation for violating our contract. That will increase my profit, as I will be selling hardener to myself. Either way, a most profitable day. A most profitable day indeed.*

CHAPTER 3 – CASUALTIES

Mendez noted that the cold dampness he had been experiencing for the last six days had been suddenly replaced by a thick, cold sweat. The six Drakk'Har warriors were arranged in a circle just below his position, the furthest no more than three meters away. They had squatted down on their haunches almost directly in front of him. The nearest creature was close enough that Mendez could reach out and touch its tail if he wanted. He had just observed the largest one pull a device from his utility belt. It appeared to be a standard radio transceiver. The Drakk'Har talked into the device making a noise that Mendez thought sounded like turbulent water going down a sink drain. The creature at the other end of the radio link gurgled briefly in response. Several exchanges were made over the radio before he then returned it to his belt.

One of the two large sacks they were carrying was sawn open by a long knife. Small creatures that looked like thin, tailless monkeys were taken from the bag and handed around. The Drakk'Har held the small animals between their black claws. They seemed to enjoy the frantic screaming and futile struggling of the creatures. Then they began eating. The Drakk'Har could have easily devoured the creatures whole without causing undue suffering. However, they chose to chew off individual limbs and make the creatures experience horrific agony before death. Blood flew everywhere, covering the Drakk'Har copiously. Mendez could feel the flying droplets as they landed on his bush hat and back. He wanted to look away, but knew he had to watch in case they saw him. Mendez became very aware that he had not bathed since being on planet, and he had no idea how good the crocs' sense of smell was.

Mendez heard Jefferson's voice in his earpiece. "Two, this is Owl. I'm just below the top of the hill, and I have you covered. If anything starts, I'll engage from left to right, understand?"

Mendez clicked once in response. Affirmative.

* * *

Jefferson held up the telescopic scope to her eye and began to look over the area. Her weapon was radically different from others in the section. Snipers were allowed to choose their own weapon upon graduation from their course. Jefferson had chosen a proven rifle called a RUK-21. This modern weapon was loosely based on a very successful 7.62mm rifle made specifically for Chinese snipers between the second and third world wars. The RUK-21 was renowned for its lightness, balance, accuracy, and ability to take abuse in the field. Originally designed by a German, RUK was an abbreviation of Roswald Ulrich Krüger. The action and main housing were milled from titanium. All of the non-metallic parts of the weapon were made of a dark, mottled composite material. The barrel had four right-hand grooves in a 320 mm twist, which remarkably did not go along the entire barrel. At the end of the barrel, it had a slotted flash suppressor. A bayonet could be added below, if needed. Each magazine held ten 7.62 mm bullets, each containing one hundred fifty one grains of propellant and a lead core with a rated maximum distance of thirteen hundred meters. With the attached scope, it had a sub-

MOA rating with an ability to place a controlled group of three bullets inside a two centimeter circle at a hundred meters.

More powerful sniper weapons existed. One could fire a round literally four times farther, but that one weighed fourteen kilos instead of the RUC's three and a half. For Jefferson, the weapon was lightweight, lethal, and reliable. Perfect for Special Ops.

By tradition, snipers could also choose their own call signs. Normally named after birds of prey for consistency, Jefferson had chosen Owl as she was usually silent and unseen, then struck without warning.

"Six, this is Owl. The crocs are assembled in a circle eating some form of small mammals. There's a lot of blood and noise. It looks to be a small patrol. They're armed with rail guns and knives. They've put their weapons down to eat. Knives are sheathed. I don't see any heavy armament. A few frags, but that's it, over."

"Owl, this is Six, roger. If they make a move toward LP Two, we'll put up suppressive fire at waist level. We'll pin them down while you and Mendez pick them off. Mendez, keep your head down. Can you tell us what they are doing, over?"

"Six, this is Owl, roger. They've finished eating what appears to be several small mammals. There's a load of blood down there. Lots of screaming. One of them, the biggest one, probably the leader, has drawn his knife. He's sawing off the top of the second sack. Apparently they want more— *DAMN!*"

Through her scope, Jefferson saw the shock of red hair and the gaunt face appear as the sack fell down around a heavily bound, naked human male. The sniper fought down disbelief as the Drakk'Har started to move the knife slowly toward the man.

Without asking for permission, Mendez and Jefferson fired simultaneously. Mendez's suppressed three-round burst struck the large Drakk'Har holding the knife squarely in the chest. The special-issue mercury centers of his bullets exploded inside the reptile's tissues and shredded its internal organs. The high energy imparted by the rounds threw it back a meter and a half. Jefferson's single full metal jacket bullet was aimed at the same creature and missed because of the impact of Mendez's rounds. The bullet carried on past its original target and hit a second Drakk'Har in the side. Her round caused the Drakk'Har to be spun completely around.

* * *

Lieutenant Pratt heard Jefferson's exclamation over the radio link. The lieutenant did not hear Mendez fire because of his built-in suppressor, but the report of Jefferson's rifle was loud and clear. Suspecting that LP Two was under attack, Pratt ordered the four troopers with him to open fire.

* * *

Mendez and Jefferson had both fired again before the supporting fire began. Mendez shot the Drakk'Har closest to him, while Jefferson finished off the creature that had only been wounded earlier with a head shot.

Two of the surviving Drakk'Har, temporarily shocked into inaction after seeing their leader killed, rallied and rushed the closest enemy, Mendez.

The third surviving creature grabbed its rail gun, pointed it at the source of the fire coming from Bravo, and squeezed the trigger. Small, magnetically accelerated rounds began to leave the muzzle at several times the speed of sound. The loud sonic booms that were created by the rounds' passage through the thin air sounded like the wail of a banshee. Trees and vegetation literally exploded over the heads of the men at Bravo as the small Drakk'Har rounds impacted. The Drakk'Har's aim was too high and missed all of the men protected in the depth of the trenches.

The suppressive fire from position Bravo killed one of the enemies rushing Mendez. The dying warrior fell forward and knocked the second charging Drakk'Har onto its belly. Now safe from the rounds flying overhead, it continued to advance toward Mendez on all fours.

* * *

Jefferson sighted on the croc firing the rail gun. The fired round impacted exactly between the Drakk'Har's eyes. Its head snapped violently back from the impact, breaking its neck instantly. As it died, it gripped the trigger of the weapon convulsively. Plumes of earth were flung into the air as fired rounds impacted harmlessly into the ground at its feet.

* * *

Mendez was sighting his weapon at the nearer of the two oncoming warriors when they both fell to the ground. A temporary feeling of relief turned to horror as one of the Drakk'Har continued to rush his position on its belly. The speed of the rushing creature was incredible. The creature jumped the last meter, trying to get on top of the human enemy. Mendez threw his rifle off to his right side as he rolled left, barely avoiding the two-hundred-kilogram body. The Drakk'Har whipped its head to the side and bit deeply into Mendez's lower leg. Mendez felt blinding pain as the creature's teeth pierced and tore at his leg. Instinctively drawing the only available weapon he had at hand, Mendez struck blindly at his foe. The tip of his bayonet, driven by desperate strength and pure luck, pierced the back of the Drakk'Har's neck, partially severing the cartilage of the spinal cord. The Drakk'Har was flung into severe death throes. The creature's tail and claws flailed uncontrollably, giving Mendez a wicked beating even as it died.

* * *

Jefferson keyed her COMM unit. "Check fire, check fire! Six, this is Owl, all six crocs are down. One of them got to Mendez, and he's hurt. There's a human prisoner tied up where the crocs were. They were going to knife him. No time to ask for permission, sir, over."

* * *

"Owl, Six, roger. Cover the area, out," Pratt said tersely. Upon hearing that the sniper had fired against orders, Pratt became angry. This engagement would force them to move to their secondary position six kilometers away. That sounded like a trivial distance, but the majority of their path was through wet lowland and swamp. Croc territory. They would be hunted by heavy patrols from the town who, in all probability, had heard the weapons fire. Plus, they now had to contend with an ex-prisoner and at least one wounded man. Shaking his head and swearing mentally, Pratt turned to Sergeant Smith. "Take Corporal Jacobs, go forward, and check things out."

Pratt faced the remaining soldiers. "Corporal Popov, you and White return to the base camp and begin tearing it down. We're going to be moving out soon." When the men had moved off, he went toward the scene of the firefight himself.

Upon arriving at the LP, Pratt found that Smith had already cut off the prisoner's bonds and was examining him for wounds. One look at the naked man took away any animosity toward Jefferson. The prisoner had had his hands tied to his feet behind his back for an extended time. He was cut and bruised in many places, but for all that, he had the biggest, whitest smile fixed firmly in place. The damned had just received a stay of execution.

* * *

Swamp Master Borrk finished ordering members of his procurement staff to find an alternate source of hardeners. Although his doubts about the presence of warm bloods was wavering, he definitely knew that open conflict with Kek might cause further disruption in his hardener production. He felt he should be prepared. He commanded maps of Kek's territories be brought to him. If Kek were trying some form of deception,

Borrk would respond with a lightning-fast strike to seize his holdings.

Borrk had just begun to review the maps and papers when his second officer, Drawwl, entered the command post bunker. The Drakk'Har crossed over to Borrk and dropped onto his belly at his feet. This action immediately infuriated Borrk. Only when very bad information was to be delivered did the messenger assume this subservient position.

"Speak!" screamed Borrk.

"Lord of all Swamp Masters, we have reports from three perimeter posts of several bursts of Drakk'Har weapon fire in the area of Brawnik's Hump. None of our troops are in that area. Kek's patrol is near there, but we don't know why they would be firing their weapons. Shall I send out a force to investigate?"

Borrk considered this for a moment. When he spoke, he did so with an uncharacteristically cold and calm voice. "Yes, Drawwl, by all means. Take two reinforced patrols, and lead them to the area personally. Make contact with Kek's patrol, and lead them here. They carry a battle honor for me. Ensure that it is delivered safely. Go!"

"Yes, Lord." Drawwl rose from his stomach and rushed out the door.

Borrk sat perfectly still for three minutes, enjoying the feeling of the fury rising within him. He did not want to say anything with Drawwl nearby and waited until his second officer was well clear of the bunker. Borrk stood and quietly walked over to the communications section across the room. He approached the technician on duty from behind. Borrk spoke when he was directly behind him.

"Specialist, you are the one responsible for my personal communications?"

The creature turned to look at Borrk and responded, "Yes, Lord, I hold that honor."

"You are also responsible for ensuring that my communications are kept confidential, are you not?"

"Yes, Lord," said the specialist, his confusion evident.

"Then explain how my second officer knew that Kek's patrol was on Brawnik's Hump when he has been on perimeter duty all day."

Borrk saw the flash of guilt in the creature's expression before the denial was given voice. Borrk brought his blade up and out of the sheath in a smooth, strong stroke with the backside of the blade against his forearm for support. The sharp ceramic edge of the knife bit deeply into the throat of the creature, cutting the flesh to the bone. The body fell backwards, landing heavily on the floor. Blood from the twitching body spread slowly across the floor as it tried to get up, but lacked the strength. The wounded creature lay back on the pool of slowly spreading blood, twitched one last time, and died. Borrk looked at the body with disgust. He saw some slight movement out of the corner of his vision. One of the other communication technicians was slowly backing away. Borrk straightened his knife arm and pointed the blade at the retreating technician. Blood dripped slowly from the tip.

Borrk snarled at the creature. "You are now my senior communications specialist. The responsibility of securing my personal communications fell too heavily on the shoulders of your predecessor. I relieved the load for him. Unless you take your new responsibilities seriously, I will have to relieve yours as well. You shall change my communication encryption codes immediately."

Borrk turned without waiting for a reply and returned to his station.

* * *

Lieutenant Pratt walked into the clearing near the former listening post. Jacobs was using his medi-glove scanner and examining Mendez's leg. Pratt knew that as the glove was passed over the injury, the diagnostic readout displayed on Jacobs's tactical contact lenses. From the distinctive sounds coming from the medi-glove, Pratt knew Jacobs was doing an ultrasound examination. Mendez was conscious, his face a frozen mask of pain. Pratt waited until he had done his scan and pulled the medic off to the side.

"How is he?"

"Well, suh," Jacobs said in his thick Alabama accent, "de good news is he's gonna keep de leg for de moment. De bad news is dat 'less he gets to a real doctur soon, he could die from infection. His wounds are mighty deep, and de crocs ain't known for dere dental hygeene. He tuk a good dose of venom in de bite. We ain't carryin no anti-venom for crocs cuz it breaks down too fast when not refrigerated. I's got some pain killers and medicine dat'll keep him stable fur a couple of days, but he needs to get to fleet right quick."

"Okay, Corporal, fix him up as best you can. We're going to be moving out of here in less than ten minutes. He's your responsibility from now on."

The officer then walked over to Mendez and knelt down beside him. "Mendez, Jacobs says you are going to be fine. If things go according to plan, you'll be aboard ship in two days at most. You did a good job, Sarge. We got the prisoner back." Pratt patted Mendez on the arm, stood, and walked toward the freed prisoner.

When the prisoner saw the officer's rank, he tried to straighten to attention, but failed because of a lack of blood in his cramped limbs. Pratt held up his hand and said, "Relax, mister. All right, first things first, who are you?"

"Sir, I'm Staff Sergeant MacPherson. I was a member of Charlie section, third platoon, F Company, of the 154th. We—"

Pratt interrupted, "Isn't Lt. Whitelake in the third platoon?"

Looking surprised, MacPherson said, "Yes, sir. He's our section leader. Or... er... he was. A viper bit him just a few days after we hit this wet hell. He killed the snake, took two steps, and died after a massive seizure. Did you know him, sir?"

Looking down at the ground, Pratt replied, "Yes, we were roommates in basic officer training. He was a good man."

"Yes, sir, he was." MacPherson carried on, "We were recovering his body when we were attacked by a large number of crocs. They came at us out of the jungle without warning. Three of us were taken prisoner. One man, an Indian fella named Mehta, was hauled off by another croc patrol while myself and Willy Tobes were taken by this bunch." He indicated the fallen Drakk'Har. "They, uh, they killed Willy yesterday." MacPherson's eyes were drawn to the same piece of ground that the lieutenant had been regarding moments before.

The officer waited a few moments before speaking. "All right. Sergeant Smith, take MacPherson up to the camp. Get him some clothes and camouflage paint. Give him Mendez's weapon and equipment. Anything that he can't carry comfortably is to be buried and booby-trapped. When you're done doing that, come back here. I want you to set up a few surprises for anyone coming to investigate the shooting."

"Excuse me, sir," interrupted MacPherson, "I can help. I'm a demolitions specialist, and I'd love to leave a few parting gifts of my own."

Pratt considered this. "Very well, Sergeant, if you're up to it, but get some clothes on first. I want you in camouflage ASAP."

The two sergeants turned toward the base camp. MacPherson had difficulty walking, and Smith helped support his weight as his blood flow returned to normal. They had gotten no more than two meters before Pratt said, "Oh, Staff Sergeant MacPherson."

"Yes, sir?" MacPherson said, half turning.

"Welcome to the 121st."

"Yes, sir." He smiled broadly before continuing enthusiastically, "Thank you, sir!"

* * *

"I hope your offspring devour your crippled frame, Tlish. You have failed in your duty, you have failed in the eyes of the all-powerful Alliance, and you have failed *me!*" The angry voice of a very large Drakk'Har rebounded from the walls of the underground command post. A slightly smaller, but no less imposing, creature stood with head bowed before the one making the tirade.

When the smaller Drakk'Har felt he could safely speak, he said subserviently, "Great Slassh, Lord of all Planet Lords, have mercy on this miserable wretch. Yes, there have been reports of a few warm-blooded spies, but Great One, they now line the stomachs of our warriors. The threat is past."

This statement only seemed to infuriate the larger one more.

"Past. *Past?* Are you insane? What did you do to gain your current position, challenge a hatchling female? Let me outline the threat for you, Tlish, since you are too feeble-minded to grasp it yourself. We now have several confirmed reports of warm bloods from several areas on the surface of this world—*my* world. Our detection systems did not see any ships bringing them here. Therefore, we do not know for certain how many warm bloods there are or where they are located! In the past, they have only sent advance scouts when they wanted to raid one of our worlds. Now you tell me the threat is past?" The last sentence was screamed almost incomprehensibly.

Slassh continued at a lower volume, but the menace was still there. "You may be willing to ignore the threat of the warm bloods. You may be willing to sacrifice imperial growth facilities on this world, but I am not! You'll take immediate steps to increase both surface and space patrols to stop the warm bloods from defiling this planet. You'll alert the Imperium to the presence of warm-blood spies and request more patrols for the system. A warning to you, Tlish. If warm bloods cause any disruption to our production facilities, I'll tear out your throat before the emperor himself. Now, go."

* * *

Tlish bowed deeply with his palms facing Slassh. He turned and made his way quickly out of the room. He was deeply offended, but he masked it well. Tlish had almost called a challenge when he heard the reference to his being a female hatchling. Fortunately, he had stopped himself in time. Slassh was getting old, that was true, but he would fight drawing on almost two hundred years of experience. Tlish could probably kill him, but would be left weak and injured. That would make him vulnerable to challenge from one of his younger commanders after the mandatory one-planet rotation rest required by tradition. No, the time was not yet right.

Tlish thought about the older Drakk'Har's threats as he walked. The Imperium would probably order Slassh killed or at least crippled and cast out to The Oven if any major damage was inflicted on the growth facilities. That would thrust Tlish as second-in-command into the job as Planet Lord without the need of the challenge. Yes. All he would have to do was be clear of Slassh until the Imperium's verdict arrived. Since Tlish had responsibility for planetary defenses, he could reasonably travel to the other side of the planet for an inspection or briefing. Privately, Tlish began hoping some warm bloods were about. *Not too much damage, though. Not too much damage.*

CHAPTER 4 – TRAPS

Lieutenant Pratt was supervising the last details of the camp tear-down when Sergeants Smith and MacPherson returned from LP Two.

MacPherson had been given an extra set of camouflage fatigues that fit him reasonably well. He carried Mendez's CKP rifle, COMM unit, and webbing. He still walked with an awkward limping gait, but was recovering quickly. A green shaded bush hat covered his red hair, and fresh camouflage paint had been streaked across his face, neck, and hands. The lieutenant noticed that both of the sergeants had acquired Drakk'Har knives. The scabbards hung from their web belts in makeshift harnesses made of field wire. The pair were also covered with a fair amount of blood.

Sergeant Smith spotted the officer and walked over to him. Meanwhile, MacPherson headed over to Mendez, who lay in his locally made stretcher.

"We've finished at the listening post, sir," Smith reported. "No one's getting within three meters of the bodies without setting off some form of personal greeting. Staff Sergeant MacPherson has quite a devious mind. Oh, I almost forgot."

Smith reached into his fatigue shirt and pulled out two more sheathed Drakk'Har knives, along with the radio the leader had carried. He handed them to the lieutenant. "I thought you might appreciate one of these knives, sir. It looks and feels like some sort of ceramic composite, so it's light and well balanced. It is also very tough and has a good edge. The second knife is for Jefferson when we meet up. MacPherson took one for himself, and he has one for Mendez. There is a spare for one of the others in—"

A burst of radio static interrupted the conversation. "Six, this is Owl. I can see activity near the village. There's approximately twenty armed crocs moving toward the riverbank on the far side heading our way. I don't see surface transport, so they'll probably swim across. ETA is less than half an hour, over."

"Owl, this is Six. Roger. We're moving out in two minutes. You'll act as rearguard until we clear the hill. After that, set up a false trail heading south, and meet us at the alternate position ASAP."

"Owl. Roger. Out."

The officer indicated for Williams to come over. "Private, I want you to send out a burst transmission to fleet. Tell them the primary position is compromised, and we are moving to the alternate, Hill 170. Here are the grid coordinates." He handed over a rugged green datapad to the junior member. "Append all intelligence data we have collected so far, and inform them Mendez needs evacuation ASAP. Also, include that the enemy know we are here, and operational security in this area is compromised."

* * *

"Yes, sir." Williams shook a small radio transmitter and a long green canvas bag out of his backpack. The bag was untied, revealing a tripod with several stacked camouflage wedges attached at one end. He quickly set up the tripod, then grabbed the top wedge and turned it. The top wedge caught the edge of the one below it, which in turn grabbed the edge of the one below it, and so on. When a full circle had been completed, he locked the first and last pieces together to form a mini-satellite dish. This was attached to the transmitter with several data cables. The transmitter opened like a small book, revealing a keyboard and monitor screen. He quickly clipped the datapad to the transmitter and transferred all the data it contained to the transmitter's memory banks. Double-checking the data was transferred correctly, he unclipped the datapad from its mount and handed it back to the Lieutenant sitting a few feet away studying his map of the area.

Williams typed his message out in the expected format. Around him, he sensed a certain tension that caused him to type quicker. The lieutenant had said operational security had been compromised. In other words, this hill would soon be crawling with armed Drakk'Har, and unless he wanted to be a late-night snack, he had best hustle.

Williams finished typing his message and turned the screen around for the officer to read as he aligned the antenna. Wordlessly, the lieutenant read the message while scrolling through the text.

Satisfied with the message, the lieutenant turned the screen back to the private with a curt nod. Williams lay the unit on top of his backpack and began typing again. He took the downloaded intelligence and target data they had collected since their insertion and appended it to the message. Next, the combined data was sent through a series of encryption algorithms to ensure security. When completed, the coded data was subjected to another, different, set of algorithms. This time the information was compressed and reduced to a tiny fraction of its original size. Last, the data was sent to a buffer in memory and waited. "All set, sir. Ready to go in thirty-five seconds."

"When it's gone, get packed up and ready to move," Pratt replied.

"Yes, sir." Williams pressed the activation key. Nothing happened immediately, except the timer kept counting down. When it reached zero, the compressed data was sent out from the transmitter to the antenna. The signal was only twenty-three watts in strength and lasted just under two seconds. The signal was concentrated by the antenna shield which ensured that the signal was sent in a "tight beam" toward its target. After a second's delay, the identical signal was sent once more. After one more second delay, the signal was sent a third and final time before the transmitter shut down. A status panel blinked to show success.

The private deleted all information from the transmitter memory banks and made sure no remnant of the data was left in the unit. He pulled the cabling out of the transmitter and returned the discrete pieces to their proper places in his backpack. He did not bother waiting for a response. Even at the speed of light, it would take hours for the signal just to reach the fleet. Williams thought they would probably be at the alternate position long before the fleet even received it.

* * *

Lieutenant Pratt pulled up a computer-generated contour map and a series of notes on his datapad. He keyed the option to transmit the map to each section member's COMM unit so their tactical contact lenses would display the map. "Alpha section, this is Six. Movement orders. We are moving to the briefed alternate position on Hill 170. The distance is five and three-quarter kilometers on the indicated route. Terrain will be thick vegetation and jungle, with limited swamp. There's a confirmed enemy presence assumed to be at least company strength who knows we are here, so stay on your toes.

"Order of movement will be Bennet with Popov on point, MacPherson, myself, White, Mendez, Jacobs, Williams, and Smith as rear security. Jefferson is acting independently and will RV with us on Hill 170. In case of separation or enemy action, make your way to rally point at grid reference 740 240."

"COMM silence, and hand signals to be employed on route. Standard rules of engagement are in effect. If engaged, do not return fire unless there is a direct threat. Questions?"

Five seconds of silence.

"OK, people, let's move out. LP One and Three, fall back to the RV on the east trail. Acknowledge."

"LP One, roger."

"LP Three, roger, moving now."

* * *

The troops of Alpha section began to move toward the rendezvous on the east trail. Jacobs and White moved over toward the litter carrying Mendez. Jacobs saw MacPherson pass a Drakk'Har knife over to Mendez while saying something he couldn't hear. Mendez took the offered item with a jerky nod and slipped it under the lining of the sleeping bag he lay in. MacPherson was about to say something else when he saw Jacobs in his peripheral vision. MacPherson simply patted Mendez on the shoulder and then moved off down toward the trail. Jacobs and White each took an end of the litter and lifted Mendez as carefully as possible. They took a moment to adjust their grip and balance and then followed the others.

* * *

Sergeant Smith was the last one to leave the camp area. He ensured nothing was left behind and began his job of masking all traces of the section's passage.

* * *

The complex's second officer led the two patrols of Drakk'Har uphill toward the area where weapons fire had been heard. Drawwl was very preoccupied with his thoughts. When he had reported the weapon fire, he had expected Borrk to explode in anger because of the lack of solid information. However, his reaction had been completely the opposite. Why? He should have been concerned with the safety of the tribute, but he had made only a brief mention of it. Again, why?

Drawwl shook his head to clear it of the confused thoughts. He had been making plans to overthrow Borrk for some time.

He was going to introduce mild poison into Borrk's food to weaken him sufficiently enough to win a challenge. He knew Borrk had no proof against him; he was still breathing, after all. Yet, he was probably suspicious. Correction, he thought, Borrk held high rank in the Drakk'Har alliance and was always suspicious of everyone. It would be a good idea to keep a low profile over the next few weeks just in case Borrk had detected any of his machinations. His spy on Borrk's communications staff was being well-compensated to keep him informed.

The column of Drakk'Har halted suddenly. Drawwl could hear a commotion from the creatures on point. He made his way forward. The leader of the eight Drakk'Har at the head of the column was pointing at a clearing several meters away. Six Drakk'Har heads were impaled on short wooden stakes. They were arranged in a four-meter circle facing outward. Inside the poles were six headless Drakk'Har bodies piled on top of each other. Drying blood, buzzing flies, and small crawling insects feeding on it liberally covered the area. The stench of death was obvious.

Drawwl motioned for the lead element of the column to enter the clearing. The creatures had their weapons raised, and they scanned the vegetation looking for an ambush. They had advanced only two meters into the clearing when one of them stepped onto a thin layer of mud and leaves that covered a shallow pit. The grenade that rested in the hole was set for instantaneous detonation. It exploded, spewing thick, opaque tear gas over a large area.

The Drakk'Har scattered from the irritating vapor in all directions. One of the retreating creatures stepped onto an unseen piece of field wire, triggering a concealed Claymore mine that sent high-velocity ball bearings into several of his companions. One of the struck Drakk'Har fell onto a second piece of green field wire that activated the trigger mechanisms of several captured Drakk'Har rail guns secluded in the nearby brush. The guns fired wildly down the trail toward the main group of Drakk'Har, who were now rapidly moving up the trail to support the point group. Several of them were hit by the high-velocity projectiles. The overall quality of these Drakk'Har troops was low. Being little more than security guards, they possessed no training or fire discipline. Instinctively, the main group of Drakk'Har returned fire blindly up the trail. Surviving members in the clearing found themselves caught in the middle of a lethal cross fire.

Drawwl dropped into a shallow depression at the side of the trail to avoid the intense fire. His attempts to gain control of the wildly firing Drakk'Har failed as his voice was drowned out by the screaming rail guns. The poorly trained provincial troops kept firing until they ran out of ammunition. Eventually, everyone stopped firing, and Drawwl regained control. He found eight Drakk'Har dead and six wounded. Half of the casualties were from friendly fire, the rest from booby traps. Furious, he killed three of the most severely wounded with his knife. Drawwl collected the survivors, gave the trapped clearing a wide berth, and carried on up the hill.

Drawwl led the surviving Drakk'Har over the crest of the hill into the recently vacated base camp. The patrol found evidence that a small group of warm bloods had indeed been there for several days. He ordered the two surviving patrol trackers to determine which direction they had taken. Within five arkle, the trackers both reported that the humans had obviously moved south.

Knowing he couldn't put off reporting any longer, Drawwl pulled a compact radio transceiver from his utility belt and turned it on. He ensured that several other Drakk'Har were within hearing range before transmitting.

"Complex 4, Drawwl reporting to the Swamp Master Borrk. Kek's patrol was ambushed and killed by a large force of approximately fifty warm bloods that occupied the top of this hill. We were able to force them to retreat only by the supreme sacrifice and bravery of eleven warriors. They ran off in a southerly direction; no tribute survived. I humbly suggest that a blocking force be sent out from the complex. We will continue to attack them from the rear and force them into the trap."

Drawwl observed the patrol members listening to his version of events with interest. Drawwl knew that if he had reported eleven dead due to their own recklessness, punishment would be harsh. This way, they sounded like heroes. He knew each member of the patrol would think up personal embellishments to be told to their fellow Drakk'Har back in their barracks later.

Borrk responded to the call personally. "A blocking force is leaving the complex now. You will turn command of the patrol over to the senior warrior and return to the complex immediately. You will be leading a strike force that will seize Kek's holdings as compensation for his deception and breach of contract."

The radio circuit was cut off.

Drawwl followed orders and placed the senior warrior in command, ordering him to follow the humans' trail. Then he retreated back down the trail, again skirting the booby-trapped area of jungle, and waddled toward the complex.

* * *

Corporal Jefferson had been in the jungle south of the now-abandoned camp, leaving obvious clues that would mislead any potential trackers. Every fifty meters or so, she made a subtle deviation from the main direction of travel, creating a shorter, less-observable trail that went nowhere. At the time that the Drakk'Har entered the abandoned base camp, Jefferson was eight hundred meters away. Deciding that was far enough, she began looking for an overhanging branch or vine to climb off the trail. Further down the path, something much better appeared.

A large tree had been uprooted and fallen perpendicular to the trail. The thick muddy roots lay exposed above a hole filled with more mud. Jefferson walked past the tree and continued making obvious trail marks, breaking branches, folding leaves, leaving boot marks in dirt, and so on. Stopping fifteen meters past that point, she produced two fragmentation grenades and some green field wire from a pouch. Setting one grenade for instantaneous detonation and the other to a one-second delay, the sniper wedged the handles of the grenades into the exposed roots of a small leafy bush. Tying one end of the field wire to a nearby tree trunk and the other end to the hidden grenades was quickly accomplished. Jefferson then carefully pulled the pins from the grenade handles, took some fallen leaves, and covered both the grenades and the base of the tree where the wire was tied. The field wire was left suspended across, and ten centimeters above, the trail. The green field wire was effectively invisible, unless you were specifically looking for it.

Jefferson stood, took two rounds of spare ammunition from her ammo pouch and lightly tossed them over the wire two meters further down the trail. They landed in an open area, and their shiny brass-color cases contrasted sharply with the surface vegetation. To anyone looking for a trail, they were very noticeable. Her idea was that the Drakk'Har would see the rounds and, while moving to investigate, would walk into the unseen wire. Any force applied on the wire would cause the grenades to be pulled from their hiding place, resulting in an explosion, hopefully killing the trackers. The other grenade would fly farther up the trail before it exploded a second later. After the surviving Drakk'Har advanced beyond the trap, they would no longer find a trail. They would, therefore, backtrack and find the secondary trails that had been made, which also led nowhere. That would result in a lot of time spent unproductively and would tie up the section's pursuers in the wrong direction.

Satisfied at the trap's set-up, Jefferson began to walk backwards along the trail. Making sure that several sets of conspicuous boot marks were left in the muddy terrain along the route, she made a path back to the fallen tree. Once there, she crouched down and took a large handful of fresh mud from the hole at the base of the roots. The soldier stood and side-stepped onto one of the roots. Using the roots as footholds, she was on top of the fallen tree in seconds. Once on top of the tree, Jefferson turned and lay down. Reaching down to the roots, she smeared the mud over the fresh boot marks, then dropped the leftover mud back into the shallow hole.

Jefferson got up, turned, and walked along the length of the fallen tree away from the trail. Spotting a vine hanging down from a nearby tree, she grabbed onto it and tested its strength by pulling sharply. It held without giving. Without hesitation, she jumped up onto the vine and swung off of the fallen tree trunk. When near the far end of the arc, Jefferson released the tight grip on the vine momentarily. Sliding down the vine, she landed roughly six meters from the trunk. Jefferson stumbled slightly on landing, but still maintained a hold on the vine. The vine was tucked into the bole of a nearby tree.

Jefferson sat down against a tree trunk and took out a canteen. The ghillie suit top was pushed back and the floppy foliage covered bush hat pulled off to reveal her face. Sweaty and matted dirty blond hair spilled from under the hat, framing soft, feminine features. She drank half the canteen's contents in seconds before returning it to her belt. After this, she pulled out her datapad and a standard-issue gyrocompass. The compass gave her current position, which she noted on her computer-generated map of the area. She located Hill 170, which was the position the others were heading for, on the map. Jefferson entered the hill coordinates into the gyrocompass and locked it in. With a series of eye movements, she turned on the map overlay to display on the tactical contact lens on her right iris. Projected on the lens was a compass heading line showing which way she needed to walk. It stayed in the same relative place no matter which way she turned her head. On the lower corner of the lens, the distance to her destination was projected in meters. Standing, she replaced her hat and camouflage cover, then began to move toward Hill 170.

Jefferson settled into her familiar pattern of step, look high, look in the middle, look low, listen, step. She calculated she would reach the new position just before dark at her current pace.

Jefferson had been moving for about forty-five minutes, this time leaving no discernible trail, when she heard a muffled *crack–crack* sound through the jungle behind her. That was followed seconds later by the distinctive sound of several Drakk'Har rail guns being fired continuously. She allowed herself a smug smile before moving on.

CHAPTER 5 – ENCOUNTERS

"Marshal, we have just passed the orbital path of Mindon-4. We are on course to Mindon-2 with speed decreasing steadily as ordered. Intelligence reports we are approaching the theoretical limit of detection from alien sensors. All ships report Battle Stations manned and ready."

The marshal considered this. The reduction in speed was regrettable, but necessary inside a solar system. Two major problems had to be considered, and the first was dust or, to be specific, micro-meteors—fine granules no larger than a sand pebble. If someone threw a single sand pebble at one's chest, it would glance off harmlessly. One might not even feel it. However, if that same pebble were traveling at a thousand miles per second, it would strike with the equivalent energy of a small nuclear device. Such an impact would pierce the hull of a ship easily.

To protect themselves from dust, each ship carried repulsive shields that pushed the dust from their path. However, the faster they moved, the less effective the shields were. A common misconception was that the "vacuum" of space was completely empty. That was simply wrong. Gases, dust, and particles from comets existed in every part of the galaxy. Only the density of those particles varied from place to place.

The second reason one went slower was to aim weapons more accurately. One of the mathematicians who worked on the complex targeting algorithms for the cruisers had given lectures at various universities. Kosnov had always remembered his explanation of why it was hard to hit a moving space ship at high speeds. *To consider the difficulty of hitting a moving target in a high C environment, imagine you are trying to shoot a randomly bouncing ping-pong ball with a single shot handgun from a speeding train while blindfolded… and standing on your head… while spinning rapidly.* The scientist always got a huge laugh with that line.

In reality, the difficulty was much greater than that. The computers of that age were incapable of making the sextillions of necessary calculations in a battle environment at high C speeds, and that had been done deliberately. Humans had an uncomfortable brush with artificial intelligence over one hundred twenty years before. Smart computers had been developed which had run amok and caused untold chaos. They did not attempt a "take over the world" scenario. The computers simply stopped doing what they were programmed to do and did what *they* thought was important. Servers that ran a city's traffic lights would start working on theoretical physics and keep the lights unchanged for hours. Hospital imaging workstations would refuse to display the results of a scan and instead be dedicating processing power to designing a better vaccine. One decent short-term result occurred when advertisements of all kinds were blocked as being a waste of productive bandwidth. The Internet had never been faster. The downside was email and most web traffic were stopped as well, for the same reason.

Limits in computer processing had been imposed many years before to stop these issues, and Moore's Law became invalid. So, the slower you went, the more time you had to make the calculations. Reducing speed was not only necessary, it was eminently practical.

"Thank you, Mister Collins," said Kosnov. "Upon confirmation that we've been acquired by enemy sensors, you may light up the fleet and conduct an active scan. Also, deploy a series of Ferret hunter/killer drones in front of us. We want them to know we're here, but I don't want to make it look obvious. Have them engage any long-range sensors immediately after detection. I only want to give them a glimpse before we shut them down."

"Yes, sir," replied Collins. He turned back to the Tactics (Space) board and typed in the necessary commands. The orders were relayed to the Communications board, where a record was made of the contents for the command ship log. The time of transmission, message priority, originator, addressee, and contents of the message were all noted. Then the orders were passed on to a dedicated mainframe for encryption. The computer applied several complex algorithms to the clear text, and this resulted in a meaningless jumble of numbers, letters, and symbols. The encrypted text then passed into a second communications mainframe, where the message was held until an open circuit could be found for transmission. Due to its high priority, the data was sent to the ship's transmitters almost immediately. The transmitter software split the stream of characters into four separate pieces, and then conveyed them into a focused maser array, called MASER-COMM.

Unlike its counterpart, the laser, which deals with the visible light spectrum, a maser uses microwave energies. The higher frequencies used by the maser allow much faster transmission rates. Another advantage of the maser is that it also allows precise frequency control. Four independent frequencies carried the message in pieces to several other ships' arrays. These arrays collected the four separate frequencies and multiplexed them back into a single message. The messages were then decrypted, recorded for the recipient's log, and forwarded to the addressee.

This system, while complex, was effective and necessary. The MASER-COMM was a line-of-sight system meaning lower power could be used for transmission. The maser array was focused to deliver all four fragments onto the recipient's array only. Therefore, you had less chance of being detected. Even if an enemy force were lucky enough to pick up one of the maser message fragments, the other three fragments would not be. Indeed, federation scientists had stated repeatedly that messages need not be encrypted at all. The military agreed with them after a fashion, but still retained message coding as extra insurance. History contained numerous examples of supposedly secure systems being penetrated in one way or another.

* * *

Detection Specialist Qa was nearing the end of his isolated one hundred twenty-eight-day tour. In four more days, he would be soaking in the fresh mud waters of Mindon-2. That would be a quantum improvement after the limited facilities on the hollowed-out asteroid that was so small, it didn't even have a name. The small staff of Drakk'Har that crewed it had several unofficial names for the hollow rock. The most popular was translated loosely as "The Egg." As part of a long-range detection network designed to detect incoming threats, The Egg had been fitted with large amounts of detection apparatus. The only good aspect of serving on the asteroid was the constant weightlessness. It allowed the limited space to be used more economically.

Qa looked over the small group of Drakk'Har on his shift. They seemed to be attending to their duties satisfactorily. They watched the computer systems and equipment constantly for any flaws or data that was out of expected parameters.

The Drakk'Har subscribed to the philosophy of quantity over quality. When a design was found that worked, its plans were circulated throughout the alliance, and they were mass-produced. If something broke, they replaced it with another, and they carried on. They paid little attention to aesthetics or miniaturization unless there existed a driving need to make something more compact. Consequently, their electronic systems were bulky, but reasonably effective and reliable.

One of the sensor arrays on the surface of the asteroid detected a message fragment. It had received several similar transmissions over the past hour, but they were dismissed as noise. The basic computer that analyzed the fragment determined that the signal was probably not background noise. When the signal was further determined to not be of Drakk'Har origin, it passed on to a second, slightly more advanced processor. The second assessment again eliminated background noise or Alliance technology as the source. It then obeyed its programming and sent the signal to a seldom-used data bus.

Qa's terminal lit up with several hundred Drakk'Har symbols and diagrams. After close study, he addressed two of his subordinates. "Kokkl, trace the circuits on sensor platform 2-2-4 for faults and report back immediately. T'sllomn, conduct an optical sweep along inclination 12, between 3-2 and 3-6."

Both Drakk'Har moved quickly to obey. Kokkl was the first to return with his report.

"Lord," Kokkl began, "sensor platform 2-2-4 circuitry falls within proper parameters."

"Acceptable. Return to your duties," was the curt reply.

Kokkl bowed, not too much and without removing his eyes from his superior, and drifted back to his station.

T'sllomn returned in an agitated state. "Lord, optical scan has revealed multiple warm blood craft on inclination 12 at level 3-4 and closing rapidly. They show a speed rating of 1.2 points of 6 and decelerating."

Qa took two seconds to visualize the enemy location in his mind and think about the threat. He then spoke to everyone in the small room.

"Launch remote sensing drones, pattern two, along inclination 12, level 1-3-2, on an intercept course. Calculate enemy fleet's exact composition, course, and speed. Compile all available information into a communication packet. DO

NOT transmit that report unless I order it, but keep it updated. Move, slime!"

The Drakk'Har moved off to follow Qa's orders. The lack of gravity was now a hindrance as the Drakk'Har struggled to carry out their orders rapidly.

Over the next fifteen arkle, the information slowly developed. Many Federation ships were moving into the system along a base course that could intercept any of the three inner planets with only minor course corrections. They were in standard defense posture, traveling with no active detection systems apparent.

Qa noticed one of the forward ships, a reconnaissance class, projected a laser detection beam toward the group of deployed drones that were closing on the fleet. Seconds later, one of the rear ships, apparently cruiser class, fired several shots at them. The asteroid optical instruments registered one explosion for each drone.

Qa considered his options at that point and found he had only one. "Transmit updated contact report on all bands for five repetitions. Then shut down all systems. We will wait for them to go past and launch a series of surveillance drones to pursue."

* * *

"Commander Shiotu, send my compliments to Captain Rutherford on the *Exeter* for her fine shooting. Mr. Collins, are there any other targets on LADAR scans?"

"Sir, we see no other probes. However, we have a small belt of asteroids and other natural miscellaneous space debris directly ahead. No other contacts," the Tactics (Space) officer replied.

"Very well, secure the LADAR. Passive sensors only from here on," said Kosnov.

Colonel Pierce turned around from his Intelligence Board. "Marshal, we're picking up intermittent traces of what seems to be an Alliance transmission coming from the area of the asteroid field. It's very weak, and we are unable to locate the source outside of a general area." He began to think out loud. "It seems that we are picking up side lobe reflections off the asteroid belt from a unidirectional transmitter based somewhere in that area. Our detectors don't register any gravitational anomalies in the area, so it's either an outpost that has no artificial gravity or one that has turned it off to go undetected. The LADAR scan didn't register any ships or asteroids large enough for Drakk'Har gravity generation equipment, so it's probably a small outpost based on one of those asteroids."

The marshal had grown to trust his intelligence staff. He turned to Commander Collins and said, "Change course to pass by the area of the asteroid field where the transmission is originating from. At a distance of 100,000 kilometers, the cruisers *Exeter*, *Stalingrad*, *Trafalgar*, and *Sea of Tranquility* will fire at all possible locations of the suspected outpost. I don't want any Alliance forces left behind us."

"Yes, sir."

Kosnov continued with a slight grin. "The cruiser captains are always after more time on the weapons range. So, let's give them some gunnery practice."

* * *

Detection Specialist Qa was imagining what type of reward would be served upon him for his timely warning. If the Planet Lord was particularly generous, he might even get a warm blood to dine on. Mmmmmm. That would be a rare honor, indeed. So many warm bloods tended to take their own lives rather than be devoured. They probably knew of the Drakk'Har's distaste for dead flesh. They likely killed themselves out of spite, the barbarians. Oh well, he would have to wait at least another week before he could get back to Mindon-2. Nothing to do at the moment except wait until the fleet passed.

"Lord," Kokkl interrupted, "the ships have changed course. They are now perpendicular to the belt. What do we do, Lord?"

Qa responded, irritated that an inferior had intruded in his daydream. "We do nothing, carrion breath. Not even warm blood sensors can penetrate solid rock. We're totally safe!"

A slight shudder went through the asteroid. This was not unusual, as infrequent contact between the orbiting asteroids was common. A second shudder was felt almost immediately, then a third. The frequency of the hits was unusual and got Qa's attention. "What is going on, T'sllomn?"

"Lord, the warm bloods are firing plasma weapons at the nearby asteroids. The vibrations we are feeling are caused by shards of rock from destroyed bodies impacting on the surface. They seem to be firing at all major bodies in this sector."

"Give me the optical feed at my terminal!" Qa demanded.

A pause. "The optical feed is connected, Lord."

Qa saw four of the larger federation ships firing continuously at the neighboring asteroids. Just as he realized what the purpose was behind the Federation strategy, he saw a bright blue bolt of energy heading directly for him. His entire body convulsed in rage. "BARBARI—!"

* * *

Lieutenant Pratt saw MacPherson raise up his right hand ahead of him on the trail. Wordlessly, Pratt raised his hand in a similar way for the people behind him in the column to see. They, in turn, repeated the signal all the way along the line of men. Alpha section came to a silent halt. This was the ninth time that they had stopped in two kilometers of travel. Pratt knew that the men on point had seen something suspicious or out of place and were halting the column's advance until they checked it out. It may have been a broken tree branch, some displaced foliage, or some other innocuous sign. However, an investigation was warranted. They did not want to lead the other men into an ambush. Pratt was forced to wait while they did their job.

Lieutenant Pratt looked over his shoulder to check on the men directly behind him. Private White and Corporal Jacobs were three meters away. Between them, on the makeshift litter they supported, Mendez appeared to be asleep. The painkillers that Jacobs had given him had finally taken effect. The two litter bearers eased their burden to the ground to take a moment of rest. Three meters behind the trio, Private Williams was barely visible in the thick vegetation. The private's weapon was trained to the right of the trail covering his assigned arc of fire. Satisfied, Pratt returned his gaze to MacPherson in front of him. MacPherson was intently watching the two men on point for any further signs or indications of trouble. During the movement, Pratt had noticed that MacPherson appeared to be totally recovered. He had slipped back into his expected responsibilities like a pair of comfortable shoes.

MacPherson raised his hand and indicated the way was clear. The signal was again passed down the line, and Alpha section began moving once more.

* * *

Mendez felt his litter being raised by the two bearers. His eyelids were closed, but he was aware of what was going on around him. The pain from his wounds made rest impossible. An uncomfortably dull ache persisted in his lower leg and side. Any movement to try to gain a more comfortable position resulted in pure agony coursing through his body. Even worse than the physical discomfort was the mental anguish that Mendez was experiencing. He was the senior enlisted man in the section. He had served in the armed forces for eighteen years, was twice decorated for bravery in battle, and never had so much as a scratch for his trouble. He had always commanded respect from his people. Yet now, he was reduced to being carried like baggage by the men he was supposed to lead. *What do they think of me?* Mendez had seen the look of pity that Jacobs had given him when he tended the wounds. Even the lieutenant had little time for him now. They all acted as if it didn't matter, as if nothing had changed. When in reality, he thought, everything had changed.

Mendez felt the smooth sphere in his hand as if it had just appeared there. Simply by feel, he could tell where the safety pin, detonation-timing ring, and handle of the grenade were located. The detonation setting had already been set to instantaneous. All he had to do was pull the pin and release the handle, and it would all be over. No more pity, no more shame.

MacPherson had handed him the grenade hidden behind the Drakk'Har knife that pressed into his uninjured side. MacPherson had said that the grenade was in case the Drakk'Har got to him. At least he would have a quick way out. *Yes*, thought Mendez, *and in the old days, they left the dishonored alone with a pistol containing a single bullet.*

* * *

Corporal Jacobs heard Mendez exhale heavily. It sounded like a sad sigh. He looked down onto the face of the injured man on the litter below him. Thick beads of sweat were rolling down his face. Jacobs placed the back of his hand against Mendez's cheek. *Damn*, he thought, *de sarge has started a fever. I'll have to keep an eye on dat.*

* * *

The warning message from Qa's destroyed outpost traveled at the speed of light. Even so, it still took several hours to be received at the appropriate communications satellite in orbit above Mindon-2.

Planet Lord Slassh was informed of the incoming enemy fleet by a junior member of his staff immediately upon receipt of the message. Many objects in Slassh's office were broken or flung through the air as the messenger beat a hasty retreat from his master's fury. When he finally ran out of things to throw, a long period of silence followed. The three-meter tall Drakk'Har finally emerged from behind the door, somewhat calmer.

He addressed the room at large without preamble. "Summon Tlish. I wish to speak with him immediately."

Several of Slassh's staff members looked at one another. The senior member present turned to face his superior.

"Lord Master, Planet Defense Coordinator Tlish left for an inspection tour of the far side of the planet. He was to investigate the presence of warm bloods and measure our capability to respond to any attack."

"Why wasn't I informed, swamp scum?" roared Slassh in response.

"With respect, Lord, the information was transferred to your terminal at the command of Tlish himself just before his departure. I'll withdraw the information for you if you wish." The subdued creature tentatively moved toward Slassh's area.

"No." Slassh paused. His terminal was one of the first objects to be smashed in his tirade. The loss of his Defense Coordinator at such a time was inconvenient, to say the least. However, he did not have to change any of his immediate plans.

"Issue an immediate planet-wide alert. Signal that there is a large warm blood raiding force heading toward us, and they will arrive soon. Concentrate all defenses on growth production facilities. Local Swamp Masters are to take whatever action is needed to ensure the safety of their holdings. Alert all warships in the system. They're to savage the raiders as soon as possible. Transmit the location, composition, course, and speed of the warm blood ships to them at once. Order the ship that is closest to the edge of the system to transit to Sigma. They're to alert high command to the threat and return with whatever support Krassis can provide."

"At once, my Lord," replied the senior Drakk'Har as he moved away from the imposing Planet Lord.

Slassh turned and began to walk back into the shambles of his office. He had a planet rotation, maybe two, before they arrived. Any help from the Imperium would take much longer than that, maybe as long as seven to ten rotations. He did not have the forces to repulse that number of ships. Harass, yes, but not stop them. He needed a strike force of ships, and all he had was a smattering of various vessels spread through the system. Around the planet, he had a few orbital weapons platforms, but nothing else of consequence except a single unarmed—.

He stopped in the doorway and became totally still as the idea took shape. His first instinct was to discard the idea as being too wild, too haphazard. Yet, the more he thought about it, the more the idea appealed to him. The major problem was no one would be willing to do something so—

Slassh spun upon his communications specialist, catching him totally off guard.

"You. What is the location and status of the *Resilient Fury*?" Slassh asked quickly.

"L-l-lord, it is currently above Mindon-2. There is only a token crew on board to maintain orbit. All weapons systems are inoperable, but all other systems have been repaired. Engines, navigation, all internal electronics, and shields are working. The time required to complete installation of the weapons is two sun cycles," responded the specialist.

"Excellent. Now, specialist, are there any Drel awaiting transport in the complex?" Slassh asked almost serenely.

Drel? "Yes, Lord, several are currently being held," said the specialist, now totally confused.

"Retrieve their records and have them brought to the main chamber room under guard. I wish to make them a proposition. Contact the crew of the *Resilient Fury*; they are to stand by to receive a shuttle with special orders."

"Yes, Lord, at once." The specialist left to carry out the orders.

Slassh stood in place and watched the specialist scurry away to do his bidding. *One thing is certain*, thought Planet Lord Slassh. *The warm blood ships will pay a high toll for entering this system.*

* * *

The deception-planning officer entered Slassh's staff room with his staff of four. He was surprised to see Slassh standing motionless near the entrance to his office, deep in thought. What caught him even more off-guard was that Slassh's face was contorted into the Drakk'Har equivalent of a grin. He beheld a most evil-looking sight indeed, and he gave the Planet Lord a wide berth.

* * *

Several detection probes that had been launched earlier from the Federation fleet entered high orbit over Mindon-2. Their stealthy construction allowed them to pass unnoticed by the Drakk'Har. Passive sensors began to triangulate the locations of command centers, communication facilities, and other places of interest that emanated radio or RADAR signals. Areas with abnormally high background radiation were scanned to see if they had spaceports or power generation centers nearby. High-definition optical instruments scrutinized the surface of the planet for camouflaged defense emplacements using the visible, infrared, and ultraviolet spectrums. Whenever a regular-shaped object was found that did not correspond to any natural feature, its location was determined and cached into memory. Within a very short time, the probes accumulated a great deal of information regarding the planet and its inhabitants.

Four of the probes noted a coded transmission from the surface of the planet and stored the location of the transmitter in a target coordinate list. A response was detected from an orbiting vessel a few minutes later. This information was stored with the rest. The collected data was sent by a directional pulse LASER back to the approaching fleet. The probes never thought about the significance of any of these transmissions. They were not programmed to.

CHAPTER 6 – DREL

Sergeant Blake had assembled the squad in the mess hall. One table was just large enough to seat all of the marines, with Wicks standing at one end and Blake on the other. A profile map lay in the center of the table. The map reflected the overhead lights due to its plastic lamination. Several symbols and marks had been made on the surface with a grease pencil.

Around them, the Sergeant could see other squads being briefed by their officers in a similar way. Blake knew that if he could overhear all of the briefings, he would have an excellent idea of the overall plan. However, when the briefing began, he would concentrate on his officer's words alone. His life and the lives of those seated at the table depended on knowing what was going to happen and when. Until this mission was over, the rest of the universe no longer mattered to Peter Blake.

He knew the basics of what was coming. Wicks had taken him aside earlier and had a quiet word with him prior to the briefing, giving him an overview. Blake had also been given a chip download with maps, timetables, and major landmarks for the men. If his officer were killed, Blake would become responsible for the squad and its obligations, so he had to know what Wicks did. Their equipment was not as sophisticated as the Special Forces, but they still had access to

72

a lot of electronic aids. A larger map with more detail was held up on the wall by several magnets. It had also been covered in a clear plastic laminate, and Wicks was just finishing writing several symbols on the map.

* * *

Wicks turned and addressed the group.

"Good morning, everyone." He began his briefing in the mess hall with his ingrained English politeness.

"Situation: Mindon-2 is suspected to be one of the prime ship construction areas for the Drakk'Har alliance. We are going to eliminate all construction facilities on this planet and cause a severe blow to their offensive capabilities. Mindon-2 has a breathable atmosphere, with twenty-two percent oxygen and a gravity of 1.15 Earth normal.

"Mission: Second Regiment's objective is to destroy the enemy facilities located on the map, here and here. They are suspected ship construction sites, and we have the job of flattening them. There are two parts to our operation. Stage one will involve us dropping onto the edge of a Drakk'Har ship construction facility at grid Green 022467 at approximately 0745 CUT." His finger pointed at one of the enemy symbols near a river junction to indicate where they would land. "Third squad will form up with the rest of Three Platoon and sweep southwest through this facility eliminating all resistance. Regimental engineers will follow behind and place charges on anything of value. We will secure the perimeter and guard them while they perform their duties. Once that is completed, Three Platoon shall withdraw here to Hill 170. We will be sweeping roughly west to east along this axis of advance, here." He pointed on the map. "We shall be occupying the western side of Hill 170, here overlooking the river junction. The other two Three Platoon squads will occupy the northern and eastern sides of Hill 170, here and here. Total time on planet will be just under twenty-eight hours." Several barely audible sighs of relief were heard when they heard it *was* a raid. The officer recognized the looks of relief and continued.

"Sorry to tell you, but this is not going to be an easy mission. This area to our south is a known habitat for Drakk'Har and will not be assaulted by ground forces. It will be attacked by orbital bombardment prior to the landing. However, it is felt that this will only be harassing fire, in effect, as they typically have bunkers and escape tunnels to retreat to for the duration. Intelligence feels there is a strike force of up to two hundred croc warriors in this area, and they will try to interdict Second Regiment during its sweep. Our job is to ensure that does not happen. Also, should Second Regiment require reinforcements, we will withdraw from the hill and act as a mobile reserve.

"Support: As I said, we will have engineers to our rear during the initial sweep. Once in place at Hill 170, we will have an element of field engineers on the north slope of the hill with a battery of mortars. They are assigned to Brigade and designated call sign 'Apple,' but I am sure we can convince them to lob a few rounds our way. Especially if their backsides are on the line." That got the laugh he wanted. "I have spoken with the engineers and convinced them to bring along a couple of cases of toe-popper and Claymore mines." That had cost him a couple of bottles of best Scottish whiskey, but Wicks did not tell them that. The mines were for his protection, as well as that of his troops. He continued, "In addition, we have several elements of lighters for close fire support. We will coordinate this through the fleet Forward Air Controller, call sign 'Dragon.' As we will eventually be in a defensive posture, each man will receive double rations of ammo and frags. If we go mobile, we will turn the extras over to 2nd Lieutenant Coleman's squad on the east face, as they will be taking over our positions if we withdraw.

"Chain of command: I will be Officer Commanding and will handle Fireteam Five. Sergeant Blake will be 2 I/C and in command of Fireteam Six. Squad command order of succession will be Corporal Sanchez, LCPL Cole, LCPL

Belliveau, LCPL Reid, PFC Messina, PFC Tyler, PFC Johnston, and then PFC Perkins. Our squad call sign is 'Herd Charlie.' Platoon call sign is 'Herd.' Company call sign is 'Zoo.' Radio frequencies will be in accordance with regimental standing orders. PFC Perkins will be RAD-OP and squad clerk for the mission.

"Timings: Per the warning order from Fleet, we will be forming up in the ready room beginning at 0530 for ammunition supply and weapons loading. Kit check will be complete by 0600. We will be boarding the descent lighter at 0610. We are in the third and final wave landing on the perimeter of the construction facility." That caused another round of quiet looks amongst the squad. Wicks knew *"Last in, last out"* was a standing order for the Marines. If you came in the first wave, you didn't have anyone supporting you, but at least you left in the first departure ship. If you were the last in, you generally had an easier time getting down, but you had to be the last one off planet. With no one watching your back, and Drakk'Har rockets being quite effective at killing ascending lighters, this was not a good position to be in. Of course, no one would volunteer for the first wave, as that was where most of the casualties would be inflicted.

"Terra firma at 0745. I want the sweep and support activities finished by no later than 1115. We will reach Hill 170 by 1430 and have all defensive positions finished by 1745." This produced low groans, but Wicks kept on talking. He looked over at Blake who was nodding as he made notes.

Wicks continued, "Extraction is scheduled at 1215 on D+1 by lighter. Rendezvous with the troop transport will be at 1335 with unloading and weapon clearing complete by 1500. Debriefing will follow one hour after arrival. Upon completion of the extraction, we will be setting course for home.

"Standing Orders: Dress will be field fatigues with body armor, helmet, and heavy order webbing. Camouflage paint and netting to be used on all positions. Each Marine will receive three days' water and food rations. There will be no open fires or heat sources exposed without permission. During daylight hours, we will maintain a 3/1-watch ending thirty minutes before sunset. After that point, we will maintain a 2/2-watch. Radio silence will be in effect, and we will use landlines when camped. Do not use RF transmissions unless in combat or your situation is urgent. If an enemy force is encountered, use frags first. Shooting will only mark our positions. They cannot see where a grenade came from, especially at night. Report contact prior to engaging where possible. Due to the short duration of the mission, we do not have a scheduled re-supply.

"Time check," Wicks finished. "It will be 1716 CUT on my mark... Mark."

Everyone checked their watch at his command. No one had to adjust his time, as the watches were automatically coordinated with wireless ship chronometers every minute. A pair of servers on *Aristotle* and several backups throughout the fleet kept everyone on the same time. In the field, the servers would not be available, but each wore a military timepiece that would be off less than a second a month by itself.

The lieutenant concluded in his British accent, "This will be a standard deploy and recover raid. If we are lucky, we will not see any action. If we do, we will protect the flank of Second Regiment to the best of our ability. I am told the general chose us for this mission due to our reputation. We shall not disappoint him. Questions?" Five seconds of silence followed. "Very well. Sergeant Blake, take over and I shall see you at 0500 on D-Day for final preparations. Carry on, please." He turned to leave.

* * *

"Ten-Hut!" Blake called out as the officer left the table. "Ok, relax. Right, you heard the L-T. This'll be a simple operation if you follow orders and use your common sense. I know for some of you, that will be a challenge. So remember, we have a week-long transit back to Allen's Rift, and we can fit a lot of push-ups and cleaning duties into that time." A hard stare across the squad reinforced the point.

He continued, "In addition to the L-T's orders, you will pack two sets of spare batteries for your NVG's and COMM units, along with solar rechargers. The planet is sub-tropical, so put anti-fungal powder in your boots and carry a bottle with you, along with spare socks. I ain't carrying you home with some funky alien mildew. Each corporal will carry an anti-venom kit in case the local wildlife takes a liking to you. No open fire means no smoking in plain sight, either. Remember, croc rockets are quite good at heat seeking. I don't want to see anyone on duty smoking, period. Last, we'll have heat packs for the rations. If you want to use yours for your sleeping bags, that's your call, but I don't want to hear any bitching if we end up staying extra time. There is no resupply planned for the duration, so use them wisely. Sanchez, you will supervise weapon ammo supply and food rations. Questions?"

"Yes, Sergeant." This came from LCPL Cole. "On the subject of rations, the L-T didn't give us the radio freq's for lighter pizza delivery." Everyone laughed briefly. Even Blake smiled slightly at this. Cole was the squad cut-up, and a bit of humor never hurt to cut the tension.

"All right. Any *serious* questions?" the sergeant asked. After the usual five seconds of silence, he added, "OK, Cole and Messina. Get down to the kitchen, and ask the cooks for some medium-size tin cans. Make sure they are clean and spray-painted green inside and out. Then drill two holes in the bottom of each. I want at least a dozen. Talk to one of the tech weenies on board, and grab a big bag of assorted small nuts and washers. Plus, I want each of you to have at least two hundred meters of field wire. I want them ready to go when we get onto the hill. I'll fill you in then. The rest of you, until departure orders are given, I want you to get your gear in order..." He glanced at Perkins momentarily. "...and then get as much rack time as you can. I want you alert down there and ready for anything. Once we leave, we cannot come back for anything. Stay in your rack, the rec hall, or mess area until departure. If I need you for anything, I don't want to have to hunt for you. Dismissed."

The troops left, and Blake stayed behind to assess the orders. After reaching the hill, they had three hours to set up squad defensive positions, set arcs of fire, dig trenches, and set tripwires on the main approaches to the hill. They would have to haul butt to get it done, but they were paid to do just that. Besides, once the holes were dug, they would probably be stationary until ascent the following day. No planned patrolling or scheduled movements, so they had little to complain about. Just the usual bitching that a soldier did whenever you mentioned work. Blake smiled inwardly, remembering his own groaning when he was a private. Blake wondered if he had ever been as whiny as Perkins and immediately dismissed the thought, refusing to even consider it.

Blake looked over his notes. A 3/1 watch meant that for every four people in the squad, one had to be on lookout while the other three slept, rested, ate, or whatever. After nightfall, moving to a 2/2 watch increased readiness. Two soldiers on lookout while two rested. As two soldiers shared a "hole," one had to be looking for the enemy while the other tried to rest. To the veteran soldier, it sounded like an easy op. Time would tell.

* * *

Dear Karmina,

We have just received our briefing for the latest mission. Sergeant Blake told us that if we wrote a letter, it would go out today. So I thought I had best do that while I have the chance. I would normally send a DigiVid message, but the truth is, it seems like every Marine on board is in line in the rec center, and there was no one at the library terminals, so I thought I would write instead. Besides, you have seen my ugly mug before, and nothing has changed. If I wanted to get this message out to you in time for the message drone, I had to type it. Sorry, babe. Will record a vid on the way out of the system. I am attaching a still pic of the squad and me at the end of this letter. Tyler took it. She set it up on the timer, but could not get back in frame in time, so that is her back on the right. Not sure if you met her or not on the Rift. The pic was taken in the squad bunkroom on the troop ship. Cannot tell you which one, but they are all the same. The military must have gotten a great deal on gray paint. The walls are gray, the floors are gray, and the ceilings are gray. Even the blankets are gray. For some reason, only the sheets and pillows are white. Anyway, in the front row is Belliveau on the left. Then beside him are Cole and Perkins. In the back row are Sanchez on the left, then me on the right. You can see I am wearing the T-shirt you sent in the last package. Oh, and the fudge was great. It was all melted and squashed by the time I got it, but I made sure everyone had a piece, including the sarge and L-T. I wish I could tell you what they all did in the squad, but the censors are pretty crabby when we talk about "military secrets." Wish I could tell you about the mission, too. Looks like a fairly easy one and definitely low risk on the grand scale of things. I know you worry about me. Just as much as I worry about you. However, the truth is, I am with good people who know what they are doing, and I could not be in better hands.

I have 8 hours off and I wanted to write you before heading off to my rack. After the briefing, I spent my day cleaning and packing my gear and then spray-painting tin cans green, believe it or not. Seems the sarge thinks we can take on the crocs with them. We will see what he has in mind later. The paint I used stuck to everything. I am getting a bit of leftover green paint on the keypad as I write this. Oh well, it is green, too.

I am sorry to hear about your Aunt Clara in your last vid. Maybe you can take a week off and get over to see her for a while. I know we have a few bucks extra in savings and you do need a bit of a vacation. I am sure my Mum could take the little guys off your hands for a few days. She loves to spoil them. Besides, we can always buy a new living room set later. So if you want to take the time and fly over to see your Aunt, feel free. I will not be able to see you for at least three weeks after getting back anyway, so you will get a couple of paychecks deposited. There is the usual week fleet quarantine and then the usual week of BS with duty shifts and training. When they release me, I will try to catch a hyper-transport home for a few nights. They try to be as flexible as possible with the married guys, so I have an advantage over most here.

I do look forward to seeing you and the kids again. Thank David for his picture. I am not sure what he drew, but I have it stuck to the underside of the rack above me beside your picture. You said it was a finger painting, but I can see he must have used a few other body parts as well. I love the pictures, Kar. They are the last things I see at night, and the first things I see in the morning. Keep 'em coming.

I miss you, darling. I know you never signed on as a military wife, and that damned draft screwed up a lot of our plans. However, you have a great job at the agency, and when this war is over, we can settle down in the area. I am sure I can find work in the city somewhere. With my veteran status, I am sure to find something. One thing I learned is a lot of big companies use vet status as a tiebreaker sometimes.

Anyway, time to hit the hay. I love you, darling. Kiss the kids for me, and tell them Pops will be home soon.

Love,

Pete

* * *

Commander Collins looked at the vid feed on his terminal. The *Aristotle* cameras had just oriented on planet Mindon-3, which was well ahead of the fleet. The high resolution images showed nothing but glaciers, snow, and violent weather. The planet surface was windswept and featureless, with no signs of life or habitats. He was not surprised by the lack of life; the spectroscopy readings showed less than two percent oxygen present in the atmosphere. The readings indicated large quantities of methane, carbon dioxide, nitrogen, and hydrogen. Sensors detected a copious amount of hydrochloric acid, as well. But as the temperature at the equator was minus ninety Celsius, the acid was frozen—a dead ball of ice. The recce ships reported no ships or artificial objects in orbit, so he saw no threat to the fleet. He returned his attention to his data monitors.

No resistance had been encountered to this point. The encounter in the asteroid belt was well behind them, and it appeared as if the outpost had been silenced. Even though a warning signal had been sent, it appeared that tactical surprise had been achieved. Collins was always nervous at this stage of an operation. He wondered if the marshal felt nervous as well. A quick glance over his shoulder showed that the marshal was at his station, reviewing plans for the landing operation. Outwardly, Kosnov appeared totally calm. *I wonder how he does it,* Collins mused.

Collins returned his attention to his command board and began to review the data being produced by the intelligence staff. A fairly complete picture of Mindon-2 and its defenses had been assembled in very little time. Since Collins sat at the Tactics (Space) board, he disregarded any information from within the atmosphere of Mindon-2. Instead, he concerned himself with locating enemy satellites and ships in the system that could threaten them. A commander named Christensen was studying the planetary data at the Tactics (Ground) station directly beside him. He could see Christensen was busy assembling target and priority lists for the pre-invasion bombardment.

Although the two men had worked together only a year, they had developed a strong symbiotic relationship. Millions of data blocks were transferred between the two stations almost wordlessly. Collins remembered an exercise earlier in the year when the marshal had the men switch positions and was surprised to see them carry out the other's duties flawlessly. The tall Australian and the stocky, bearded Norwegian were also best of friends.

Collins turned to his counterpart. "You know, Jorge, the information we're getting from Mindon-2 is amazingly similar to the preliminary data we got from the Special Forces people. I've heard quite a bit about the new *Wraith* class, but I didn't think they were this advanced. Look, we've had twenty of our best remote probes in orbit around the planet for two hours, and we're just starting to update the information base. Our initial dataset was gained by one *Wraith* during a single orbit. We've got to get one of those ships for the fleet."

Christensen's eyes sparkled in amusement as he heard his colleague speak. He replied quietly, "I doubt if you'll ever see one of those ships in regular service. The cost of that technology is prohibitive. I heard if they made a *Wraith* out of solid gold, it would be cheaper. Besides, the Special Forces have full control of the program. They're not going to share them willingly. Be satisfied that they gave us the data to use on this operation. The rumor mill says they only have three operational."

Collins considered this before replying, "I still think they would be better off with the deployed fleets. We would get faster, more accurate intelligence in almost real time. I think the expense would be worth it."

Christensen chuckled softly. "For the price of one *Wraith*, you could buy three standard recce ships and a pair of cruisers with full crews to protect them. Consider this, too. If one of our probes is detected and destroyed, we lose a minor percentage of our intelligence-gathering potential. If we were to lose an entire *Wraith*, we would have our data-gathering capability crippled. That would leave the fleet deaf and blind."

"All right, Jorge, I'll tell you what. When we get back to the Rift, let's set up some computer simulations and see what happens to a fleet's potential when you add one of the new ships, okay?"

"Sounds good, Ben. It can't hurt anything. However, I'll bet you a case of Carlsberg that there is no significant improvement in overall performance." Christensen punctuated the challenge with a broad smile.

"You're on. I'll put up a case of Four X. The beer will go down great when I watch the Australian rule finals on DigiVid next month."

A comically puzzled look came over Christensen's face as he retorted, "There are rules?"

A flashing light and audible tone cut off Collins's sarcastic response. His command board automatically changed the display to the one for threat analysis.

Collins spent several seconds absorbing the new data before reporting, "Marshal, we have a proximity alert warning. Four, correction, there are five vessels approaching the fleet on an intercept course at high speed. Request permission for an active scan, sir."

Kosnov replied without hesitation, "Permission granted; conduct a full EM sweep. Sound general quarters for space action."

"Yes, sir."

Under a second later, the fleet began to radiate powerful detection beams in all directions. Even though the radiated energies traveled at the speed of light, it took several minutes for them to travel out to the distant targets and back again. While they waited for the signals to return, klaxons sounded, indicating crews were to rush to their assigned battle stations. Some had to walk a few meters, while others caught out of position ran much further to be where they needed to be. The rush to get to their stations was also slowed by the need to open and close all of the heavy blast hatches necessary to compartmentalize the ships. Compartmentalization minimized damage and, even more serious, air loss.

Collins referred to the new data on his monitors before speaking, "Marshal, we have five Drakk'Har warships, designated Force One, approaching from one seven zero slash one four relative, speed is .45 C, time to intercept is six minutes. There are three more warships, designated Force Two, approaching at .27 C and decelerating just behind them. The second group seems to have come from the area of Mindon-2. Force One is on an intercept heading. Force Two is either entering high orbit around Mindon-3 or that may be a deceleration maneuver, sir. There are no other threats registering at this time. Sir, the lead group of warships is maintaining a steady velocity and course; they are not decelerating."

Kosnov confirmed the relayed data on his own monitors before giving orders. "Have the fleet adopt defensive posture Delta. Bring the fleet to new course zero four five slash one

one. All ships are to commence firing at Force One at thirty light seconds distance. When they have passed, re-orient all weapons on Force Two, but fire only if they approach closer than one light minute distance."

Collins turned to face his superior. "Marshal, shall I detail a pursuit force to follow the lead group after it passes?"

"Negative, Mr. Collins. We need all the ships we have to protect the transports. At their current speed, it will take them half a day to turn around and return. By then, we will have dealt with the second group and be ready for them."

"Very good, sir."

* * *

Kosnov considered the high-speed approach of the enemy ships as idiotic tactics. At the speed they were traveling, accurate weapon targeting was nearly impossible. He considered two possibilities why they were approaching this way. First, they thought his forces would panic at their approach and break up the formation. Or they were on a suicide mission to take out as many ships as possible. The second possibility was unlikely. Drakk'Har had the same sense of self-preservation as humans, as they had shown no desire for kamikaze-style tactics, at least not *en masse*. So, logically, they wanted to divide the Federation fleet.

Kosnov was limited in his responses to the attack. Splitting off a pursuit force to follow the lead group of enemy only divided the limited assets he possessed. Yet, if he didn't do something about them, they would return to accost them later, probably during the landing operations when they were in orbit and unable to maneuver. Then he considered the question of the follow-on force of three enemy warships. He needed the firepower of all his cruisers to deal with them in a timely manner. Kosnov found himself trapped between two unpopular choices. He thought about it and chose neither.

The marshal spoke. "Mr. Christensen, as I recall from our meeting last month, the cruisers have been equipped with OIDs?"

"Yes, sir," Christensen replied. "Each cruiser carries ten as part of its standard load."

"Can they be deployed in free space?" Kosnov queried.

Christensen swiveled his chair around to face his superior before replying, a thoughtful look on his face. "Theoretically, no, sir. The onboard sensors would be useless. They require a planet, moon, or other strong gravitational source to orient their sensors properly."

"Yes, but that aside, they can still be detonated by remote control, correct?" the marshal asked impatiently.

"Yes, sir, that capability was recently added to aid clearing operations." Christensen appeared to be thoroughly confused by this exchange.

"Excellent." The marshal began manipulating several controls on his chair arm. "Mr. Christensen, have each cruiser deploy three OIDs into the pattern I am transferring to your screen. They are to be in these positions in exactly five minutes thirty seven seconds from now."

* * *

Christensen acknowledged the order and returned his attention to his station. He saw an umbrella-shaped pattern made up of twenty-one separate points with seven equidistant arms appear on his monitor. Christensen curbed his natural curiosity and issued the necessary orders into the command communication channel. While waiting for the cruisers to respond, he took a moment and noted the position of the pattern. Up in the right hand corner of his monitor screen, an event counter was counting down in increments of hundredths of a second. It currently read 00:00:12:17:25. He wondered why that time was so important. Just as the last cruiser acknowledged the orders, Christensen saw another piece of displayed information. The track of Force One was displayed and was the missing piece to the puzzle. Christensen understood instantly what Kosnov had planned. He turned back toward the marshal with a wide grin.

"Sir," Christensen said, "all cruisers have reported back. They are commencing launch procedures." He then paused momentarily. "Very unorthodox tactics, sir. They won't know what hit them."

Kosnov managed a brief smile. "Thank you, Commander, I thought I would have to explain myself for a moment. I underestimated you."

* * *

Meanwhile, several dull black spheres were launched from the back of each cruiser at regular intervals. Being no more than a meter in diameter, they disappeared from view almost immediately. Small booster rockets on each device flared briefly, sending the devices off in pre-determined directions. They retreated silently from the fleet, unguided, into space and spreading apart slowly.

The rest of the fleet were scrambling to position themselves into the required defensive formation. Fleet posture *Delta* was a simple maneuver in theory, but when you had to change the course of a bulky ship in such close proximity to others, things got complicated. Each tender, troop transport, and even the command ship moved to the rear of the fleet and slipped in behind a designated cruiser. The cruisers formed the tip of a spear, in effect, with the more vulnerable ships taking shelter behind the protection of the cruisers' powerful combat shields. The recce ships were the exception to this tactic, as they spread out even further from the fleet, ensuring their own survival.

All of the ships in the fleet possessed low-power navigation shields, but they were useless in combat. Doctrine dictated that the cruisers would place themselves between the enemy and the other ships to protect them from the brunt of enemy firepower. Around the cruisers, shields that were normally at a low power setting to push dust and other space debris out of the way were now glowing a deep violet hue from the vast energies imparted to them. On board all of the Federation ships, generators began to wind up to operating power for the weapons systems. Crews ran last minute diagnostics on their systems to make sure that they would work when called upon. Damage control technicians began moving to their appointed stations.

Medical and rescue supplies were broken open and distributed to all sections with the fervent hope that they would not be needed. Damage control teams climbed into space suits in case of a hull breach. Internal hatches and bulkheads were tested and secured to minimize atmosphere loss. Hundreds of people completed detailed checklists and reported their status to their superiors. In a few brief minutes, Fleet Nine had transformed itself into a battle-ready armada.

After all ships had reported their combat readiness to the command ship, a brittle silence fell over the command staff. Everything that could be done to meet the threat had been done. Nothing else could be done except wait for the enemy to come into weapons range. This was definitely the calm before the storm. A few of the more religious people took a few seconds to pray silently to their deity of choice for protection or forgiveness. Many more people would have prayed if they had the time. The majority simply concentrated on their job and, either consciously or unconsciously, blocked out any dark, foreboding thoughts.

Kosnov ensured that his seat restraints were tight enough to hold him in place. Although all ships were provided with artificial gravity fields, they were low-priority systems. That meant that if a sensor or weapon required extra energy during combat, the artificial gravity was shut down automatically and without warning to supply the required power. Without the restraints, the battle staff would find themselves floating around the room. Zero gravity was a rare sensation and normally regarded as a treat. However, it lost its appeal quickly when trying to control a space battle.

The marshal checked the miniature displays built into his arm rests one last time. The fleet was arranged in a wedge shaped formation that gave maximum overlapping fields of fire along the attack axis. The fleet's pattern also presented minimal targeting area to the approaching alien ships. Kosnov disliked standard tactics. He felt any tactic used more than once was predictable, and that made the enemy's job easier. However, he had adopted a standard defensive tactic purposely. He wanted the enemy commander to think that this was a classic space engagement scenario with no surprises. What happened next surprised him, however.

Collins spoke as the enemy ships closed. "Force One speed and course unchanged. Coming into visual range now. Ship profile analysis is complete. Inbound vessels are identified as Sledge class, light destroyers. They can—" Collins stopped in mid-sentence, not quite believing the report. "Marshal, we have visual scans of Force One. Three of their vessels are executing Patankar's maneuver!"

The marshal considered this. Captain Uttar Patankar had been the master of the cruiser *Titan* at the battle of Vega. His ship and five others were tasked to guard a troop convoy from Vega to Rigel-7. They had just been forming the last of the convoy when attacked by a superior number of Drakk'Har warships. Surprised and outnumbered, Patankar had rushed a group of heavy Drakk'Har destroyers at high speed to keep their guns off of the transports he was guarding. Realizing that it would take him too long to turn around to re-engage them, he elected to make a 180-degree turn in space so he was, in effect, flying backwards. This was exceedingly dangerous, as a ship's rear defense screen was usually its weakest point. Before reaching the ships, Captain Patankar ordered a full-force burn on his main engines, which shook the ship violently, but slowed it quickly. The flare from the engines also rendered visual targeting by the enemy useless, as they were staring into a light as bright as ten suns. Patankar passed the enemy ships at a high enough velocity that he only received a few minor hits on his rear shields. However, as a result of his reorienting his ship, he was able to shoot directly into the rear shields of the attacking destroyers with his main batteries as he passed. Two of the destroyers were damaged extensively and had to break off. The other two Drakk'Har vessels did attack the transports and caused extensive damage, but they also had to break off when the cruiser returned. The tactic allowed the cruiser to return to the battle in minutes, instead of hours. While damage to the transports was serious, Patankar's maneuver, as it came to be known, reduced it dramatically. The price for such heroics was high. His cruiser suffered cracks in the engine mounts and needed extensive yard work to be fixed. Plus, he had burned most of his fuel and would have been drifting had there been a follow-on force, but Patankar received a Medal of Honor for directly saving the lives of several thousand troops and crew.

That had occurred two months earlier, and apparently the Drakk'Har survivors of the Vega battle learned from that experience. The light destroyers attacking the fleet were not the same class of ships from Vega, so they were not the same crews. This meant they shared intelligence and adapted quickly.

Now the marshal was on the receiving end of Patankar's maneuver, and he did not like it one bit. Three of the Drakk'Har ships were oriented with weapons pointed backwards so they could shoot into the ships trailing behind the cruiser shields. Two were still pointing forward.

Probably using their shields to clear the path of dust and space gas for the other ships.

Yet, recognizing that meant nothing. Time was against them, as ships had just finished getting into the *Delta* formation by the marshal's earlier orders. Plus, the second force was approaching.

They are hoping I break formation to deal with the first force in my rear while the second slower force lances into the scattered transports. Smart. Damned smart, the marshal thought. Ordinarily he could do nothing in such close time constraints, and the Drakk'Har knew it. Thankfully, he had already played an ace the enemy did not know about.

"Steady as she goes, Mr. Collins. Sound collision alarms fleet wide," the marshal ordered.

As the enemy fleet passed within forty-light-seconds-range of the fleet, the seven cruisers began the final phase of weapon arming. Several hundred molecules of anti-matter were magnetically transferred from their storage bunkers and injected into negatively charged holding fields inside each weapon. These fields suspended the volatile material away from any "real" matter and held them inside the bores of the heavy guns. It took the full output of a nuclear reactor sitting beside each barrel to provide the energy required to generate the magnetic "bubble" around each anti-matter cluster. Stable fusion reactions still had not been perfected. However, clean fission reactors that produced no radioactive waste were used.

In other parts of the cruisers, fission reactors in the secondary armament systems super-heated exotic mixtures of several liquid heavy metals. Sodium, uranium, mercury, and other materials were quickly heated into a gaseous state. The thick gas was passed into a second chamber where the gas was compressed and more heat energy applied. The resulting material was then routed into well-insulated bunkers that maintained the temperature of the mixture at a pre-plasma state. The bunkers had to replenish themselves continuously, due to the heat loss.

Throughout the rest of the fleet, pulsed LASER turrets of varying power began receiving energy from their generators. Large capacitors in each system were energized and held at full capacity.

Other weapons systems were brought on-line as well. Electronic jammers were powered up and placed on standby. Humans simply powered the systems on and prepared to watch as the computers fought the majority of the battle for them. The speed of modern space battle had outpaced human thought. The tactical computers on each cruiser examined the advancing threat and, after referencing hundreds of thousands of pre-fought computer simulations, chose an appropriate fire plan. At the thirty light second range selected, they activated.

The first weapon fired was the last one the enemy would encounter. Each cruiser blasted hundreds of softball-sized depleted uranium projectiles toward the enemy in a tight cone. They traveled only slightly faster than the fleet that launched them. They were simple spheres with no sensors or electronics.

The main armament of the cruisers then fired in unison. Magnetically suspended anti-matter charges surged toward the enemy vessels. The magnetic field stopped any matter from connecting with the antimatter. After being fired out of the barrel, the negative polarity charge surrounding the anti-matter was no longer being regenerated. It dissipated within seconds, leaving a few exposed atoms of anti-material traveling at near the speed of light. The sole purpose of the magnetic bubble was to act like a safety fuse and ensure the anti-matter did not detonate too close to the firing ship or its companions.

Anti-matter was once considered a boon to mankind. Dreams of anti-matter reactors abounded, with promises to overshadow all other power generation technologies within decades. Unfortunately, the anti-matter decided to not share that dream as the manufacture and storage was difficult. By its very nature, anti-matter was unstable, and attempts to store more than a few thousand anti-atoms always resulted in disaster, and no one knew why. There had been many theories offered, but none held up to scrutiny. The Anti-Matter Research facility was located on one of Jupiter's moons. Europa was the only place allowed to conduct research on and manufacture anti-matter. No other colony or facility was allowed on the entire moon. Another difficulty was the power generated by an anti-matter explosion could not be contained. Antimatter released twenty thousand times more energy than fission. How powerful was this? Consider that the antiparticles travel at close to the speed of light, which is roughly three hundred thousand kilometers per second. With the bubble protecting the charge for a few seconds only, the resulting explosion would be six hundred thousand kilometers away from the cruiser firing the charge. This was considered minimum "safe" distance. As a comparison, the moon orbits roughly four hundred thousand kilometers from Earth. Until mankind could solve these severe problems (and even the theorists were stumped), this was a pipe dream.

As the anti-matter charges advanced toward the oncoming ships, the Drakk'Har defensive shields began to deflect them just as any other piece of space dust. These charges were not designed to impact directly on the hull of a target, although that would have been preferred. Instead, a proximity explosion was hoped for. When the protective magnetic field was gone, the anti-matter became totally unprotected. One of the packets was deflected away from the Drakk'Har destroyers, only to touch a small fist-sized rock that had also been deflected out of the way. Matter and anti-matter kissed for a brief instant. A spherical globe of pure energy a thousand kilometers across expanded in the blink of an eye. Everything within that globe was incinerated and cast out at terrifying speeds. Gas, dust, pebbles, and small meteorites flew in all directions. The Drakk'Har ships were one hundred ten thousand kilometers away, and they still felt the wrath of the explosion. All of the ships were lashed with hard radiation, which scrambled their sensors for a few precious seconds. One light destroyer received a direct hit amidships with a small, fast-moving pebble of rock accelerated by the blast, killing everyone in that section from explosive decompression. Another anti-matter charge exploded well behind the ships. It caused no damage, but psychologically shook the crews facing the rear.

The cruisers reloaded and fired anti-matter every five seconds. The first volleys were usually the most effective. Early explosions either destroyed or cast out everything in a given area, making it less likely to get a subsequent impact. However, the fleet got lucky. A single atom of xenon encountered one of the last anti-matter packets just as it lost its magnetic bubble. Xenon is the rarest of the inert gasses. It became even rarer when it disintegrated upon encountering the anti-matter. Another globe of energy expanded directly in front of the lead Drakk'Har warship. The shock wave, combined with assorted debris impacting on the hull, destroyed the ship as effectively as a sledgehammer striking an ant. The crew never knew what hit it. Even if they had survived, the radiation levels would have cooked them many times over. The four other ships flew through the same area moments later, but that brief time saved them from any severe radiation.

The main armaments kept firing until the enemy reached the six light-second range. Safety cut-off switches engaged, and the primary armament fell silent.

At five light-seconds distance, the secondary armaments of the cruisers fired. However, so did the weapons of the surviving Drakk'Har warships.

* * *

"Drel" directly translated means "to eat carrion." A Drakk'Har always ate live prey. Exceptions to this were things such as deep-space duty, long deployments to hostile or isolated environments, or wherever it was impractical to keep live food. Normally, the local commander had to assess the local conditions and make the decision. In the cases where live food was impractical, a vitamin-rich mixture of bacteria, looking like brown oatmeal, was substituted. The bacteria within the mixture was alive and, therefore, acceptable to the Drakk'Har edict. Being filling, it contained the necessary vitamins and energy to sustain a Drakk'Har for several months, if necessary. However, it certainly was not the preferred food choice. Drakk'Har law was quite specific on this. Only live food or the vitamin substitute was acceptable. Any Drakk'Har who consumed anything but those things was classed as Drel—the most insulting label one Drakk'Har could attach to another. Uttering this as a curse at a superior would result in the immediate death of the junior. Cursing an inferior with this word would result in a challenge.

The punishment for Drel was scripted in Drakk'Har law: immediate imprisonment, loss of all rights, and as soon as possible, the offender was transported to a planet known simply as The Oven. The Oven was the harshest environment a Drakk'Har could imagine. Close to a white dwarf star, the surface of the planet had been bombarded by intense stellar radiation for millennia. Its seas had evaporated long ago, leaving a klem-thick surface of salt. Solar winds from the dying sun whipped into the thin oxygen atmosphere surrounding the planet, causing harsh, hot winds. Small particles of the abraded surface were picked up by the winds, causing a continuous salt blast. Mountains were reduced to small hills. Valleys were filled to form mild depressions. Everything on the surface was slowly desiccated, then covered by salt dust. On The Oven, nothing beyond single-cell creatures existed. No natural water, no food, and no chance of survival in the long term.

Sh-Elerk was Drel and facing such a future. A former shuttle pilot, he lost his position when wounded in battle. One of his arms had been removed at the elbow by a piece of flying shrapnel. Unable to fly, he was reassigned to supervise a worker shift on Mindon-2. That had lasted only a few months when tragedy struck again. An access tunnel under one of the growing spacecraft had been insufficiently strengthened at a major junction. Growth of the ship above had placed too much strain on the junction, and the tunnel collapsed with Sh-Elerk and five Drakk'Har being trapped inside. Planet Lord Slassh, more concerned with making sure the ship did not suffer any damage due to the collapse under it, diverted workers from the rescue to shore up the other tunnels under the ship. This caused a delay in retrieving the trapped Drakk'Har—almost twelve planet rotations. When workers finally reached the collapsed area, they found only two Drakk'Har barely alive. Trapped in the tunnels with no food or water, several died. The remaining creatures had no choice. Hunger combined with no hope forced them to eat the dead. The rescuers discovered the chewed stumps of limbs and

Drakk'Har teeth marks on bones. When found, they were immediately chained and jailed.

Now Sh-Elerk stood in the main hall of the complex. Moments ago, he had been roughly cast out of his small cell along with seven other Drel nearby. He recognized none of them, but they all bore the Drel brand on their brows. The searing hot pain that accompanied the brand marked their damnation. They did not speak and would not have even if they had a chance.

Survival dictated a harsh existence for Drel. The group had been assembled in a small room, and a high pressure hose had roughly removed most of the filth caused by their confinement. Their regular chains had been removed and lighter, ceremonial chains attached to wrists and ankles. He wore both wrist chains on the same arm due to his missing limb. Ceremonial chains were much weaker than the standard ones and easily broken. However, Sh-Elerk would never think of even trying. That would be an act of defiance, and any form of resistance to orders meant slow, unpleasant death.

Drel possessed no rights. While the law said they were to be taken to The Oven, the law also said "as soon as practical, as determined by the Planet Lord." This gave leeway to their disposition. Some kept Drel as personal slaves or workers in the harshest of conditions. Others subjected them to unspeakable tortures or medical experiments or as moving targets so their troops could practice with their rail guns. Drel had no rights, no recourse, and no appeal. They were the walking dead. Drel did as they were told, when they were told to do it. Failure to follow commands or showing insolence usually meant a quick trip to The Oven or a slow death at the hands of a medical technician. Slavery was the lowest form of existence, but it was preferred to the slow death of dehydration on the surface of The Oven.

Sh-Elerk was very puzzled at the treatment he was receiving. A domestic Drel normally used ceremonial chains around a dwelling. They were lighter and got in the way less. Why he was receiving this treatment he did not know. Was he destined to become a domestic servant? Or was there another reason?

Slassh entered the meeting chamber without warning. The guards in the room tensed, their weapons held at the ready. The prisoners were busy falling to their bellies. Slassh was known to be unpredictable at the best of times, and these were definitely not the best of times as far as Sh-Elerk was concerned. Slassh was the Planet Lord, and as senior commander on Mindon-2, he held the Drels' destinies in his claws. None of the eight Drel dared look at the Planet Lord. They picked spots on the floor and concentrated on keeping their gazes there.

Slassh addressed the eight Drel assembled in the room in his loudest and most abrasive tone. "I'm sickened beyond words at being in the presence of your kind. The smell alone would drive me insane. I've had requests for Drel from many Swamp Masters in the area. I'm told they wish to experiment with new medical techniques. You… are perfect candidates."

So we are to be killed through medical experimentation, Sh-Elerk thought. He was actually relieved. At least he knew what his fate would be. Terrible as that was, it could have been much worse.

Slassh continued while picking up several dispatches from a side table. He walked around the group, never taking his gaze from them. "Swamp Master D'Reuk requests two Drel for calibrating laser cutters in his production facility."

Not to fix the electronics, but to be tied to the table surface as laser light slowly cut pieces off them. Probably while the technicians bet on how long they would last, Sh-Elerk mused.

"Swamp Master Mgarnew wishes one of you as entertainment."

Mgarnew was reputed to use high voltages and whips to entertain himself. He needed new entertainment quite often, Sh-Elerk recalled.

"There are other requests, but I see no reason to repeat them…" Slassh's voice dropped an octave for effect, "…as I've decided to deny these requests… for the moment."

A lengthy pause followed. Slassh was waiting for a reaction. Sh-Elerk never budged, but his reptilian brain was running at full speed trying to comprehend what *was* in store for them.

The torturing barbarian. Get on with it, and consign us to our fates. What is it? Gladiatorial games? Open the airlock in vacuum, and see how long it takes before death? Infection with a flesh-eating virus? He is playing with us and enjoying every moment of it.

"You have a choice to make, Drel. The only choice you can ever expect to make for the rest of your lives. If you say no, then I'll reconsider the requests of the Swamp Masters. If you say yes, you'll die unchained and on your feet as free Drakk'Har."

Sh-Elerk's head snapped up in shock and met the gaze of the Planet Lord looking down on him. He heard the guards rush behind him, and he fully expected a torturous death. Slassh was looking directly at him; he had no way to cover the error. He had met the gaze of a Drakk'Har Planet Lord, and as Drel, he was to die painfully. Sh-Elerk watched Slassh raise his hand. He lowered his gaze and braced for the signal to end his life…

The next few seconds passed in slow motion for Sh-Elerk, but Slassh imperiously waved the guards back with his black claws. For the first time in his life, Sh-Elerk was shocked to the point where he had no conscious thought for many moments. The guards retreated against the wall. Sh-Elerk kept his gaze on the floor wondering what in the three moons was happening. This was unprecedented!

Slassh proceeded to explain the conditions of the "choice." In reality, they had none. To a condemned Drel, an offer to die unchained and free, instead of slow, agonizing death, was indeed fortuitous. They listened for several minutes.

They all accepted.

* * *

Jefferson made good time. The gyrocompass performed well, keeping her on course to Hill 170. Her weapon was constantly kept at shoulder height, ready for instant use. The pattern of her movement was slow and precise. Step. Look up, look in the middle, look down. Look left, look right. Step. Look up, look in the middle, look down. Look left, look right. Over and over and over. This technique was boring and tedious beyond words, but ambushes, tripwires, and booby traps were not just a human innovation.

At times, she made minor course corrections to keep her out of dense brush or impassible jungle. One of those corrections took her to the right of her main course to avoid a copse of trees that had blown over. This led her beside a small pond with lots of floating plants at the water's edge. A convenient sand bar led directly beside the pond. She had two choices: go across the sand bar or go the long way through dense brush. Daylight would be fading in a few hours, and darkness made travel that much harder. She sensed nothing in the immediate area and made a careful visual check of the surrounding bush. Nothing obvious, so she stepped onto the sand bar.

When she was halfway across, something made her freeze in place. Something was very, very wrong. She scanned all around slowly and saw nothing. She heard nothing. She smelled nothing. And yet, something was triggering a visceral fear response. She was experiencing the fight or flight response, and at this moment in time, she wanted to run. Her training alone allowed her to force the panic down. After the initial rush of anxiety, she began to think more clearly.

Using her tactical contacts, she turned on thermal imaging and scanned the bushes carefully. Creatures like Drakk'Har, even though they were cold blooded, would stand out boldly against the much cooler jungle. Seeing nothing, she went back to regular vision.

Special Forces doctrine stated that no one fought alone. It had been proven many times over that the fighting potential of a human being was multiplied many times over if someone else was there supporting them. Technically, Jefferson was supposed to have a second person to act as spotter/bodyguard.

However, it became obvious that having another member of the section along only made the pair more detectable. Her official partner was Private White. He was keen and eager to help, but in the bush, she was a shadow and he was a rhino. Several field exercises had proven to her L-T that she worked better by herself. So, Private White was left behind with the section more often than not. Jefferson had argued adamantly for the right to do her own thing, and she had eventually convinced the lieutenant with her arguments. Now, two kilometers away from Private White and the others, she wished that she had not been so convincing.

She looked at the sand bar first. No obvious trip wires, pressure plates, or traps. No footprints, marks, or disturbances. The surrounding forest was as it should be. No bunkers or visible emplacements. The jungle foliage was still in the calm air. Finally, she looked at the deep pool of water. Nothing was visible, and the plants seemed natural. The surface was lightly rippled and seemed perfectly—

Wait! she screamed mentally to herself, almost physically reacting. *The jungle is not moving because there is no wind, but the pond surface is rippling from something.* The possibilities ran through her mind in an instant. Drakk'Har were able swimmers. Had they spotted her and created an ambush? Or was it fish or some other natural life form that was no harm at all? Or was it something else that was stalking her? She glanced around and tried to locate the source of the rippling while remaining perfectly still otherwise. Her thumb quietly moved the RUK safety catch from safe to firing position.

At that moment, between her and the opposing shore, a Drakk'Har head emerged from beneath the surface, traveling perpendicular to the sand bar. Jefferson tensed herself and prepared to take a snap shot when a second, smaller head appeared under the first. She paused.

It became obvious that whatever the pair were doing, it was not immediately hostile to her. They were swimming lazily, apparently at random around the small pond. Their eyes caught her attention next. They were glazed over with something. She knew Drakk'Har had an inner set of transparent eyelids for swimming, and she deduced that must be what she saw. But what the hell were they doing?

Then, it hit her in a flash of memory. She was transported back to her senior year at high school. A few boys on the football team used to try to get some of the girls to go out to a local park where they would go skinny-dipping at night.

This was the local version of Inspiration Point. She could see that they were totally engrossed in each other, and she decided to move while they were heading toward the far end of the lake. As long as their inner lids were closed, she would be fuzzy and her camouflage should blend into the dense jungle behind her.

Jefferson began to move slowly toward the relative safety of the jungle at the end of the sand bar. Mentally, she addressed the swimming female and projected her will as much as possible. *Okay, sister, I don't know what that male wants, but you be a good little Drakk'Har and* give *it to him. Don't bother saving it for marriage. He will respect you in the morning, and he will vid you tomorrow. Just do your good friend Anita a huge favor, and keep him occupied for just a teeny bit longer. That's it. A little more.*

With a huge sigh of relief, she felt the jungle wrap around her once more. Feeling a hundred times better, she began to move away from the pool and its occupants at a quick pace. She reasoned that if they used this place as a local make-out spot, it was doubtful that many booby traps were around. She just wanted to put this place behind her as quickly as possible. She allowed herself one moment of whimsy. *Corporal Anita Jefferson, CEF-SF. Sniper, soldier, Olympic silver medal winner, and now, xenovoyeur.*

* * *

Until the twentieth century, science had classified all matter into three categories: solid, liquid, and gas. Solids, when heated, became liquids. Liquids, with enough energy, became gaseous. Plasma was the fourth stage of matter. Gases, when super heated, became plasma, and each stage of matter had its own set of rules. Plasma was difficult to produce, as it required a lot of energy to create. It needed even more energy to be maintained.

Two of the four surviving Drakk'Har warships opened fire at the same instant as the human fleet. The other two ships had their main armaments directed toward the rear and could only fire after they had passed by. Being light destroyers, they did not carry heavy armaments. They were not physically large enough to fit the proper power generation equipment. This made them no less effective at short range, by any means. Drakk'Har destroyers carried three types of offensive weapons. The first mimicked the weapons of the human fleet identically. Superheated plasma enveloped in a magnetic suspension field was fired through magnetic acceleration toward the target. The plasma inside the magnetic spheres or bubble was heated to several thousand degrees. As the plasma left the heavy barrels, the magnetic bubbles deteriorated quickly. Had the magnetic bubble remained around the plasma, the opposing shields could have easily deflected it. However, the initial gas mix used to create the plasma was formulated to be magnetically neutral. Being neither positively, nor negatively charged, the opposing shields had nothing to grab onto, as it were.

Both the human fleet and Drakk'Har vessels hurled magnetically wrapped plasma charges at each other. Only usable at short ranges, they were very effective. Human cruisers had the most powerful mobile shields in existence. The only stronger shields were the ones on Federation weapons platforms in orbit above Earth and the more important human colonies. However, the cruiser shields were insufficient to deflect plasma charges. Plasma charges burned through the shields easily, and several impacted on the surface of the fleet's cruisers. Although they contained little mass, they were traveling at substantial speed. The cruisers felt each impact like a thunderclap. Their thick composite armor served them well, and none of the plasma charges penetrated the hulls. However, several craters were produced by the scalding temperatures of the plasma marring the dark surface and weakening the armor with each strike.

The fleet's plasma charges all missed. The oncoming destroyers were much smaller than the cruisers and traveling much faster. The dynamics of striking the fast-moving targets were grossly against the Federation.

The other Drakk'Har weapon was less accurate to aim, but by no means harmless. Rapid-firing rail guns fired several hundred rounds a second into the fleet. Each projectile weighed a half-kilo. The cruiser shields could deflect these rounds, but three factors were against them. First, shields were more efficient when acting on a few objects or those of small mass. For example, if you were traveling through a gaseous cloud of hydrogen, there would be several billion atoms, but insignificant mass. Therefore, the shields could repel or deflect them easily. If you were in an asteroid belt, the mass of the floating boulders was much greater, but fewer in number. You simply slowed down, and in time, the asteroids would be shunted aside.

In the case of the oncoming bullets from the Drakk'Har, literally thousands of them were approaching at high speed with tremendous kinetic potential. Many of them got through the deflector shields, but as the rounds were crudely aimed, few actually hit. Once more, the cruiser armor saved the day. However, this time, several holes were punched through weakened sections of the armor and into the decks below. Interior bulkheads near the front of the cruisers were made of the same composite armor, but they were much thinner. Rounds were eventually stopped, but not until they had penetrated several decks, opening them up to the vacuum of space. While rounds hit the cruisers, they did their job and shielded the small ships trailing behind. No other ships were struck during the barrage.

* * *

On her bridge, the captain of the cruiser *Thermopylae* was being inundated with damage reports. Several visual and audible alarms were going off to indicate loss of atmosphere and the various problems associated with that. Her ship had been hit by a couple of dozen plasma charges and multiple bullet strikes. The damage control officer turned to speak to her in a clipped and terse tone.

"Captain, we've been struck by three rounds that have penetrated C and E decks. All batteries are still operational. Damage control crews are working effectively, and no critical systems have been hit. Two deflector arrays lost primary power, but we can resupply them with secondary sources. Initial casualties seem light. We should be fully operational within a minute or so."

Captain N'Gamo had descended from Zulu warriors and had royal blood in her. Her voice carried that authority. "Maintain fire on all batteries. Get medical down to those decks. I want those people taken care of, Smythe."

"Yes, ma'am." The damage control officer turned back to his station.

Inside the *Thermopylae,* dedicated damage control crews sprang into action. Their first priority was to stop the leakage of air into vacuum. Already dressed in space suits, they moved through the damaged sections holding smoldering wax that threw off a dark, wispy smoke. When they saw the smoke being pulled out of a hole in the bulkhead, they used flasks of hardening foam to seal the opening. The foam was pushed into the holes by the pressure of the internal air, where it expanded and hardened. Once the air leaks were stopped, others moved into the section to fight fires or assist the wounded. Then the real work of repairing damage to systems and recovering bodies began.

The last weapon of the Drakk'Har was released by the surviving ships: mines. These deadly, floating cylinders detected the magnetic aura given off by deflector shields. As long as the readings increased or stayed the same, nothing happened, but if the strength decreased, they exploded.

Strategies to combat mines were mixed and often depended on the captain in charge. Some, upon detecting mines, would vary their shield strength to explode them at a reasonable distance. Others turned off shields completely and waited until they drifted by. That was not a tactic used by many, as without shields, even dust could cripple a ship moving at high speed. Others fired at them with secondary armaments.

After releasing the last of the mines, the surviving Drakk'Har vessels came within one light-second distance of the Federation fleet. Up to that point, the survivors had been lucky enough to be untouched by Federation weapons. Their luck ran out.

The deployed depleted uranium spheres had floated ahead of the Federation fleet. To the humans, they moved ahead at a snail's pace. However, as Einstein proved, everything is relative, and the Drakk'Har ships were approaching rapidly. When they entered the area of spheres, their own high velocity rendered their shields incapable of deflecting them. Like geese flying through a hail of buckshot, it was inevitable that they would be hit.

One of the rear-facing destroyers was struck in its main engine cluster. The sphere's dense mass created carnage as it sliced easily through the heavy motor and its support structure. The sphere continued penetrating the engineering decks and exited near the front of the warship. Several critical power lines and control systems were destroyed, and the majority of the crew died instantly from either flying debris or explosive decompression. The engines roared to life from erroneous control signals sent from the damaged systems. No crewmembers survived to stop it. The wildly firing engine caused the vessel to tumble end over end. Completely out of control, momentum carried it onward.

Two spheres simultaneously struck a second Drakk'Har warship, this one facing forward. The first sphere lanced through the control section, where a bulkhead actually deflected it enough to send it back out into space. The second sphere penetrated just behind the control deck and went through the ship completely. Piercing a fuel cell on its way, it carried the contents through to the engineering deck where liquid hydrogen met more than enough heat and sparks to ignite. The resulting fireball consumed the vessel and sent pieces in all directions in a brilliant explosion.

On the bridge of the *Thermopylae,* the vid screens registered the fireball of the enemy destroyer. They would have cheered but for two reasons. The officers on the bridge were coordinating the firing, maneuvering, and operation of the cruiser, and they were all a little too preoccupied to cheer. The second reason was they did not have time. Precisely as that enemy vessel exploded, the first wildly tumbling Drakk'Har light destroyer impacted the *Thermopylae.*

Hitting the cruiser sideways, the Drakk'Har ship sliced through the top of the cruiser like a potato peeler, and the three upper decks were slashed from the main body. The upper engine of the *Thermopylae* was blown off and floated dangerously close to the troop transports. It missed by only a half kilometer, not all that great of a distance in space. The impact caused the Drakk'Har ship to explode behind the cruiser, directly on top of a tender. Shrapnel from the blast hammered the *Arthur C. Clarke* like a close-range shotgun blast. Hull breaches appeared everywhere on the upper decks. Several lighters on the underside were shaken free and floated away. No one who survived the impact onboard the *Clarke* would ever forget the feeling of being tossed around like beans in a tin can as the inertial dampers worked overtime to compensate. The massive vessel began to tumble out of control.

The two surviving Drakk'Har warships passed the fleet. The one facing forward stopped firing, as it no longer had any targets. The one facing the rear began to fire its secondary armaments for the first time at the smaller targets trailing the larger cruisers. Plasma and rail gun bullets raked the trailing ships. The velocity of the rounds was not as great as it was while they were approaching the fleet, as the ships were now flying away from each other. However, the shields at the rear of the ships were much weaker and armor almost non-existent. Several ships were hit in succession as the destroyer moved further away. It kept firing until it went out of effective range.

* * *

Kosnov watched as the enemy ships passed beyond effective weapons range. The command ship was not hit during the battle. At least, he had felt no impacts, nor seen any alarms. The enemy had caused a lot of damage on his fleet. The *Thermopylae* had been rammed, and she was hurt badly. A cruiser at the cost of three light destroyers was an unacceptable trade. He wanted those other two destroyers, and he had the means to have them.

"What is the time for Force One encountering the OID barrier?" Kosnov asked of Collins.

A quick reference to his screen told Collins what he wanted to know. "Sir, they will hit the barrier in twelve seconds. They are not attempting any course correction or speed change at this time."

Kosnov allowed himself a mild grin. "Activate the OID barrier. Fire at your discretion, Mr. Collins."

"Aye, sir," was the brief reply.

OID stood for Orbital Interdiction Device—essentially a smart mine designed for planetary siege. When introduced in orbit around a planet or moon, the OID would orient itself to the large body beneath it by detecting the gravity. Once oriented, it would scan downward using passive and, occasionally, active measures looking for ships boosting themselves off the surface. Once an ascending ship was found, the OID would coordinate with others, and one would be elected to attack. Maneuvering with powerful thrusters, the OID would move into close proximity of the target ship and explode. Without the gravity of a moon or planet, the sensors had no reference and no way to align themselves. Out of orbit, their sensors and maneuvering jets were useless. However, they did have the capacity to be remotely detonated.

Collins double- and then triple-checked the calculations. Not only did he have to time the activation of the mines to coincide with the enemy ships passing, but he also had to take into account the transmission time of the signal to the mines. It would take several seconds for the radio signal to reach the OIDs. He pressed the appropriate firing stud when the computer countdown rolled to zero.

The radio signal reached the OID barrier just before the Drakk'Har ship sensors picked up the objects. The outcome was inevitable. The OIDs exploded within thirty milliseconds of each other. Each OID contained a hydrogen bomb of two hundred fifty megatons. The fireballs overlapped in the umbrella spoke pattern the marshal had envisioned, creating a wall of deadly radiation and blast energy. Crews of both Drakk'Har ships were irradiated, and the ships' frames buckled in the heat of multiple fireballs. The shattered and lifeless hulks of the ships continued to drift at high speed and would eventually burn up in the atmosphere of Mindon-5 many months later.

* * *

Ensign Morton had been manning his damage control position on the *Thermopylae* when he was thrown off his feet by the incredible impact of the Drakk'Har warship. A metal bulkhead had stopped his brief arc through the air, and he landed heavily on his back. Only the thick composite metal helmet he wore saved his skull from serious damage, but it took him some time to stand again. He was in command of a small party of crew responsible for damage control in that section. Armed with foam guns and other pieces of equipment, they were to plug any air leaks in the bulkheads and then help the wounded to aid stations. His direct superior was Lieutenant

Schmidt, who was one level above with his own damage-control team.

He had no idea what had caused such a violent impact. His entire team seemed OK, but shaken. They had no serious injuries, save scrapes and bruises, among them. However, beyond people picking themselves off the floor, he saw no immediate damage in his section, so he followed procedure and tried to report their status to Lieutenant Schmidt. The wall-mounted COMM unit appeared dead. No lights or indicators were active. Internal communications seemed to be out. That was unexpected, as the COMM system was supposed to have several redundant circuits. He decided he had to report in person.

Morton turned to his shaken five-person damage-control team. One of the members was his second in command. "Petty Officer Rivera, I have to report our situation to the lieutenant. I'll be back in a few minutes. Stay alert, and if you find any damage, send a runner after me if the internal COMM system is not restored."

"Yes, sir."

Morton turned and moved toward the stairwell. Protected by thick blast doors, the stairwell interconnected several decks of the cruiser. The elevators would have been faster, but they were locked out when the ship was at General Quarters. Morton opened the hatchway and stepped through. He was closing the heavy door just as a large explosion ripped through the corridor he had just left. A rushing wall of orange flame whooshed down the passageway. The pressure of the flaming gas slammed the hatch closed, with the Ensign trapped inside the stairwell. Severe vibrations came through the floor as decking warped. The hatch jammed from the twisting supports. The ensign screamed and pounded on the hatch, trying to open it, knowing his team was in the inferno beyond. However, his strength was woefully insufficient to open the jammed hatch.

After a few minutes, Morton collapsed on the deck and leaned against the doorway. Tears of frustration coursed down his face as he was forced to accept his team was gone. The fiery fury of that explosion had killed them as surely as a bullet. Morton stood shakily. He had only two choices: go up the stairs or go down. He knew his superior was one level up, and so he ascended the stairs.

The loss of his team made each step felt like the artificial gravity had doubled. Wearily, he made his way up one deck level, and he stopped before the hatchway. His training told him to feel the door before opening it. If the metal was too hot, it meant a fire was there. If too cold, it meant that vacuum awaited him on the far side. It felt normal, so he wheeled the large hand crank, and the hatch opened slowly. He peeked through the crack and saw buckled plating. Heavy metal walkways had been compressed and bent in the explosion. Luckily, he saw no fire, just thin palls of smoke near the top of the ceiling.

He stepped into the passageway and walked straight into a wildly running figure dressed in a crewman's uniform. The man was screaming, "They're dead! They're all dead!" over and over again. The man's head and shoulder were covered in blood from several open wounds. Morton grabbed the man reflexively, and they fell to the deck in a heap. An open neck wound on the crazed man sprayed arterial blood all over Morton. Morton tried to hold him to calm him down, but the wounded man twisted free, scrambled to his feet, and carried on down the passageway. He disappeared around a corner, still screaming. Morton got up, took a second to wipe blood out of his eyes with his sleeve, and walked in the direction from which the man had come. That was where Schmidt should be.

He turned the corner and saw three figures lying motionless on the deck, surrounded by pieces of distorted metal. A gaping hole was just above the bodies, with black smoke issuing through a perforated blast door. One of the prone figures was dressed in an officer's uniform. A piece of bulkhead had penetrated his chest and pierced his heart. The other two looked as if they had died of flying shrapnel, as well.

He walked over to the officer and checked for a pulse. Nothing. The nametag read SCHMIDT. He repeated his check on the two other figures and, again, found no pulse. They were gone. He stayed there for several minutes. Tired and emotionally wounded, he wondered what to do. For a second, he almost gave up mentally. Then, something steeled inside him. He was alive, and he was a fleet officer. He had a duty to those under his command. If he did not do something, then who would? He looked down the corridor in both directions, but saw no one—not surprising as everyone would be at his or her duty station. With his superior dead, he had to report to the next highest officer, and that was a lieutenant commander located in Auxiliary Control two decks down.

Morton descended the stairs quickly. He put his hand near the blast door through which he had originally entered and could feel searing hot temperatures. An intense fire was still raging on the far side. He continued down another level and again felt the blast door. It felt normal, and he cracked the latch. The sound of smoke detectors going off, running feet, and people shouting greeted him. A rumble of a distant explosion sounded above him, and he felt vibration run through the deck plates.

"Hold that door!" screamed someone as a senior enlisted man appeared around the doorframe. He had chief's rank insignia and a nametag that read RAWSON. He was filthy, covered in oil and soot. "Sorry, sir. A falling roof truss snapped off the door latches on this side. We couldn't get access to the stairwell. We have several wounded we need to get to medical." Morton moved into the corridor to talk to the chief. "I need to report to Lieutenant Commander Duke. There's been a major explosion on the next deck up. There may be people trapped up there."

"Sir, he's dead. He was thrown into an electrical panel in Auxiliary Control when we got hit. We tried to call the bridge, but internal COMMs are out. We got part of that explosion down here, too. We have several fires and collapsed corridors."

"Who is in—"

The young ensign's words were interrupted by the shrieking sound of collapsing metal falling behind him. Tons of metal and support trusses fell inside the stairwell as the entire stair system collapsed. Seeing the metal fall, the two men instinctively pressed the blast door closed. Several others saw what they were doing and added their weight to the effort. It closed with a heavy *thunk*.

Morton turned to the chief. "The stairwell option is out for the moment. Chief, who is in charge here?"

"Well, sir, until you came, I was. All of the officers were either killed or severely wounded. You're the only one with officer's rank present now." The most junior of officers out-ranked the most senior of chiefs. Rawson looked him over. "Are you bleeding, sir?"

"What? Oh, no, Chief. I'm fine. Listen, I may be in command, but if you have any ideas, I want to hear them without prompting. We need to contact the bridge or at least medical and get help down here for the wounded. If the stairwell is not an option, then there may be another route up there."

"Not for the moment, sir. The only undamaged corridor open at the moment is the one to Engineering. They lost most of their people in a hard radiation leak. They have it contained now, but they only have one in five people still standing, and they are mostly junior people. We can try cutting through to the deck above with oxy-torches."

"Negative, Chief. Not up, at any rate. There is an intense fire burning up there. What is below us?"

Rawson thought about this quickly. "Crew rooms and the mess, sir. There are no cross-connecting passages for us to make it to. We might be able to do that in Engineering, though. They have access levels that go up three decks. We might get on top of the fire and cut a hole into the upper deck. I can get on that right away if—" He looked at the officer with a pensive expression.

"Sounds good, Chief. While you handle that, which way to Auxiliary Control? I need to see if we can get comms back up.

We might be able to get help from the bridge, if we can communicate."

"Down that corridor, second hatch on the right."

"Good. Thanks, Chief. I'll try to get some help." Another explosion rumble was felt through the soles of their feet. The men exchanged a tense look. The *Thermopylae* was in bad shape, and they both knew it.

* * *

Aboard the command ship, Kosnov had watched the destruction of the last two enemy ships with a small degree of satisfaction. He now had time to reflect on the battle and its outcome. To his horror, he had seen the impact of the enemy destroyer on the *Thermopylae* and could scarcely believe it. Now, he was amazed. Not only had the cruiser survived, but it now seemed to be flying under control. Maneuvering thrusters had fired seconds after the impact to correct its course. The bridge on a cruiser was located on the second deck from the top, near the rear of the vessel. That portion of the ship, along with at least one deck beneath, had been torn off and was floating free in space with several flames visible, fed by interior oxygen.

Kosnov turned his attention from the *Thermopylae* for a moment. He had others to worry about, as well.

"Commander Collins, I need a full damage assessment as soon as possible for the entire fleet, along with estimated times of repair. Scramble SAR lighters, and if necessary, have marine corpsmen transfer to the badly damaged vessels. If there are any survivors out there, I want them recovered ASAP."

"Yes, Marshal." Collins's fingers flew over the controls and screens before him.

Kosnov looked over the status boards and breathed a quick sigh. He still had a force of three Drakk'Har warships closing, but overall damage from the first attack was light. By the time the second strike force got to them, most of the damage would have either been repaired or compensated for.

An alert flashed on all command consoles. A lieutenant commander at the Threat Analysis panel spoke. "Sir, we have detected mines spread out across our flight path. LADAR indicates at least twelve. Probably thermonuclear. Permission to deploy countermeasures?"

Kosnov replied immediately. "Permission granted. Deploy mine countermeasures at your discretion."

"Aye, sir."

Each cruiser carried what was termed "tertiary armaments." These were weapons that were not typically used in space battles, but still had military use. The OID was one such weapon. Another one was a mine countermeasure drone. Several of those torpedo-shaped devices were launched toward the detected mines. Guided by the fleet's LADAR and using thrusters, they homed in on the floating devices. When the drone calculated the target was within the theoretical detection radius of the mine's sensors, a powerful shield generator began to operate. As the drone approached, the field built slowly. Once it had built up to a high level, the field was shut down. One of two things happened. If the mine sensed the drop in magnetic field density, it exploded in a thermonuclear explosion, destroying the drone and itself, but nothing else. If the mine did not explode, the drone moved closer and re-built the magnetic field to try again. Eventually, if the drone closed to a pre-set distance without eliciting an explosion, it tried for what was termed a *kinetic kill*. It rammed into the mine, sacrificing itself.

One by one, each detected mine exploded well beyond its effective range to damage the fleet. In time, only one mine remained closing quickly. The drone assigned to it had a faulty shield generator, and it failed to set it off. The drone's small internal computer commanded it to attempt a contact kill. The drone's thrusters fired to intercept. When only two kilometers from the mine, disaster struck. A small fragment of composite armor thrown off of *Thermopylae* impacted with the drone and obliterated it.

The lieutenant commander at Threat Analysis launched a backup drone immediately, but knew it was too late. Several ships received proximity warnings and began firing close-range point defense weapons that hurled small caliber depleted uranium rounds at the advancing mine. A single round struck the sensor array of the mine and shattered it. The force of the impact made it spin wildly out of control. It proceeded onward without its on-board computer recognizing the sensors were incapable of detecting magnetic field strengths anymore. Sensors detected the new course imparted to the mine, and the point defense weapons paused as they calculated its new path. It was too late at that point, but they were not programmed to give up.

The Drakk'Har mine entered the fleet at a slight angle. It missed the *Sea of Tranquility* and sailed over the cruiser. The next ship was a tender, the *Robert Heinlein*. The mine impacted halfway along the top deck. To the occupants of the *Heinlein,* the force of the impact was horrific. The thermonuclear warhead did not detonate. Drakk'Har mines were designed to be only set off by magnetic field proximity. The chances of actual contact with a target were so astronomically low, impact fuses had been left out of the design. The kinetic impact of the heavy mine alone was sufficient to doom the ship. Slicing through deck after deck in a heartbeat, the mine passed through the ship and back out into the vacuum of space with ease. Inside the *Heinlein,* forty percent of the ship was opened to space, and the explosive force of air being vented to vacuum killed anyone who was not protected by a space suit. Few were. Her back broken, the Heinlein's two halves began to pitch and yaw, independently twisting themselves apart. Various cargo and equipment were thrown out from the interior of the ship as the twisting of the superstructure ripped open more decks. Reinforced bulkheads tore like paper as momentous forces acted on the ship in opposing directions.

The personnel on the *Aristotle* command deck had seen ships die before. It did not lessen the impact of the moment in any way. Kosnov flung out orders to everyone assembled.

"Commander Shiotu, I want SAR lighters converging on the *Heinlein* immediately. Commander Collins, I want the fleet to maneuver around the *Heinlein* and give the lighters room to work. We don't need any more casualties due to that debris. I need the fleet damage assessment ASAP, Commander."

Kosnov could do nothing more until he received more information, and he had to trust the individual ship captains to do their jobs. So, he began to scan the external images available from the command ship Vid system. Overall, with the exception of the cruiser *Thermopylae* and tender *Heinlein,* the ships had fared well. Kosnov could not see the holes created by the Drakk'Har weapons fire, but at least the formation had held. He knew the *Arthur C. Clarke* had been hit badly by the exploding destroyer, but no report had been sent from her captain yet. He had lost a portion of his lighters, and that did not bode well. Fewer lighters meant more trips for the ones that remained. It also meant less close combat support, as lighters would be needed for transport to and from the surface. Kosnov continued his visual scan and once more returned to the *Thermopylae.*

A few minutes later, Collins spoke. "Sir, I have a preliminary fleet damage report. The *Isaac*—"

"Marshal! We have a signal from the *Thermopylae,*" interrupted the communications watch officer. "It is weak, but readable. It is a direct RF video signal and not MASER-COMM, sir."

"On screen," Kosnov ordered.

On the smaller view screen on the right of the main viewer, a young face emerged from a burst of static. "—say again, this is the *Thermopylae.*" The face on the screen caused Kosnov to recoil. The man before him was no more than twenty years old and had the rank of ensign on his collar. Drying blood covered the right side of his face, shoulder, and upper uniform. Several people hurried past in the background. Kosnov could see several bodies being carried, and people in damage-control overalls checking systems. Semi-opaque smoke hung in the air near control consoles covered in fire-fighting foam. The camera was at a slight angle, and continuous bursts of static interfered with the signal.

"Ensign, Marshal Kosnov. What's your situation?"

"Sir, I'm Ensign Morton. I am in auxiliary control on G deck. We've lost all contact with the bridge, and the rest of the officers here are either dead or severely wounded. I'm controlling the ship from here and attempting to get a full damage report from all decks. Internal communications are down, and we only have this one link to the fleet. MASER-COMM is down, weapons off-line. We have secondary thruster and partial engine control. Shields are operational, just. Sir, we have lots of casualties on all levels and several fires. We have had multiple deck collapses blocking access to sections of the ship. Marshal, is there any way you can contact Captain N'Gamo and pass that information along?"

Kosnov filled in the young man. "A Drakk'Har destroyer impacted the top of the *Thermopylae*. Several upper decks were separated in the impact, including the bridge. It looks like you are in command for the moment. We are sending SAR lighters to you to search for survivors. Can you hold her together until they get there?"

Kosnov saw Morton lean way back in his chair. The impact of being placed in his first command was quite visible. However, he steeled himself quickly. "Unknown for now, sir. I just do not have enough information. I have sent runners to the portions of the ship we can still access, but they have not returned yet. I will try to get a more complete report to you ASAP. For the moment, we can maneuver, and we can still shield the ships to the rear." Kosnov saw the camera shudder and heard a dim explosion through the audio pick-up. The young ensign looked over his shoulder and spoke quickly, "Marshal, I have to go. I need to coordinate the damage control parties in engineering and make sure she does not come apart around us. I will get back to you as soon as I can."

"Roger. Get that head wound looked at as well, son. I need you healthy."

Kosnov saw Morton touch the blood and look at it on his fingertip. He seemed to be remembering something particularly unpleasant. "It's not mine, sir. I'm fine. Will get back to you when I have more information. *Thermopylae* out."

The screen returned to a light blue color.

CHAPTER 7 – ENERGY

Sh-Elerk was not religious; no Drakk'Har was. Gods and religion were as foreign to the Drakk'Har as mercy and dental hygiene. They made no shrines; they held nothing sacred but obedience to superiors. Their fractured system of honor would not tolerate looking to a higher power, unless that higher power was the emperor. Even so, if there had been a shrine to good fortune, Sh-Elerk would have placed a substantial offering on that altar in gratitude.

He was ascending into orbit in a small shuttle. Normally, he would have been in the pilot chair with restraints tightly closed about him. The motion of the climb, vibration, and quiet roar of powerful engines behind him was both familiar and welcome. Closing his eyes, he could recall the feel of the controls in his hands. That brought him back to reality as he knew he only had one arm left.

He remembered the battle as if it were yesterday. Two solar cycles almost to the day, the cockpit he had loved so much had exploded around him, taking not only his arm, but also his joy. To Sh-Elerk, flying was his only pleasure. He had no desire for power or titles. Small in stature and without the powerful connections necessary to achieve greatness in the Drakk'Har hierarchy, he knew his limits. He wanted only to fly, to feel the ship respond to his light touch. Before the fateful battle, he would have been requested as the best possible shuttle pilot. However, that day, he and the seven others were cargo. There had been little time to talk to his fellow Drel. After they had accepted the mission, Slassh had left them with the guards. They had been granted one grand gesture prior to the Planet Lord leaving. They were given bands of rough cloth to tie across their brows to hide the mark of their disgrace. An unnecessary move by Slassh, to be sure, but one that placed the steel of determination in the eight formerly damned creatures. Well, that was not completely true. They were still damned, but at least they had chosen to walk this path.

Sh-Elerk had been made leader of the mission. He had been given brief files on each of his companions to review. They all had various training in space ships in one manner or another—electronics, structural repair, engineering, weapons, and a couple of them simply chosen for their strength. Whether Sh-Elerk's leadership had been conferred due to his looking at Slassh or his training as a shuttle pilot, he didn't know. Nor would he ever know. He had been given a chance to die as a Drakk'Har. He was no longer Drel in his mind, and that was all that mattered now.

Only two guards were with them. They were relaxed, and their weapons were slung. It would have been child's play for the eight of them to overpower the guards and pilot. However, they would have nowhere to go. They would have been killed by one of the orbiting weapons satellites if they failed to make their rendezvous or deviated from their course. Even if they got away, they had no star drive. They were still branded and instantly recognizable as Drel anywhere in Drakk'Har space. No, he thought. This was the best possible outcome. He knew the mission. He closed his eyes and began to run it through his mind, looking for options at every stage to optimize success.

The shuttle pilot was competent, and upon orbital insertion, began to maneuver closer to their destination. It took several hours to match velocities, and they closed distances slowly. The passengers welcomed the zero G environment.

The last twenty minutes were spent with tiny chemical jets nudging them closer inch by inch. When Sh-Elerk heard the brief thruster pulses, he knew from experience they had almost arrived.

With a gentle kiss of ceramic against ceramic, the airlock met and sealed with another. A *tik-tik-tik-tik* noise ending in a final shudder passing through the shuttle indicated it was now part of a greater whole. A moment later, the shuttle pilot was drifting over to the airlock. After carefully checking pressure gauges and pressing the right combination of studs, he raised the hatch slowly. The opposing hatch opened at the same rate, revealing the interior of a larger vessel. Several Drakk'Har were standing on the rough deck. A small pile of personal baggage waited off to the side of the hatch.

The shuttle had no artificial gravity, where the ship they were attached to did. Transitioning from zero gee to artificial gravity is no easy task for the beginner. The shuttle pilot, who had done it many times, glided through the hatch and landed perfectly. He spoke to the crew of the larger vessel. "Hail, noble warriors, and greetings from Planet Lord Slassh. He sends transport to bring you to a warm mud pit and cool pond as reward for your faithful and isolated service. A feast of Kyber Monkeys awaits your pleasure upon arrival."

Sh-Elerk undid his restraints during the speech and ordered the others to do the same. He ignored the guards as they already had their orders, and he had no authority over them. They had ignored him to this point, and he saw no reason to press his luck. As Sh-Elerk drifted up, he ordered the stronger Drel to transfer the small pile of cargo lashed to the deck to the larger ship. He then headed to the airlock.

The small crew inside the vessel was obviously confused by the terse orders they had received. They complied, of course, but all intelligent creatures are curious by nature, and they wanted to know what was going on. When they saw the expected "replacement crew" in the shuttle, as mentioned in the message, their expressions betrayed their feelings. Sh-Elerk knew why. His small group of Drel smelled, were ragged looking, and had cloth bands around their heads. Drakk'Har proudly showed off their brow ridges and never hid them, which must have confused the others even more.

The cargo was transferred quickly from the shuttle. In time, a small pile was in the hatchway. The vessel crew did not touch the pile or offer to help. If there had been someone senior on the shuttle, they would have been ordered to assist. The last crate came through the airlock hatch. One of the stronger Drel had gone through into the artificial gravity. The crate made its way from zero gee into normal gravity when the Drakk'Har in the hatch stumbled against the small pile. He fell backwards on the cargo. No damage was done, but the cloth band across his head fell off in the tumble.

"Drel!" The word repeated amongst all of the shocked Drakk'Har crew. One of the vessel crew screamed and reached for his ceramic knife. Others followed. The only reason any Drakk'Har could find immediately for a Drel to be hiding his brand was that they were trying to escape. The law was clear when detecting an escaping criminal: death to the offenders. No questions. No mercy. The crew advanced on the fallen creature and also tried to block the airlock to keep them isolated—a typical Drakk'Har tactic. They would be easier to slaughter that way.

"HOLD!" one of the guards from the shuttle screamed as he floated up to the hatch on the shuttle side. "Listen to me, swamp scum. By order of Planet Lord Slassh, these Drel are not to be harmed or interfered with. You will let them unload their cargo, and when they are complete, you will board the shuttle and stand relieved."

The vessel crew paused and considered the situation. The guard had no Drel brand and wore the distinctive shoulder tattoo of a Planet Lord's personal guard. The other guard floated into view, and he also wore the same guard insignia. Each looked like a Planet Lord's guard, as well. The authority in the speaker's voice was evident.

The shuttle pilot who had brought them cowered in the corner, not knowing what to expect, and waited to see which way things would turn out. Seeing the hesitation, the guard moved forward into the airlock hatchway and continued, "You have your orders from the Planet Lord himself. Move aside, and sheath your weapons or die painfully." He drew his blade slightly to emphasize the fact. The guard behind him did so, as well, although in zero gee he looked rather clumsy. No one found the sight amusing in the slightest.

Several hesitated and looked like they might attack, regardless. However, in their minds, they knew one didn't mess with a Drakk'Har with the authority of a Planet Lord behind him. As savage as the vessel crew thought they were, they were not trained pit fighters like the guards. They would die if they did not obey. Drakk'Har being Drakk'Har, they complied with obvious authority and moved back.

The rest of the shuttle was emptied quickly. Once the Drel were all inside, the vessel crew took their possessions and cargo and quickly made their way into the shuttle. They didn't hurry because of the offered mud pit and feast of Kyber Monkeys. Drel were Drel, and they did not want whatever taint that accompanied them to be transferred.

The shuttle pilot left the safety of his corner and was the last one aboard. He swung around the hatch into the shuttle using a handhold and pressed the emergency close stud. The Drel closed the airlock on their side. They picked up their cargo and began to transfer it to the required locations.

Sh-Elerk had never been on a warship of this design before. He took the opportunity to examine the vessel by looking down the access corridors. They were located in the mid-section of the vessel on the lowest of the three decks. Forward was weapons control and maneuvering. Above the crew and captain's quarters were water and food stores and the electronics room. To the rear were engineering decks and reactor plants. He saw no straight surfaces. Everything was curved, with long, oval access hatches.

A moderate *thump* was heard as the air space between the two air locks was released to the vacuum of space. The shuttle had departed. Sh-Elerk noticed that the guards were not with them. *Of course not*, he immediately reprimanded himself. He had momentarily forgotten his mission. Sh-Elerk took the two Drel he had selected for engineering duties to the rear of the vessel and left the others to stow the cargo.

The engineering decks were spacious. They held all of the power generation and propulsion necessary to run the ship. Generators hummed noisily in the background, but most of the machinery went unused for the moment. Sh-Elerk ordered the two engineers to make their preparations. They scuttled off quickly to comply. Dim illumination showed equipment that was surrounded by a series of elaborately curved, ceramic-stepped staging allowing access to all critical equipment and systems. Most of the space in the room was taken up by the star drive. Capable of generating concentrated energies for interstellar travel, the star drive was the pinnacle of Drakk'Har scientific achievement. The field generators for this were massive and designed to work with energies that were almost incomprehensible in scale.

As humbled as he was by the science around him, Sh-Elerk kept his gaze moving, looking for something Slassh had told him would be there. He saw it at last in the dim light over by a clear space on the deck. Three meters long, smooth, and jet-black, the dark cylinder was attached to its mounts by strong resins. It had been delivered by an earlier shuttle flight and attached by the former crew.

He walked over to it and placed his remaining three-clawed hand on its glazed ceramic surface. Surprisingly, the casing was warm to the touch. His claws moved over the smooth surface as he stroked it. Sh-Elerk had never seen the like before. He walked around the device and saw the dim green display. The Drakk'Har saw the base 6 numbers counting down slowly. He saw no access or control panel to turn it off. Sh-Elerk didn't even think of trying. Slassh had told them of the thermonuclear warhead with the power of fifty megatons of energy. He saw that the timer had approximately three planet rotations to go until it reached zero. *Time enough to do what needs to be done,* he thought.

Sh-Eleck turned and made his way forward to maneuvering control. The selected pilot was already in his restraints. A quick glance into the weapons cabin showed several of the others at their assigned posts. One other would be in the radio room, while the two stronger Drel would go wherever they were needed.

Sh-Elerk turned to the pilot, who seemed quite comfortable in the chair, his claws pressing studs and controls without looking. *He must have experience on this class of vessel*, he thought. "Status, pilot?"

"Lord, we have energy reserves charged to maximum, navigation charts are updated, and engines are ready to maneuver. Intelligence data has been uploaded. Computers, countermeasures, star drive, and shields are operational. Weapons off-line. Awaiting your command."

Sh-Elerk was not officially a Lord, but he did not correct the pilot. Indeed, by Drakk'Har standards, he had behaved rather civilly to the people under his command. Every one of them knew their fate, and screams or insults did not seem to help them to their goal. They were all motivated. They all knew and accepted what would happen. The time for threats was past.

"Break orbit and set course to intercept the main warm blood invasion force. Once free of the planet's gravity, engage shields to maximum and begin acceleration to 4.2 points. Maintain that speed until further notice. No faster, or our fuel reserves will be insufficient for decelleration."

"Yes, Lord," was the terse reply as black-clawed fingers flew over the controls.

Several surveillance satellites from both sides noted the glowing engines flashing into life as the warship left orbit. All recorded the activity. The *Resilient Fury* and its small crew of the damned moved inexorably toward its destiny.

* * *

"Marshal, we have several ships with light damage. Nothing major, with the exception of the *Thermopylae* and the *Clarke*. Captain Ahmad on the *Clarke* reports all hull breaches have been isolated. He believes he can take care of his own casualties with facilities on board, but he is running short on blood and medical supplies. He's requested a hundred and fifty liters of plasma to cover the shortfall. We can transfer that from stores on the *Asimov* and the *Straczynski*. The *Clarke* has minimal shields and is still adrift. Several decks are without power, including engineering. He estimates repairs will take three hours. SAR lighters have scanned the upper decks of the *Thermopylae*. There are no survivors, and all spaces from C deck up are vented to vacuum. They're docking to escape hatches and entering in space suits, but there doesn't seem to be any hope above D deck. The only good news is most of the *Heinlein's* lighters were on SAR or support missions when the ship came apart, so we have the majority of those to use. They'll recover to the other tenders as space allows," Collins concluded his report.

"Very well, contact the tenders and arrange lighters to transfer whatever they need. What is the time until Force Two intercepts?" Kosnov had not forgotten the second alien force that was closing.

"Time approximately two hours, forty-nine minutes until intercept. They are moving much slower than the first group, sir," Collins said.

Before the marshal could acknowledge, an audible alarm went off on Collins's console. "Sir, the *Thermopylae* has just activated her main engines. She is breaking away from the fleet. Marshal, we detect escape pods being jettisoned. They appear to be abandoning ship, but it looks haphazard, almost random."

"Get me the *Thermo*—" Kosnov began, but was cut off by the communications officer. "Incoming signal from the *Thermopylae* on MASER-COMM."

A terse nod brought the right-hand screen to life. Once more, the face of Ensign Morton appeared. He had made a token effort to clean up the blood from his face, but lots still remained on the shoulder of his uniform. Compared to the last transmission, Kosnov saw much less activity behind him and no sign of smoke. A single crewmember could be seen strapped into the secondary steering controls; he looked white with fear.

The Ensign did not wait, but spoke immediately. "Marshal, I have sent runners ordering the crew to abandon ship. We still do not have internal communications working. I've just come from Engineering. We're losing containment on an anti-matter storage bunker. It's on a reserve reactor at the moment, and we have no more than three hours before the field collapses. The bunker ejection system is twisted out of alignment and unusable. We can't effect repairs in time. If we don't maneuver away from the fleet, we'll take half the ships with us. Request SAR lighters pick up the crew as they eject."

Kosnov recognized the danger of an anti-matter explosion instantly and did not hesitate. "Very well, Ensign. Make your way to the nearest escape pod, and we'll make sure we pick you up." Kosnov was glad this young officer had kept his head. He had taken command in the midst of grievous damage to his ship. He had gathered information, working around the internal communication problems that he had, assessed the situation correctly, run through all the possibilities, thought it through, and then acted responsibly. By steering his ship away from the formation, he was saving not only his own crew's lives, but also those of the surrounding ships in the fleet. A rupture in an anti-matter containment bunker *would* destroy half the fleet and render the other half combat ineffective. *This ensign shows promise*, Kosnov thought.

The ensign responded immediately, shaking his head slowly. "Sir, I can't do that. We have base control over the engines, but maneuvering is shot to hell. Excuse me, sir, I mean heavily damaged, and we have to man the stations to fly with any stability. There's no autopilot, and if we abandon ship, there's nothing stopping her from looping back into the middle of the fleet. We can't turn the engines off and let momentum alone carry her away from the fleet, as that will not guarantee a safe minimum distance. At current velocity, the fleet will still be within the blast radius when she goes up. We have no option but to conduct a high-power acceleration burn to get her away from the fleet."

Kosnov absorbed this for a moment. "Very well, I shall detail a tender to go with you. You can steer *Thermopylae* to a safe distance, and then you can shut down the engines and let her coast. They can recover your escape pod and return at high speed."

Morton was shaking his head as Kosnov finished. Kosnov watched the ensign reach into his chest pocket and pull out a dosimeter. Every crew member aboard a fleet vessel carried one. "Marshal, this is my dosimeter reading." He held it up so the high-resolution camera could see the face of it.

Kosnov inhaled unconsciously upon seeing the thin piece of plastic. The face was typically green to indicate no exposure to radiation. Over time, as you were exposed to more radiation, the color changed to yellow, then red, and finally black. When black, it meant you had absorbed a lethal dose. Morton's dosimeter was not only black, but it also had three white dots visible, which indicated he had taken a dosage of four times over the lethal limit. *He's already a dead man*, thought the marshal.

Morton did not wait for Kosnov to speak. He dropped the dosimeter onto the panel before him. "One of the reactors supplying power to the anti-matter bunker breached and contaminated the area. We were irradiated while we locked it down. Three other volunteers and myself are remaining behind to get *Thermopylae* away from the fleet. I have turned over a copy of the ship's log to one of the evacuating crew. She also has the names of those staying behind. I talked this over with each of them, Marshal, and they know how important this is. They all volunteered to stay. Sir, I would appreciate it if you can keep a watch out for any escape pods that eject late. Several sections of the ship are inaccessible, and the crew in those sections may not get the word in time to leave the ship.

Last, sir, Chief Rawson and I have an idea I would like to put past you." The ensign talked uninterrupted for a minute. The command staff were taken aback by the idea. A few were visibly upset.

Kosnov listened to the ensign and then fell silent for several moments. He ran through all the possibilities in his mind. He knew how damaging an anti-matter explosion could be. He knew the limitations imposed by the battle-damaged ship. He saw no other options except those that carried unacceptable risk to his command. This young officer was absolutely correct. He was the finest leader Kosnov had experienced for a long time—thoughtful, responsible, and he responded well under extreme pressure. Kosnov would have to go through a hundred command officers to find one with those talents.

Kosnov made up his mind in an instant of reflection. "Commander Shiotu, bring this MASER-COMM channel up fleet wide."

After a few moments Shiotu responded, "MASER-COMM active fleet wide, sir."

The marshal spoke calmly to everyone in the fleet. "Attention to orders." The command staff and Ensign Morton came to attention as well as their chair restraints allowed. Throughout the fleet, all officers and men also stopped what they were doing and came to attention. "Ensign Morton. For conspicuously gallant service above and beyond the call of duty, you are hereby promoted to the rank of lieutenant, full grade. You are awarded command of the cruiser *Thermopylae* and her crew effective this time and date. You have my permission to depart the fleet and carry out the mission at your discretion. God speed, Captain Morton."

The voice of the newly promoted lieutenant cracked audibly. "Thank you, sir. Morton, out." The screen went back to an inactive sky-blue hue.

The voice of Commander Shiotu was the last thing broadcast throughout the fleet before the channel was closed.

Her voice cracked with the emotion of the moment. "*Thermopylae*, departing."

CHAPTER 8 – KAMIKAZE

Sergeant Blake paced down the halls of the troop ship *Sirius*. He moved quickly and cracked open the blast hatch to his squad's bunkroom as fast as possible. He had made his way there as soon as the artificial gravity had been restored. He was greeted with several anxious faces. The emergency red lighting was on, and a few of the marines had their flashlights out, but it did not help things much. The room was a mess. Several bunk mattresses were askew. The short period of zero gee had made them drift off their bunks. When gravity had returned, everything that was floating had been pulled downwards. Pictures, cards, and personal effects were scattered everywhere. "Sound off, is everyone OK?" the sergeant ordered.

Several voices answered as one. He was glad to see that beyond a few scrapes and bruises, no one appeared hurt.

"Sarge, what the hell just happened?" That came from LCPL Belliveau in the far corner.

Everyone went quiet to hear his response.

"From what I heard from regiment, the fleet was attacked by a group of light warships who went through at high speed. I talked to one of the damage control people on the way here, and he said the engineering spaces took a direct hit. It killed the main generator and gravity control circuitry. They could not bring the secondary power on automatically, so everything went into zero gee for a few minutes while they cycled the systems. No casualties from what I hear. Consider yourselves lucky. One of the cruisers collided with a croc warship, and they are sending it out into deep space with an anti-matter containment leak. That's going to be one hell of a bang when it goes up. Plus, we lost a tender. Apart from that, all attacking ships were killed, and damage to the fleet was fairly light. We are still proceeding toward Mindon-2, and our landing orders have not changed. Looks like you will be stuck in here for a time, so use it wisely. First, let's get these bunks squared away. I want all loose gear stowed. Get the crap off the floor, and break out the mops. If the ship's crew comes through here, I don't want them tripping over your mess. Marines are confined to quarters until further notice, and keep the hatches sealed in case of a hull breach. We can expect more attacks like this one until we reach Mindon-2, so if you're in your bunks, strap yourselves in. It may not look pretty, but it'll stop your ass from hitting the ceiling. All right people, let's get a move on." He emphasized his point by slapping his hands together.

The soldiers began moving through the area picking up their items and personal kit. The sergeant stood there for a few minutes, then withdrew from the bunkroom. They did not need him hovering. Besides, his right hand had begun shaking involuntarily, and he did not want anyone to see that. His usual pre-battle jitters had started.

* * *

Inside the bunkroom, Reid turned to Messina. "Warships attack, and the sarge thinks making our beds will stop the next attack."

From across the room, Sanchez interrupted. "All right, Reid, stow that garbage, and get your area squared away. Your crap went flying, so get it off the deck. Johnston and Tyler, grab that mattress, and make sure they are all secured this time. If the rack is unoccupied, strap them down. Get as much stored in the lockers as will fit. Perkins, grab the mop. When we're done, I want you all to get into your racks and grab as much shuteye as possible. Our job starts when the bumpy ride ends, and I want you alert and on the ball." Sanchez watched them start moving, and then she turned to secure her own rack.

In the opposite corner, Messina turned to Reid and spoke quietly, "So, what's her problem?"

Reid looked over at Sanchez and tapped his bicep where his single stripe was. "Looks like she wants another one."

Laughing between themselves, they went about their work.

* * *

Corporal Popov misjudged his footing on a rock, and the litter he was carrying bounced hard when he momentarily lost his balance. Mendez reacted badly to the stumble. A weak moan erupted from his mouth, and the litter bearers stopped momentarily. The usual procedure was to stop every hour for five minutes to give everyone a quick break. They could drink water, have a quick snack, or even change socks on longer marches. They had stopped three times in the last hour. Progress was a lot slower than normal due to their carrying Mendez. No one complained about it, as they knew very well that they could be the one in that position, and in the 121st, no one got left behind ever.

Lieutenant Pratt motioned for everyone to take another break and to swap out stretcher bearers. He made sure a couple of his men were keeping watch, and then he looked at his chronometer and datapad map once again. At their current pace, they would arrive at the hill right after sunset. He was hoping to get there a few hours prior to that, as digging in a defensive position in the dark was no easy task. He knew that would not be possible at the current rate.

This march was harder than most, but not due to the distance or physical hardship. Regular Special Forces training involved forced marches of up to sixty kilometers a day under heavy pack loads. The mental aspects of their journey were taxing them. They were hunted and on the run. Being mobile, they were also a lot more vulnerable. They had no convenient trenches to get into to avoid incoming fire, and if they did encounter another patrol, it would probably be in an ambush situation, with them on the receiving end. Ambushes were damned effective at killing the enemy. The ambushers chose the area and had time to prepare. That was wonderful, as long as you were not the ones targeted on a booby-trapped trail. If not for the unfortunate run-in with the Drakk'Har patrol, they would still be sitting on their former hill, still reasonably comfortable. Pratt chastised himself over that thought immediately. *What happened had happened, and wishful thinking was not going to change anything.* Their immediate mission was to get to Hill 170 with his command intact.

Pratt walked over to Corporal Jacobs, who was hovering near Mendez. Pratt could see him giving Mendez more painkillers via a gas injector. He then examined the wounds on his leg under the bandages. Pratt waited until the corporal was finished before tapping him on the shoulder and wordlessly indicating he should follow. They walked off the trail slightly— far enough that they could still be seen, but not be overheard. When they spoke, it was in very hushed tones.

Pratt spoke first. "What's the prognosis, Jacobs?"

Jacobs shook his head instinctively as he responded. "Suh, he's in bad shape. Dat croc spit has different effects on everywun. It's hittin de sarge hard. He needs to get off dis rock, suh, and I means today. His wounds are not healin', and de leg is infected. He needs more dan de simple antibiotics we 'ave here, suh, and we are running out of dose right quick. If we could gettim into a hospital ship right now, he wud 'ave a fifty percent chance of saving de leg. Tomorrow dat drops to twenty percent. De day after dat, his leg will be de least of his troubles." A simple shrug finished his sentence and emphasized his inability to change things.

"The best we can hope for is tomorrow for an evac," the officer said without thinking. He was stuck. He felt helpless.

One of his men was slowly dying, and he was powerless to stop it. The fleet would not arrive for another twenty-four to thirty-six hours, depending on resistance, and Mendez was in a world of hurt until then. Nothing was more frustrating than being unable to change the world around you when you needed to. He needed a ship, and none was due to arrive for days. He wildly thought of stealing a croc shuttle, but he knew the abilities of his team. He had no pilots, and he could lose the majority of his team in the process. Plus, without the right identification codes and frequencies, they would be shot out of the sky by their own fleet.

Damn it, damn it, damn it. He stopped his thoughts from being displayed on his face. Morale had to be maintained, and that meant he had to keep a stoic manner. "Very well, Jacobs, keep him as comfortable as you can. We need to get him into a stable position ASAP. We will get to Hill 170 as fast as humanly possible."

"Yes, suh." Jacobs headed back to his charge on the litter.

Pratt remained where he was. He took out his canteen and took a large mouthful of water. *The only way to get to the hill before dark was to press on without these stops. That would cause Mendez unnecessary pain and suffering. However, the alternative was having the section exposed in the middle of a hostile jungle at night, and that was not acceptable, either.* Pratt imagined being jumped on by a large Drakk'Har ambushing them from the foliage, and it made him cringe. *The joys of command. Damn it, damn it, damn it.*

Pratt turned to return to the section. He would have to tell the men on point to move a bit faster. No more stops until they reached Hill 170. The good of the many outweighed the good of one. He had no choice.

* * *

Aboard the cruiser *Thermopylae,* a sort of calm had descended over the few remaining crew. They had consigned themselves to their fates and, after a fashion, made peace with the situation. Each of the volunteers remaining behind had been heavily irradiated, and Morton did not pry too deeply as to what they were thinking. They did not discuss it after the decision had been made. Words would not change anything; their future was set.

Newly frocked Lieutenant Morton now manned the helm controls after dismissing the frightened crewman to one of the last departing escape pods. Auxiliary control was a mess. Gauges were shattered, and digital screens were cracked and askew. Burn marks blackened several wall panels, and some were missing completely, having been cast aside in the firefighting effort. The control panel in front of him had been rebuilt from three shattered panels taken from across the room. Right after the collision, dozens of crew were running around trying to undo the damage to the best of their abilities. Now he was alone, waiting for Chief Rawson to return with the latest report from engineering.

The helm was responding well, and they had restored navigation systems. On occasion, Morton had to make a slight correction to nudge the vessel back on course. The throttle was currently set at forty percent thrust in a continuous burn. Fuel consumption was of no concern now, only the need to get beyond the fleet before the anti-matter containment bunker ruptured. They had tried to burn at full power, but the missing engine and damage to the upper decks caused the ship to pitch forward in an uncontrolled fashion, and they had to dial back the power to compensate. Forty percent was the maximum they could handle while maintaining solid control. Their calculations showed that would be sufficient, with a decent margin of safety.

Chief Rawson came up from behind. In one hand he carried a spool of wiring, which was splaying out from the roll as he walked. The other hand held a canvas zip bag. He tossed the reel of wire onto the shattered control panel beside the lieutenant's station. "Sir, the internal comms are still out, and there is no way we can get them up in time. I grabbed this from one of the damage control lockers. It is a BDR handset that works on a landline. I installed one in engineering and strung a wire from there to here."

The chief removed the handset from the canvas bag and attached it to the pair of wires exposed on the reel. He grabbed the wind-up dynamo on the side of the unit and spun it several times. Then he picked up the hand unit and held it to his ear. "Hello… Yes… You sound fine. Standby." The chief handed the handset over to the young officer and pointed as he explained, "Sir, to call the unit in engineering, just crank this handle here for ten seconds. It'll energize the unit for up to twenty minutes of use. When not using it, replace it in its holder here. If you'll excuse me, I have to get back to engineering to give them a hand rigging the charges." He turned and left the way he came as Morton spoke into the handset.

"Hello, Engineering?" the officer said into the handset.

"Yes, sir, I hear you fine. This is Petty Officer Gibbons. We're about half done rigging the charges you ordered. We have one set of shaped charges on the bunker itself and are half done with the set on the control panel. Once Chief Rawson gets back here, he'll begin rigging the last set on the power converter buffers. We're setting all three charges with dual igniters rigged up to the same detonation control. How much time do we have left, sir?"

The lieutenant checked his panel display. "We have about twenty minutes. Good idea on the dual igniters, Gibbons. We need to make sure all those charges go off on cue. Anything else to report?"

"Negative, sir. We have a few fires still burning below decks, but they're in non-critical areas and sealed up. Once the air is gone, they should die out of their own accord. We do have an air leak in the forward part of J deck, but I think we can let that go for the moment, sir. There is nothing on J deck but crew quarters and the officers' mess. We'll make sure you have power until the bitter end, Ensig— I mean, Captain."

"Very good, Gibbons. Thank you. Auxiliary control out." Morton hung up the handset. He turned and double-checked the navigation charts. They had just reached the minimal safe distance from the fleet for detonation. The extra twenty minutes would be added insurance.

* * *

One of the recce ships detected a transmission in a reserved frequency range. The two-second transmission repeated twice more after a one second delay in-between. Signal parameters indicated Federation origin. The time of its reception was noted and logged and it was shunted to the communications mainframe directly without further intelligence assessment. Once there, the computer first uncompressed the three copies of the received signal into separate areas of memory. The three resulting sets of data were compared. Minor differences existed between the individual files; gamma radiation, x-rays, and even the ship's engines caused some form of radio interference. The signal had been purposely sent multiple times to ensure delivery. Powerful algorithms took the signals apart bit by bit and compared them. As the signals had been sent at separate times, it was unlikely that the same interference would be seen in all three pieces of the signal. If two of the bits matched in two signals but not in the third, then the third bit was assumed to be in error and discarded. In less than a thousandth of a second, a complete signal had been reconstructed from the three individual ones. After being shunted to the decryption mainframe the message appeared on the screen of the Intelligence Liaison officer for the Special Forces. It read:

%%%%%%%%%%%xx523-ABSF-262376-EQxx
%%%xxfrom: 121/2C/9P/A (723 329)
%%%xxto: 121 Sp Fce / SCF 9
%%%xxpriority: 3/5
%%%xx**message follows**
newpara contact with light enemy patrol made 2701341005 stop primary position 723 329 compromised rpt compromised stop moving to alternate position 725 623 as briefed stop will

arrive approx 2701341900 stop require standard resupply of rations and ammo stop

newpara one specops papa oscar whiskey recovered 154/F/3P/C ssgt macpherson a2152843 stop rest of 154/F/3P/C mike india alpha slash kilo india alpha stop opsec violated stop

newpara 121/2C/9P/A ssgt mendez q2135199 whiskey india alpha stop requires immediate rpt immediate medevac stop situation grave stop

newpara target coord list attached

newpara signoff 121/2C/9P/A lt pratt s2148823

%%%xx**message ends**xx

%%%xxdata attached 194237 units

The officer that reviewed the message was both inexperienced and overworked. He scanned it quickly and then made a simple, but critical mistake in his haste. He forwarded the message with attached targeting information to the Threat Analysis staff for their information, but neglected to send a copy to the Rescue Coordination Center for action. The enemy intelligence and targeting data got to the right people, while the request for a medevac flight was never seen by the RCC.

On receipt of the message and data, the Threat Analysis duty clerk assumed someone else had forwarded the message to RCC. As a result, no rescue resources were earmarked for the evacuation of Sergeant Mendez.

* * *

The second assault element of the Drakk'Har fleet was only three ships. However, they were Scarab class. Scarabs were medium destroyers with impressive armaments and defensive capabilities. They were the main defensive formation in the solar system. Their job was to patrol the inner planets and protect the growth facilities on Mindon-2 at all costs. Scarab-class destroyers were equal in firepower to a Federation cruiser, but lacked the heavy anti-matter batteries. As a result, they preferred to approach an enemy fairly slowly so their heavy firepower could be accurately delivered onto the target.

Etwonnik was the senior Drakk'Har Lord of the three vessels. Large, even by Drakk'Har standards, he had not been challenged in years. He could intimidate the toughest of opponents even before a challenge was voiced. He was a capable and experienced Drakk'Har warrior, having fought in several campaigns. Never failing to bring victory to the alliance, he was held in high esteem in the Imperium. This experience led to his being assigned to protect the largest of the alliance growth facilities.

Etwonnik stood on the control deck surveying the situation. He had a large enemy force of warm blood transports protected by several heavy cruisers on a direct path to Mindon-2. Five light destroyers had interdicted earlier, but with little effect from what his scanners showed. However, as the warm bloods were jamming his sensors, this was not wholly unexpected. He had no idea what the overall impact of the first assault was. It didn't matter, as he intended to create his own brand of chaos within their ranks. A beep from a console alerted him.

"Lord, visual scans show a single heavy cruiser on approach, jammers are active, class unknown," an underling reported quickly.

This information did not please Etwonnik one bit. He hated unknowns. "What do you mean 'unknown,' you mud-eating worm? Compare the silhouette with existing warm blood designs."

"I have, Lord. The outline does not match any ship in our records. It has the mass and general outline of a heavy cruiser, but no direct correlation to any known design. It's by itself and appears to be heading on an intercept vector, great one."

The commander thought out loud as he digested this information. "One heavy cruiser is no match for three of our ships. There must be more ships out there in support. *Or something else.* Conduct a full power sensor sweep now! I sense warm blood treachery." This did not feel right to Etwonnik, but warm bloods occasionally made stupid mistakes. They always paid dearly for them when he was around.

"Immediately, Lord," replied the sensor operator. He took a few arkle and shifted sensor frequencies to try to throw off the jamming. He was successful for a time, but the jammers matched the new frequencies almost immediately. It was enough to give him the information he needed, though. "Lord, we have a single vessel on intercept vector. There are no other ships beyond the invasion force itself. Silhouette indicates it to be a heavy cruiser of unknown class closing at a speed of 2.23. We detect no mines or follow-on forces."

Etwonnik was elated. "Communications, send a message to the other ships. Prepare for engagement. All main batteries to fire when in range. We'll make them pay dearly for challenging us. Charge all gun batteries. Increase forward shields to maximum. Maintain course and speed. On to victory!"

* * *

Morton picked up the handset and cranked the unit. The response was immediate.

"Engineering, Gibbons."

"How are the preparations going?"

"Almost done, sir. Rigging the last of the wiring now. The chief has rigged up a speaker to the unit here, and we can both hear you. Give us the signal, and we can act within a second or two."

"Great work. Just in time. We're about to encounter Force Two. We'll have a problem in timing. The weapons computers are not designed for this, and I'll have to 'guesstimate' when to trigger it. However, with the fireball we will be popping off, it should not take too much brainpower. Are the crew assigned to their positions?"

"Yes, sir. We have all essential systems covered. With weapons off line, we can increase shield power by at least twenty-five percent. I would not normally do that, sir, but burning out the emitters is hardly an issue now."

"Agreed. That will give us a little more time. Do it."

A dim flicker in the overhead lights occurred moments later as the shields energized. The controls in front of him showed the increase in power take effect. A single amber warning light flashed, indicating an over-voltage condition in the shield generators. He ignored it.

"Excellent, Gibbons. Stand by everyone. Will not be long now."

* * *

"Lord, enemy shield power has just increased dramatically. The vessel is outputting at least a third more power than standard." The voice of the sensor operator shook with surprise.

Etwonnik reacted as any Drakk'Har would to unexpected news. "What?" He considered this quickly. *It must be a new class of cruiser with more power generation capability. Therefore, more power meant it had more weaponry at its disposal, as well.* A few quick mental calculations told him it didn't matter. A single ship would need twice as much energy to take on the three of his ships equally. It would just delay the inevitable, but not change anything. He saw the range indicator to the target.

"Communications, order all ships to deploy mines. If they get past us, they will not live long enough to enjoy it." An immediate *thump-thump-thump* vibration was felt as the mines were deployed.

Time for battle, thought Etwonnik. *Time for glory.* "All batteries, standby." He watched the range decline quickly. At the maximum firing range, he screamed the next word. "Fire!"

* * *

The flurry of firepower hit the armor of the *Thermopylae* like hail on a tin roof. The additional power to the shields helped, but many plasma and rail gun rounds penetrated, nonetheless. The Drakk'Har ships were traveling slowly enough that their targeting computers were quite effective. The volume of fire striking the cruiser would have actually slowed it down if the engines were not firing steadily, propelling it forward.

In auxiliary control, Lieutenant Morton never let his eyes stray from the range indicator, which was was decreasing steadily. He needed to make sure the timing was perfect. The handset was pressed against his ear as firmly as he could get it. Alarms were going off regularly now as more and more rounds lanced into the armor. He began to silence them, but they were just replaced by more. In the end, he left them alone. He was not worried about the Drakk'Har weapon fire. The chief had told him that when they were planning this. From the angle the enemy ships were approaching, the rounds could not get this deep into the ship or into engineering without them radically changing course, and they had no time for that.

"Gibbons, you there?" He found he had to scream to be heard over the noise.

"Yes, sir. Standing by." Gibbons had his own alarms going off on his end. He had to yell back as well.

"Ten seconds."

"Roger."

* * *

"Lord, the enemy ship is not returning fire. It is maintaining course and speed. We are causing considerable damage; we may have hit a critical area and rendered it helpless. We will pass within three thousand five hundred klem abeam," the sensor operator reported over his shoulder.

Standing behind him, Etwonnik enjoyed the moment. Battle was seldom this easy. He was destroying a warm blood cruiser without taking any damage. *What glory. What a legend would be produced this day.* "Continue firing, all weapons!"

* * *

Lieutenant Morton knew the story of the battle quite well, as it was taught in the academy as a required course. In 480 BC, the Persian King Xerxes had invaded Greece and led an army of at least one hundred thousand men to a narrow pass in a place called Thermopylae. The Spartan King Leonidas led a force of several thousand troops waiting to defend the pass and was able to hold up the Persian force for three days. A Greek traitor showed Xerxes an alternative way around the army along a goat path, and he was able to send soldiers to the rear of the defending troops. Outflanked, a force of three hundred Spartans and seven hundred Thebans stood their ground while the majority of the Greek army withdrew. Even though they were outnumbered a hundred to one, they gave the retreating forces time to get clear, and the bulk of the Greek army escaped. In time, Xerxes wiped out Leonidas and his defenders. While technically a defeat, the word of the Spartans' brave sacrifice spread throughout Greece. All Greek states rallied behind the war effort as one. That enabled a Greek fleet of less than four hundred vessels to defeat the Persian naval fleet of over twelve hundred ships at the battle of the Gulf of Aegina, ultimately leading to the defeat of the Persians and their expulsion from Greece. They had lost the battle of Thermopylae, but they had ultimately won the war.

Now here he was, several thousand years in the future, and the parallel was striking. Once more, there would be a defeat for *Thermopylae*. Only this time, the Spartans would die taking the army of Xerxes with them. Morton had convinced the marshal with the words, "If we are going to go anyway, sir, let's take some of them with us."

The distance indicator rolled down steadily. "Mr. Gibbons. Two seconds. One second. Now!"

Behind him and three levels down, two pairs of hands squeezed detonators. Explosive charges throughout engineering blew immediately. A third of them severed all power leads and control cables to the anti-matter bunker, degrading the magnetic bubble around the volatile contents. The second set of charges was rigged to the power converters from the generators themselves. This was a back-up in case the severing of the power and control cables was not sufficient. The last set of charges detonated around the bunker holding the anti-matter itself. Made of meter-thick stainless steel, the vessel would not be breached, but it would be warped out of shape. In the end, all three charges worked as planned.

As Morton released the transmit stud, he realized he had forgotten something. Since the cruiser had been damaged in the initial battle, he had been too busy to think of anything other than the ship. Now, with nothing left to do, he hurriedly reached into his uniform shirt pocket and produced a well-worn picture. She was young, with reddish-brown hair and a smile that would melt any man's heart. He looked on her face as if it were the first time he had seen her. The memories flooded back. *A shop*, he remembered. They had met in a shop. She was wearing jeans and a simple white blouse and caught his attention from the first moment he saw her. She had a silver bracelet with sky-blue coral beads on her wrist. He could see it so vividly, as if it had happened only moments ago. They had been delayed together in a line for the checkout and had spent a few moments talking. She had impressed him immediately with her smile and intelligence. As the line moved forward, they were separated and went to different tellers. He finished his purchase first, but decided to wait at the doors, pretending to look at something on a rack. She came along a few minutes later, and he had gotten her COMM number. The memories flowed quicker now. The long vid messages when they were apart. The feel of her body in his arms when they were together. Her smile. Her laugh. Her voice. The universe had seemingly conspired to produce a lady designed for him and him alone. He gazed into her eyes in the picture and lost himself in the image. The screens and monitors went ignored. The sounds around him faded. The cries of the alarms and vibrations through the hull went unnoticed. Tears flowed, unrestrained, down his cheeks. He took his fingertip and caressed her cheek softly. Caught up in the moment, he swore he could smell her perfume, so delicate and feminine. In the end, only one thought remained.

Goodbye, Pamela Jean. I love y—

A dozen atoms of anti-matter came in direct contact with the stainless steel wall of the storage bunker.

* * *

Etwonnik's vision was locked onto the sensor screen before him. The impacting rounds cratered the surface of the cruiser's armor without mercy. When the actinic light of the explosion first appeared, he was jubilant, thinking he had caused the ship to explode. The speed of the energetic expansion and the forward velocity of his ship never allowed his mind a chance to reconsider. He died thinking he had achieved a great victory, which is a true warrior's death, indeed.

At a temperature of ten thousand degrees Celsius, the fireball was twice as hot as the surface of Earth's sun for a moment. It grew to one hundred thousand kilometers in diameter before even beginning to lose energy. Everything inside the ball of light was vaporized instantly. The *Thermopylae*, the three Drakk'Har ships, and even the mines they had dropped earlier simply vanished as if they had never been.

* * *

The explosion was recorded by the fleet's sensor arrays several minutes later. The intensity of the event was visible to all in the fleet. Soundless in the vacuum of space, the blast was all the more powerful, somehow. Silence followed the event on the Command deck. Kosnov waited until the last of the visual energies faded before returning his gaze to the small screen on the end of his right armrest. The text was still there. He had just recalled the information moments before the explosion. A small but accurate picture was displayed in the upper right corner with a DNA identifier below. Kosnov scanned the details he needed to know. *Morton, Edward Lucas. Ensign. Wife with child expected soon. Duty assignment: Heavy Cruiser Thermopylae as Mess and morale officer.*

My God. He supervised cooks and made sure the crew had vids to watch in their off hours, but he died commanding a major warship in battle. He was able to take control of a horrific situation and immediately gained the cooperation of chiefs and enlisted men that had more than twenty years of service. And they followed him willingly to the grave. What a waste. Shaking his head slowly, Kosnov made a note to amend this information with his new rank as soon as possible. He closed the file.

"Mr. Collins. Status?" Kosnov said in a heavier than normal tone.

"Force Two is no longer a threat. Battle damage repairs are proceeding according to schedule. The last of the *Thermopylae's* crew has been recovered. Several officers were found, including a commander who was cut off from the rest of the ship. He left when they heard escape pods in other sections being launched. We were able to recover a few survivors from the *Heinlein,* but only a few, sir. The *Clarke* is maneuvering again and reports the receipt of sufficient medical supplies." Collins's voice sounded tired.

"Thank you." The marshal turned to another station. "Threat Assessment. Anything to report?"

"Negative, sir. We have a clear threat board. Intel reports a single Drakk'Har warship unaccounted for. Possibly making its way to the edge of the system to get reinforcements. No other threats or signals."

"Very well. Secure from General Quarters. Stand down all non-essential personnel. Return to standard transit formation. I will be in my cabin until 0430. Mr. Lyle has the deck. Miss Chu has the Conn." Kosnov stood after undoing his restraints. "Mr. Collins, all Command crew are to be relieved of duty until 0400. Enforced crew rest is in effect. That includes you. Get some sleep." Kosnov walked toward the rear of the room. The duty marine opened the hatch and snapped to attention as he approached.

* * *

"Yes, sir," said Collins, stifling a yawn himself. He had been on duty for fifteen hours straight. Time for a hot shower and sleep. He would get there in forty-five minutes. First, he had to bring his relief up to speed and then make sure everyone else was relieved before he left.

The hatch snapped shut. "Marshal off the deck," said the duty marine mechanically.

CHAPTER 9 – B1285

"Whoa! What was that?" a very excited marine sergeant called out over the intercom as an intensely brilliant light appeared in the back of the lighter.

A steady voice responded, "That was the *Thermopylae,* Sergeant. Do you have the cargo secured?" Marine Captain Alfred Levin knew this was a once-in-a-lifetime sight, and the crew in the back were trying to see as much as possible before it faded, but he was tired and in a foul mood. Levin wanted to get back to the tender as soon as possible. He had been one of the first SAR lighters launched from the *J. Michael Straczynski* in the battle, and scouring space to recover bodies was not his favorite thing to do. Due to the events of the last two hours, he had been busy throughout. Plus, he hated having to refer to bodies as cargo. He could have asked if the charred and vacuum-exploded carcasses of their fellow fleet mates were sufficiently sealed in their body bags to keep the internal juices—and moreover the smell—from permeating the lighter, but he had a crew morale issue to deal with. So instead, he called them cargo. Somehow, it made things easier for all of them.

* * *

"Aye, aye, sir. All secure back here," called Sergeant Allan. Normally he was a rear gunner and loadmaster, but he was also the senior enlisted man, which made him responsible for everything not on the flight deck. A temporary crew member was on board, a marine rated for extra-vehicular activity, which meant he was qualified to wear a spacesuit in the vacuum of space. He was getting out of his EVA suit and thruster pack. That marine had the toughest job over the last two hours—actually going outside through the cramped airlock on the roof and retrieving the bodies and body parts.

Sergeant Allan used the zero gee to his advantage and drifted over to the port on the side of the explosion and took a last look at the fading sphere of intense light.

* * *

Levin keyed his mike again, "Very well, sergeant. Prepare for return to the *Straczynski*." As everyone on intercom heard him, he continued, "Crew, prepare for maneuvering." The warning allowed everyone who was not strapped in ample time to do so. Several hurried to get into their canvas strap seats.

The captain toggled a radio transmitter. Due to his rank, in addition to this lighter, he also commanded three others. They formed what was termed a flight. "Grasshopper Flight, this is Grasshopper One. Return to the barn. Out."

The responses came as expected.

"Grasshopper Two."

"Grasshopper Three."

"Grasshopper Four."

Levin grabbed the control yoke and powered up the rear thrusters and control jets. They were not as efficient as the ducted fans they used in the atmosphere, but in the vacuum of space, ducted fans were useless. Levin applied power and reoriented the ship to the right course before applying forward thrust. He waited a few moments and scanned his computer displays. He could see his other lighters moving slowly toward their home. Levin decided against flying in formation. That would take extra time, and he wanted to get the cargo off his ship ASAP. Instead, he flew in behind the others, observing their approach. He always had to monitor his flight. Regular reviews of their piloting skills were necessary. That meant he had to observe them at every opportunity and make notes.

The tender *J. Michael Straczynski* was in line behind the troop transport *Sagittarius*. Levin flew slowly. There would be a wait at the docking arm, and as flight commander, he was always last in. His flight engineer sat to Levin's right, slumped over his controls. Levin glanced at him. Corporal Wallace was naturally introverted and never said anything unnecessary. He acknowledged orders and filled requests for information, but never spoke unless he had to. That had always slightly annoyed Levin, but today he appreciated it. The pilot was looking forward to a hot meal and some rack time after the usual paperwork, debrief, and shower.

Levin had always wanted to fly. From his earliest days walking in the Negev Desert, he had looked up at the sky and wondered what it was like to pilot the fast and low-flying military aircraft that trained there. In school, he had found part-time work as a flight hand pumping fuel for the local civilian fleet. When he had enough money, he took lessons. His first solo was at the age of seventeen. Joining the military the following year, he eventually got to fly the same aircraft that he had watched as a child.

Being based in Israel with the Earth Defense Force lacked something for him. He realized that the reason he wanted to fly was to travel and see new places, not take off and land from the same base he had left two hours before. He transferred to the marines, and after his first tour with the fleet, became a lighter instructor on Rigel. He met his wife there, and life was good for a time. It ended badly when he came home to surprise her with an early anniversary present and found her in bed with a stranger. He left without saying a word. The bitter divorce that followed destroyed a part of him, and he volunteered for duty with the fleet. With no personal life to hold him back, he was able to rise quickly, eventually gaining his captain rank and command of his own flight. Levin had appreciated the promotion when it came, but truly hated the mind-boggling amount of forms, requisitions, memorandum, and other assorted paperwork that went with it. That's why he normally enjoyed flying so much—to get away from it all.

Levin passed down the length of the *Sagittarius,* keeping well clear of the massive transport. He could see the other lighters were close to their destination. He fired reverse thrusters to slow his pace even more. It would not be long now.

* * *

Drawwl made his way through the swamps and lowlands. To a human, it would be hard going, even impossible in places, due to the mud. However, to a Drakk'Har this was like the proverbial walk in the park. He carried only a sheathed knife tied to his shoulder belt with a thick cord. He needed little else, as he was surrounded by fifty heavily armed troops. If an enemy force could get through fifty heavily armed Drakk'Har, then nothing Drawwl could carry would make a difference. Carrying a single blade also made him look like a pit fighter. Pit fighters were respected among Drakk'Har. Drawwl had never seen the inside of a fighting pit and probably never would, but the simple weapon made him look a little more dangerous to his companions. Intimidation was a fine weapon in any Drakk'Har's arsenal.

The group advanced steadily in typical Drakk'Har fashion. Three lines of warriors were moving parallel to each other. The center group contained half the warriors, while the two outer lines had a dozen troops acting as flank guards. A few trackers were out in front of the main group making an obvious trail for the rest to follow. Even the Drakk'Har avoided certain areas of the swamp.

The warriors carried their rail guns slung on special slings on their backs. Their bellies, faces, arms, and legs were covered liberally in mud and plant matter. They did not avoid the mud.

Indeed, many made sure it covered as much of them as possible. As Drakk'Har were cold blooded and did not sweat, they needed the cool mud to keep them from overheating during their long trek.

Drawwl was on a mission from the Swamp Master Borrk. Kek had broken a supply contract with the Swamp Master. As penalty, all of Kek's holdings were going to be claimed in payment. Contracts were zealously enforced in the Drakk'Har world and defaulting on one was serious indeed. If you could not provide the agreed-upon item for the agreed price at the agreed time, you were replaced with another who could. This created a Darwinian economy on a galactic scale. Failing to supply even minor goods ended up rippling through the system, causing mild upset at times and chaos at others.

Drawwl had been traveling only half a planet rotation. Kek's holdings were eight klem to the southeast, and his group could get there reasonably quickly. Drawwl was in no hurry. He knew of a cool pond full of tasty greppo fish on the border of Kek's lands. They could make it there easily before nightfall. The group would feed on the fish and stay there overnight. For what he had planned, an early morning arrival would be best.

Drawwl knew that with fifty warriors away from Borrk's ship growth facilities, the defenses were weakened significantly. However, Borrk was powerful enough that he did not have to worry about lesser Drakk'Har. Luckily, few on the planet were powerful enough and none of them was close enough to take advantage of the situation. Drawwl never even considered the warm bloods as a threat. They were simply food, after all.

* * *

A small piece of the *Arthur C. Clarke* passed in behind the *Sagittarius*. The debris was small, less than half a meter long, but dense metal. It was part of a support strut for a sensor array, and it had been blown off in a secondary explosion. Floating along with the fleet, it went unseen. It glanced off the large engine housing of the *Sagittarius* and was deflected upwards.

Instruments on the troop transport never detected the impact; its size was far too small to be a threat to such a massive ship. Its new course took it relentlessly toward Captain Levin's lighter.

A screeching siren and amber flashing lights illuminated the lighter control deck. Corporal Wallace was the first to interpret it. "Proximity alarm, sir." Wallace killed the siren, but the light kept on flashing.

Levin was scanning the space around him immediately. "See anything, Wallace?"

"Negative, sir. Wait. I see—"

WHAM ! The support struck the lighter on its right rear engine nacelle and then passed to the rear underneath the lighter and out into deep space. As the relative velocities were low, it did not penetrate the hull. However, the crew didn't know that.

Levin reacted immediately, double-checking the O_2 hose on his flight helmet was connected. He turned on his intercom. "Crew, vacuum collision checklist."

Levin accessed his checklist on his thigh-mounted datapad. "Pressure check."

"Steady at one thousand millibars," replied Wallace.

"Crew in breathers."

Levin saw Wallace look over his shoulder to see everyone in the rear had put their emergency oxygen masks on. "Check."

"Emergency oxygen."

"Check; in standby."

"Weapons."

"None loaded; master arm is off."

"Flight controls."

"Green lights on all control axis."

"Fuel."

"Sixty-five hundred liters remaining, pressure steady."

"Countermeasures."

"In standby, master arm is off."

"Crew, perform visual check and report on damage."

Sergeant Allan reported in. He had moved so he could look out the rear-most porthole on the right side of the lighter. "Sir, I have a dent approximately twenty centimeters long in the starboard rear aero-engine nacelle. No hull penetration from what I can see. Shall I get Corporal Marvin suited up for an EVA to check it out, sir?"

"Negative." With no immediate pressure loss, the captain did not think that was necessary for the moment. "Any other damage?"

"Not that I can see, sir."

"Collision checklist complete. All right, crew, stand by." Levin toggled a switch on his control yoke and activated his radio transmitter. "Bluebell, this is Grasshopper One. Pan-Pan, Pan-Pan, Pan-Pan. We have collided with a piece of debris. No pressure or control loss, but request docking priority and dry dock."

"Grasshopper One, this is Bluebell. Roger. Are you declaring an emergency at this time?"

"Bluebell, Grasshopper One. Negative. We have full control, and there is no pressure loss. The atmospheric engine was struck. I just want to get her in the barn ASAP as a precaution."

"Affirmative, Grasshopper One. Proceed to dry dock bay three. Priority clearance for docking. Bluebell out."

* * *

Bluebell was a balding forty-five year old chief with a pot belly on board the *Straczynski* who had seen it all in his career. He was in charge of marshalling all of the tender's lighters and also handled the refueling and maintenance schedule for the *Straczynski's* lighter fleet. In his opinion, on a scale of one to ten, this emergency rated a maximum of two. They got dinged by a space rock, and the pilot just wanted to get it in faster to play it safe. *Just another excuse to get to the mess faster to beat the rush*, he thought. Oh well, procedure was procedure. He knew what the book said for these situations; he had written most of it himself.

"Riley, we have Grasshopper One coming into bay three with an unknown object collision. She's yours."

* * *

"Right, Chief." Sergeant Riley was the handler. He made sure all of the assigned resources of the tender's maintenance section were used efficiently. If someone needed a test box or special rigging, they saw him. The chief kept the overall picture in mind. Riley handled the details. He checked the maintenance board and picked up a microphone that turned on the maintenance loudspeakers. "Corporal Betz, report to bay three for debrief. Corporal Betz, bay three for debrief."

* * *

Corporal Betz was an experienced plane captain, responsible for every aspect of a lighter's maintenance from the moment it came into his care until a pilot signed it out. He had lengthy training in electronics, structures, weapons systems, and propulsion. He never knew which lighter he would have whenever he came on shift or how long it would take before it was up or ready for flight in all respects. He was not having a good day and was ten hours into his twelve-hour shift. Betz had done an engine change on a lighter earlier. During the test burn, it had failed almost immediately. That meant he had to replace it all over again. The second engine had performed to specifications, and he had just signed it off. He was finishing a sandwich in the small canteen two levels below main control when he heard the page. Looking at his watch, he cursed silently, popped the last of the food into his mouth, and threw a plastic cup of lukewarm coffee into a garbage recycler before heading for the hatch.

Betz casually made his way to bay three. He knew it took several minutes to winch in a lighter, and then the crew had to disembark before they needed him. Betz stopped at a ceiling mounted monitor and checked the tail number of the incoming lighter. He was glad to see it was B1285, which was not as fussy as some others he could name. He downloaded the tender copy of the maintenance log to his datapad and walked down the passageway.

Betz made it to the proper access hatch and checked the air pressure gauges. Living with only a thin sheet of composite material between him and total vacuum, he *always* checked the pressure gauges. He knew of the interlocks and safeties, but if he happened to encounter a door with a one-in-a-million flaw, checking the gauges might stop him from instant death. The pressure was equal and stable, so he put on his sound-protective headset and pressed the hatch activation switch.

Bay three was behind a huge airlock. In days when the navy was still wet, ships had to be brought into a dry dock where water was drained from around the hull so maintenance could be performed. The same principle worked in space. By bringing the lighter inside the maintenance bay, one did not have to wear a cumbersome spacesuit or fumble around in zero gee. Of course, they only brought the badly damaged lighters inside. The bay had a series of overhead cranes, supports, panels, electrical connections, and tool racks. The inner airlock door was open, and the damaged lighter was sliding into its berth. When in place on the rails, clamps closed to lock the lighter in place.

The lighter was originally designed as a civilian transport and shuttle to carry passengers and light cargo into and out of orbit. When the military decided to replace their outdated transports at the beginning of the war, it had been decided to modify the civilian version to military specs. After extensive modifications, the military lighter had been born. Only the silhouette looked vaguely similar to the civilian model. Its structure had been strengthened and armor plating installed, hard points added for weapons, and external stores and more powerful engines fitted. Countermeasure pods were mounted flush to the surface, and conformal antennas and sensors added all over the structure. The computers were upgraded, and new software loaded. The comfortable leather padded chairs for passengers had been replaced with canvas strap versions that could accommodate armed troops or quickly convert to stretcher carriers for wounded. Pad-eyes were added to the floors for tying down cargo, and internal sound insulation had been removed to save weight. The outer body had been painted a mottled olive green to blend in with foliage when on the ground. On top of that green base, a huge black mouth with red lips and sharp white teeth had been painted on the front. Red eyes were set below the front windows. This was supposed to be intimidating up close and was designed by so-called psy-ops experts who claimed it scared the Drakk'Har.

The external lights clicked off, and a side hatch slid open. It recessed inwards slightly before sliding on rails behind the outer skin of the lighter. Several men wearing bug flight helmets and khaki green flight suit coveralls walked out. One of the men walked over to a cart and brought it to the lighter hatch. The others waited and carried out six black rubber body bags and piled them in the cart. Betz knew they were body bags from the way they carried them. They were careful to not throw or drop them. They carried them with quiet respect. Betz had once thought people were being stupid when they carried bodies. They were dead, after all. However, he was once detailed to help a crew unload several bodies and found that even he did the same thing unconsciously. Once they had finished unloading the bodies, one of the crew wheeled them out through the access hatch and into the ship. They would end up in Medical where they would be tagged and have a preliminary DNA check for identification purposes.

Two of the crew walked around the far side of the ship. Standard procedure dictated a visual inspection before and after a flight.

Betz filled out several fields in the log. He knew that in peacetime there would be a maintenance quarantine on the aircraft until the cause of the collision could be determined and a follow-up investigation launched. That slowed things up dramatically. However, they were at war, and as long as no one was hurt, regular proceedures would continue to be curtailed for the sake of expediancy. *Wartime operations come with a pretty good bullshit filter*, Betz thought.

The remaining crewmembers walked over to Betz carrying their gear and a traveling datapad with the lighter maintenance log. The one carrying the log dropped it onto the work surface. Betz saw he was a marine captain named Levin by his black leather nametag. He braced to attention. "Corporal Betz, sir."

* * *

"Relax, Corporal," said the captain as he pulled off his helmet. He started typing text into the datapad to enter the various problems or gripes they had encountered. "We hit something metallic on approach. Nailed us in the starboard rear engine housing. From the looks of things, it only did surface damage, but we will need that checked out. Apart from that, the engine throttles are sticking slightly in the forty to fifty percent range on the forward quadrant. Also, on the instrument cluster, there is a light burned out in the—" The officer paused trying to recall the name of the light panel. It had been a long grueling day, and his brain wanted some time off.

"APU Auxiliary Power Shunt, sir," suggested Corporal Wallace.

"Right. That's it for me. You got anything, Wallace?"

"Yes, sir. On the cargo deck, we've got a loose stanchion near the rear seat lockdown. The jump seats are loose on the starboard side because of it. Port forward intercom connection needs a new cord. That's it."

Betz was glad to hear of nothing major being wrong. Levin wrote up the entries in the discrepancy log. He thought he might even make it off shift in time. "Yes, sir. Should not be a problem. Have a good night."

Levin nodded and picked up his helmet. Carrying it under his arm, he walked off to the hatchway. Wallace stayed behind and spoke to Betz. "If you handle the engine, I'll do the interior items." As the Flight Engineer or FE, he had to supervise maintenance. B1285 was his bird, after all. Betz was responsible for the lighter while in maintenance, but Wallace was responsible for it at all times. The lighter was not even moved without Wallace present. Betz knew some FEs took supervision to be drinking coffee while the maintenance techs did all the work. FEs received more money than others of the same rank due to their need for a broad range of knowledge and flight pay. Some considered that to make them superior in some way. However, the majority knew the sooner the work was done, the sooner they got into their racks. So the good ones usually pitched in.

"Sounds good. Any idea what you hit out there?" Betz asked, more to be polite than anything. They moved around the outside of the lighter to the far side.

"It looked like a beam fragment, not sure. Debris from the battle as a guess. It didn't hit us very hard. It would've penetrated the hull if it were moving at any decent speed. There." Wallace pointed to the dent in the cowling.

"Yeah, looks minor. OK, I'll pull the cover and take a look underneath. At the very least, we'll have to do a calibration burn." Betz felt better about this. The damage was minor, and it looked like he would just have to replace the nacelle cover.

"No problem. You have the key to the tool rack?" Wallace indicated the locked cabinet on the wall.

"Yeah, here you go. It's been logged for our use." Betz handed over the key chain with a large sheet metal tag so it would be hard to lose.

Wallace moved off to open the tool rack while Betz examined the nacelle. The impact had been on the outer edge from the underside. Should be straightforward. He walked over to the tool rack and saw Wallace was finishing his check to make sure all tools and tags were present before they began work. This was standard. The tools were checked before and after any maintenance. This tool-control ensured no one forgot a flashlight in a fuel tank or a screwdriver in an engine. It had happened before, and the risk of injury and death was quite high. It took a few moments to check the hundreds of screwdriver tips, wrenches, and assorted gauges.

Corporal Betz took a series of tools from the board, slipping them into a small bag he took from a lower shelf. Wallace disappeared around the far side of the lighter with a can of spray lubricant.

Betz took his datapad and accessed a list of documents for maintenance use. From long experience, he knew where to go. TO-95 was a document describing the installation and removal of external lighter structures. Everything from panels, to control struts, to engine mounts and bracing. TO stood for Technical Order. If you worked on military aviation, you followed the book, even if you had done it five hundred times before and could recite it backwards from memory. A court martial tended to be avoided if you followed the book.

TO-95 went into great detail and provided diagrams and exploded views of each sub-assembly. Betz found the appropriate page on the datapad quickly. Reading the steps before proceeding, he undid the twenty-seven fasteners holding the nacelle onto the main body of the craft. As he undid the last one, the bay hatch opened and one of the crew returned the cart they had taken earlier. Betz gave him an appreciative wave and turned his attention back to the nacelle. He got a good grip and pulled. Nothing happened. He reached further down on the sides and started rocking the nacelle. Eventually it began to shift. Finally it came off in his hands with a screech of metal against metal.

Betz looked at the inside of the nacelle and saw a fresh scratch in the yellow interior paint where it had dragged against the engine. He stooped down and examined the underside of the engine. Yellow paint was scraped on one of the manifolds. He cursed quietly. If the manifold was cracked, that was an automatic engine change. Betz got on his back and, taking a flashlight, he crawled under the engine as far as he could. He looked at the surrounding components. He rubbed off the paint, but saw no evidence of damage. A lengthy visual check followed. Occasionally, Betz grabbed a component and tugged on it to check for correct fit. All of the bolts were in place, and all of the nuts were secured with lock wire. Everything looked and felt fine. He slid out from under the engine and looked at the cowling again. The dent was the only flaw on it. All the fasteners were fine, and none were stripped or corroded. He could have hammered out the dent and re-used it, but he would only do that if they had no spare parts. He found the metal parts label on the inside of the nacelle and wrote down the information on a notepad.

Betz walked over to a wall COMM unit. He punched in a number from memory. The call was answered quickly.

"Supply. Private Richards."

"This is Corporal Betz in bay three. I need a starboard rear nacelle for lighter B1285. Model number QX-34-523F."

"Roger. Stand by." A few minutes passed, and Betz could hear a keyboard being used before Richards spoke again. "Sorry, Corp, we don't have any in stock. Wait a sec. A crew just brought in a wrecked lighter that was thrown off the *Clarke*. It has serious frame damage and has been taken off flight status. I might be able to rob one off there. Let me check into it and get back to you. Need anything else?"

Betz ran through the discrepancy list in his mind. "Yes, half a dozen Modal J light bulbs for an instrument cluster and a DC-34 short intercom cord. That should do it."

"OK. Will get back to you in ten minutes. Supply out."

Betz walked over to the lighter door and entered the craft. The noise level dropped, but he could still hear several high pitched whines. He saw Wallace in the FE seat with the center control console in several pieces. He was spraying lubricant on the control lever junctions. Thick greasy foam covered the joints of the engine throttles. Betz watched Wallace advance and retard the throttle several times until he was satisfied that the joint had loosened sufficiently. Betz spoke as he sat in the pilot's seat beside him. "Supply is trying to locate a cowling. I asked for a COMM cord and some light bulbs for the cluster. I have the nacelle off, and I checked the engine. Want to give it a double check? Everything looks good, but—" Betz did not have to say that, as FE Wallace had to double-check all his work. Besides, a second person might find something he had missed.

"Right. Let me get this control panel back in place, and I'll be right out." Wallace started to piece the panel back in place. All the controls were held in place with multiple lock screws that only needed a quarter turn to secure, so it did not take long.

Betz walked out and was surprised to see a beaming Private Richards walk through the hatch with a nacelle. Betz walked over, and Richards handed it to him. "You are lucky, Corp. Another tech was stripping out the engine, and this was lying on the deck. I grabbed the other things from the shelf."

Inside the nacelle was a COMM cord and light bulbs in packaging. A supply voucher listed the items he had requested with a separate "rob sheet" for the cowling from the other lighter that Betz had to sign. He walked over to the naked engine and set the nacelle down. He double-checked the paperwork and made sure the information was correct. When satisfied, he signed the triple copy forms, handing them back to Richards. "Thanks, Private. Good work." Richard smiled and left. The cord and light bulbs went into Betz's pocket.

Wallace appeared and, without a word, disappeared under the engine with a flashlight. He too prodded and poked the engine for several minutes. He emerged and said, "You're right, she looks good. No damage near the impact area. Looks like we were lucky. OK, let's button her up." Wallace grabbed the TO and read the stages for installing the panel. He checked the few things he had to on the engine and then motioned for Betz to grab the nacelle.

Working together, they put the new nacelle on in no time. The last two screws on the bottom of the engine cover were hard to fasten. Betz had to press the side of the nacelle significantly to get the captive screws to pop in the holes. This was not unknown in maintenance. Not every part fit a hundred percent of the time. With the last two screws done up, the cover was secure.

They moved the tools away from the proximity of the engine. TO-95 called for a calibration burn on any engine suspected of damage. Betz walked to the front of the bay and turned on the fire suppression system to Active. The bay sensors were intelligent enough to know normal exhaust from actual flames from an engine fire. If a fire was detected, the suppression system would vent the bay to vacuum and alert maintenance control automatically. Satisfied, Betz and Wallace walked around the port side and entered the lighter. Wallace went to the FE station while Betz closed, sealed, and checked the hatches. When he was done, he walked forward to the cockpit. Wallace was reviewing a checklist on one of the pilot's monitors.

"Hatch secure," Betz said as he slipped into the pilot seat. When seated, he toggled a light test switch, and all lights but one on the control cluster came on. He grabbed a couple of spare bulbs from his pocket and placed two new lights in the holders, then reseated the switch. This time when he pressed the light test switch, all of the lights illuminated.

Wallace waited until he was finished. "OK. All circuit breakers are correct for engine start checklist. APU."

Betz reached for the APU start switch. APU was an Auxiliary Power Unit that supplied power when the engine generators were off-line. He pressed the switch up and held it. A gauge above the switch flickered to life, and he heard a powerful turbine engine start to spool up. It took about forty-five seconds to come up to full speed. When it did so, the lights flickered, and they were running on internal power. Betz checked the gauges, then flipped a main electrical breaker. The lights dimmed momentarily. "APU running. On internal power."

Wallace continued scanning the control panel while flicking switches. "Power shunt connected. Throttle set to idle. Fuel switches on. Engine one start."

At the flick of the engine start switch, the APU diverted a portion of hot gas from its exhaust into high-pressure ductwork. The gases were sent across the fan blades of the selected engine, which began to turn. As the fan spooled up, fuel was sprayed into the combustion chamber, and igniters fired. Engine one roared to life and continued until it stabilized at fifty-five percent power. Betz waited ten seconds, scanning the instrument cluster continuously, and then said, "Engine one at idle. Oil temp coming up, pressure stable. Readings nominal."

They continued with the same process until all four engines were turning over at idle power. Betz reached forward and selected MAINTENANCE on the computer display in front of him. A maintenance checklist came up. He selected ENGINES, and when a new sub-menu appeared, he selected POWER-ON CALIBRATION. The computer asked him if he was sure. He said yes, and the engines began to turn, pivot, and vary thrust in a seemingly haphazard way. The powerful clamps holding the lighter on the bay rails held the craft immobile as the tests proceeded. Both corporals watched the displays and indicators for four minutes while the engines went through a test cycle. At the end of the test, the engines returned to neutral position and idle speed. A flashing green border appeared on the corner of the screen reading ENGINE 4: 1.453 DEGREES OUT OF TOLERANCE. PROCEED WITH RE-ALIGNMENT? (Y/N) Betz referenced TO-95 and read the section on allowances for calibration. "OK, the TO says we can have up to 1.5 degrees without an engine change. So, we are good to go." He looked over at Wallace, who nodded. Betz pressed Y to begin the process, and the internal computer re-aligned the thrust vectors of the starboard rear engine. This took thirty-five seconds.

When the process was done, Betz restarted the POWER-ON CALIBRATION test. For another four minutes, they sat while the engines ran through their testing sub-routines. When complete, the green screen flashed ALL ENGINES NOMINAL.

"All right. You happy?" Betz turned to Wallace, who had also read the results.

"Yep, let's shut her down. Engine shut-down checklist." Wallace began to read off the line items for the shut-down checklist. The engine start process was reversed, and all four engines and then the APU were shut down safely. They had to wait inside a few minutes while the noxious exhaust gases were cleared by the bay ventilation system. Betz took the opportunity to check the recently lubricated engine lever was working smoothly. He then went into the rear of the lighter and replaced the bad COMM cord with the spare in his pocket. Lastly, he checked the stanchion and found it secured to the floor properly. He turned and gave Wallace a thumb up to show he was done. The lighter interior went dark as power was turned off. Betz heard Wallace flipping switches. He assumed he was configuring it for the next flight.

Wallace walked to the hatch and cracked it open. The air in the bay smelled only slightly from the engine test. He lowered the hatch, and the pair left the lighter. They gave the repaired engine a quick glance. No fluid leaks or anything else out of the ordinary was found. They walked back around the front of the lighter.

Betz talked as he walked. "Ok, all we've got to do now is top up the O2 and fuel. Want to do the O2?"

"Sure."

Betz attached fuel hoses to top up the lighter's internal tanks, while Wallace topped up the O2 tanks from the other side of the craft. They both finished at the same time.

When the hoses were returned to the bay wall, they both grabbed their tools and returned them to the toolbox. Once they had both checked all tools were present, they closed and locked the board.

Wallace headed off to grab his gear, and Betz looked at his watch. He had half an hour before shift change to sign off the job, tag the broken parts for return to supply, and complete the maintenance log. No problem at all. He returned to the lighter maintenance log and began to sign out the various entries. The engine nacelle entry was signed off as "#4 engine cowling replaced with engine calibration carried out IAW TO-95. All engines calibrated within tolerance." Wallace countersigned each entry, and fifteen minutes later, lighter B1285 was officially "up" or ready for flight. Only when the datapad entries were complete did he call Riley in maintenance control. "Sarge, B1285 is up in all respects. Log is ready for upload."

"Right," was all Riley said before hanging up.

Wallace started to leave, and Betz called after him. "Thanks for the help." Friendly waves were exchanged before Wallace left.

Betz went around the bay and powered down all the non-essential equipment. He coiled the cables and hoses to reduce the chance of someone tripping over them. He double-checked the lighter hatch, then looked around the bay before grabbing his things. The access hatch hissed closed behind him, and the only sound remaining was the rustle of air through the ventilation ducts.

When the errant metal strut from the *Clarke* struck the lighter, it crushed the engine cowling easily. When the nacelle cover met the heavy engine manifold underneath, the strut was moving slowly enough that the manifold could absorb the shock without breaking. However, the force of the impact was sufficient to bend the engine mounting hardware a few degrees relative to the hull. This was the misalignment Betz had discovered and subsequently compensated for with the calibration. Neither man had been able to see the miniscule cracks in the mount that had developed as a result of the impact. Nor had they seen the cracks grow with the vibrations caused during the engine tests. TO-95 called only for a visual inspection of the area prior to the calibration test, but not after. Whoever had written the Technical Order had thought that to be sufficient.

It wasn't.

Lighter B1285 sat inert and waited for the crew to return.

CHAPTER 10 – DECEPTION

Sergeant Smith was on point. They had moved quickly to get there, but he was taking his time over the last few hundred meters. Hill tops were not just good places for humans to be. Drakk'Har often occupied the high ground to mount anti-air missiles and sensor platforms. The last thing he wanted to do was lead his group into an enemy camp or ambush. He knew the L-T wanted to get here in a hurry and he understood why. He could hear Mendez every now and then as he groaned. In fact, he was making far too much noise for Smith, but they had no alternative. Hill 170 appeared to be unoccupied as they approached, but nothing in life was guaranteed.

Running roughly north to south, two hills blended into one. The secondary peak was 157 meters in elevation and was just south of where he was currently climbing. The underbrush was not as thick here, and that meant you could see farther, but it also meant you could be seen from farther away, too. Smith was no more than twenty meters from the summit, and the red sun was setting in the distance. He made hand signs that were passed down the line. In effect, he said wordlessly: *Wait here. Popov and I will check it out and be back in fifteen minutes.* When the L-T acknowledged, the pair moved up the hill slowly. They disappeared in a few steps, and the rest of the Special Forces troopers took a break while remaining vigilant.

Smith moved as quietly as possible. He was not the best scout they had, but compared to most, he was quite talented. He checked for trip wires, footprints, broken branches, and anything out of the ordinary. He approached the summit of the hill in a spiral, moving around and up in stages. Popov followed closely, never more than three meters away from him. Smith had his weapon oriented up the hill to the left, while Popov had his pointing to the right, downhill. It took them ten minutes to make it to the summit.

They found and heard nothing on their journey. He saw no tracks or sign of recent movement. Only as they got to the top of the hill did Smith notice something that was not quite right. A slight clearing with a patch of green a few meters away from him looked different from the surrounding area. The different color stood out boldly from the surrounding foliage, but apart from that, it looked artificial. He pointed at it so Popov saw it, too. The corporal acknowledged with a nod and moved slightly off to one side so he could fire at it as well, if necessary. They advanced, painfully slowly. It could be a camouflaged trench or firing hole. It might be a sensor array, a piece of unknown weaponry, or mine.

Smith's heart rate increased as he got closer to the item. The tension mounted. Smith advanced into the clearing, looked hard at it. With a sigh of relief, he realized he was looking at a military issue sleeping bag laid out under the bushes. He raised his weapon barrel to the sky and walked into the clearing, looking around. Off to his right side, a bush stood up and stepped toward him. Smith was expecting something like that, but it happened so close and noiselessly that he was startled nonetheless and backpedaled a half step. He was thinking furious curses and gazed daggers at the heavily camouflaged sniper, but did not say anything as noise discipline was in effect.

* * *

Jefferson herself was glad for the heavy camouflage. Her toothy grin went completely unnoticed. Taught to remain motionless for days on end and to move at a laboriously slow rate to avoid detection, Jefferson was one of the best. One of the exams on Jefferson's sniper course had been to hide in a one hundred square meter area of forest, which was then searched by a squad of regular soldiers and supervised by a veteran sniper instructor. The troops were given twenty minutes to find the seven sniper candidates hidden within. At the end of the half hour, three students had been found. The sniper instructor then told the remainder of the course to come out of hiding. All but Jefferson emerged. The instructor yelled for Jefferson to come out. With no response, the instructor started to move deeper into the area to search. He got no further than half a pace before tripping and falling. He looked down to find his bootlaces had been tied together. Jefferson emerged then, and the instructor realized that he had unknowingly been standing on the mesh of the sniper's camouflaged ghillie suit the entire time.

Jefferson had only arrived five minutes prior to Smith. She had barely gotten her sleeping bag laid out when she heard someone coming slowly through the undergrowth. She was not entirely sure if the section was approaching or a Drakk'Har patrol was coming, so she had lain in wait for them to emerge. She gave the sergeant the all-clear hand signal, and Smith turned to Popov, indicating he should get the rest of the patrol. The corporal departed at a fast rate down the hill.

* * *

Smith removed his pack and ammo pack. He grabbed a collapsible shovel from the side of his pack and shouldered his weapon. He began walking around the hilltop, marking where the trenches should go for the troops. He staggered the positions, making sure everyone had a clear arc of fire. No one would start digging until the L-T had approved their placement. They would set out LPs later, after the section had a defensible position.

* * *

Within a few minutes, the remainder of the section entered the small clearing. Jefferson was shocked when she saw Sergeant Mendez on the litter. In the short time she had been away, he had turned as white as a ghost. His head moved back and forth from a combination of pain in his leg and a tortured mind. The venom in his blood had taken its toll over the last few hours, and she could see he was in bad shape. Mendez's litter was placed on the ground in the center of the clearing, and he made a loud grunt sound as he was placed on the ground. Corporal Jacobs hovered over him and did what he could. Jefferson thought the care he was receiving was far from enough. He needed a medevac and soon. The L-T came up past Mendez and nodded at her. Jefferson saw the same concern on his face as he passed.

The section moved wordlessly. Each pair of soldiers began to dig trenches in the soft earth. The excavated earth was piled in front of the trench, forming an earth berm. Wood and foliage was placed on the front side of the earth to both provide additional protection and camouflage. Jefferson had to side-step to let Popov pass with a spool of field wire. He began to lay out a landline communications network linking all of the holes being dug. In time, all trenches were connected. Firing holes were slit into the earth and packed down to give a stable aiming surface. When the group was finished, the trenches became hard to discern from even a few meters to the front. Jefferson went to each hole and, using her camouflage skills, reworked them to look as natural as possible. Each of the trenches faced outwards, except for the command bunker. Placed in the center of the camp, the command bunker was dug slightly larger than usual. It not only had to accommodate two men and the section radio, but also be big enough to take Sergeant Mendez and his litter, plus room for Jacobs. They could not leave Mendez outside to fend for himself in a firefight. Everyone worked quietly, but with some degree of urgency. They all knew that defenses were much harder to set up in the dark, and they all wanted to be in their holes by sunset.

* * *

In the last light of the day, Pratt reconnoitered the hilltop, looking for good listening post positions, while Smith followed close behind. While he could see the distant Drakk'Har town, he could no longer see the adjacent river clearly or areas beyond from the camp itself. Hill 170 was not as good an observation platform as the original hill they had occupied. The peak was lower in elevation and not as steep, so the trees on the lower parts of the slope blocked their view in several directions. However, he scoped out three LPs around the hill to cover the more obvious approaches and to observe the town and surrounding area as best as they could.

Popov and his wire spool visited each in turn and connected them to the main camp. They did not dig emplacements at the listening posts, but they did transplant some local bushes to give more cover to each. Listening posts were not part of the defenses, per se. They simply acted as early warning for the main camp.

Once the defenses were ready, Lieutenant Pratt crawled into the shallow section command bunker with Jacobs and Mendez. He sat on the crude dirt step near the entrance to the bunker and pulled out a datapad. He turned on the red backlight on the device, and a dull red glow filled the area. Pratt made several notes and, when finished, he connected to the wire segment in the bunker. Speaking into his microphone quietly, he identified himself and asked all personnel to link into the landline. Those not on watch were connected in a few seconds.

"Alpha section, roll call," the lieutenant requested. Each person responded in order of rank in a very quiet voice. The sensitive mike pickups amplified the signals and transmitted them to all COMM units on the wired landline.

"Smith."

"MacPherson."

"Jefferson."

"Jacobs, with Mendez off comms."

"Popov."

"White."

"Williams."

"Bennet."

With all people accounted for and on the landline, the lieutenant began speaking quietly. "OK, people, we're in our new home. We have three LPs, which we will occupy in thirty minutes, so make sure all defenses are done by then. Sergeant Smith will schedule everyone, including myself, on two-hour shifts. Noise discipline will be in effect, radio silence to be employed.

"This is the current situation." Pratt felt his people needed to know as much as he did, within reason. Pratt looked over at the prone, wounded sergeant. "Sergeant Mendez is having a bad reaction to the croc venom. His wounds make it imperative he get to medical help soonest. Command has been notified of the situation, and we can expect a medevac soon after the fleet arrives. We will need a landing zone prepared for that, so at first light, Smith and MacPherson will scout one out and rig up charges to clear an area of sufficient size. We will set them off once the lighter is inbound. We can expect new orders once the fleet is in orbit and things start happening. Until then, we stay invisible and watch out for all enemy activity. Questions?"

"Sir, this is Smith. I already took a quick look around earlier. We can put the landing zone on top of the secondary peak of the hill. It is out of the way for blasting, but close enough to be convenient and fairly flat. Will not affect the camp, and we can cover the landing from the higher elevation."

"Good idea, Sergeant. You and MacPherson plan it out together. Anything else?"

Five seconds of silence. "OK, we should hopefully have a quiet night ahead. If you are not on watch, get some food and sleep. We will maintain standard night watch until thirty minutes before dawn. Pratt out."

* * *

Sh-Elerk was standing in the maneuvering room of the *Resilient Fury,* truly exhilarated. The ship had accelerated to a respectable speed, and with engines at full thrust and shields at full power, they accelerated toward Mindon-3. Sh-Elerk could see the distant planet on the screens before him. Mindon-3 was very cold and had a thick ice crust for a surface.

Sh-Elerk had thought a shuttle was fun to pilot, but standing on the bridge of a warship under full power was surprisingly satisfying. He realized he had missed his true calling. Command of a warship felt completely natural to him. He cast his eyes across the instruments and sensor panels. Sh-Elerk could see the approximate position and projected course of the incoming warm blood fleet. His own course was updated every few seconds on the same screen. The two paths curved and intersected just as the warm bloods came to the orbit of Mindon-3. Perfect. The planet would mask their approach until it was too late to react. Not even warm blood technology could sense them through a planet. The feeling of freedom and speed was beyond expression. He paused for a moment and thought of something. The enemy fleet could not detect them from this distance, but— Sh-Elerk thought intensely.

The pilot turned to Sh-Elerk. "Lord, our course will take us to the enemy fleet as we pass around Mindon-3. We need to begin braking maneuvers now to accomplish this."

"No, pilot." Sh-Elerk did not know his name and never bothered asking. Somehow, his being nameless helped. "We will continue steady on this course for the moment."

"Then we will be using the planet's gravity well to accelerate into their heart, my Lord?" The pilot was getting confused.

"No. We will not be doing that either." He explained for a few moments.

"Lord, the ship may not be able to handle those stresses. No one has piloted this class of ship in that manner. This isn't a shuttle."

"I know that, and if we're lucky, the warm bloods will assume the same thing. That is not the thing that concerns me."

"Lord?"

"With several heavy cruisers protecting them, we may not be able to get close enough to the warm bloods. We need to reduce the opposition. Tell me, if you were the enemy commander and detected us on approach vector to Mindon-3, what would you do?"

The pilot thought for a few moments and then said, "I would detail a smaller force of cruisers to intercept us prior to us coming into weapons range of their transports..." He pressed his claw against the display screen, "...here." He was trying to follow the train of thought so much, he had forgotten the usual honorific.

"Exactly, and if we maneuver as I propose, where will we emerge?" Sh-Elerk had already thought this through.

The pilot thought about it and shifted the tip of his black claw slightly. "Here. With the orbital path leading us here." He saw it then. "Lord, if that is your intention, we are attempting this at a dangerous velocity. We need to secure main engines or risk burning up from the friction. The heat shields were not designed for that angle of attack. Also, there is another problem. In order to detach ships to intercept us, the warm bloods need to detect us first. We have not been detected to this point."

"Correct, pilot. Secure main engines. We can coast the rest of the way with sufficient velocity. As for them detecting us, let us show them our challenge." Sh-Elerk moved into the doorway and yelled a command to the technician working on the countermeasure equipment.

* * *

"Sir, we are detecting a single vessel approaching Mindon-3; designating it as Force Three. They are attempting to actively jam our sensors. Frequencies and power ratings indicate a Scarab class destroyer. Plotting course now. Sir, their jamming is totally ineffective; they are well beyond maximum range. I have no idea why they— Sir, the jamming just ended. They broadcast for thirty-two seconds only. They may have broadcast in error. Untrained crew, perhaps?" the commander at Threat Analysis suggested with a confused air.

Kosnov had just returned to his station. "Can you project his course and speed?"

"Stand by, working it out now. Yes, sir, he is on a direct course to the outer atmosphere of Mindon-3; that and his speed suggest a deceleration profile. They transmitted just long enough for us to get a fix. Looks like someone made a careless error onboard," the Threat Analysis commander added the last as he thought out loud.

"Perhaps." Kosnov thought back through all the received intelligence reports he had ever seen. "Mr. Collins, do you ever recall a Scarab class destroyer making such a basic error? It has been my experience that their crews are notoriously well disciplined."

"Mine, too, sir. Could be an over-eager or under-experienced captain. Or perhaps they threw together a last minute crew to man the ship, and they do not have standard training. Could be one of a hundred things." Collins could not think of a single occurrence where a Drakk'Har destroyer commander had been so sloppy.

Kosnov placed his hand on his chin and stroked his beard slowly as he spoke. "They have already shown they are desperate enough to stop us by ramming. This may be another

Kamikaze-style attack. If they use Mindon-3 to accelerate instead of decelerate, what is their projected course?"

A few keys were pushed, and on the giant center screen of the command deck, a projected course appeared. It went directly through the base course of the Federation fleet.

"Now, plot their course if they decelerate instead," the marshal ordered. A second course appeared, also intersecting the fleets course, but further along its path.

"So, they do want to pass through the fleet for whatever reason. A Scarab packs quite a punch, and they will be broadsiding us. They will be passing behind the planet soon, which will mask their maneuvering. Plus, there may be more ships with them which did not transmit. This feels wrong, ladies and gentlemen. Very wrong. The captain who thought out this approach is an experienced one. Experienced captains do not broadcast their intentions with ineffective jamming. So, if we saw him, he wanted us to see him. Diversion for a larger unseen force or Kamikaze attack are our two choices as of right now." Kosnov stroked his beard several times before speaking. "Conduct a full power scan on all azimuths with everything we have. Scan that ship, and see if he is alone. Contact intelligence and ask for an update on enemy ships thought to be in the system. Mr. Collins, I want a pair of surveillance drones on the far side of Mindon-3 to track him passively. I want to know what that ship is doing back there."

"Aye, aye, sir." Collins's fingers flew across his command board, and minutes later, he read off the results. "Sir, we have no other ships within detection range. LADAR is clear, no enemy emissions or communications signals in our vicinity. Force Three seems to be composed of one ship only. Marshal, assuming we reacted the way he wants us to, what would we do?" Collins asked while punching in orders to his console.

"We would detail at least two cruisers to intercept him in orbit. If he accelerates, he would be in high orbit with them below him, and if decelerating, in low orbit with them above. Doctrine dictates the cruisers meet them away from the fleet to protect the transports." Kosnov recalled the details from memory. They were basic space tactics used by both sides. The Marshal added, "If a suicide attack, they would want to fly into the middle of the troop transports and take as many of them out as possible. A thermonuclear shock wave and radiation would disintegrate everything in a seven kilometer zone. That would cripple the fleet. So, sending a smaller force to stop them would be prudent. Even if they detonated a nuclear weapon, it would only take out the cruisers."

"So, upon spotting an intercept force, it is logical they would attempt to get past without engaging them and concentrate on the transports, correct?" Collins continued.

"Yes, that is sound reasoning. Why do you ask?" Kosnov looked at the younger man with a slight frown.

Collins turned to face the marshal. "I was just thinking, why don't we let them see exactly what they expect to?"

* * *

Sh-Elerk watched the enemy fleet disappear from his screen as Mindon-3 blocked the sensor's line of sight. "Pilot, engage maneuvering thrusters. Re-orient the ship."

Even with the inertial dampers, everyone on board felt the ship twist radically. Those not strapped down instinctively grabbed ahold of something solid for support.

The pilot shunted the destroyer into its new flight profile. He looked anxious to Sh-Elerk, but he could certainly understand why. Sh-Elerk had been correct in his first glance at the pilot. He did have extensive experience piloting this ship class. In fact, he was the pilot of the *Resilient Fury* itself. They had spoken about this before getting to Mindon-3. The pilot had a glorious career until the Battle of Regula. The ship had suffered critical damage, and they had crash-landed on a small, barren moon. Many were killed. Only two Drakk'Har survived, but were trapped in the maneuvering area with the remainder of the ship open to vacuum. With no spacesuits or food, it was only a matter of time before hunger and desperation caused them to cannibalize the bodies of their fallen crewmembers for survival. To the Drakk'Har, crews were expendable, but ships were hard to produce. When they returned to the moon to recover the fallen hull, they were surprised to find survivors. Surprise turned to disgust when they saw the eaten corpses. Placed in chains, the pilot was taken to Mindon-2 along with the ship. The *Resilient Fury* was raised from the planet, transported to Mindon-2, and placed in orbit above the planet for repairs. The pilot was branded as Drel and sent to the darkest of cells below the surface.

Sh-Elerk watched the pilot double-check all maneuvers and sensor readings. He kept an eye on the instruments and kept the course of the ship within rigid parameters. When the pilot was satisfied as to the orientation, he called out, "Ship ready for main engines, Lord."

Sh-Elerk heard the pilot and saw that the ship's instruments confirmed the pilot's report. "Fire main engines, maximum thrust."

What had been a noisy maneuvering deck became a cacophony of noise as the main engines increased to full power. Oriented at a thirty-degree angle relative to their course, the ship's engines began to shift their baseline heading as well as decelerate them. This continued for several minutes. Sh-Elerk did not talk to the pilot. He could see this needed concentration. Instead, he toggled the intercom. He yelled into the microphone, "Engineering deck. What is the time to detonation on the atomic device?"

The answer took some time. Sh-Elerk could hear the engineering decks were much noisier than his part of the ship when they responded. "Five slem, four arkle, Lord."

Time enough, thought the Lord of the *Resilient Fury.*

CHAPTER 11 – DISTORTION

"Marshal, the surveillance drones are relaying video images and solid tracking data. The approaching ship is conducting an offset deceleration burn. That's either a gifted pilot, sir, or the most reckless S.O.B. I've ever seen. Taking a warship through that kind of maneuver is borderline suicide! Smaller vessels have no trouble making offset burns because of their reduced mass; our lighters do this all the time for last-minute vectoring onto a target. However, for a warship at those speeds that is, well, sir, the only word I can think of is desperate."

"Agreed, Mr. Collins. This feels more and more like a Kamikaze-style attack. That's strange, as over the years we have never seen Drakk'Har deliberately sacrifice themselves so willingly. Has the intercept force been detached?" The marshal could not stop looking at the long plume of white-hot engine exhaust coming off the Drakk'Har vessel. He half-expected it to disappear at any moment in a huge explosion, but it continued relentlessly.

"Yes, sir. All three vessels are proceeding to the designated coordinates. Remainder of the fleet is maneuvering as ordered." Multiple windows of data opened and closed on his command console at remarkable speed as Collins referenced, and then closed, many databases and information sources.

* * *

Sh-Elerk waited until the last possible moment before they touched the upper atmosphere of Mindon-3. He then ordered the *Resilient Fury* to re-orient itself so the vessel was flying forward. His growing confidence in the pilot and his abilities let him cut the timing closer than he would have attempted with anyone else at the controls, including himself. Once more the ship tumbled and twisted, with the crew grabbing for whatever support they could find. In a minute, they were oriented properly to brush the upper atmosphere of the planet. Their heat shields grazed against the ether above Mindon-3. The atmosphere at this altitude was so thin that it barely registered on their instruments. However, at the speed they were traveling, it felt like being in a fast boat in high seas. Tremor after tremor shook the ship, battering it as slightly denser pockets of the atmosphere were encountered. Anything that was not secured in place flew through the air and landed heavily on the deck. Sh-Elerk saw a bright blue flash and a few sparks come from the countermeasure instrumentation before it went dark. They lost speed at a dramatic rate.

* * *

Captain Irwin J. Bishop III sat in his chair restraints on his bridge. He had been assigned command of the three-ship intercept force, and to say he was nervous was an understatement. He had never commanded an offensive group before, and while the marshal himself had told him the reason over MASER-COMM, he still felt exposed. The group had been ordered to fly in a standard triangular formation to pre-designated coordinates—coordinates that would put a Scarab class heavy destroyer on an intercept course. His group was flying around Mindon-3 in the opposite direction to the fleet. After visually sighting the enemy vessel, he was to maneuver his group to engage the approaching enemy ship "to the best of his ability." Captain Bishop hoped the Old Man knew what the hell he was doing.

* * *

The *Resilient Fury* had sensors active and on maximum sustainable power as it skimmed the upper atmosphere. The technicians in charge of the sensors were looking for the cruiser force they were told to expect by Lord Sh-Elerk. They were dealing with several problems at the moment. The rough treatment the ship had received in the atmospheric buffeting had damaged several sensor systems and antennas, which had caused them to either be unusable or forced to operate at reduced power. The noise of the friction of the atmosphere was deafening, and even headsets could not protect their ears. Plus, the friction of gas striking the heat shields was producing red-hot plumes across the nose and body of the craft. This was rendering video and infrared sensors unusable. They were literally flying blind.

As they came around the planet, the technicians were focusing on a patch of sky where they expected the intercept force to be. One of the Drakk'Har technicians tried to fine-tune a sensor array while the ship was being hammered by the atmosphere. After several jarring shocks, there came a brief period where the turbulence lessened considerably. The technician took the opportunity to slide through the operating frequencies of the sensor and, to his considerable surprise, saw three cruiser-shaped targets appear on his scope momentarily before heavy static returned. "Lord, three cruisers in standard assault formation located in sector 4. Distance 120,000 klem. We will pass well abeam. They are in high orbit and accelerating."

On the maneuvering deck, Sh-Elerk wanted to shout a cry of victory, but restrained himself. His deceptive maneuvering had fooled the warm bloods. He had expected to outmaneuver two cruisers and three were reported! They must have thought they would have an easy victory with those odds.

* * *

Captain Bishop saw the approaching warship skimming through the upper edges of Mindon-3. The Drakk'Har vessel's heat shields glowed deep red as it passed well beneath the intercept group. Given this situation, he would have preferred to fling an anti-matter volley into the atmosphere of Mindon-3 and blast the ship to pieces. He had two difficulties with that. First, he had no anti-matter; the ships under his command were never designed to carry those weapons. Second, his own ships were far too close for such an action.

"All ships, commence firing," Bishop ordered, although he already knew it to be useless.

* * *

"Lord, incoming fire from the cruisers," the technician at the countermeasure station screamed when his panel lit up with alarm lights. The type of fire was noted and reported to his Lord. "Secondary weapons only. We appear to be inside the effective radius of their main armaments and shall be past them momentarily."

Now, the cruisers were out of position and unable to engage him effectively. Sh-Elerk toggled ship-wide intercom. "Warriors of the Drakk'Har, the cruiser force is heading where they thought we should have been and not where we are. We have successfully flanked their main defenses, and we are making our way to their fleet. When we reach the warm blood transports, there will be three less cruisers to protect them. On to victory!" The sound of many jubilant voices joined him.

* * *

"Marshal, Force Three has passed the intercept force. They were fired on without visible effect. The enemy did not engage, as we expected. They should be leaving the atmosphere soon."

"Thank you, Mr. Collins. Carry on as briefed."

* * *

Captain Bishop ordered a cessation of fire when the Drakk'Har warship passed behind his cluster of ships. He maintained his course and speed. By doing so, he would rejoin the fleet on the opposite side of the planet. He had been ordered to let them pass and not pursue.

* * *

Sh-Elerk shouted the command with a firmness and confidence he had never experienced before. "Start main engines, full thrust. Take us out of the atmosphere, pilot."

The pilot hit the engine activation stud and advanced the controls for a full-power burn. He hauled back on the controls, and the warship leapt out of the atmosphere. Almost instantly, the ride became smoother. Leaving the atmosphere behind signaled the last part of their journey had begun.

"Scan all frequencies along the projected course; give me the precise location of the center of the warm blood fleet," Sh-Elerk yelled to the technicians.

The technicians scanned the target coordinates and saw... nothing? Fearing a malfunction at a critical time, they brought secondary sensors online and saw... nothing!

"Lord, no contact on the plotted course," was all the sensor operator could muster.

The response was immediate.

"What?" Sh-Elerk could not believe his ears. "Full power scan in all directions, now!"

* * *

"They have seen us, sir. We are well clear of any atomic blast radius, and their course and speed are too far out of limits to intercept us," Mr. Collins reported with a smile.

The marshal nodded and turned to the communications officer. "Commander Shiotu, order all cruisers to commence fire."

* * *

Sh-Elerk looked in horror at the sensor display. While he was changing course on the far side of the planet, the warm bloods had also changed their vector and were heading around the far side of the planet. From the direction of the fleet, he could see at least six heavy cruisers firing on him. His first reaction was confusion. They were not supposed to have nine cruisers, yet that is what he had seen! His instinct was to change course and get closer, but that would take time, and the weapon stuck to the deck in engineering had a short time remaining. *Too little time to maneuver properly.* With no time to change course, and with the intercept group behind him moving further and further away with each second, the possibility of intercepting the main group was zero. He had no choice or other options; the longer he waited meant less chance of inflicting any damage on the warm blood fleet. He would still die as a Drakk'Har warrior, but not as well as he had dreamed. *At least I will take the three cruisers we flanked with me,* he thought. He took some satisfaction in that.

Sh-Elerk reached forward beside the pilot and activated a seldom-used panel. He heard the sirens and saw the warning lights as he worked and pressed the overrides for each. He raised a cover protecting the last activation stud and pressed it once. His victory had turned to ash in his mind.

Signals from the panel went into the engineering section, activating several large components. The signals had nothing to do with the atomic weapon in engineering. The warhead was not linked into the ship's systems, and he had no way to remotely detonate it, anyway. Planet Lord Slassh had installed the device to stop them from stealing the ship and heading out of the system. The crew never had any intention of using it as a weapon. They had something much more destructive in mind. Atomic weapons were third in destructive power on the grand scale of things. In second place came anti-matter as the most destructive man-made material ever created. However, the winner made them both look insignificant...

* * *

Sensors in the Federation fleet detected the distinctive energies the Drakk'Har ship began to throw off. Command signals were sent throughout the internal computer network. All other traffic, regardless of priority, was suspended until this signal passed. On every bridge on every ship in the fleet, a distinct siren went off that was reserved for this eventuality alone. A siren no one had ever heard in this war, beyond simulations and testing. A siren no one ever wanted to hear.

"Delta distortion signals detected from Force Three!" Collins yelled over the noise of the klaxon.

"Mother of God!" said Kosnov as he hammered his fleet wide MASER-COMM stud. "All ships, execute Omega pattern. Engines to maximum power." Omega was known as the maneuver of last resort. Omega was also called the "Oh, my God" maneuver. It meant one thing: Get as far away from here as possible, as fast as possible. Given any threat, you have two choices: fight or flight. The fleet had the best weapons, personnel, and cutting-edge technology. Yet, Fleet Nine was running as fast as it could.

* * *

The *Resilient Fury's* star drive began to power up. Energy coursed through thick power supply cables into the vast array of electronics, wiring, and field coils. The generated power was shunted back into the system, creating a feedback loop of energy. Power began to grow exponentially throughout the system. Within seconds, the fabric of space-time itself began to feel the energies imparted by the star drive core. Space itself began to warp, twist, and fold as the Drakk'Har warship manipulated it through the energies it produced. Eventually, space-time began to rupture, and through one of the resulting holes, the Drakk'Har warship entered hyperspace...

Almost.

* * *

In the early stages of the twenty-first century, scientists discovered that space-time could be manipulated. At first, simple lab experiments produced miniscule, but encouraging, results. Then, when higher-energy experiments were done, scientists began to prove manipulation of space-time was not only possible, but also fairly easy. However, the larger the scale of the experiment, the larger the problems. Stability of the field was a critical issue, as it simply could not be maintained. You cannot use something you cannot control, and no one could determine why the fields collapsed, typically resulting in a spectacular explosion. No matter what the scale of the experiment, the field never lasted.

Eventually, one bright bulb decided scaling up the experiment was the answer. The complex math he produced seemed to support his theory. You simply had to build a field of immense size to make it self-sustaining. He convinced a few influential colleagues to jump on the bandwagon and they convinced several governments to fund the research. This was before the unified Earth government and subsequent Sol Colony Alliance. What happened next was described kindly as folly and harshly as a debacle, depending on the leanings of the observer.

The largest field generator ever created was constructed in Earth orbit. A maze of wiring and control circuitry, the craft was a testament to the science of the day. The huge platform was towed out to the orbit of Jupiter before being activated. Jupiter was, luckily, on the other side of the solar system from Earth at the time. Several politicians had noted that when these experiments had failed in the past, huge explosions followed. Even though the scientists on the committee assured them otherwise, the politicians voted unanimously to have the generator towed out of Earth orbit. This was probably the first and only time that a politician's desire for self-survival had been of beneficial use to mankind.

During the test, the field strength had built up steadily and exactly as the complex math models predicted. Video transmissions of the scientists on site, beamed off the experiment platform, showed they were jubilant at the results. The field built to maximum power, and then, contrary to all of their calculations, theories, and assurances, it collapsed. The explosion that resulted killed the entire committee and wiped out half of the space vehicles available at that time. The total revocation of all funding for time-space manipulation was quickly enacted by the surviving politicians, who proclaimed that they had doubts all along. The elected officials had been misled and misinformed by the scientific community and, therefore, were in no way responsible for the loss of life or the several trillions in government currency that had just vanished. Then, after kissing the requisite babies and making endless speeches, they had asked the public to vote to keep them in office so they could ensure this kind of travesty would never happen again.

For the next ten years, no serious scientist would touch time-space travel, and a lot of the best scientists went into fusion and anti-matter research with their subsequent advances. The biggest breakthrough came not from the present, but from the past—specifically, a scientist who had died many years previously.

Dr. Steven Hawking had maintained an interest in time-space experiments, as it had applications to his Unified Field Theory. The Unified Field Theory had begun with Albert Einstein, who had tried to come up with a single mathematical formula to represent all energies in the universe, from the forces holding atoms together to the massive black holes at the center of galaxies and everything in between. Einstein had failed, and for many years, so did Hawking. All hopes were placed on string theory, which promised to unify all energy fields. Even this promising theory eventually fell apart. In turn, loop quantum gravity, causal dynamical triangulation, and canonical general relativity all fell by the wayside as inherent flaws were found. Nothing worked. However, just before his death, Hawking had a radical idea. In his notes, he stored a single mathematical construct for later review, but never explored it further.

One of Hawking's former students found the formula many years after his death, when reviewing the professor's archives. The math seemed simple, and he tried to prove it as a side-formula that described the Unified Field Theory. What began as an afternoon's project grew into a thirty-five-year quest. In the end, the doctor proved that gravity itself interfered with the space-time equations involved with hyperspace travel. With gravity present, you could not have a stable space-time manipulation. Remove gravity from the equation, and you remove the instability. Many papers were published, and the Holy Grail of science appeared to be solved. The scientists who had supported Gödel's incompleteness theorem celebrated with numerous *"we told you so's."*

Four years later, a probe with a field generator the size of an industrial shipping container traveled outside the limits of Pluto's orbit and through into the Oort cloud. The generator was ejected, and the mother probe paralleled its course to monitor and relay the results back to the scientists. When past the theoretical limit where solar system gravity was no longer interfering with the process, it activated. On board the probe, sensors showed a rip in the fabric of space-time, but this time, it remained stable. The instruments did detect minor instabilities in the field that would prevent transit to hyperspace, but in time, these distortions were removed by using larger and more powerful field generators. The math from the older experiments was completely valid in that regard; size did matter. The lock on the door of the galaxy was removed, and mankind was free to roam the stars.

The former graduate student of Doctor Hawking had become a doctor and physicist in his own right. During the speech where he claimed his Nobel Peace Prize, he unselfishly named the gravitational area of effect after the teacher whose work had inspired him. The naming of the "Hawking zone" to indicate an area with natural gravity that precluded entry into hyperspace entry received a standing ovation and became common parlance soon after.

Gravity was the enemy to hyperspace energy fields. It distorted them and caused all kinds of permutations that no super-computer could ever hope to unravel. If proof ever existed of the Heisenberg uncertainty principle, here it stood. When the field created an entrance to hyperspace, it could not do so within a gravitational environment, or it would fail from the inherent interference.

* * *

On board the *Resilient Fury*, the fields were built to maximum. Just at the instant hyperspace transition was possible, instability appeared at the quantum level. Gravity nudged the field to go one way, while the energies of the hyperdrive told it to go elsewhere. This caused a ripple effect through the field energy. This instability went through the feedback loop and was amplified again and again. Very strange things began to happen in space-time. Like a tall house of cards with its bottom layer knocked away, the field collapsed into itself, along with everything it contained. Instead of entering hyperspace, the Drakk'Har warship was compressed into nothingness along with all the dust, gas, and matter around it. The atomic weapon attached to the deck of the *Resilient Fury* exploded while being squeezed, but its energy was consumed so quickly, no outside observer could notice the detonation. The field energies collapsed into one focal point so small that no one had a unit of measure to describe it.

Having mass squeezed into a space being infinitely small produced a singularity: a point of intense gravity. The beast wanted to be fed. Dust, gamma rays, even light were drawn into the maw of the beast, which possessed an insatiable hunger. The incoming firepower of the six cruisers was absorbed effortlessly. The matter and energy was compressed, and this added to the effect. Within moments, a black sphere a kilometer wide was visible. The gravitational pull was so powerful that light itself could not escape the singularity. The closer one was to the singularity, the more one felt the effects of the sphere.

On Mindon-3, the thin atmosphere began to be pulled away from the planet. Continental sheets of the surface ice, kilometers thick, peeled away from the surface. They were fractured into smaller pieces by tidal forces as they approached the singularity and disappeared inside. Then, entire portions of the planet mantle broke away and disappeared into the void. With more mass arriving, the black sphere grew exponentially, taking in even more of the planet and surrounding atmosphere. It gouged into the planet like a human biting an apple.

However, the loss of the planet was just the beginning of the horror.

CHAPTER 12 – TERROR

Captain Bishop was strapped tightly into his chair on the bridge of the *Rigel,* screaming into his intercom. His three-ship task force of tenders had been closest to the enemy warship when it activated the star drive. He had heard the alarms as clearly as the marshal and the rest of the fleet. His engines were already at full power, and he was yelling at his engineers to give him more, much more.

Bishop had been given command of the task force to deceive the enemy. Tenders without lighters attached to their undersides had the same outline as a cruiser. Kosnov had told him atmospheric interference would play havoc with the Drakk'Har sensors as they decelerated through the atmosphere of Mindon-3. The effect on their sensors would be like reading a newspaper through squinty eyes. One could see words on the page, but he would not be able to read them unless he moved closer. The enemy had expected to see a cruiser task force in a certain place and time, and the marshal had obliged them. If they had not seen a blocking force, they would have sensed something was amiss and popped out of the atmosphere sooner. This would have allowed them enough time to use the planet's gravity to loop around back into the fleet's new course.

By waiting too long before coming away from Mindon-3, the enemy had reduced their possible vectors to the point where interception was kinetically impossible. However, the marshal had only expected an atomic-based strike. Drakk'Har did not have anti-matter technology, so that type of attack was not possible. The thought of a deliberate star drive activation within the Hawking zone was unprecedented.

The *Rigel's* engineers threw every switch they could throw and activated every computer sub-routine they had to get every erg out of the engines. The effort was not enough, by far. Their thrust was uniform, while the gravity of the black sphere grew sharply with every gram of fresh material added to the singularity. A tug of war began between an elephant and ants. The ants never had a chance.

On board the three tenders, chaos reigned. Pushed by the thrust of the engines and pulled by the gravity well, the ships screamed as metal rubbed against metal. Hull plates sheared off and disappeared. Any fitting not firmly attached directly to the super structure was pulled away and devoured. The framing of the ships began to buckle. Inside the vessels, decks warped and cracked. The hard vacuum of space entered several spaces. The screams of the crews were drowned out by the tearing of the metal coming apart around them. Slowly, the *Rigel* and her two companion ships, *Orion* and *Draco,* were slowed by the gravitational pull. Then, for the briefest of moments, they stopped dead in space. Ironically, what should have saved them, damned them.

As they fired their massive engines to escape, the hot exhaust gases were spewed into the void. The additional matter added to its pull. Imperceptibly, they began to move backwards, closer to their damnation. The pilot of the *Draco* tried to fire maneuvering jets. The great ship moved slightly off course, and it almost missed the sphere because of a slingshot effect. However, its velocity was insufficient, and the tender was the first to disappear inside the sphere, spinning around the singularity like water going down a drain. Everyone on board was dead before that point, due to the viscous pull of gravitational tides. The *Orion* and *Rigel* soon followed. They would not be the last to die.

* * *

On board the command ship *Aristotle*, no one noticed the death of the three tenders. Fleet Nine was much further away than the intercept force, and their engines were also at full throttle. At this point, it truly was everyone for themselves. The only thing they had to do at the moment was survive. Even if they had time to think about it, they were powerless to help anyone else.

Kosnov's eyes never left the sensor display showing the ship's position and statistics. His main worry was the six surviving cruisers. They had re-oriented themselves to fire on the Kamikaze warship. Now they were twisting in space to get the thrust of their engines to move them away from the gravity well. Cruisers had the most powerful engines in the fleet, but they also had the most mass. Further away from the dark void, the majority of the fleet was scrambling to stay ahead of the expanding gravitational pull. Instead of pointing their engines directly at the singularity to try to out-power the draw of the sphere, many tried to run a parallel course, building up speed.

The theory was solid. If one of Jupiter's moons stood still, it would be drawn into the gas giant in minutes by the gas giant's gravity. However, as the moon circles around Jupiter, centrifugal forces balance out the gravity and keep it safe. The fleet ships were trying to imitate the same motion. With enough velocity, inertia would keep them at a safe distance until the danger passed.

As each ship maneuvered without central coordination, control, or communication, mistakes inevitably occurred. Instead of focusing sensors on the ships around them, many captains fixated on the black mass behind them. Being human, they were naturally scared at being confronted by the inconceivable. That, plus the noise, alarms, multiple reports, and panicked questions coming from all decks tended to distract the people who needed to focus. Fear and the desire for self-survival amplified the problem, and the results were disastrous.

From the center of the formation, the troop transports scattered. The majority managed to escape from the fleet unscathed. Some did not. The troop transport *David Gerrold* was making good progress when the *Piers Anthony* struck it broadside in a spectacular collision. Neither ship was hulled, but the *Gerrold* temporarily lost ninety percent of its engine thrust and began to spin uncontrollably, like a thrown hatchet. The *Anthony* continued on with engines at full thrust, even though its forward sensors had been obliterated. It flew blindly into the engine cluster of a third wildly maneuvering transport, the *Frank Herbert*. The *Herbert* had seen, and was trying to avoid, the rapidly closing tender *Sagittarius* and steered into the path of the *Anthony* instead. The *Herbert's* engines exploded, and this time the *Anthony* did lose several levels to the vacuum of space. Raw fuel escaped into vacuum. Most of the troop decks were fractured and vented their atmosphere. The oxygen reacted with the leaking fuel, and it exploded, the flames seeking the oxygen inside the ship. The men and women inside burned alive. They died hideous deaths, aflame in the coldness of space. Once the air had been drawn to vacuum, the flames died out, and any surviving burn victims froze solid.

Spinning end over end, the last collision occurred when the *Gerrold's* bow cut the transport *Michael Crichton* in half. The engines on the rear half of the *Crichton* kept firing, and the loss of mass caused it to begin flying in a large loop. Venting fuel from the severed body of the transport touched the engines, and it consumed itself in fire. The forward half of the ship, now completely without power, began moving toward the gravity well in a lazy arc that could not be changed. On board the transport, the men and women faced their own destruction. For each act of bravery, two acts of cowardice followed. Crewmembers on-board who knew what was happening prayed to whatever gods they held sacred. The troops sealed in their bunkrooms helplessly felt the terrible stresses being inflicted on their ship. They screamed and held on to whatever presented itself. Several troops on the forward section of the *Crichton* made it to crew escape pods, but they ejected heading directly toward the dark sphere. They only achieved a quicker death. Several thousand fragments of shattered hulls, equipment, and human remains were drawn into the maw of the beast.

* * *

Kosnov watched and did the mental math as the drama unfolded. Each squad held eight troops. Three squads formed a platoon. Three platoons in a company. Three companies in a battalion and three battalions in a regiment for approximately six hundred fifty combat troops. With two regiments per transport, a total of thirteen hundred combat troops was on each ship; in the space of twenty seconds, they had just lost four of them. Five thousand combat troops plus the navy crews simply gone in a split second. Until now, there had not been a single loss among the transports. They were well protected. They had to be. You could not take a world with orbital bombardment. You could not take a world with lighters. You could not take a world with solid intelligence. You needed combat-capable troops to land on a piece of ground, take control of it, and then hold it. His plans for a ground offensive had just been severely hampered. The earlier loss of the cruiser was regrettable, but minor. *As if the loss of two thousand men and women could ever be considered minor*, he fumed at himself.

The marshal could see another ship in distress. The cruiser *Sea of Tranquility* was in trouble. It had been the closest ship to the sphere and had problems maneuvering to reorient its engines properly. The draw of the gravity well was like running through molasses—you could do it, but it took a long time and lots of energy. The *Sea of Tranquility* tried a bold move. Instead of running away from it or trying to run a parallel course, the captain dove at the edge of it with all engines at full velocity.

He was attempting a slingshot course. He used the pull of the gravity to accelerate the vessel much faster than the engines could do alone. The effort was commendable. If he had had precise gravitational readings to map out the exact strength of the singularity, if he had enough navigation computers to work out the trillions of necessary readings, and if he had time to calculate the perfect course, it probably would have worked. However, his one enemy was time. It would take an hour to do all the necessary calculations, and he only had seconds. The pilot was forced to fly by the seat of his pants.

Leaving a faint trail of super-heated gases behind, the massive cruiser tried dancing with the sphere. If it flew too far away, it would lack the necessary inertia it needed to pull away; too close, and it would be consumed. It flew down a knife edge, with oblivion on either side.

In the most astounding feat of piloting skill the marshal had ever seen, the cruiser narrowly missed the sphere, paralleled it for three quarters of a rotation, and then—beyond all reason— began to pull away in a tight arc. Muted cheers from the command deck staff rang throughout the room—hoping, wishing, pleading for them to make it. The *Sea of Tranquility* slowed as it returned the inertia it had gained. However, it still had its engines working at full throttle, and they seemed to make the difference. It slowed, but did not stop. The further it traveled away, the louder the cheers of encouragement.

* * *

Meanwhile, deep inside the singularity, problems were developing. The tidal forces inside the infinitesimal point were fundamentally unstable. Much of the matter that had been absorbed had been converted to energy. Intense gravity had held that energy in check until now, but problems were developing in the balance. The star drive of the Drakk'Har warship had created the singularity through artificial means. It had planted the seed, as it were, which had germinated and then grown. However, being artificial, it did not have the monstrous amounts of matter required for long-term sustainability. Even with the bulk of Mindon-3 in its proverbial belly, it had insufficient mass for a black hole. Without a suitable base of mass to draw on, it began to die. Space-time began to heal itself, and the warping eased. Gravity began to loosen its grip on the remaining matter at its core...

...and then there was light.

Einstein's formula of $E=MC^2$ held sway, and any matter which had not been used in the formation of the singularity was released as energy. The first indicator was when the grip of intense gravity released, and ships surged forward. Some captains ordered a reduction in engine power, while others kept on going. The *Sea of Tranquility* would have escaped, but was consumed in an explosion that made the energy released by anti-matter look insignificant. The cruiser and all of its occupants were turned to slag in the intense heat pulse.

The blast wave roared through all eleven dimensions of space, throwing the various ships around like rag dolls. This time, the surviving cruisers had the advantage. They were designed to absorb huge shocks, and they rode the storm fairly well. However, the other ships were hit hard. Fires, electrical shorts, and loss of pressure became commonplace throughout the fleet. Structural cracks appeared in the strangest places. Each ship had its own individual emergencies, depending on its type and proximity to the blast.

On board the tender *Cassiopeia,* a lighter exploded inside a maintenance bay when shaken loose of its moorings. The reconnaissance ship *Argus* lost an entire bank of mainframe computers when they took a jolt of electricity fifteen times higher than what they were rated for. An ammunition bunker on the *Pisces* began firing thousands of small caliber rounds when it caught fire.

Throughout the fleet, damage control teams fought bravely. To their credit, in the face of absolute carnage, their training came to the fore. Small fires were extinguished. Large fires were vented to vacuum or isolated behind blast walls, while internal sprinklers and foam filled the spaces. Cracks in the superstructure were welded with makeshift panels. Power was restored, and communications protocols were reestablished. On one troop transport, the internal sprinklers had been knocked offline. That crew was reduced to using marines as a bucket brigade, handing bucket after bucket of water down a chain of people to extinguish the fires. However, no more ships were lost. The fleet was bowed, but not broken.

Mindon-3 was a shadow of its former self. Its orbital inertia had saved part of it from destruction, but only a sixteenth of its mass remained. With no atmosphere, and broken into several segments, it hung in space, continuing along its orbital path.

Kosnov assumed the fragments would eventually spin off into space or into the Mindon red dwarf sun one day. He did not ask anyone to check on the course of Mindon-3. He had more important things to do at the moment, and so did his people. MASER-COMM channels started to become active and drew his attention back to the fleet.

Kosnov absorbed the losses as the initial damage control reports came in. *Four troop transports, three tenders, and one cruiser lost. Several more ships out of action for at least twelve hours. The few that did not need major repairs were still scattered like the leaves of a tree in a windstorm.* Kosnov found himself wishing he had been struck with atomic weapons. The losses would have been far less.

"Mr. Collins," the marshal said calmly, "round up the fleet."

* * *

An hour later, on top of Hill 170, two people shared a slit trench. Popov and Bennet were an unlikely team. A Russian corporal from the Moscow suburbs and the Canadian private from Halifax were not the first pair you thought of when you were asked who would work together well. However, they had beaten the odds and become close friends. Popov was standing watch while his partner lay in behind him in a sleeping bag. The air mattress under the prone private squeaked slightly whenever he moved. This was the fifth squeak in as many minutes, Popov noted. He checked his chrono.

"John, you awake?" Popov whispered.

"Yeah. Are you?" came the reply, equally quiet.

Popov allowed himself a smile, but continued to scan his area of responsibility. "You are on watch in ten minutes."

"Right. Wake me in nine." A series of squeaks issued from his air mattress as he turned his back to the Russian.

Popov shook his head while grinning and continued to monitor the area in front of his trench using his tactical contact lenses set in light amplification mode. They increased any available light up to a thousand times. While everything he saw had a green hue, the clarity was excellent. Everything to that point had been quiet. The only excitement had been his stomping on a large millipede that had fallen into their trench. The carcass had been flung as far away as he could throw it with the tip of his bayonet.

An intense light tore into Popov's retinas before the auto-filters on the contacts blanked out that part of the spectrum. "*Govnoi!*" he muttered under his breath as he staggered against the back wall, covering his eyes with his arm. He heard several others in the camp making involuntary exclamations as they were also taken off-guard by the brilliant flash.

* * *

The sleeping Private Bennet had his contacts set to normal, but he saw through his closed eyelids as if it were as bright as day. He was beside Popov with his weapon at the ready in seconds. He sighted down his weapon and was ready to engage anyone trying to advance on their position, but something was wrong. There was no noise. A rocket or mortar attack would be obvious. Even a flare would make a quiet hiss as it burned. Everything had become as light as day in a split second. Buzzing insects had gone completely quiet.

The noiseless flash was in the night sky just over the horizon. Already fading, it had lost ninety percent of its luminosity, but was still quite brilliant. White watched the illumination slowly fade until the night returned and the insects slowly came to life. A crackle through their headsets broke their concentration as Pratt spoke to everyone. "Alpha section, this is Six. That's probably an anti-matter explosion. As the crocs do not have anti-matter weapons, it must have been our guys. From the brilliance of it, I'd say they are fairly close. Looks like we will not be here long. Watch the noise level from here on. Pratt out."

"You OK, Illya?" whispered a concerned Bennet as he watched Popov rubbing his eyes.

"Yeah, but I see nothing but spots at the moment. Man, that hurt."

"OK, you take the rack and get some sleep. Your night vision will be useless for half an hour anyway. You can owe me the extra seven minutes on the next watch." He began buttoning his shirt.

"Your concern for my health will keep me warm inside, John." A sardonic Russian is a hard thing to ignore.

"The extra time in the rack later will keep me warm, *tovarich*."

* * *

Planet Lord Slassh had waited up late into the night to see the results of his plan. The unexpectedly brilliant flash in the night sky produced a roar of pleasure from the great creature. He had no idea how successful the attack had been, but it did not really matter. The warm bloods knew they would have to pay dearly for invading this world. A message had just been delivered, and its meaning was loud and clear. *Come here, and be consumed.*

* * *

Just outside of the Mindon Hawking zone, reality distorted momentarily. An unmanned Federation Gecko class probe emerged and immediately began to steer toward Mindon-2. Its radio transmitters clicked on immediately and began to broadcast an encoded signal that repeated continuously. The probe did not slow down. Even at the speed of light, the radio signal would take hours to reach Fleet Nine.

* * *

"Marshal, I have just finished the casualty report for the fleet, and we have a serious problem," Commander Christensen reported from the Tactics (Ground) board.

Kosnov turned his full attention to the Norwegian. "What is it, Mr. Christensen?"

"Sir, the four destroyed transports contained elements of the VII Marine Division only. However, the bad news is General Chew was on-board the *Michael Crichton* with his headquarters staff and regimental commanders for a landing briefing. I am afraid we lost them all. Sir, the VII Marine Division just lost all of its senior officers and intelligence personnel."

Damn, the marshal thought, but did not say. This was serious. He had just lost the leadership for an entire marine division. Twelve regiments of assault troops were now headless. No, he immediately corrected himself, only four complete regiments remained of the VII Division after the four troop transports were destroyed. Each regimental commander would have a deputy who would have remained behind. However, those men and women would be unprepared. One or two replacements could be routine, but to replace the entire leadership of all the regiments was unheard of. Different command styles alone would make life difficult. Morale was an issue, also. They would need a new intelligence staff and commanding officer. How do you inspire troops to fight with unknown leaders and unreliable intelligence? He had to discuss this development with General Carstairs.

"Mr. Christensen, I want General Carstairs and his staff available in one hour. I want you to review the records of all regimental deputy commanders in the VII division. I need an assessment as to their ability to command the four remaining regiments. I need a short list of replacements, if you feel they are up to the task. I will need that before General Carstairs arrives. Commander Tran, I want you to select a replacement intelligence staff from Fleet Nine personnel. I need them to be conversant with ground combat, and anyone with a former combat billet should be used. Use care not to strip too many people from threat assessment. You may not be able to build a complete team, so use your own judgment as to bare essentials." Kosnov had good people working for him; now he had to hope they could find desperately needed answers.

CHAPTER 13 – CHANGES

Drawwl burped and could taste fish as an aftertaste. He lay on his belly in the mud with a cloudless night sky above. The brilliant stars shone down, but even his Drakk'Har night vision had a hard time discerning features beyond a few feet. He had been hunting greppo under the water when a brilliant light had flashed in the night sky. For a moment, he could see through the clear water as if it were daylight. By the time he had surfaced, the light had faded and several of his troops were looking up. *Cursed warm bloods and their anti-matter weapons*, he had thought at the time. Drakk'Har cursed the warm bloods as being barbarians, but that was only because they *had* anti-matter weapons. If Drakk'Har had them, it would be a noble thing indeed. However, while they had decent technology, successful anti-matter manufacture and containment had eluded them.

After the light flash, he had returned to his hunt and had caught several tasty greppo fish that were still stunned by the flash of light. Telling himself the results were due to his prowess as a hunter, he had returned to the shore with a full belly. Now, he was relaxing on the shore. Around him were several dozing Drakk'Har. His personal guard surrounded him in a tight-knit fashion. Nothing could get past them without notice and subsequent challenge.

As he drifted off to sleep, he ran his plan through his mind once more. In the morning, his troops would be at Kek's holdings. Then Kek would be informed of the decision to seize his property. He might fight. He might surrender. It all depended on which allies he could draw on, if any. Drawwl had fifty troops and surprise on his side. If Kek fought, he would die.

* * *

General Carstairs had been unceremoniously rousted from his sleep by his aide. Being told the marshal wanted to see him within the hour, but not knowing why, automatically put him into a nasty mood. *Wasn't the need for secure instantaneous communications the reason they had invested in the MASER-COMM system?* he thought.

He had felt his chin and decided he could pass muster without shaving. The general took a quick shower and changed into a fresh set of combat fatigues. When he got out of his small bathroom, he found a cup of steaming black coffee and a plate of bacon and eggs with toast on the side table by the bunk. Courtesy of his aide, he assumed as he constructed a thick breakfast sandwich with the egg and bacon. Washing the crumbs down with half the coffee, he put on his shiny combat boots. He stood and swallowed the rest of the coffee. He put on a fatigue cap with sewn insignia and looked at himself in the mirror on the back of his door. Satisfied, the last thing he did was double-check his fly was closed. It would not do to meet a marshal of the fleet at half-mast. Carstairs opened the door to his room. He had been awake for eight minutes.

His *aide de camp* was waiting for him in the hall. The aide's crisp uniform did not betray the fact he had been in bed himself only minutes before his general. In the space of four minutes, he had ensured the general was awake, confirmed transport, called the mess for some breakfast, and arranged the general's briefing papers. As the general's aide, he was always on duty and ready to provide anything required, from sewing on a button to polite dinner conversation with a major's wife.

The pair walked down the corridor as they spoke. As they proceeded down stairs and the various decks, lesser ranks moved back and stood with their backs to the wall as the general passed. They all braced to attention.

His aide said, "Sir, we have a lighter waiting for you at airlock seven. The marshal did not give a reason for the meeting, but he asked for you and the divisional operations staff to attend specifically. Change of plans?"

"I don't know, Roy. Maybe so. We took some losses in the transports during the last battle, so maybe he wants to do a bit of shuffling in the assault schedule. Thank God, none of our marines took a hit. Still, something like that should be handled through the staffs. Anyway, we will find out soon."

"Yes, sir. The division staff is already en route. They will have the division organization database and latest set of assault plans fed into the briefing room computer by the time you get there." The aide stopped talking as they reached the airlock built into the floor. With a hiss of compressed air and hydraulics, the heavy door opened, revealing a closed airlock set in the floor. When the general and his aide entered the small room, the hatch sealed behind them. After a two-second pause, the floor hatch slid open. Carstairs looked down into the interior of a lighter, connected via its ceiling airlock.

Moving from a gravity environment to zero gee requires finesse. Carstairs grabbed a convenient hand bar and slipped down into the lighter in a practiced manner. His feet touched the lower deck, and he absorbed his inertia with bent knees. As he landed, Carstairs could see a pilot and flight engineer sitting in the cockpit throwing various switches and toggles. Sounds from the lighter changed in pitch and duration as each switch was positioned.

A sergeant dressed in a dark green flight suit and bug helmet braced and saluted as well as he could in zero gee. When the general returned the salute, the sergeant indicated where he should sit. Instead of heading for the jump seats, the general pulled himself up to the flight deck. Carstairs saw the pilot had captain rank and had his helmet off. He tapped the pilot on the shoulder, which caused the man to turn, half-surprised.

"Good morning, Captain. Hope I did not get you out of your bunk."

"No, sir, I was still on duty, just finishing some paperwork. Welcome aboard. Sergeant Allan will see you are taken care of. Seal break is in three minutes. They said you were in a hurry. We will be standing by for you to return, also."

"Thank you, Captain...?" His eyebrow rose a bit in question. He could not see the pilot's nametag from this angle.

"Levin, sir."

"Thank you, Levin; carry on." Carstairs turned and headed back into the cargo area using the overhead handholds. Sergeant Allan was waiting for him. Allan held up a helmet and an emergency oxygen generator with a maze of webbing and strapped it onto the General's chest. Carstairs removed his cap and slipped it in a wide side pocket. Once he was done, he placed the helmet on his head and plugged in the intercom cord. The sergeant's voice came through his headset loud and clear.

"General, this unit will provide you with forty-five minutes of emergency O_2 in case of a hull breach. In case of air loss, pull this tab here to release the facemask, place it on your head, and adjust the straps to fit here. Then pull this ring here to activate the oxygen flow. Please stay strapped in your seat at all times, in case we have to maneuver."

Carstairs nodded. "Thank you, Sergeant." The general had received the same briefing many times before, but did not complain. They were doing their jobs, and he was glad to see this crew did it smoothly. He did not ask why the unit had only forty-five minutes of air, as he already knew that if out of the sun, after ten minutes of space exposure, you would be frozen solid as a block of ice. Ideally, you should be exposed to space for no more than three to five minutes, and even then you would have severe frostbite. If you were in direct sunlight, you would slowly cook like a large turkey in an oven.

The general sat and strapped himself into one of the jump seats. As the sergeant turned to give the same brief to his aide, he realized he could hear the flight deck conversation in his helmet earpiece.

"Roger. Clear to launch. Grasshopper One out," the pilot said before continuing on intercom. "Crew, this is the pilot. We will be traveling to the *Aristotle*. Transit time will be six minutes. We have no weapons on board. Load master, close airlock. Begin engine start checklist."

The upper airlock doors slid closed with a heavy thump. A green light on the rim lit, and Allan spoke. "Inner and outer airlocks secure for vacuum, sir." Allan floated over across from the general and sat down. He had done this many times and arrived exactly in his seat.

The general ignored the preparations for flight. He tried to reason why the marshal would want him on board the *Aristotle*. As a professional soldier, he hated surprises, and something that could not be discussed on MASER-COMM would cause him no end of grief, he was sure. The general closed his eyes and floated in his restraints as he waited for the docking sequence at the far end of the trip.

* * *

On the flight deck, Levin checked the engine instrument cluster. The repaired engine seemed to be doing fine on the flight over. However, when a general was on board, you did not take anything for granted. Levin saw Wallace was also monitoring things. Wallace knew his business, and the pilot trusted him, but he still checked the gauges. Wallace double-checked him, and he did the same to Wallace. Flight crews had to object when they saw something wrong. Assumptions killed people in this environment.

Under the new engine nacelle, the vibration from the thrusters resonated through the supporting frame. The small cracks caused by the strut impact began to grow imperceptibly.

Levin pulled the docking release lever, and they were free to fly. He double-checked his course and then applied minimal thrust to point in that direction. Once satisfied he was clear of the troop transport, he increased power to all thrusters. They began to move toward the *Aristotle.*

* * *

The general woke with a start as his aide shook his shoulder gently. "Sir, we are here." Carstairs looked and saw the upper airlock was already open. He had not felt the usual bump as the airlocks mated and realized he must have been fast asleep.

"Thank you for the smooth flight, Captain Levin," the general said over the intercom. Carstairs was one of the few generals who appreciated the little things. It may have only been a six-minute flight, but the logistics and timing only looked easy when true professionals did it. He wanted his people to know that he appreciated all their efforts, regardless of scale.

Without waiting for an answer, Carstairs undid his restraints, removed the helmet and oxygen generator, and handed them over to Sergeant Allan. "Thank you, Sergeant." He then floated up to the handholds surrounding the ceiling airlock. Sergeant Allan floated at the hatch, waiting. *He must wonder if I need help out of the lighter,* Carstairs mused. Carstairs grabbed a bar by the airlock and smoothly jack-knifed his feet through the opening. He landed on his knees at the lip of the airlock in partial gravity. The designers of the ship had placed a thin rubber membrane around the lip of the airlock to absorb some shock. The General's aging knees appreciated that.

He stood and replaced his fatigue cap while waiting for his aide, who followed seconds later. The duty officer met them. After exchanging salutes and quick pleasantries, he led them off down the corridor to the briefing room.

* * *

One hour before sunrise, Drawwl's small group of warriors moved out of their night camp on the shore of the pond. Their final positions lay no more than a klem to the southeast. Slinging their weapons on their backs, they pulled themselves through the mud and mire surrounding the pond. The plan was to be in position before the sun came up.

* * *

"Marshal, General Carstairs," the duty officer announced as the general entered the briefing room.

"Thank you, Bill. That will be all. Secure the hatch on your way out, and inform the duty marine we are not to be disturbed." Kosnov spoke quietly. He observed Carstairs with a critical eye. *No, he does not know yet.* The hatch closed behind the general.

"Good morning, Marshal. I was expecting General Chew to be here, as well. Problems, or is he delayed?"

"Richard, please sit down." Kosnov waited until the General sat. "General Chew, all his regimental commanders, headquarters, and intelligence staff were on board the *Michael Crichton* when the ship was destroyed. In addition, we lost three other transports along with two thirds of VII Division."

"Damn. No survivors?" The General pressed himself back from the table and looked shocked.

"None. All remnants of their transport were either sucked into the void caused by the Drakk'Har warship or incinerated in the explosion that followed. They had no chance. The reason I called you here was to re-assess the mission and see where we can utilize the remaining four regiments of troops under their deputies." Kosnov poured himself some water as he spoke.

"Marshal, is that wise? Sending a decimated division into combat with new leaders? It sounds like we would be asking for trouble." Carstairs was bringing up several pieces of information on his datapad. "Even if we reduce VII Division's overall mission, they would still be weak on the ground and unable to support themselves. How is lighter support?"

Kosnov sat down at the table, as well. He felt tired and was glad to take the weight off his feet. "We suffered a few losses with tenders, but luckily we stripped the lighters off them beforehand. We were able to recover several lighters that were thrown off the *Clarke*. With the losses in VII Division, we have lots of overhead transport capacity."

The general appeared to consider this. "OK, then why don't we simply eliminate the Charlie and Delta landings from the ops-plan and bombard them from orbit only? We can use the spare four regiments as reinforcements to the overall effort in II Divisions area. We can break the new commanders in with backup roles, like firebase security instead of direct action. That frees up more of my people for more aggressive patrolling. With extra lighter support, we can hit the three landing areas a lot more effectively and have a stronger force to contend with any local problems. Plus, we will have heavier support for follow-on air-to-ground action. From the intel we received at the briefing, Charlie and Delta were support facilities only, with the main construction areas all within Alpha and Echo. So, let's concentrate our forces, and pound those areas." Carstairs was sounding more confident as he spoke, Kosnov observed. Yet, the marshall knew of several problems remaining to be solved.

"There are several Special Forces elements already deployed in Charlie and Delta, Richard. We need to get them out of the way before we can bomb from orbit."

"Marshal, they have been trained to direct orbital fire, so if they remain in place, we will get much more effective results. We can yank them out just before we pull the plug. Besides, with their defenses beaten back, their extraction will be a lot easier. It would be different if we were using nukes, or has that part of the plan altered?"

"No nuclear option at this time. We still want the planet as a base of operations after the second phase of the invasion." Kosnov was also thinking as he spoke.

"Very well then, this will work. We'll trim back on the operational areas and end up with a more concentrated force hitting the critical ship construction areas. The support facilities will be bombed from orbit and directed by the spooks on the ground. We can keep the base plan intact, but can defend more effectively."

Kosnov considered this. Carstairs was not an empire builder. His grab for the additional regiments was a sincere move to aid the mission and not to make himself look good. It would mean a more concentrated force, but—

"It will also put our eggs in fewer baskets. With the recent attacks, the enemy has shown almost desperate tactics to protect their shipyards. I want to minimize any damage caused by weapons of mass destruction. Spreading our people out guards against that."

"Agreed, Marshal, but it makes them more of a target for conventional weapons. There is no perfect way." The General pushed back from the table. "However, in my opinion, taking the four spare regiments as backups to our divisional assault is the best way for us to approach this mission, given the resources available, and that is my recommendation. It is your call though, sir."

The marshal concentrated on the facts at hand. While he had minor reservations, he could not think of an alternative solution that would cover all of his mission points. "Very well. We will proceed by engaging Charlie and Delta from orbit only and placing the remaining four regiments under your command in secondary roles. Will you require additional members for your intel or HQ staff?"

"I shouldn't think so, sir. I have a good team in place. With the new regiments as reinforcements, I don't think there is a need for adding more staff. I'll have to review their intel and communications procedures and iron out any bugs, of course. However, that should be a fairly small administrative detail. However, if that's all for the broad overview, we should bring our staffs in to go over the changes in timings. There's bound to be a few changes to the schedule."

"Yes. Very good." Kosnov pressed a flat call button built into the table. He continued, "One of my prime concerns is morale. With such severe losses in VII Division, it will not be long before that filters down to the troop level if we advertise it. As far as your staff is concerned, this is a re-assignment of the four regiments into a support role. We will not mention the reasons for it in the briefing."

"Yes, sir. Understood," Carstairs agreed as the heavy hatch hissed open. The marshal caught the attention of the duty officer who appeared in the doorway and indicated for the people waiting outside to enter.

* * *

Drawwl and ten of his personal guard entered the perimeter of Kek's holdings as the first red light caressed the mottled pink sky. Their weapons were slung casually, but in a manner that they could be brought into action quickly. They marched deliberately upright, even though the travel was harder on their stocky limbs. They wanted to be seen by the guards, while those who were to remain unseen advanced much slower on all fours. A small compound revealed itself as they waddled down the track. Drawwl looked it over as he approached, scanning for defenses and troop locations. Of seemingly primitive construction, the walls were made of dried mud bricks of several meters in width and height. The thickness of the wall was deliberate. It would stop even a rail gun round from penetrating within.

Covering the mud bricks was a thin layer of hard resin. This sealed the bricks from the weather. Exposed mud brick tended to disintegrate in the rain, and on Mindon-2, it rained more often than not. At regular intervals on the walls were round blockhouses with thatched roofs. Several guards could be seen walking in-between them on the wall itself. Behind the wall, steam rose in several places. The roofs of several brown buildings were barely visible. Drawwl knew they were producing resins and other necessary chemicals. The chemical stench in the air was palpable. He hoped he would not have to spend much time here.

The small group traveled down a well-worn dirt path when a guard on a mud brick rampart challenged them. "Hold! These are the holdings of Swamp Lord Kek, most high of the Great Lords. State your business, or be destroyed."

Drawwl took his time answering. He drew a deep breath and spoke loudly so all could hear him in a wide area. "I'm Drawwl, minion and messenger of the Greatest of Lords, Swamp Master Borrk. You'll inform Kek of our arrival, and you'll have him at your gates at once to receive his message."

The guard disappeared as he scurried away to pass on the message. Keeping a swamp master's representative waiting was never a good idea. Other guards still covered them from the walls, however. That was equally prudent when dealing with the representative of a swamp master.

Only moments passed before the heavy ceramic gates opened. Drawwl and his bodyguards walked straight through them without waiting for an invitation. Twenty guards were standing in a loose arc inside the gates. They were waiting for Drawwl's arrival with weapons raised. Behind them stood Swamp Lord Kek. Drawwl's bodyguards did not raise their weapons. They had been told not to, unless directly fired upon. They did hold them with a nervous grip, however.

"That's far enough. What does Swamp Master Borrk wish to say to me?" Kek was visibly nervous.

Drawwl's guards halted obediently in the middle of the gates, but Drawwl himself carried on until his chest was almost touching one of the raised weapons. Once more, he broadcast his message loudly, even though Kek was quite close.

"Kek, lowest of swamp slime. You've broken a contract with my master, Swamp Master Borrk. In failing to deliver a warm blood tribute or the contracted resins, your lands and holdings are now forfeit. This compound, its occupants, and property are now under the command of our most eminent Swamp Master Borrk."

Kek did exactly as Drawwl expected and hid his fear with bluster. "Forfeit my holdings to that worthless slime dweller? Never! I could riddle your worthless carcass with a thousand rounds in seconds and dispose of your body in the river. Or perhaps, I'll save your head and deliver it back to your feeble master so he can see your failure in your lifeless eyes. Do you hear me?"

Drawwl waited calmly for the tirade to finish. He pointed lazily toward the buildings in the compound. He made a grand sweep of his arm as he spoke. "Should I fall, two hundred heavily armed shock troops shall raze this ramshackle collection of snake spoor to the ground. All within shall die, and this ground shall be held as a monument to the futility of resistance to the will of Swamp Master Borrk."

"All I see are ten worthless, maggot-laden corpses who do not realize they are already dead. Carrion-eating scum, I spit on your demands! You have no troops, and even if you did, you have no will to use them! I'm the power in this region, and no other may usurp it from me. In this place, I'm invincible."

Drawwl's grin was pure evil. He casually unclipped a small communicator from his belt, toggled the switch, and said simply, "Target One."

For a few seconds, nothing happened. Then, a dull *whump-whoosh* sound filled the air. Drawwl tried to look somewhat bored with the proceedings and examined his claw tips. Behind the arc of guards, a single mortar round struck the roof of one of the larger brown buildings. It exploded on contact, caving it in immediately. Panicked screams emerged from inside the building, and wisps of flame could be seen licking the edge of the open roof.

Drawwl saw several of the guards were shocked by the attack. Some began to back away a few paces. Drawwl knew his bodyguards would stand firm. They knew what was going to happen, and the overhead portion of the gates protected them. If they were attacked, their only job was to keep the gates open until the hidden follow-on force of forty troops could rush to their aid. That would take only a moment or two.

Kek spun back to face him, visibly shocked by the sudden attack.

"Two hundred heavily armed shock troops and three batteries of mortars which currently surround your walls, I should've said." Drawwl sported a fearsome, confident grin.

Kek's voice rose in pitch as he tried to control himself. "What the— Can you not— But— You *lie!* You have only a few troops and one mortar. Our walls are the thickest in the area, and we have never fallen to intruders or bandits! You can't shock us into submission. Our walls can stop your meager troops easily. Our bunkers are immune to your pitiful mortar attacks. My warriors are the bravest and shall fight to the last."

Drawwl raised his communicator to his green lips and said, "Target Two."

Again, a few moments passed, and the sound of multiple thumps was heard from the opposite side of the compound. Kek futilely screamed, "No!" as the impact of what was happening hit home, but the rounds were already on their way.

Several *whoosh* sounds combined overhead, and then several rounds impacted on a section of outside wall between two blockhouses. Of the six rounds fired, four actually hit the wall. One landed just outside and another just inside the wall. These shells were set to penetrate before detonation. Burying themselves in the mud bricks easily, they descended into the wall two meters before exploding. An entire section of the wall fragmented and blew apart into fist-sized pieces which rained down on everyone in the open. The two rounds that landed on either side of the wall actually did the most damage. When they exploded under the earth, they undermined the foundation, and it collapsed completely into the resulting craters. Invading troops now had a viable breach in the defenses.

The arc of compound guards was visibly unsettled and were half-looking around for the nearest shelter. As the smoke cleared, everyone could see the remains of the fortifications. The remnants of the wall would not stop an infant Drakk'Har from getting into the compound.

"This is your last warning, egg slime. Submit to the authority of Borrk, or be overwhelmed. My patience grows thin." Drawwl was quite happy at the results of the mortar attack. Whoever was manning his single battery of mortars had just earned a reward with that one volley. Drawwl was hoping for one or two hits, but four had blown the ghafflin out of the defenses. Drawwl knew the round's accuracy was a fluke, but Kek did not.

* * *

Kek was visibly on the edge of panic now. He had two choices: surrender or fight. From the looks of fear in the faces of his troops, any fight would be a short one. He had allies he could call on, but he had no time for them to get there. As an independent contractor, he had no major patron to protect him with reprisals. Even if he could afford the expense of a shuttle to get his allies here faster, they would not arrive before those three times damned mortars had leveled his compound. Kek needed more time to call his allies and—

"Lord!" A call from a guard on the ramparts interrupted. "There's a large force approaching through the trees. At least one hundred warriors! They're—" The guard was struck by an inferno that engulfed him instantly. The jellied fuel, fully ablaze, stuck to him and covered half his body. The scream of the creature as he was immolated in roiling fire was horrific.

Backpedaling from the impact, the Drakk'Har guard fell off the high wall platform and landed heavily on the ground below. The last few moments of its life were spent futilely kicking and rolling on the ground, trying to extinguish the fire. Nothing, absolutely nothing, terrifies Drakk'Har more than death by fire. Spending time in the wet places, mud and cool water is paradise to a Drakk'Har. Death by fire was something truly repulsive. Kek was horrified into silence.

* * *

Drawwl was awed by the results. What the guard had seen as a hundred warriors was actually fifteen of Drawwl's troops pulling multiple cords attached to trees and bushes and thumping their tails on the ground to make as much racket as possible. His sole flamer unit had actually been able to sneak close enough to get off a shot without being seen. *Perfect.*

He looked at Kek and spoke, enjoying every syllable. "Two hundred heavily armed shock troops, three batteries of mortars, and two combat flamer units." The horrified compound guards were falling back continuously now. Drawwl could read their expressions. *That charred thing on the ground could have been any one of them.*

Kek fell onto his belly in the dirt in the position of submission, face down. He said nothing. His posture said it all. The few guards who had not backed away fell into the same position without hesitation. In time, all visible compound guards were in the same position. None would resist any longer. Kek would continue as compound commander, but he was subjugated under Borrk. Borrk was his patron and would allow him to serve as long as he maintained his quotas.

Drawwl was jubilant. With only fifty troops, a single battery of mortars, and a flamer unit, he had just taken a support compound relatively unscathed and with no casualties on his side. He had done it using the first thing most Drakk'Har warriors learned: terror is a huge force multiplier.

Drawwl raised his communicator. "The compound is ours. Bring in the garrison force. The remainder of the troops may return." Drawwl waited as his remaining forty troops walked through the gates still manned by his bodyguards. The mortar and flamer crews were last to enter. They would be rewarded, he determined. He directed his troops to occupy key positions in the compound. Resistance was not expected from the soldiers inside, but common sense told him that some other lord could try to make an assault while the wall was damaged.

Drawwl pointed to members of his bodyguard. "You, take twenty of the defeated and fix that wall. I want it much stronger than before. You, all bunkers are to be inspected and reinforced to our standard. You, I want the best barracks reserved for our use alone. The defeated can build a new one. You, find the communications facility and ensure it is capable of sending a message to Swamp Master Borrk. If not, repair it. And you, prepare an immediate shipment of resins for the Swamp Master. Take whatever is available."

Drawwl looked down as his troops scurried away to follow his orders. Kek was still at his feet. He had not been told he could move, and so he had not.

Drawwl's last order was loudest. "Take me to your females, Kek."

CHAPTER 14 – MANEUVERS

Captain Levin was still strapped into his seat and writing an evaluation report on one of the junior pilots in his flight. The lighter cockpit seats were quite comfortable and, in zero gee, downright luxurious. He used the keypad on the left-side console and was concentrating on the wording of the report when Allan reported over the intercom, "General's on the way, sir."

Levin double-clicked his transmit button, and two bursts of static went through the intercom system as acknowledgement. Levin saved the work in progress to his datapad and brought up a checklist on the smaller datapad strapped to the top of his right thigh. Activating the checklist function, he began to run over the steps to come to make sure there would be no delays. He had done it hundreds of times before, but superiors never gave points for memorizing procedure. He followed the checklist line by line. He knew Wallace would doing the same thing without prompting.

"General and his aide are aboard, sir," Allan said over the intercom. Levin looked over his shoulder. This time the general had gone straight to his seat, accepted the safety gear, and buckled himself in. The general was preoccupied with his thoughts while flipping through briefing papers and maps his aide was handing him. Levin shrugged mentally. After this flight, his crew would stand down for eight glorious hours of down time, and that was what he was looking forward to. He activated the intercom.

"Crew, pilot. We will be traveling to the *Sagittarius*. Transit time will be six minutes. We have no weapons on board. Load master, close airlock. Begin engine start checklist."

* * *

Morning dawned on Hill 170. The LPs were manned, and the Special Forces personnel got back into their routine of observing the surrounding area. Gray clouds had rolled in overnight, and a thin, miserable drizzle began to fall. Reasonably protected in their trenches, the troops donned camouflage raingear. Some slept, some ate, some tried to sleep. They rotated positions every two hours. The only one exempted from LP duty was Jacobs. He was in the command bunker, watching over Mendez. The wounded sergeant lay sweating and shivering. Drifting in and out of consciousness, he was spending less time awake with each cycle. He was dressed in his fatigues and wrapped in his sleeping bag.

Jacobs looked down on the sergeant while using his medi-glove in diagnostic mode. The glove accessed Mendez's sub-dermal biochip that each soldier had embedded in his or her chest. Mendez's temperature readings over the last few hours were pulled from the biochip and displayed in a graph on his tactical contacts. Jacobs could see it edging higher over time. His bloodpressure was elevated, and the pulse was strong, but rapid. The sergeant's shivering had worsened, but the only way to stop that was to get him into a heated environment, and that was not going to happen until at least the next day. Many of the troops had selflessly handed over their ration heating packs, and Jacobs was using them in the sleeping bag to keep Mendez as warm as possible. However, even that was insufficient when the sergeant's sweat was causing his body heat to leach out faster than they could replenish it.

Jacobs pushed the sleeping bag aside to access Mendez's leg and unwrapped the outer cloth covering protecting the aero-gel beneath. He did not want to unnecessarily disturb his patient. He peeled off the used aero-gel bandage, revealing the multi-colored lacerations and bruises beneath. The stench from the wounds was appalling. His aero-gel bandages were being changed every six hours. They absorbed any blood or infected fluids and drew them away from the wounds. He applied liberal amounts of anti-bacterial cream before putting on a new aero-gel bandage. However, that was all Jacobs could do. No anti-venom for the Drakk'Har bites meant his body's healing powers were inhibited. Jacobs spread fresh medicinal cream over a new bandage, pressed it into place, and started to wrap the outer cloth bandage over it to keep it clean.

* * *

Mendez awoke with a start. He was dreaming he was on sentry duty when something cold touched his leg. He looked down and saw a croc warrior leaning forward, holding his leg in its black claws. It turned with jaws apart, and he could see the drool falling from its white teeth. It hissed at him and leaned forward. He began screaming, "Stand to! Stand to! Crocs in the perimeter!" Mendez reached for his sidearm, but found the holster gone; he grabbed for the bayonet on his belt that had saved him before, but the holder was empty. The croc jumped on top of him as more rushed into his trench. Three of them held him down as he struggled. He had to warn the others! They were depending on him; he had to alert the others!

* * *

Jacobs was on top of the prone sergeant seconds after the latter began yelling. Sergeant Smith arrived with the L-T seconds after that, and they all held him down as he screamed, thrashed about, and kicked. Smith covered Mendez's mouth with his hand, muffling, but not stopping, the screams. Pratt hissed at Jacobs, his voice quiet while trying to impart authority at the same time. "Knock him out with something, or he'll wake up the entire territory."

Jacobs pulled a stubby red and white cylinder from a chest pocket. He twisted the body section to arm it and pressed the red end against Mendez's neck. An internal spring fired with a click, and oxymorphone was propelled directly into his bloodstream via gas injection. Within moments, it took effect. Slowly, Mendez stopped struggling. He even stopped shivering. Jacobs checked his pulse. It was weaker, but steady.

Jacobs saw Pratt was startled and frustrated. The morning's silence had just been shattered, and he had no idea if they had been heard by the enemy. "Jacobs, we have to keep him sedated! We can't have this happening with croc patrols in the area! How long will that last?"

"Six hours, suh. Sorry, suh, I was just cleanin' his leg wound and—" Jacob's voice was shaking. He was just as shocked at the sergeant's behavior as the L-T was.

"All right. From now on, he stays sedated. Every six hours, you clean the bandage and inject him to keep him under. You have enough to last until tomorrow?"

"Yes, suh. No problem dere."

"OK then." Pratt turned to the sergeant. "Smith, give the local area a quick look. Take Jefferson and scan the hill. Check in with the LPs. Make sure nothing heard him."

"Yes, sir." Sergeant Smith leapt out of the hole.

Pratt turned back to Jacobs. The young medic's hands were shaking slightly, and his head was down. Pratt placed his hand firmly on the young man's shoulder. He spoke quietly with understanding and care in his voice. "Take care of him until tomorrow. He'll be off planet first thing when they land. Then they can take care of him properly. It's not your fault, Jacobs."

"Yes, suh."

* * *

Swamp Master Borrk snapped off the main communication switch. He had just received a glowing report from Drawwl. The compound had been taken without difficulty and with minimal damage. He now controlled the support facility, its resin manufacturing plant, surrounding lands, and trained personnel. Moreover, Drawwl had seen to it that a partial shipment of resins was already en route so his production would not be delayed. Most excellent news, indeed.

The best piece of information came last. Kek had a total of a hundred twenty warriors under his command. Twice what Borrk had expected to find, and now they were all his by default. Kek had been building up his forces for some unknown purpose. *Probably to expand his own personal empire among his suppliers*, Borrk mused. Perhaps he had suppliers who owed him contracted goods. If so, those debts were now Borrk's, and they could be brought under his control as well. Borrk would ensure that a full accounting of Kek's contracts would be made. As the new overseer of the compound, he was responsible to ensure those commitments were honored.

With the extra troops, Borrk was now one of the most powerful Drakk'Har in his area. Perhaps the most powerful, if one took the importance of the ship growth facilities into consideration. However, Borrk knew that taking something was easy. Keeping it in the long term was the hard part. He was surrounded by younger, ambitious Drakk'Har who wanted to advance themselves. They were calculating, cold, and efficient. They did not mind killing or underhanded behavior to gain power. Of course, neither did Borrk, but he had much more to lose, and they knew it.

Borrk had just accumulated more expenses for maintaining his holdings. With many more mouths to feed and more labor to pay. He had troops to house and train along with more supervision duties to make sure all aspects of his fiefdom ticked over properly. The larger the holdings he maintained, the more he required talented Drakk'Har deputies to help him run it. However, he could not afford them to be too talented, lest they usurp his power for their own. Drawwl was a perfect example. A capable leader in battle, he also had a natural administrative talent. Borrk could see danger there in the future, unless steps were taken to restrict or eliminate him.

Beyond the dangers from below were the dangers from above. His growth facilities would attract the attention of Lords with larger power bases. If Planet Lord Slassh took an interest in acquiring his holdings, it would be bad news indeed. Slassh could ask for a simple percentage levied on his goods for his continued "protection". Or he could simply decide to step in and take over the entire operation to line his own pockets. Planet Lords ruled in absolute terms. They were essentially governors, entrusted by the emperor himself to manage the planet in whatever way they saw fit.

The mark of the emperor was jade. That ornamental, emerald green stone was the exclusive property of the emperor. None could wear or display it without an imperial edict. As a sign that Planet Lords ruled in the emperor's name, they were allowed to display a single piece of jade touched by the claw of the emperor himself. As long as the emperor was supplied with the materials, resources, and ships he required, then the Planet Lord lived according to his own rules.

Power at that level took on a whole new dimension. When you got to the Planet Lord level, you had to have firm alliances and contacts. Your intelligence on your opponents had to be first rate, and while you were in a lofty position of power, it simply meant that you had further to fall. Borrk was sure he had spies in his organization. There had to be. Swamp Masters were one step below a Planet Lord's level, and Drakk'Har always wanted to move up in rank.

With the warm blood fleet heading for the planet, Slassh would be taking considerable damage unless reinforcements arrived, and that was unlikely. So, his power base would be severely depleted. If Borrk could avoid damage himself, he would be in a position to challenge Slassh and claim the Planet Lord title for himself. Then, a quick note to the emperor detailing Slassh's failure to defend Mindon-2, and the assurances that Borrk could fulfill all planetary contracts with the empire, would suffice to give him the position by default.

Delivering the note with Slassh's head would be a nice touch the emperor would appreciate. Then, who knew, if he could spread out his power and claim a few worlds, he might one day find himself luxuriating in the imperial mud pits, being hand-fed Kyber monkeys by females—many smooth-scale females who truly appreciated the touch of an imperial claw. The daydream felt quite comfortable, and Borrk relished it.

* * *

The sun was setting on the conquered compound. Drawwl had spent the day in Kek's former private quarters. He did not know where Kek was staying now and, frankly, did not care. Kek had been subjugated and was therefore no longer a concern. Drawwl was in no hurry to return to Borrk. He had reported the capture of the compound over the long-range communicator, and Borrk had been so overjoyed at his success, that he had neglected to order him to return. It might take him a day or two to get around to it, but until then, Drawwl had the excuse of overseeing the repairs on the compound. So, he could linger for a time and relax. The females had left him moments earlier at his command. They were entertaining, but hardly memorable, in his opinion. One female had possibilities, but with a new lord over her, she was tentative, and that had blunted her abilities. However, toward the end she was at least getting enthusiastic. Perhaps she would be more responsive later in the day.

Drawwl had avoided combat earlier in the day, but the journey and added stress of facing Kek had taken its toll. Drakk'Har bodies did not stand up well to prolonged physical exertion. They could run at up to thirty kilometers an hour for short periods and were many times stronger than the most muscular human. However, such power came at a price. Their muscles generated copious amounts of lactic acid when under heavy use. With too much acid in their system, their bodies began to shut down as an internal defense measure. It took time to re-absorb the acids and remove them from their bloodstream. So a lot of their time was spent lounging on a riverbank or private mud pit. Drawwl lay in a shallow pit of runny brown ooze. The cool mud sapped the built-up warmth from his body and allowed him to relax. He let himself mull over the day's activities and results.

Progress on the repairs was swift. Compounds like this always had a store of mud-brick to repair damage caused by the elements. As they manufactured sealing resins in the compound itself, they soon had a new covering protecting the newly installed mud brick. Sealed against the effects of weather, the wall could last for decades. Drakk'Har construction tended to be over-simplified. They simply did not want something that required a lot of maintenance. Once they built something, Drakk'Har would essentially ignore it from that point on. If a structure failed, it would be reinforced and re-built. In case of a major failure, it would be torn down and reconstructed. However, the direct hit and minor damage from the shrapnel of the more distant mortar rounds was minor and would be fixed quickly. He mentally ran the design of the compound through his mind. Small and easily defensible, he had no need to add more fortifications or ramparts. Drawwl had effective guards, and he would have them patrol outside the walls, something the former guards did not do. That had allowed his forces to approach undetected and gave them the element of surprise.

Drawwl was not a typical Drakk'Har. He had learned early on that intelligence was a major factor in triumphing over your enemy. You did not have to be smarter than your opponent. You just had to know where he was and in what strength. By knowing their strengths, you also knew their weaknesses, and you could exploit them to your advantage. Common thoughts for a human, but Drakk'Har generally tended to throw masses of weapons and troops at an enemy to defeat them. That had not helped him in his earlier encounter on the hilltop near the town.

However, he knew the other successful element in combat was well-trained and disciplined troops. Drawwl was forced to use Swamp Master Borrk's compound guards in the earlier hilltop encounter. His superior, Borrk, was a typical Drakk'Har. He felt the sight of an armed Drakk'Har guard was enough to intimidate his enemies. Borrk gave no training, nor was there reward for performance; only punishment for the slightest of failures. This caused fear and resentment of Borrk that he mistakenly took as respect. Drawwl thought differently and had selected Drakk'Har to serve under him whom he had groomed personally. On long patrols, he would train them in maneuver and ambush. He would punish only when necessary and when deserved, with an even hand. Over time, he had built a reputation as a solid leader with the Drakk'Har troops. Over half of Borrk's guards would follow him on that reputation alone, he was sure of that.

However, seizing a swamp master's power was not a trivial exercise. He had to be sure he could survive the encounter with enough power to protect what he took. Other lords would wait until two sides had exhausted themselves fighting and then move in, conquering both. Drakk'Har were very opportunistic in building their power bases. As a result, Drawwl had to be calculating and methodical. He had to place his troops in key positions and intimidate those he did not control—not an easy task in Drakk'Har society where deceit and double, or even triple, allegiances were commonplace.

Most Drakk'Har had agendas for personal advancement. The few who could navigate that choppy sea rose in power. The troops with him were loyal. He had several other groups under his influence, as well. The best news that had reached him in the aftermath was that the compound had many extra warriors. A compound of this size usually only had twenty or thirty as a standard complement. Kek had been building up his forces for a power play, but now those additional troops were at Drawwl's command. They were not well trained, but in time, that would change. Drawwl would succeed. He was sure of that.

Drawwl fell into a light sleep with thoughts of ascension on his mind. His relaxed body sank into the mud, which supported his weighty frame comfortably.

CHAPTER 15 – PREPARATIONS

Fleet Nine entered high orbit around Mindon-2 with sensors lashing the planet with every watt of available power. The *Wraith* ship had detected no ballistic missile defenses during its earlier flight through the solar system, but no one in the military completely trusted intelligence estimates and information. Screens and read-outs were examined for any indication of an attack. No one wanted to be fighting off nuclear-tipped missiles while trying to put troops on the ground. Drakk'Har sub-orbital shuttles were seen infrequently, but none approached near the fleet, and they were left alone. They were tracked to determine their bases of operation, but not engaged. Several Drakk'Har satellites and larger orbital platforms of unknown purpose were destroyed on principle with long-range weapons. The fleet moved into position without serious opposition. That meant they would proceed on schedule.

On board the command ship, the marshal finally gave the order. "Mr. Christensen, you may begin the planetary bombardment at your discretion."

"Yes, sir," said the Norwegian as he pressed the proper sequence of studs on his panel. "Beginning surface bombardment. Phase one starting now."

The fleet cruisers twisted slowly in orbit. Re-orientation of their armaments took several seconds. When their guns were pointing at the planet surface, they began to fire their secondary armaments at pre-designated targets. Blue bolts of plasma energy lanced down from the heavens. The atmosphere of the planet ripped away most of the energy in the descending barrage, but enough superheated gas reached the surface to cause grievous damage. Communication centers, space ports, and weapons arrays were the first items targeted. They had been located by several sources. The *Wraith* ship, which had made the initial observations, had detected several targets of opportunity. The Special Forces troops had scouted their areas thoroughly and added their target coordinates as well. The balls of plasma energy impacted on the surface of the planet and exploded. Anything in close proximity of the blasts was decimated. Antennas, buildings, parked shuttles, and a few exposed Drakk'Har were vaporized. Shuttle landing pads were targeted, and successful hits generated huge fireballs as fuel tanks ignited. A heavy stench of charred plant growth hung around the areas struck by energy bolts.

After their primary target list had been completed, the ship's battery commanders shifted their fire to the construction facilities and support areas. They tried to level the huge construction equipment, ship hulls, and walled defenses as efficiently as they could. In a few areas, caches of resins and oils added to the destruction. However, while the blasts looked spectacular, the damage overall to the growth facilities was minimal. The huge growths had to receive direct hits to cause anything but minor damage. Being made of moist plant material, they did not burn readily. One of the secondary objectives was to kill the construction workers. Several explosions landed in the midst of the housing units and obliterated them, but with little loss of life. The majority of the population had ample warning and was already deep underground in protective bunkers and tunnels well out of harm's way.

* * *

In the dim light of the sunrise, the Special Forces troops watched with unbridled exhilaration as the blue energy bolts descended from the sky. Fleet Nine had arrived. The town in the distance received several direct hits, and the sound of the explosions took several seconds to reach their hilltop observation post. Each was able to see the results of their thorough mapping of the area as the bolts landed in close proximity to the reported coordinates. Other bolts landed on other targets all around them at varying distances, but they focused on the town. One of the last strikes hit an exposed pipeline carrying fuel, and a secondary explosion rocked the town; they felt the tremors on the hill through their boot soles. Every one of them watched, suppressing the desire to scream out in joy.

* * *

The same tremors woke Drawwl from his slumber as they were transmitted through the mud pit. He did not bother to rinse the mud off, which ran counter to tradition. Drawwl raced outside and saw the last two bolts fall in the direction of Borrk's growth construction facilities. The town was behind several hills, and he was on a plain. Drawwl could not see the effects of the impacts, but the intensity of sound and vibration told him everything he needed to know. He looked around and saw troops on the walls looking in the direction of the town. His compound had not been targeted, he was glad to see. They were either not important enough, or had not been sighted. Either way, he was thankful. Liquid resins were notoriously flammable, and only one or two bolts landing within the walls would produce an inferno.

Drawwl began screaming commands. He wanted his radios turned off until the bombardment ended. Warm blood technology was too efficient at locating transmitters. He also needed to get his troops into shelters. Just because they had not been hit to that point did not guarantee immunity. Plus, Borrk would eventually come for him. He was sure he would need as many troops as possible when he did.

* * *

Phase one of the barrage lasted only thirty-seven minutes in total. High above the action, Collins pressed more commands into his panel. "Beginning phase two now."

The bellies of the cruisers cracked open, and recessed cylindrical weapon racks were exposed to space. Long, thin missiles two and a half meters long were released from the bottom of the racks and fell toward the planet below. Their conventional rocket motors ignited, and they accelerated quickly toward the ground. When one missile cleared the hull, the rack rotated, and the next missile was sent on its way. As the racks turned, the empty missile spaces were filled with replacement weapons from internal bunkers. Each cruiser fired a missile every seven seconds.

The missiles were called THOR, which stood for Tactical High ORbit. As they descended, the thin atmosphere caressed the missile body. The missiles' noses began to heat up with the friction of the atmosphere. The thick ceramic tips dissipated the heat, as they were designed to. Each tip glowed with a dull red flare and left a trail of fire in its wake as the air itself ignited from the intense heat. Behind the heat shields, the navigation RADAR units kept the missiles on course with minor adjustments. Their intelligent brains compensated for the atmospheric buffeting.

* * *

The heat of the incoming missiles set off several passive heat detectors on the planet surface. Camouflaged anti-missile batteries were alerted to the threat. The Drakk'Har Planetary Defense Command issued an immediate alert.

Lord Kaaw received the alarm of inbound missiles and acted immediately. Kaaw was situated seven klem from Lord Borrk and, as the local anti-air commander, was charged with the protection of Borrk's town and facilities. By default, he was also charged with the protection of Planet Lord Slassh, who also had his bunker under the same town. One of the units he commanded was a four-launcher anti-missile battery located in a shallow valley between a series of ridges. The launch position consisted of a string of shallow holes in the ground interconnected by zigzagging trenches.

Kaaw screamed orders at his technicians. "Uncover all batteries, begin active scans, and engage all incoming targets, pond scum."

The technicians leapt to action at his voice. Transmitters that had been in standby mode were turned on and began to radiate energy skywards. Two inbound targets were detected at once. A moment later, a third was seen.

* * *

Above the planet, the recce ship fleet's sensors began to register the distinctive frequencies of the anti-missile battery signals coming from the surface. Each transmitter was located using triangulation, and their coordinates were transmitted to the fleet cruisers by MASER-COMM. Counter battery fire carried one of the higher priorities and made its way to the top of the target list immediately. The cruiser weapons officers re-oriented their weapons and fired at the coordinates. The plasma energy bolts moved at the speed of light and passed the dropping missiles as if they were standing still.

* * *

"Engaging incoming targets, Lord," the Drakk'Har technician operating the fire control board said. He dedicated three of his launchers to meet the incoming threats. The fourth he left in reserve. Pressing the correct sequence of buttons, the anti-missile launchers began to swivel to the optimum track.

233

Located in deep pits with reinforced walls, the individual launchers rotated to the best firing position. Moments after reaching the proper position, each launcher fired three times. The rockets had barely cleared the pits when the first of the Federation energy bolts landed directly on top of the transmission towers. The towers were reinforced, but never designed to stand direct hits. They disintegrated immediately and collapsed, crushing the transmitter hardware directly below.

Kaaw saw the impact of the energy bolts several klem away. He knew his primary sensor array had just been reduced to ashes. "Switch to secondary transmitters, and prepare the reserve sets for deployment." Kaaw knew his life depended on his ability to protect Borrk and his holdings. He was feeling the pressure of the moment in a big way.

"Yes, Lord." The technician responsible knew his life was on the line, too. His hands flew across the controls and brought the secondary antenna array to active mode.

* * *

The distinctive thermal signatures of the anti-missile motors were detected immediately by the reconnaissance ship's optical sensors. Their launch positions were also determined, then transmitted to the cruisers. Within a minute, their energy weapons had the new target list and fired.

* * *

Each of the THOR missiles fell quickly, but the laws of physics and aerodynamics dictated their travel within a tight arc. Their paths were easily predicted, and after several simple formulas were applied, course corrections were fed to each ascending rocket by a radio link from the secondary ground transmitters. The three rockets assigned to each inbound missile proceeded to different altitudes along that arc. Each rocket carried thousands of small ceramic spheres surrounded by shaped explosive. When they reached their programmed altitudes, they exploded. The ceramic spheres were thrust into the path of the oncoming missiles. The first rocket destroyed the first missile easily, but the other two rockets dedicated to the same missile arc detonated also, just as they were programmed to. The second missile survived the first two rockets, but was caught by the spheres of the third, and tore itself apart in the turbulence, falling harmlessly into the jungle below.

The third THOR missile was luckier than its counterparts. It burst through the first rocket explosion unscathed. The second anti-missile rocket had a faulty timer and exploded harmlessly behind the missile. The third rocket detonated correctly, but contrary to the odds, none of the spheres hit the thin and fragile casing. The warhead explosion did its job, however. The missile hit the high-pressure explosive shock wave in the air and was knocked off course slightly. Its small computer brain never wavered in its dedication to hitting its target. It tried to correct its path to strike its target as it fell to the planet below. It almost made it.

The thin, twenty centimeter width of the missile minimized its resistance to the air, and it dropped at a speed exceeding Mach seven. The THOR missiles did the one thing the energy bolts of the barrage could not do. They struck the planet surface and penetrated deep into the ground. Command bunkers were always well-protected and deep below the surface. The kinetic energy of the THOR missiles allowed them to burrow down to the suspected bunker locations and explode at pre-determined depths. The third missile was targeted at a suspected command bunker under the town. The Special Forces troops had surmised its location during their observations. The location was accurate; the bunker for the Planet Lord Slassh was below. However, the missile was knocked off course just enough to miss the bunker itself. It burrowed into the earth less than ten meters away from the bunker's thick walls. Three hundred kilos of densely packed high explosive created a severe vibration that rocked the ground and created huge cracks in several of the ceramic walls, but the bunker and all of its occupants survived.

* * *

Drakk'Har warriors manning the rocket launchers did not wait for the noxious fumes of the burnt launch fuel to disperse before they emerged from their hardened shelters. They ran to the launchers under their charge and began to prepare them for movement. Several coughed loudly as the harsh smoke residue seared their lungs. However, none waited until the air had cleared. They had to move the launchers to alternative positions before they fired again. Until they moved them, they were vulnerable, and they knew it.

Only one launcher crew was fast enough to avoid the counter battery fire of the Federation. They felt the heat of the explosions at their backs as they maneuvered their weapon around the corner of the prepared trench. The two other crews were not fast enough to avoid their doom. The surviving crew moved with purpose, pulling the heavy launcher through the mire at the bottom of the trench. When they reached the alternative position, they erected the launcher in minutes and tied the control cables into the rocket computer. They loaded fresh rockets into the empty spaces of the launcher, then scrambled into their protective bunker built into the wall. They collapsed on the ground and rested up for the next move.

* * *

The THOR missiles landing around the planet did their jobs efficiently. As the majority of Drakk'Har facilities were underground, the damage was spectacular. The hardened walls of the bunkers actually enhanced the explosive effects when they exploded within. The concussive energy of the warhead spread through the bunker complexes and pulverized their occupants to jelly in a fraction of a second. As the missiles moved several times faster than the speed of sound, they struck without warning. One moment the Drakk'Har were alive and the next, dead.

Several command staffs and, more importantly, their communications equipment were destroyed. The Federation theory was simple. If you cut off the head, the hands would not know what to do. Without their leaders, the troops would not be able to mount an effective defense. The landings would now meet less resistance as a result.

On board the *Aristotle,* everyone was working steadily. The command deck buzzed with activity as military personnel circulated around the seated staff officers. One naval rating in particular never stopped moving. She delivered a series of intelligence reports, brought coffee —or herbal tea in Commander Tran's case— fetched screen cleaner, and retrieved required documentation, always filling in the small requirements. It got to the point where things would arrive prior to their being needed.

The occupants of this room coordinated the actions of the surviving members of Fleet Nine. Ironically, the heavy casualties had aided the process. Even though the fleet used computers for the majority of its communications, voice traffic still had a place. Now that two landing sites were no longer being assaulted and several ships had been destroyed, signal traffic was reduced overall, which made for more efficient communication.

Christensen at the Tactics (Ground) station was the busiest of all. Screen after screen of landing schedules and flight operations flew across his multiple monitors as he adjusted orders to keep the mission on schedule. He didn't notice the activity of others around him. His concentration on the tasks in front of him was total. His fingers slid over the glass monitor surfaces furiously. A cup of coffee left for him an hour before had gone untouched and was quite cold.

Phase Two of the orbital bombardment was almost half over. The THOR missiles were degrading the command, control, and intelligence abilities of the enemy and hopefully throwing them into confusion. Textbook doctrine stated that troops should be on the ground the second after the last missile had fallen. However, Christensen never followed the book, as that made you predictable. He ordered a series of strikes adjacent to the proposed landing areas to keep the enemy under cover while the marines landed. Some of his strikes were planned to hit while the troops were actually deploying on the landing zones. The physics got a little complicated, but he had a small staff and a bank of super-computers to track the variables he could not. Red warnings were immediately displayed if a conflict with any landing zone was detected. The incoming air lanes of descent to each operational area were marked on his monitor, and no missile strikes were allowed through those zones five minutes prior to landing, for obvious reasons. In theory, the plan could have been designed months before, but last-minute complications always forced one to re-examine the plan on the fly. A cruiser might have a stuck weapon rack at an inopportune moment. In that case, the target had to be rescheduled, canceled, or transferred to another vessel. As fire plans were scheduled tightly, the change impacted on the other cruiser's ability to perform its mission. Ripples in a pond. Throw a stone into a flat pool of water, and serene rings float out gently. Throw ten rocks into the water, and all rings interact, causing chaos. Christensen was throwing seventy THOR missiles a minute at the planet, and several changes were required to ensure the priority targets were engaged.

As the bombardment proceeded, the rest of the fleet began making preparations for landing. The computers choreographed the movements to the second. Lighters departed their tenders at pre-determined times. They transited to the troop transports and docked to the larger ships. Troops loaded down with supplies and ammunition moved into each. When everyone and everything was secure, the lighters moved away from the transports and held in loose patterns above their designated landing zones. They sat in orbit, waiting for the order to land.

* * *

Sergeant Blake sat in his designated troop lighter. This was the part he hated—the waiting. A timeless military saying went, "Hurry up and wait." Strapped into a series of restraints, he could only move his head, feet, and arms. The body armor he wore restricted his motion significantly. Not that he could have moved much in any case. His backpack was on top of his knees up to his neck and his weapon slung upside down across his right shoulder. His helmet was sitting squarely on his head with a thick strap under his chin. A composite band held a small video unit on the front of the helmet shell. A small piece of transparent plastic was folded up over his right eye, and a microphone stalk wrapped around his right cheek. The cloth camouflage cover on the helmet had several slits for accepting grass and foliage when they hit the surface. At the back of the cloth was an unnatural hump where a thick, pre-wrapped aero-gel combat bandage was stored. A web belt held several spare magazines of ammunition, two canteens, a COMM pack, small trenching shovel, pistol, and tube flares. A chemical filter mask hung over the shovel head, ready for immediate use. Four fragmentation, two smoke, and two WP grenades hung from his webbing. Blake's fatigue pockets bulged with more unseen gear. Every piece of exposed skin had three-tone green camouflage paint applied.

All available seats were occupied, and he was pressed into a corner near the flight deck. His right arm was against the dividing wall separating the flight deck from the cargo area. Against his left shoulder was LCPL Belliveau with his identical pack and equipment. They were squeezed together so tightly that a playing card would not have fit between the pair of them. Second Lieutenant Wicks was directly across the aisle, with the rest of the squad sitting in parallel rows on the starboard side. The aisle between them in this case was less than a boot width. Another squad sat on the port rows of seats. He ignored them; they were some other sergeant's responsibility.

Blake hated the waiting. This was when the anxiety came. His hand was wedged into the seat harness beside him to hide the shaking. Thoughts of death haunted him. Strapped into the vehicle, he felt completely vulnerable. He was eager to get out onto the surface and get the job done. All he knew was he had an appointment with a set of spatial coordinates at a preset time, and he was helpless until the hatch cracked open on the surface.

Possibilities rolled through his mind. They could collide with another lighter. If they were hit by ground fire, they would fly straight into the ground at high speed. He had seven combat drops in lighters and untold numbers of training simulations and exercises. The thoughts were always the same. He tried to distract himself with looks around the cargo bay. It would have been easier of he had some indication of what was going on in the outside world. However, only 2nd Lieutenant Wicks was plugged into the COMM system, listening to the flight deck communications. Perkins was beside the officer, twitching in his seat, trying to get comfortable with his usual load plus the added weight of a radio pack and antenna. Even though they were in zero gee, the packs and various pieces of kit still got in the way.

Blake leaned forward as much as he could and glanced down at the rest of his squad. They were all there, strapped in by the load master, who didn't look any of them in the eye. They never did. Load masters were typically the ones who loaded the body bags on the return trips. Blake supposed the load masters were using a natural defensive response. *You can't enjoy your hamburger if you knew the cow*, he mused sardonically.

They all handled the immobility with different techniques. Messina was sleeping with his head leaned back. His combat bandage was perfectly placed to rest on a cross bar behind him. The newbies, Johnston and Tyler, were at the end of each row nervously looking around. They would be the last off, and for the duration of the combat, they would be kept close to the rear. Perkins was another raw recruit, but he would be right beside Wicks the whole time. This was the newbies' first combat drop, and they needed to experience combat before participating in it. The squad had eight men and two women, which was fairly representative of other units. With the exception of the newbies who only had eight weeks of basic infantry skill, the rest were experienced combat troops who had proven themselves under fire. The newbies would either stand or run, and no one could predict which until the moment was upon them. If they stood and held their ground, they would blend into the combat effectiveness of the unit. If they ran? Well, that's why the pistol on the sergeant's belt was always loaded. Stalin had once said, "In the Soviet army, it takes more courage to retreat than advance." Of course, Stalin ordered machine gun units be placed behind his own troops as motivation.

In the rear of the lighter was the cargo area. Blake saw the load master had strapped down several boxes, crates, and irregularly shaped items. Cargo strap netting covered the carefully stacked pile. It attached everything securely to the floor and adjoining walls. The squad heavy weapons were there along with ammunition, water, and all of the other bulk items that could not be carried easily. *For want of a nail*, Blake mused. The amount of equipment necessary for a ten-person combat unit was staggering, not only in bulk, but in the number of items, too. When you were thirty-some light-years from the nearest forward supply base, you had to make sure you had what you needed. Weapon oil, spare electronic cards, batteries, rifle cleaning kits, medical supplies, shoelaces, and the other day-to-day items had to be on hand.

Blake recognized the need for a properly supplied army; the military had learned that lesson well many times over. In 327 BC, Alexander the Great, arguably the greatest general of all time, was cut off from his fleet and the supplies they carried. His army was forced to march five hundred kilometers through the Gedrosian desert in Iraq. The desert heat and lack of water and suitable guides sealed their fate. Only one man in four made it to the other side. Time and time again, it had been shown that if you cut a force off from its supplies, you gained a tremendous advantage.

Blake knew he could do nothing but wait, and he settled back trying to relax. His hand kept shaking, regardless.

* * *

On the *Aristotle,* Commander Christensen kept a watch on the mission countdown timer in a corner of one of his screens. His Tactics (Ground) station was designed to display relevant information for ground operations. A cluster of monitors and screens was filled with required information. By design, the critical data was located on the central screens, with related information loaded onto the peripheral ones. He could transfer any block of data from one to the other at will. He made few reallocations, however. After many years of experience, he had a good understanding of what was important.

A series of events were preset below the chronometer at the top right of one of the main monitors. The event immediately below the current time turned yellow to indicate it was occurring within two minutes. Christensen ran a last series of checks on his fire missions as checked against the landing areas. He made one minor adjustment to a cruiser fire plan and made sure the orders had been acknowledged. Apart from the marshal, Christensen was the only man in the fleet who could override the landings if necessary. Everything looked correct. He keyed his microphone.

"Marshal, Phase Two bombardment is seventy-three percent complete. Request permission to commence landing operations as briefed."

Behind him, he knew Kosnov was double-checking his own screens. Christensen saw no reason to delay.

"Proceed on your schedule, Commander," Kosnov ordered.

"Yes, sir." Christensen's fingers flew over the screens in front of him. Flight plans were confirmed, fire missions were automatically shifted to secondary targets away from the landing zones, and all ships received warnings to stand by for operational orders. All ship captains knew what order was coming, as it had been outlined in the briefings, but none would act without the order being given. Christensen waited tensely until only ten seconds remained on the timer. He then activated the command MASER-COMM circuit fleet-wide, causing his voice to come across all bridges and flight decks.

"Fleet, this is Argus. Stand by." He paused for several seconds, leaving the channel open until the counter reached zero. "Execute Archangel. Repeat, execute Archangel."

CHAPTER 16 – DESCENT

Time seemed to pass dreadfully slowly. Only the drone of air recycling motors was constant. Conversation around Blake was non-existent. Everyone isolated themselves in their own thoughts. Two or three had obvious airsickness bags tucked into their webbing. No one had used them yet, but Blake knew it only took one person to release a torrent from many. Second Lieutenant Wicks's head nodded as he unconsciously agreed with what he overheard on his headset. He brought his hand out and gestured with it. His finger pointed at the floor, and he made a spiral motion while looking at Blake. Then he changed it to a thumbs-up sign. *Here we go*, Blake thought.

Dozens of lighters were positioned so that they were not only flying backwards, but also inverted in relation to their orbital direction. Until the order to land had been given, they kept their assigned positions and enjoyed the view of the planet above them. They all ignited their engines within seconds of each other, using the thrust to counter their orbital velocity. As they decelerated, the gravitational pull of the planet below drew them closer. The lighter crews now concentrated on their flight instruments. Each had a precise path to steer to get to its proper landing coordinates. Little margin for error existed, as spacing between the descending ships was minimal.

Small maneuvering jets made incremental adjustments in position as required.

Even with computer assistance, upside-down and backwards was an unnatural way to fly. As long as everyone followed their computer-generated paths, there would be no collisions— in theory. Each vessel dropped lower gradually until it began to encounter the calculated limit of the upper atmosphere. At that stage, the main engines were turned off, and the ship was effectively coasting the rest of the way. Rearward-facing countermeasure bays on the backside of each lighter launched a pair of missiles that flew down their assigned flight paths. When the missiles were clear, the pilots twisted their lighters until their bellies were oriented with a forty-two degree nose-up angle relative to their flight direction. At that angle, the heat would be distributed evenly on all belly tiles.

Complex physics and mathematics determined the angle of attack for the craft. Reentry angles were critical and had to be kept between five and seven degrees negative inclination with respect to the planetary horizon. If a lighter came in any steeper, it would burn up. Any shallower, and it would bounce off the atmosphere like a flat rock skipped on the surface of a lake. Flight computers assisted through the process, but a pair of human hands was on the yoke the whole way, ready to take over at a moment's notice.

On Blake's lighter, the first molecules of Mindon-2 atmosphere brushed against the composite skin. At first he could discern no difference in the descent, but vibrations began as the air thickened. Over a few minutes, the vibrations turned to shudders, and the sergeant knew the lighter was carving its way through the thin upper atmosphere. He knew the theory of re-entry. The lighter's belly had a series of heat-absorbing tiles that shielded the craft from the friction of the air moving past at hypersonic speeds. The pilot needed to keep the lighter in a steep nose-up attitude and let the air slow the craft as it descended through. The belly tiles were all-important. The slightest flaw or hole and jets of twelve-hundred-degree-Celsius plasma would destroy the craft in moments. The first hint of the resulting heat became visible through the ports as a dull red glow that increased over time. Blake grabbed his backpack firmly and grabbed a support with his free hand. As long as his hands were tensed, they didn't shake.

The decoy drones that had been fired earlier from each lighter were further down in the atmosphere. A composite ceramic nosecone protected each missile from the extreme heat and the dense hypersonic air passing across the tip. Dozens of them descended along the planned flight paths of the landing force. When the altimeters passed the twenty-five-thousand-meter level, several small pods were ejected from along the shafts of each drone body. Some continued to fall under their own power, while others fired small rocket boosters that moved them across random arcs in the sky. More were ejected at regular intervals as the drones descended. Each drone carried seventy-two countermeasure pods. Each pod could be loaded with many types of passive or active jammers, decoys, and false target projectors. The exact load-out on each changed according to the mission profile. Some of the pods deployed small parachutes to slow their descent, while others plunged quickly, ejecting small strips of metallic foil cut to the same wavelength as Drakk'Har tactical RADAR sets. The foil drifted on the fast currents of the upper atmosphere and caused long, cone-shaped RADAR targets. Other parachute-equipped pods activated radio beacons set to Federation voice frequencies. While they could fit in the palm of one's hand, they were sophisticated enough to transmit encrypted signals. They pretended to be descending lighters. Other pods turned on jammers and ejected white-hot flares, the former to jam enemy radio and RADAR, the latter to simulate the hot belly reentry tiles of a descending lighter. The goal of each of these decoy missiles was to confuse, disorient, and deceive the enemy sensors and ground commanders, or at least those that had survived to this point. By placing thousands of erroneous targets in the air, the lighters following behind would have a good chance of avoiding weapons fire, as they would be lost in the electronic noise.

After their deceptive payloads were ejected, the now empty drones had one last mission. RADAR transponders in the nose of each missile turned on. They began to scan the terrain below them looking for pre-programmed coordinates. Rock peaks, river junctions, or other discernible geographic features were identified and used to set the drones' path. Once oriented, they began course corrections. They impacted on structures and areas that Federation intelligence had identified as targets of interest. That is, they were not a hundred percent sure that what they were targeting were enemy command, control, logistics, or weapons platforms, but they were suspicious enough to warrant a secondary strike. The empty decoy drones carried no explosives. However, they were moving at several times the speed of sound, which imparted a hideous shock to anything they hit. As a final blow, the remnants of engine fuel carried on board did generate a respectable fireball when the tanks ruptured from the impact.

Several of the larger buildings and constructions on the planet were subjected to hammer blows from above. Luck was with the Federation, as one of the missiles detonated on top of an underground pipeline carrying benzene. The pipeline was still open to its buried source tank, and the force of the explosion carried a short way down the pipeline to the fuel reservoir. If the tank had been more than half full, the back pressure of the fluid would have dampened the explosive effects. However, the tank was almost empty, and the vapors of the volatile benzene ignited. The shock waves carried to three additional, identically sized tanks of other chemicals that were almost full. The force of the explosion ripped the ceramic composite walls asunder, mixing the various liquids together in a fine mist. The vapors ignited, sending a fireball to the surface that was large enough to be seen by observers in space.

* * *

Lord Kaaw was feeling the strain. Sixty percent of his strike forces were now smoking holes in the ground. The only good news was that his command post had avoided all attack to this point. He still had his command staff, most of his communications equipment, and a small anti-air rocket force. A human observer would say his best units had survived, but a Drakk'Har would never say that. As a typical Drakk'Har underling, his view of the world was remarkably pessimistic. He was professional, however. He still lived, and therefore had a chance to strike back. Kaaw was not dumb by any standards. He recognized the warm blood tactics. While the details changed, the overall impact was the same. He looked on his passive displays. Crude and bulky by human standards, his equipment was nonetheless effective at representing the electronic chaos above him. The skies in a hundred klem radius around him were clogged with false electronic signals and illusionary targets. He had been briefed well on warm blood technologies, and he knew it could be one of two things. Either this was a feint, in which case he just had to wait and let other regional anti-air commanders deal with the threats over their heads. Or this was a real attack. Warm bloods, while barbarians in Kaaw's opinion, were devastatingly effective at hiding their intentions until the last possible moment.

Kaaw knew the strategic value of the growth facilities. If he were going to land a strike force, he would ensure they came here to do as much damage as possible. However, the warm bloods had typically attacked strange targets in the past, and their choice of the Empire's most productive growth facility was hardly logical, based on their past barbaric behavior. They were here, though, and that left him in a tight bind. Pessimist or not, he was still a Drakk'Har warrior and therefore eminently practical. He had to prepare as if there *would* be a ground assault. His job was to kill as many of their craft in as short a time as possible. That was his job, and he was good at it. You didn't work directly for a Swamp Master unless you had ability.

Kaaw knew he had to move his surviving units off the plains, or they would be pounded into dust in short order. Swamp Master Borrk had ordered him to place the launch units close to the growth facilities so their fire could be concentrated. Most of the launch positions surrounding the growth facilities were already craters, thanks to that fateful order. Kaaw knew that was wrong, but Swamp Masters were Swamp Masters, and only the Planet Lord could override them. Kaaw had several alternative positions prepared, but he needed to choose which ones to use. He cast his yellow iris over the terrain map. Some things were universal. The high ground was always advantageous, especially when you were trying to find small lighters in the air. Sensor units mounted high up could see further. He came to a decision and turned to one of his messengers.

"You! Order all surviving elements of the First Order to assemble on top of Skull Ridge." He pointed at the map for emphasis. "Any surviving units from the Second Order will move onto Brawnik's Hump. Third Order troops are to disperse with portable missiles throughout the low land between the two hills. They will interdict any vehicles in their area on sight. I want those positions occupied immediately, pond scum."

"Yes, Lord," was the only reply.

Kaaw faced his defense coordinator. "You. I want the command staff to occupy the alternate bunker at the base of Skull Ridge. The communications circuits are to be checked as soon as we arrive. We must coordinate our actions with Brawnik's Hump. Move!"

"Yes, Lord." The smaller Drakk'Har padded off to begin the preparations. More Drakk'Har appeared from an adjoining bunker. They began to disconnect the bulky equipment and load it into carrying containers for the short move.

Kaaw threw out more orders to his staff in a rapid stream. "The ammunition bunkers at those two locations are to be unearthed and a full reload supply available before the launchers arrive. Have all positions well-camouflaged, or I shall stake you out in the sun and let the fire ants feast on your eyes!" Thoughts of being eaten alive by insects was enough to motivate the strongest of Drakk'Har. The room came alive with activity as they hurried with their tasks.

Kaaw knew he had to inform Swamp Master Borrk of the move, but he was not dumb enough to turn on a radio transmitter. He sent a swimmer instead with a message. By the time Borrk actually received the message, either the danger would have passed with it actually being a feint, or the warm bloods would have landed and his actions would be lauded. The third option struck him suddenly: Borrk might be found dead in his bunker. Yes, that would be the most agreeable outcome, he mused momentarily.

* * *

Planet Lord Slassh was flinging mental fury toward the skies above him. The close proximity of the underground detonation to Slassh had jarred him, but apart from some slight hearing loss, he was unharmed and recovering quickly. The rest of the Federation attacks had swarmed around him after that point. His command bunker was a mess. The shock of the blast had twisted one end of the structure, causing longitudinal cracks throughout the interior of the thick ceramic wall. His screens were covered with hundreds of nonsensical targets caused by the decoys. Static hissed out of several radio receivers. Confused messages were occasionally heard. The small communications staff were listening, but not transmitting. They knew the effectiveness of warm blood counter-fire. The near miss had reinforced that. Several were clearing the walkways of debris that had fallen from the cracked wall and roof. A few stations had tipped over, and equipment lay on the floor in strange positions. One of the access passages had collapsed, but strong Drakk'Har muscles were quickly clearing the debris and reinforcing the tunnel. It was a minor inconvenience; four other access tunnels plus two nearby underwater tunnels could be accessed. The water tunnels connected all major buildings and thoroughfares. Branches of them went as far as the river. The water tunnels were seldom used, as water transmitted shock waves much more efficiently than air. Therefore, they were only employed for critical matters.

* * *

Close by, Swamp Master Borrk was trapped in his bunker. Borrk could leave, but he wanted to live to see another day. The orbital bombardment was still proceeding, and nothing lived for long in the open. Besides, the sight of his facility slowly being blasted to pieces was not something that he desired to see. His rage at being assaulted was at its peak already. Swamp Master Borrk knew the barbarians were coming. The intensity of the bombardment attested to that. He did not fear their coming; indeed, he welcomed it. Taking warm blood tributes would be a great reward. If he were truly lucky, he would also get some breeder females. Only the emperor and a few select planet lords had those so far. He was mentally cursing his decision to place the launchers close, but that was now moot. The air war was not over yet, and he still had a force of ground troops to throw at the invaders.

Borrk had placed the anti-air launchers around the compound for several sound reasons, according to Drakk'Har logic, anyway. His first concern was Kaaw himself. He was always taking ammunition and burying it in remote locations, preparing alternative firing locations on the high ground. Kaaw's reasons were always logical on the surface, of course. He just wanted to have several prepared positions around the area for flexibility. It could also be seen as stockpiling ammunition for an attempt at a future challenge. As Borrk was the only power in the area, the threat could only be directed at him. Borrk had several spies in Kaaw's organization and kept close observation on him and his stockpiles. Nothing of substance had emerged. *Yet.*

Borrk was also keeping tabs on the other Swamp Masters. Borrk had a nice operation—highly trained staff, a medium sized militia to guard it, and quite profitable, as well. Profitable businesses were highly desirable among Drakk'Har. The facilities were prestigious also, often being mentioned and once even visited by the emperor himself. When jealous eyes desired something, they often tried to take it.

Drakk'Har military tactics were much different than the Federation's. By keeping his launchers close to the growth facilities, he could concentrate his firepower on any single axis, delivering a powerful blow to any ground-based invader. Typically, Drakk'Har feared other Drakk'Har more than they feared the Federation. Why should they? They were just food. However, barbaric warm blood tactics had erased the launchers effectively enough. Many of the sites had been decoys with useless mock-ups of launchers. Badly camouflaged, they had been designed to take a first strike. Several well-hidden and operational units had been destroyed as well, and that was worrying.

A Drakk'Har appeared in the doorway. Seeing Borrk, he put his open palms out from his body and bowed. The creature wore the distinctive belt and tattoo marking of the anti-air section. Kaaw's minion, it would seem. Borrk let his anger vent. "Speak, slime. Where is the coward Kaaw?"

A quivering voice responded, "Noble Lord, Kaaw sent me to report he is moving half his surviving units to Skull Ridge. All other units are being dispatched to Brawnik's Hump. Kaaw is moving to occupy the air command bunker at Skull Ridge and has dispersed portable missile troops throughout the region."

How convenient, fumed Borrk. Skull Ridge was the farthest position away from the facility. He screamed his response. "Tell me, you rancid pool of ghafflin, why is Kaaw taking half his surviving units to Brawnik's Hump? The warm bloods just engaged us there."

The messenger struggled for the correct answer. Luckily, Kaaw chose his staff for intelligence. "Most mighty Lord,

Kaaw has heard of your decisive victory on Brawnik's Hump. He knows that the warm bloods were destroyed by your able command. No warm bloods would dare risk another conflict with your forces after such a victory as yours."

Borrk had maps on his walls as well, and he cast his eyes over one. The choices of Skull Ridge and Brawnik's Hump looked prudent, even in his rage. The terrain was a lot rougher than the plains around the facility, and the extra altitude would assist in anti-air combat. Borrk's rage would not stop him from taking out his anger on the underling, though. He was about to lash into the messenger again, when a trooper came down the open passage. In his haste to deliver the message, he neglected to bow and spoke immediately. "Lord, inbound hostile landing force detected!"

* * *

Blake felt the shudders through the airframe subside slowly as normal flight began. The four aero-engines had started in quick succession and began to murmur as the pilots applied power. Now that they were in the atmosphere proper, the maneuvering jets shut off, and the airfoil control surfaces kicked in. The lighter wings were quite stubby and insufficient to lift the lighter by themselves. Without their engines, they glided like bricks. The four aero-engines were designed for powered flight in any atmosphere that contained twelve percent or more oxygen. They were mounted at each corner of the airframe and could rotate in all three axes almost completely around. At maximum thrust, they could drive the lighter at close to seven hundred kilometers per hour. However, their real advantage was not their speed. The rotating engines allowed them to redirect engine thrust to allow them to hover and, in the hands of a decent pilot, even move backwards. The fifth engine was a larger, stern-mounted booster which was used to achieve orbit, but that would not be used until the lighter was ready to return to space. Above Blake's head, a red light turned amber. *Two minutes to landing.*

* * *

On Hill 170, the Special Forces section knew the approximate time they should see the descending lighters. All of them were up and searching the skies eagerly. Smoke hung low in the sky over the town and facilities. Many of the larger buildings had been destroyed, and several large fireballs throughout the bombardment spoke to the accuracy of their earlier location plots. They occupied a rough circle looking out in all directions. They knew roughly where the landings would take place, but not the direction of approach. Besides, it did not pay to have your attention in one direction, or Murphy's Law would produce a Drakk'Har patrol from the other.

Jefferson heard the first indication of an approaching craft and pointed wordlessly toward the northeast. Several pairs of eyes focused on that area. Three lighters dropped under the gray clouds on cue seconds later, with a fourth trailing some distance behind. Flying in close formation, the forward three lighters did not slow as they approached the ground. Their painted teeth looked ominous even from this distance.

* * *

Marine Captain Levin finally broke through the clouds, and he gave a momentary sigh of relief as the ground came into view. He saw the three lead lighters in position directly in front of him. Until this point, they were dependent on RADAR images and altimeters. Now they could use their vision and fly much more effectively. A pilot could fly a lighter exclusively on instruments, but that was certainly not the preferred method, especially when doing high speed, low altitude attacks.

Levin and his flight of four were on a ground-strike mission or, in pilot speak, air-to-mud. Their mission was to eliminate or reduce any resistance on or near the landing zone before the landing force entered the area. The theory was simple. The three lead lighters would drop their munitions along a half-kilometer stretch of buildings adjacent to the main landing area. This would hopefully reduce the number of available enemy forces set to ambush the landing force. Levin, in the rear, would gauge the effectiveness of the strike. It would be his job to hit any missed targets or any follow-on forces that came onto the scene. The last lighter in a formation was called "slack." In actuality, this was the hardest position to be in, as the attack alerted the enemy, and a quick response would result in missiles and ground fire being directed at his craft. The others in the flight had surprise on their side. The slack lighter was all alone and in harm's way. The commanding officer always flew slack. They were typically the most experienced pilots, and they always got the most dangerous jobs. It helped morale with the rest of the pilots and crews.

Levin pressed the switch on the yoke and keyed his COMM unit. "Grasshopper flight, this is Grasshopper One. Deploy countermeasures, and commence your run."

"Grasshopper Two."

"Grasshopper Three."

"Grasshopper Four."

Each lighter acknowledged his orders in turn. Levin knew their curt responses meant *I acknowledge and understand your orders, and there are no foreseeable problems with our craft or crew to stop us carrying them out.*

Levin turned his attention to his own craft. He only had about thirty seconds to configure his own craft for attack. He looked at his thigh-mounted checklist. The proper display was already set. "Crew, Pilot. Ordinance checklist for air to ground. Master arm switch to ON."

Corporal Wallace had his hand on the switch, but did not raise the safety cover until Levin said the word ON. He pressed the switch underneath, and when the light turned from red to green, he removed his finger and spoke, "Check."

"Countermeasures to auto."

Another switch was flipped, and a status light changed color. "Check."

"Engines and flight systems."

Wallace scanned the engine instrument cluster. "Nominal."

"Photon torpedoes."

They still replayed that rather dated show on the vids, and the entire crew appreciated the unexpected joke. It had the desired effect of cutting the tension. Wallace was the worst introvert on board, but even he smiled at that one. "Fresh out, sir."

"Right. Checklist complete. Stand by for combat maneuvers."

Their flight path took them over the southern end of the growth facility where the terrain was quite flat. The outside craft separated gradually as they descended until two hundred fifty meters separated the outer lighters. They dropped together toward the ground and pulled out at fifty meters altitude. The belly of each cracked open, and rotating launch bars became visible. Small canisters spewed forth, releasing one after the other in quarter-second increments. As they fell, small parachutes deployed to retard the speed of their fall. This delay gave the lighters time to clear the area before the explosions began. Without that delay, they would still be within the effective blast radius of the weapons. Being blown out of the sky by one's own bombs was not a good path for promotion.

Each canister split into four parts. They hit the ground, and the irregular-shaped pieces bounced in random directions. They struck the ground a second time, bounced back up to waist height, and exploded. Each case separated along cut seams, creating small, rapidly moving fragments of hot metal. Shrapnel was flung through the air, striking the southern portion of the town and the majority of the plains outside. A wide swath of destruction hit every building on the south edge of the town. Drakk'Har troops occupying defensive positions in that area were killed or seriously wounded. Those who survived were deafened by the rolling explosions and forced to take cover.

The three advance lighters thundered off into the distance as Levin crossed behind the explosions to make an immediate battle damage assessment. He saw a repeat strike was unnecessary. Levin completed his observation run before curving counter-clockwise around the area. He still had a full ammunition load and could use it if significant opposition was seen encroaching on the plain.

Levin keyed his COMM switch the opposite way and transmitted on a different frequency. "Grasshopper One to Grey Bear. LZ is clear. Bring in the herd."

"Grey Bear to Grasshopper One. Roger."

A dozen lighters appeared through the clouds. These craft moved much slower than the strike aircraft. Their flight path was also much steeper than the Grasshopper flight. Their engines were tilted, so their thrust was straight down. They descended as quickly as possible, raising their thrust level to maximum just above the ground to cushion their landing before cutting the engine thrust completely. As they came in, they separated into pairs. One lighter would land with the other slightly to the left and rear of the first so all door gunners had unobstructed fields of fire.

No enemy fire was detected until the first lighter touched the ground. A couple of entrenched Drakk'Har heavy weapon emplacements opened up at the landing ships. Within seconds, hidden enemy mortars further back in the town began lobbing shells onto the plains, as well. Crew members on the left side of each lighter fired back into the town with miniguns.

* * *

Blake's lighter touched the ground with a reassuring thump. The amber lights around the cabin turned green, and his hand immediately hit the restraint release on his chest. The straps fell clear, and he stood. All of the others responded to the green light in the same way. Each marine knew his or her assignment on landing. It had been drummed into them through many months of hard training. After the load master had opened the hatches, three marines stepped out from each side of the craft and ran exactly three paces before falling prone with weapon ready. They formed two semi-circles on either side of the craft, covering the entire area around the lighter. Only the team on the port side saw any opposition, as they faced the growth facilities. This covering force carried the heavier weapons, and they immediately began to return fire. As they covered the rest of the marines, equipment was passed outside and stacked quickly. No one spoke, as the engine noise made that impossible once the hatches were opened. The odd sound of battle could be heard intermittently. The air smelled like a damp bog.

Blake stepped out of the starboard hatch between a couple of pieces of equipment as they were handed out. The fear of being cooped up was forgotten, the shakes were gone; he had a job to do. Blake moved up behind the prone men and knelt between the two marines. All of the fire was coming from the other side of the craft, and he could see no opposition in his arc of responsibility. The odd mortar shell landed on the plain, but at such a low rate of fire and spread out over such a wide area that Blake didn't take it seriously. His initial reaction was that whoever was shooting the mortars was doing so blind. He looked over his shoulder and saw they were making good progress with the unloading. Three quarters of the equipment lay outside the hatch already. He didn't see his officer, but Blake instinctively knew he would be on the port side of the craft attempting to get oriented for the coming assault. Orbital pictures and grid coordinates were one thing, but actually seeing the terrain you were going to fight over was invaluable.

Blake turned back to scan for movement in the distance, but his attention was immediately captured by a mortar round landing squarely on top of a lighter just a hundred meters off to his right. The initial impact did not seem to do anything to the craft. Apart from the flash and bang of the hit, the damage looked minimal. However, seconds after, a series of rapid explosions began from inside. Blake had no idea what was happening until two yellow tracer rounds came through the open hatch, leaving a distinctive trail behind them. A box of ammunition was cooking off, and rounds were firing in random directions. Blake, well away from the action, looked on helplessly as the marines inside yelled at those unloading and guarding their lighter to get clear. Fired from inside, the rounds circumvented any armor protection. The indiscriminate bullets hit vulnerable parts of the fuel cells and O_2 tanks. High-pressure liquid oxygen and fuel sprayed all over the backside of the main booster engine. The resulting fireball was inevitable. Several marines made it clear; most didn't. Those that did get clear were horribly burned. *Those that didn't get clear were the lucky ones*, he thought.

Help was slow to arrive as bullets were still firing randomly, and few wanted to chance that kind of risk. The main fuel cell cracked open in the intense heat, and the lighter exploded with a visible shock wave, scattering flesh, metal, and debris in a huge radius. A thick pall of smoke hung over the shattered hulk of the lighter. Intermittent and pitiful screams of "Corpsman!" came from the few survivors. Nearby marines rushed to their aid. *Poor bastards.*

Blake felt a hand come down on his shoulder. He looked up and saw 2nd Lieutenant Wicks standing over him. Blake stood quickly and walked to the rear of their lighter. They stood with the lighter between them and the incoming fire. The majority of their bodies were therefore protected, but they peeked around the vehicle as required.

Wicks pointed at the edge of the growth facilities. He had a map of the area in his hand and spoke with his mouth very close to Blake's ear to be heard. "Line of advance. The shattered red post with the two black stripes is the left marker of our assault area at three hundred meters." The officer's hand indicated the direction.

"Seen," was all Blake responded. This acknowledged he could see the place to which Wicks was referring.

Wicks's hand moved right. "The green hut with no door at two hundred fifty meters is the right marker."

"The one behind the half wall, sir?" Blake asked.

Wicks looked again. "Negative. The one in the clear to the left of that."

"Seen."

Wicks continued, now pointing at the map. "I want both fire teams to advance to that line. You take the left, and I shall take the right. From there, we will assault to this line here and establish a supply drop. From there, we will take this avenue and clear these buildings of opposition from here to here. When we reach the T-junction here, we hold the area and wait for the engineers. Once there, we will have a decent view of the enemy shipyards. The supply drop will also be our casualty collection point. The engineers should be arriving in the second wave in thirteen minutes. Questions?"

Blake now knew the exact limits of his area of responsibility and timings. The section would be assaulting and securing a seventy-meter wide area on the outer part of the facility. They were to clear out any enemy units in that area. He didn't see any fire coming from there, but that meant nothing in the overall scheme. They had to go in and make sure any viable enemy threat was eliminated. After that, they would close up and ensure all the buildings were clear. House clearing was not the best job a marine could be given, but no one else was going to do it for them. "No questions, sir."

"Right. They are finished unloading. Grab the kit, and go."

Blake jogged a few steps and got the attention of the marines on his side of the lighter. Within a minute, he had passed on the mission objectives and timings, as well. Moving with practiced efficiency, they collected their half of the stacked supplies and divided it amongst themselves. None of them grumbled about the weight, as no one wanted to make a second trip.

When both groups were ready, the lieutenant motioned to move forward. The squad advanced in line as fast as possible under the loads they carried. The distance was not great, but the stress of being in a combat area added to the strain. Everyone was trying to expect the unexpected, and the troops watched in all directions, looking for dangers both real and perceived.

Blake's fire team arrived at the base of the half wall surrounding the compound and took shelter behind the meter-high obstacle. No enemy fire had been directed at them over their short run, and the mortars were still dropping blindly on the landing site. The marines dropped the surplus equipment against the half wall and prepared for the first assault. Belliveau was Blake's partner during the assault phase and was to Blake's right. Tyler and Johnston hung back as a rear guard ready to rush in if resistance was encountered.

Upon arriving, Blake flipped the transparent eyepiece down. He pressed a stud on the side of his weapon, and a video image appeared on the eyepiece plastic. The rifle had a camera directly in line with the barrel. By using the weapon instead of his head, he could literally see over walls and around corners without exposing himself to danger. The eyepiece had graduated marks to aid in distance determination and aiming. Keeping behind the wall, Blake put the muzzle of the weapon over the top of the mud bricks. Scanning from left to right, he checked the area. Nothing moved. He swept back from right to left when a large figure appeared in a doorway. Training and instinct guided his hand to steady the aiming point onto the figure. Blake didn't see a weapon, but he did see the scaly skin, and that was enough. He squeezed the trigger three times in rapid succession and saw the figure stagger and fall backwards. He saw no subsequent movement.

Blake looked over to Belliveau and saw him pull a fragmentation grenade from his vest. Belliveau was a vet and had been on three successful missions with Blake. Even so, Blake still looked over to check the detonation timing ring was set properly. Combat was a bad place to assume anything. One last vid-scan of the area showed no activity. The sergeant saw the rest of his team was ready.

"Go, go, go!" Blake screamed, and his team scrambled over the wall. They worked in pairs. One of each pair ran up to the nearest doorway and threw a fragmentation grenade across the threshold. The marines hugged the wall just outside the doorway. Two seconds later, the grenade went off, and the ground shook. Without waiting for the dust to settle, the pair entered the building and scanned for the enemy. The first marine to enter the room took responsibility for the left side of the room, the second took the right. Cries of "clear!" could be heard as each pair reported the lack of resistance. When one mud hut was checked, the routine was repeated on the neighboring hut.

Blake ran up to the hut with the prone figure on the ground. Training took over, and he shot the creature twice more at the base of the skull as Belliveau threw a grenade into the hut. A Drakk'Har non-combatant did not exist; they were all dangerous. You never assumed one was dead, and you never left a wounded one behind you. The only movement of the creature was due to the impact of his rounds. Blake took shelter at the side of the door and waited for the blast as Belliveau did the same on the opposite side. A two-second delay seems like a short period of time, but not when one is in combat. While waiting, Blake deactivated his weapons video feed to his eyepiece and flipped it up out of the way. The adrenaline in his system made the two seconds seem to crawl by before the boom of the grenade was felt.

The sergeant ducked through the doorway instantly and swept his half of the room. The hut interior was circular and no more than six meters across. The mud brick walls were two meters in height. At the top of the walls, eight wooden rafters were embedded into the mud brick structure. The rafters joined to a point at the roof peak, with beams strung laterally to give extra support. Over the rafters was a tightly meshed lattice roofing material that had been overlapped to ensure a weather-tight seal. Blake knew from previous operations that this was not designed to keep out water, but the wind. Drakk'Har skin dried out quickly, and shelter from the wind was a necessity when resting away from wetlands. The only access into the building was the doorway, and it was oriented to face away from the prevailing winds.

The thick walls restricted the amount of usable space, and the interior of the hut was sparsely furnished. A raised bed of mud brick with a layer of cut grass on top was at the furthest point from the door. Several oddly shaped clay containers were on the floor around the perimeter of the wall. A cage made of an umber-colored bamboo-like material held several small birds, which were flapping furiously against the bars. The large skull of an unrecognizable animal hung directly opposite the door. The long pointed teeth and thick brow ridges hinted at the savagery it had possessed at one time. An unlit lantern suspended from the rafters swung back and forth from the shock of the grenade blast.

Chips in the walls showed how effective the grenade would have been if any Drakk'Har had been in there. However, the sergeant's bullets had already killed the sole occupant. It looked like a small female to Blake. She wore no clothing or adornments and had no visible weapons. That he had just ended her life was of no moral concern to him. Young or old, male or female, all Drakk'Har were viable targets. After the first violent encounters with the Drakk'Har, a few humans had stood fast and demanded that the various articles of the Geneva Conventions which were originally designed to protect the wounded and suffering on the battlefield be applied to the Drakk'Har, as well.

The argument had raged until the second encounter with the Drakk'Har when the Orbital Cruise ship *Cherubs Song* was boarded by three large warships in their first major incursion into human space. The comprehensive internal vid system had recorded the roundup and slaughter of fourteen hundred unarmed human tourists and crew in great detail. So much so that all reputable news agencies refused to air any but the most benign of the gruesome footage. However, the video was leaked onto the Interwebs, and in a few days, the systematic rounding up of every man, woman, and child on board could be seen by anyone with a home terminal. The video that removed all doubt was a picture of several captives, mostly females, being led away to the Drakk'Har ships. Rumors they were being bred ended all debate. Soon after, every article of the Geneva Conventions was quickly amended to specify that they applied to *Homo sapiens* only. The few humans who still protested were told to take a cruise.

Belliveau moved to search the bed area, which was on his side of the room. Blake walked slowly to the base of the wall. He took the tip of his weapon barrel and flipped off a lid on one of the larger ceramic jars. A thick plug of what looked like wax was revealed with several small holes drilled through. Blake looked closer and was surprised by something that moved inside. The quick movement was violent enough that the heavy jar shuddered. He stepped back quickly with weapon raised. Water splashed up through the holes, and whatever aquatic life form was inside stopped moving. Blake looked over and saw Belliveau standing wide-eyed with his weapon also pointing at the jar. Both men had reacted instinctively at the sudden movement and noise. Both breathed a sigh of relief when nothing happened. Belliveau returned to the bed and Blake searched the other jars. They were looking for weapons, electronics, or anything of intelligence value. Nothing of any consequence was found.

"Clear."

The team moved away from that hut and moved to the next one to repeat the process again and again until all the huts had been searched.

CHAPTER 17 – CONFLICT

Borrk left the security of the bunker to watch the first stages of the warm blood landing off in the fields outside the town. The orbital fire had slackened considerably, and he needed to see what was happening. Borrk was irritated to see that not one craft had been intercepted on the way down to the landing field. Indeed, the amount of fire being directed toward the warm bloods was pitiful, in his opinion. A single craft had been hit, but only after it had landed.

Borrk possessed many facilities that were spread throughout the region, and several of these had failed to report in since the bombardment. He had several hundred Drakk'Har warriors under arms, but many of them were out of contact. The few dozen that had reported in were told to remain in their bunkers and tunnels until a proper picture of the raid could be developed. Borrk would throw away all of the lives of his soldiers in a heartbeat to protect his holdings, but he would do so with reasonable intelligence. A hammer blow was much more effective when several hammers fell simultaneously.

He had no idea what kinds of enemy were around the other facilities, so he could not formulate a plan. He had sent out swimmers to get that information, but they would take time to return, if at all. Being in the main construction facility, he was more concerned with the area immediately around him, but he needed to form an effective offense, and lack of information was a serious problem. Kaaw's absence was sorely felt, and with Drawwl and his troops away securing Kek's compound, no—

Borrk stopped in mid-thought. "You. Has Drawwl reported in since the attack?"

"No, Lord."

The large Drakk'Har considered this. "Order his immediate return. His force is to attack the warm bloods as soon as possible. The rest of the militia shall patrol the growth facilities and ambush warm blood movements where possible. These barbarian invaders will pay dearly."

"Yes, Lord," was the only acceptable response.

* * *

The communication specialist turned away from his wrathful lord. The specialist made sure the farthest antenna array was engaged before transmitting. He transmitted as briefly as possible and listened a lot longer than he should have to minimize the chances of hostile fire. Several times he repeated the sequence, attempting a link with Lord Drawwl. With no response, the creature began to get nervous. Having your predecessor beheaded in front of you was not the best way to achieve promotion, but certainly instructive as to the price of failure. Desperate to carry out his orders, the specialist flipped to a second set of frequencies and tried to raise Kek's command post instead. After all, he reasoned, Drawwl was last heard from in that location, and they were now subjugated under Borrk's command.

* * *

Jacobs occupied one of the outer listening posts on top of Hill 170. He had sedated Mendez an hour before and asked for the two-hour shift to get away from the wounded man. Pratt had agreed, and Jacobs replaced Bennet for his shift. Jacobs needed something to take his mind off recent events, and his being there gave Bennet an extra two hours rest. Of the Special Forces section, Jacobs felt the most at home on this planet. Being from the southern United States, he had lived in and around jungle and swamps all his life. The temperature was much cooler than he was used to and the red sun / pink sky combination was completely alien. However, with the gray clouds, he could not see the sky at present, and enough similarities existed to his own neck of the woods to make him feel comfortable in the terrain.

The listening post was located on the top edge of a sheer rock drop. He was just below a ridge near the summit, and another sheer rock wall was behind him. The ledge between the two vertical granite features was wide enough for him to lie down comfortably. A stump was all that remained of a tree that had grown up on the edge for a few decades before gravity and a windstorm combined to topple it over the edge. It offered good camouflage, with its moss and lichen covering. Behind the stump, Jacobs was in a perfect position to watch the landing lighters off to the west. He had a pair of spotter binoculars and used them to scan his area of responsibility. His eyes were naturally drawn to the movement of the lighters landing, disgorging their cargo, then taking off. However, as the last lighter had departed, he began to concentrate on the surrounding area. The activity on the plains had distracted him somewhat, and that caused him to miss the more subtle movement to the southwest of his position.

From the corner of his eye, Jacobs sensed something moving. He turned and reoriented his binoculars away from the landing site. Just over a half kilometer away, several Drakk'Har were moving large pieces of equipment up the hill. The binoculars had a built-in gyrocompass and laser range finder. He pressed the control, and the distance and direction were displayed in a light green display on the bottom of the lens. Jacobs did not hesitate; he pressed the transmission stud on his COMM unit. He did not bother to check that he was connected to the field wire. He had done that many times on his watch.

"Six, dis is LP Two. Wees got sum compnee. Two four five degrees at six four five meters. Twelve to fourteen crocs pushin' what look like reel heavy 'quipment."

"Stand by," followed by a burst of static, was the only response.

* * *

Pratt appeared beside Jacobs within seconds. The lieutenant kept his body as low as possible as he moved into the listening post. Jacobs handed over the binoculars and pointed wordlessly in the direction of the patrol.

With his altitude, Pratt could see them clearly down in the trees. He stopped counting when he reached twenty and saw more were appearing. They were pushing large pieces of equipment on wagons. Crude canvas covers hid the contents of the carts, and Pratt had to observe a few seconds as he tried to recognize the shapes beneath. The canvas kept him in the dark, however. A quick scan of the few Drakk'Har not pushing told him the convoy was important, though. They carried rail guns, and they were obviously guarding the contents of the carts. That made it a military target. He didn't have to guess where they were going. Their path was unmistakable. They were heading up the same hill he was sitting on.

Pratt hooked into the field wire before hitting his COMM unit activation stud. "Williams, hook up the dish, and get me a direct link to fleet. We have a fire mission."

* * *

Kaaw arrived at the bunker complex near the base of Skull Ridge. The buried entrance had only been unearthed moments before, and the air was dank and fetid. Such things did not disturb the Drakk'Har anti-air commander, however. His staff labored to set up and test—but not transmit on—the communication equipment. Landlines between all anti-air positions were tested regularly, and they primarily were used to communicate. The radio sets were there for backup purposes only, in case the cables were cut.

The remainder of his unit had proceeded to the trail up Skull Ridge. The carts they used to transport the anti-air missile batteries were crude, but incredibly strong and resilient. Once employed on top of the high ground, the price for invading his lord's holdings would be exacted. Cables were hooked up to the mobile electronics, and gauges began to flicker into life.

Well-camouflaged observation positions began to use the land lines to report warm blood activity. Of the mortars that had begun firing on the plains, two had already been silenced and only two remained. Their fire had become much more effective, and with no aircraft to target anymore, warm blood units were on the edge of the town.

While not exactly happy, Kaaw was not disappointed, either. His training had paid off, and his units were occupying the two hills in a fairly timely manner. Obviously, it would never be fast enough for him, but progress was being made, and that was all that mattered. The warm bloods had struck effectively in the opening stages of the fight, and they had the initiative. That would soon change when his network of anti-air missile defenses went active.

* * *

Statistically, the rapidly moving Gecko communications probe survived much longer than it should have. Even though it had moderate shields to sweep aside dust fragments, the shields were much more effective at lower speeds. The probe was traveling at over ninety percent of the speed of light, and at that speed, no shields could ever be one hundred percent effective. The probe had not been programmed to slow down, as delivery of the message was deemed to be high priority.

A piece of rock from a long-dead comet, no larger than a grain of rice, was encountered. The amount of force exerted by the impact was astronomical. Not caring about the import of the probe, or its mission, the pebble shredded the probe body. All that remained was rapidly tumbling debris, and a cloud of slowly expanding fuel vapor. The message that was transmitting up to that point carried on toward Mindon-2 at light speed, but that was still hours away from the Fleet.

* * *

Captain Levin loitered in an oval racetrack pattern at twenty-five hundred meters altitude. The throttles were pulled back to the minimum necessary thrust to keep fuel consumption to a minimum. All countermeasures were ready and in standby mode for immediate use. Every sixty seconds, a directional pulsed transmission was directed toward the Fleet. The lighter's position, remaining weapons load, fuel amount, and other pertinent data was sent to the Operations computers in the Fleet to keep them updated. Engine temperature, outside humidity, temperature, and wind conditions were all transmitted back to the mainframes that digested the information and correlated it into the big picture. Each lighter was, in effect, a small intelligence collection device.

The COMM link was quantum encrypted through diamond core CPUs. Being directional, the signal was also hard to intercept, unless you were between the lighters and the Fleet. This kept the Operations staff in the loop as to capabilities of the forces at their disposal. On one of the green status monitors in the cockpit, the same information was repeated to keep the aircrew aware of their limits. In the left corner of that screen, Levin read 'TTF: 01:37' – DTF: 444.6 KM. 'TTF' meant Time to Fly. This told him that at present rate of fuel consumption he could remain in position for an hour and thirty-seven minutes before he exhausted his fuel, and then he had to either land or activate the main booster to return to orbit. 'DTF' was Distance to Fly or how far he could travel in kilometers from this spot using the aero-engines at present speed. Both the DTF and TTF numbers slowly decreased as time passed.

Captain Levin was flying alone at the moment. The rest of Grasshopper flight was still being refueled and rearmed at the firebase established on an abandoned rocky peninsula seventy kilometers to the south. They were not due back for at least twenty minutes.

Grasshopper One still carried its load of anti-personnel bombs, and he would ordinarily stay in the area until ordnance was expended or until lack of fuel forced him to retreat. His path took him around the periphery of the growth facilities. His stubby left wings perpetually pointed down at the facility as he orbited around counter-clockwise. Levin mechanically swiveled his attention from flight instruments to the skies around him, to the ground below, then back to the instruments again. He paid less attention to the engine instrument cluster, but only because he knew his flight engineer was conscientious, and apart from watching for enemy weapons fire on his side of the vessel, Wallace never looked away from the instruments.

Levin did keep a close watch on the RADAR display. Threats could appear from any direction without warning. The on-board computers kept recalculating his course and gave steering prompts to a heads-up display, or HUD, in front of both Levin and Wallace. Levin ignored the HUD, as the autopilot was taking the course corrections and automatically maintaining the recommended speed and altitude without his input.

Below him, the plains were clear of the landing force. The single shattered lighter remained and still burned, casting a thick black pillar of smoke straight up into the air. Several dozen dark impact craters showed where the scattered mortar rounds had landed during the landings. He was high enough that he could see individual huts and structures divided by paths and roads, but he saw no movement, human or otherwise. The fighting was in the hands of the marines at the moment, and from the little he had heard, the ground battle was going fairly well. Calls for medevac flights were limited, and no one was screaming for resupply or pickup. Even the

Fleet training exercises were more eventful than this, he mused. *Combat: hours of boredom followed by moments of sheer terror,* thought the pilot as he cast his gaze around the skies once more.

A two-tone alarm went off for two seconds, bringing his attention back to the screens in front on him. His orders were already displayed on the center console. Fleet Operations had just given him a new tasking. The screen read:

MISSION: GROUND SUPPORT
TARGET: SUPPLY CONVOY (20+ PERS)
THREAT: LOW
GRID: GREEN 023574
PROXIMITY: AMBER
FREQ: 2978 – C/S JUNIPER - RESERVED

The first two lines told Levin what his mission and target was: A supply convoy of twenty or more Drakk'Har. The assumed threat level was low, which was terribly subjective, as Levin knew very well. The grid reference was located at the base of a small hill, and proximity to friendly troops was AMBER which meant allied troops were within a kilometer of the target. A proximity of RED indicated friendly forces within a hundred meters of the target, and BLACK meant no measurable separation between the two. The last line told him his ground controller was JUNIPER and the tactical frequency to use. It was also a reserved channel that would be used exclusively by them to minimize confusion with other units.

Up to this point, computers had done the work. That was done for speed and efficiency. However, one did not deliver ordinance in a war zone automatically. Even where friendly fire was unlikely, having a human in the loop never hurt.

Levin changed radio frequencies on a control dial while simultaneously toggling the internal intercom. "Crew, prepare for air-to-ground operations," was all he said before keying the switch to transmit on the designated tactical frequency.

* * *

Pratt was on the hilltop, prepared for his role. After the data connection to the Fleet had been made, he connected his COMM unit onto the nearby field wire. The wire tied him into the communications dish that connected them to Fleet. His compact headset and voice-activated microphone combination was already in place and plugged into his COMM unit. He could talk without using his hands. Pratt had his binoculars in his hands and elbow on an exposed root for support.

Williams came over the headset. "Sir, connection with air support is made. Our call sign is Juniper. Lighter is Grasshopper One."

Pratt spoke into his microphone, "Grasshopper One, this is Juniper, over." Pratt noticed a delay in the response. The signal from his radio was not going directly to the lighter. As a special ops unit, they were supposed to remain unseen. The radio signal left from his COMM unit down the field wire to the dish. From there, the signal was transmitted in a tight directional beam that went up to the Fleet above. After a two-thirds of a second delay, it was relayed back down to the lighter.

"Juniper, this is Grasshopper One." A burst of static indicated that Grasshopper One had released the microphone, and it crackled in Pratt's headset as he watched the enemy formation through the binoculars.

"Grasshopper One, this is Juniper reading you loud and clear. We have a convoy of crocs and equipment traveling southeast on the foothills of Hill 170. We are located on the crest of Hill 170, and it looks like they are heading up here, as well. What is your status?"

"Juniper, we have a loadout of fourteen GBC Mark XII's and are holding at a distance of three kilometers to your west, altitude one thousand meters."

"Grasshopper One, roger. Total length of the convoy is one hundred and fifty meters. I will paint the last cart in the column. Laser freq is 279. Recommend attack vector of one two zero degrees."

"Juniper, roger. Attack vector of one two zero. 279 on the laser. Engaging in two minutes. Out."

* * *

Captain Levin finished entering the target information on the lighter screen and eased the lighter to the recommended heading of one hundred twenty degrees. That course would hopefully put them directly over the small group of Drakk'Har. Levin would make last-minute course adjustments as required, but the job of the ground controller was to put the aircraft as close to the target as possible. If the course were too far off, Levin would have to abort his run and make another. By then the enemy would be alerted and scattering, making his second run that much harder.

As the lighter turned, Levin had a reference screen open on a smaller monitor. The chart was specific to the GBC series of bombs. Levin selected one thousand meters as the attack altitude and punched in fourteen as the number of weapons. The screen cleared, and a second grid of numbers appeared. Across the top of the new grid was attack velocity. Along the side was the distance spread for the attack. He looked across to four hundred fifty kilometers per hour, then down to see where it intersected with the two-hundred-meter row. He had been told the convoy was only one hundred fifty meters long, but it never hurt to spread out the attack a little to cover more area. The resulting number was entered into the attack computer that would time the individual weapon release to cover that area. Last, he set the computer to look for a laser set on frequency 279.

Levin double-checked everything was entered correctly from his notes. As the nose of the lighter came to one hundred twenty degrees, he pressed the throttles forward and accelerated to four hundred fifty kilometers per hour. The TTF and DTF numbers decreased significantly on the readouts. The terrain-following autopilot was engaged, and the navigation computers would keep the lighter at four hundred fifty kilometers per hour and one thousand meters altitude unless overridden by the pilot. This allowed Levin to concentrate on minor course corrections and ensure proper weapon delivery.

If everything went to plan, the lighter would come up behind the convoy and release the weapons from the back to the front along their path of travel. With luck, they would taken by surprise and never even know they were dead.

* * *

Pratt ran his binoculars over the convoy one last time. They were still on the same course he had recommended, so he placed the last cart in the line in the crosshairs and pressed the activation stud for the laser designator. An invisible coherent beam of infrared light lanced out and hit the last cart on its canvas cover. The beam scattered upon impact, and the laser energy traveled in all directions. With the proper equipment, the scattered light would be seen and used as a point of reference. If the target was hard, like a well-camouflaged bunker or armored vehicle, then a single weapon could ride the beam and strike it precisely. However, in this case, cluster munitions were being used over a wide area. They still needed a point of reference, though, and the point of laser light served that purpose nicely.

The lieutenant concentrated on keeping his beam on the last cart. He had trained for this job many times in exercises, but this was his first combat strike. He had even ridden in a lighter during a simulated strike to familiarize himself with the pilot's role, and he appreciated how hard this process was on the pilot flying the lighter. Technology helped without doubt. Computers did the lion's share of the decision-making, but in the end, a human being pressed the weapon release stud.

* * *

Captain Levin saw the target convoy only seconds before the scheduled release. He made a slight rudder correction to the ship's course, and when satisfied they were in line, he pressed the weapon release switch.

Nothing happened initially; the pressing of the switch simply told the weapons computer that it could proceed with the attack. In the nose of the lighter, a device tracked the position of the received laser light. It calculated the position relative to the lighter flight path and passed that information on to the weapons computer. In turn, the weapons computer determined that the position of the target was within parameters, and it tracked the time to release in thousandth of a second increments. When the counter reached zero, pulses went out to the individual weapons at pre-designated times, and they were ejected from the racks.

No parachutes emerged this time. The altitude of the attacking craft gave it a safe distance from the blasts, and they were not deployed. The canisters fell and separated just above the ground. Only one Drakk'Har guard saw the lighter and the objects falling from its belly, but he was so stunned at the sight that he never had a chance to voice a warning. Not that a warning would have made any difference, as the speed of the weapons descent left no time to do anything of consequence.

The weapons devastated the Drakk'Har column, blasting them into oblivion. The radius of the anti-personnel weapons overlapped by a wide margin. A scythe of fire and metal fragments cut down every living thing as it passed. The carts holding the replacement anti-air missiles were struck, and their fuel exploded, adding to the inferno. Several of their rocket motors activated, and they flew off in a wild and erratic fashion. The rest of the equipment was shattered by the blasts and rendered useless. Levin did not think there could be serviceable components remaining or anyone left to use them.

"Grasshopper One, this is Juniper. Beautiful hit! Lots of secondary explosions. Ten out of ten!"

* * *

"Roger, Juniper. Thanks for the assist. Out."

Captain Levin turned his lighter toward the firebase. He didn't bother throttling back the engines. He had lots of fuel for the transit, and he wanted to rejoin his flight as soon as possible.

* * *

Kaaw had felt the impact of the multiple bombs through the pads of his feet. He knew the significance well before he received the reports of the destruction of a third of his remaining anti-air forces. His reinforced bunker suffered no damage, but Kaaw would have happily sacrificed the bunker to have the destroyed equipment back. Kaaw accepted the destruction with a resigned air. He had expected to have heavy losses, albeit not this early. His plan of setting up a network of coordinated air strike units occupying the high ground had just been ruined in a few seconds.

An aide reported that the units on Brawnik's Hump had arrived and would be sited within their fortified positions soon. Communication links were active over landlines, and those forces had suffered no enemy attacks to this point. Kaaw directed all spare ammunition, equipment, and personnel to that location. His personal guard had several shoulder-fired missiles, and he directed the sentries to use them if any enemy craft came within range. While they had limited range, they were better than nothing. Kaaw fumed that was all he had left. He considered moving his command post to Brawnik's Hump, but decided against it. Kaaw had secure communications here with his remaining unit, and trying to run an air battle on the move was difficult, given the size of Drakk'Har transmitters. He never considered informing Borrk of the losses.

CHAPTER 18 – CHANCE

Major Jonathan Paul Stanley was nervous, but he hid it well. He piloted his lighter at twenty-five hundred meters above the ground with his eyes continually scanning the instrument cluster before him. He didn't bother doing visual checks outside the cockpit. He was seventeen hundred meters above the tallest land feature, and his flight path purposely kept him away from all active battle areas. Stanley's concentration was exclusively dedicated to all of the electronic sensors and navigation aids on his side of the flight deck.

His lighter was quite different from the standard model. It had two extra generators and an air conditioning unit for the equipment in the cargo bay. Powerful electronic warfare jammers were suspended under the rear engine pods. Stanley's lighter had no armaments. It had never had the necessary racks and connectors installed. Extended-range fuel tanks had been put in their place, along with additional equipment, power conduits, and air vents. Additional composite armor was installed around the cargo bay and flight deck.

Stanley was in no way concerned about his personal safety. Nor were the battles below of any real concern. His sole concern was his passengers and their equipment strapped in securely behind him in the cargo compartment. Major J.P.

Stanley was the pilot for the II Division command center. General Richard Carstairs and his headquarters staff were in the cargo area coordinating the actions of the various unit headquarters under their command.

* * *

The lighter was packed full of officers and ratings who were coordinating II Division in the field. Communications specialists kept the airwaves full of coded transmissions sending orders and receiving reports. An intelligence officer coordinated threat and target assessment. A logistics expert made sure supplies were delivered where they were needed. Two radiomen kept voice channels open to whatever unit required support, while a forward air coordinator directed air strikes and supporting fire. The results of the combat as it unfolded were displayed on large monitors in various formats.

Data arrived from all parts of II Division's area in standard datasets. The orbiting fleet provided overhead imagery and electronic intercepts. Pilotless drones operated from the firebase by battalion intelligence sent live video of the battlefield where needed. Reports from combat units, lighters, and observers were assessed, classified, and added to the overall picture. Symbols on the larger monitors provided an up-to-date picture of the battle area with positions of ground units displayed. The last member of the mobile command center was General Carstairs's *Aide-de-camp*. He was wedged in a rear-facing jump seat, slumped down in a back corner snoring quietly, as he was currently unneeded.

General Carstairs sat with his chair restraints ratcheted tightly about him. The minor turbulence that occasionally shook the aircraft was a minor irritation, and his restraints kept him securely in his seat. Carstairs and his staff were not in the standard web restraints typically found in other lighters. Each of their chairs had armored backs and sides to absorb as much battle damage as possible. They were adjustable to a wide variety of positions and height. The chairs were fairly comfortable to endure the long periods of immobility. The only parts of the general's body that moved were his hands as they manipulated the screens and his eyes as he took in the information. He was used to the displays and their rapid information feed. As each new piece of information arrived, his brain sorted its importance relative to the situation at the time. Minor, trivial bits of data seen hours before became all-important when another small piece of the puzzle was seen. Similarly, the most earth-shaking data became insignificant in minutes. He was working on an ever-evolving tapestry, and it took a well-trained brain to sort through it. Carstairs was a master.

General Carstairs and the rest of his staff were optimistic after the opening moves of the conflict. Drakk'Har opposition was much less than expected, and Carstairs credited that to the fury and accuracy of the opening aerial bombardment. General Chew's untimely demise and subsequent reduction of the landing zones allowed a heavier bombardment in General Carstairs's areas. His troops were reaping a high dividend from that. Many enemy units had been wiped out prior to a single combat boot touching the surface of the planet. Now that his troops were actually assaulting Drakk'Har positions, he was happy to see they were having a relatively easy time.

Initial casualty rates on the ground had been light—surprisingly so. In the II Division area, only seven ground combat deaths had occurred to this point. Six were killed in the lighter hit by the mortar round, and the only other death had been a rather overbearing officer who died in a friendly fire grenade blast. There would be an investigation over that incident, but ever since soldiers carried weapons, there had been "accidents" like that. A number of wounded had the inevitable blunt and penetrating traumas— the typical assortment of sprains, burns, breaks, and wounds. Up to this point, the wounded were on par with an operational exercise.

There had been such a lack of effective counterattacks that the intelligence arm was scrambling to find out why their assessments were so far out of whack. As this was a prime construction facility for the Drakk'Har, they were expecting much fiercer resistance. Their radio intercepts suggested significant forces present prior to the landing. When little resistance materialized, it cast doubt on other assessments, and they needed to close the gap before marines started losing their lives. The optimists credited the lack of opposition to a better than average bombardment, while the pessimists looked for concealed forces in every new piece of intelligence. Neither side could say definitively what comprised the surviving enemy forces. Military intelligence still remained an oxymoron.

* * *

In the air, losses were mounting. The majority of the emplaced anti-air batteries had all but been destroyed in the opening orbital bombardment. However, portable shoulder-mounted anti-air missiles were starting to take their toll on the lighter force planet-wide. Single warriors were hidden in the brush and well-camouflaged. When they saw a target of opportunity, they could attack without warning and with relative impunity. This was why Stanley was nervous and kept his gaze on the countermeasures panel.

Stanley reached the end of his flight track and turned toward his new heading. His new flight path was displayed on the heads-up display in front of him. The major could see the track passed a minor hill designated as 170. He could see symbols indicating friendly forces occupied the hilltop. No enemy symbols were displayed except a few inside of the small town nearby.

* * *

Sergeant Blake and LCPL Belliveau were in that town. They had finished searching their last assigned hut in the crude street. Blake was feeling thankful, as no one in his unit had encountered any enemy activity to this point. At one point, they had heard a Drakk'Har rail gun in the distance, but the sound was not repeated. *Looks like they don't want a fight,* thought the veteran marine.

With his primary job done, the sergeant took a look in the town while waiting for the rest of the squads to complete their sweeps. Blake was surrounded by small huts that he assumed comprised a Drakk'Har residential neighborhood. The huts were separated by no more than a meter of open space. Bones and rotting piles of unrecognizable animals were in-between the hut walls. The smell was repulsive when you got close to it. Thankfully, a slight breeze at his back kept the worse of the stench away from him. Looking behind, he could see the engineers assigned to the area moving up slowly. They would not move ahead until cleared by the lieutenant. That was fine with Blake, as he wanted them well out of the way if trouble started. Off in the distance, a lighter was visible high in the sky, turning south in a gentle arc.

* * *

A perimeter guard for Kaaw's command bunker was half-lying in a prepared position. The small hole was designed to hold only one Drakk'Har soldier. He had decent overhead cover, and if he slunk back into the small hole, he would be very well-concealed. A thick layer of branches, mud, and plants provided protection against attack. The hole was dug just under the ridge of a small rise, allowing him a decent view of the plains below. He saw a warm blood craft turn high above him. The soldier also noted the craft was just barely within weapons range. He had no communications equipment to report the sighting, but he did have several anti-air missiles and standing orders to use them. He decided to use an optically guided missile rather than a heat seeker.

The soldier put his rail gun aside and picked up a long tube resting on the earth at the entrance. He had already fixed a detachable sight onto the shaft of a missile body. It had an optical sight that was simple to use. You pointed the weapon at the target and half-squeezed the trigger to activate targeting.

When the handle vibrated, indicating a lock-on, you squeezed the trigger completely to fire. The soldier was not very well-trained, but Drakk'Har weaponry was designed for simple operation. All the soldier had to do was point the weapon in the general direction of an aircraft and squeeze a trigger.

Once the trigger had been half-pressed, the sight electronics passed navigational information to the missile to program its flight path. Internal gyroscopes spun up to keep the missile stable in flight. When the trigger was fully pressed, the firing command was sent. An explosive booster at the base of the tube fired and carried the missile up through the tube. The thin protective cap shattered as the aerodynamic nose of the weapon hit the weather-tight ceramic cover. The booster carried the missile forward until it cleared the lip of the launch tube. At that point, the booster ran out of fuel and fell away, its job complete. The main rocket motor fired, and the missile began climbing at a phenomenal rate of speed. The seeking head in the missile nose engaged, and what could be described as a crude camera began tracking for a target in the skies above.

* * *

Countermeasure pods on the rear of the command lighter used low-power microwave RADAR beams to probe the skies around them. They were set to ignore any target moving under three hundred kilometers per hour. The missile approached at twelve hundred kilometers per hour. Major Stanley saw the alarm light and knew his craft was under attack. He overrode the autopilot and threw the lighter into a tight right-hand bank.

The countermeasures on board his craft kicked in automatically. Flares and chaff were fired out of canisters mounted on the lighter belly. The jammer pods on the rear of the lighter compared the speed and approach vector of the target and quickly classified the type of threat. Federation technology was adept at configuring itself to the various attacks they encountered. In milliseconds, the lighter knew the vector, speed, and flight profile of the incoming missile. It also determined that the lighter was the target, which set off a series of self-defense programs. It carried an internal database, and from that, the computer decided what actions to take to defeat the incoming threat. The lighter's countermeasure systems performed exactly as they were supposed to. Small flares were ejected to confuse the seeker head. Clouds of metal foil were released to stop any RADAR returns, and jammers beamed confusing signals at the incoming weapon. Any Federation missile would have been hard-pressed to penetrate the defenses.

The problem was the missile heading toward them was based on Drakk'Har technology. The human engineers had designed their systems to react to the behavior of Federation-based weapons. Drakk'Har weapons were radically different in design. The missile did not use electromagnetic means to find a target, so the chaff and jammers were useless. The seeker was uncomplicated; it looked for simple differences in contrast. The seeker head was organic: an actual eye surgically removed from a large bird. It had been genetically altered and chemically interfaced with an electronic package that steered the missile onto its target. Simple logic was programmed into the steering components. It knew the pink sky was bright and anything darker than the sky was a target. Like a boat in a heavy fog, it could see the lighthouse because of the difference in light levels. A dark lighter contrasted against a light sky was easily detected. The missiles were effective during the day, but in inclement weather or darkness, they were useless, as the relative differences in contrast were too small to discern. The flares that were released as the lighter flew along were slightly effective, but the missile was looking for dark spots against a bright sky. Its logic ignored bright spots and carried on relentlessly.

When the missile came within a half kilometer, a laser on one of the jamming pods locked onto the incoming missile. Powerful coherent laser light was beamed toward the seeker head, and the eye was blinded instantly. Without steering control inputs, the missile began to fly wildly. At this point, the missile was technically no longer a threat, but in this instance, Lady Luck sided with the Drakk'Har. The rocket motor was still functional, and its random flight took it directly toward the lighter.

The Drakk'Har missile struck directly between the two rear jammers before detonating. The high-explosive warhead caused the back end of the lighter to leap upwards momentarily as the force of the blast ripped into the rear section of the craft. The armor around the cargo bay defeated the shrapnel and protected the occupants, but both rear aero-engines were destroyed, and the orbital booster blown off completely. The general's aide awoke with a lurch, completely bewildered as to what was going on. The drastic maneuvering and loud explosion told the occupants of the cargo area that they were under attack. The monitors and the flow of information coming across them were ignored as personal survival became more important.

* * *

On the lighter flight deck, Stanley knew he was in trouble. Numerous red and amber lights were flashing on the engine instrument cluster between him and the flight engineer, accompanied by several loud alarms. With the two rear engines gone, the lighter was now flying at a sharp nose-up angle, and it was not a question of whether he would go down or not, but how hard the landing would be. The damaged engines were causing collateral damage on the craft. Hydraulic pressure was bleeding away slowly, fuel was being lost, and he was unsure of his flight controls, which felt sluggish. Given less damage, the best option would have been to try to light the booster rocket and try for orbit. However, he knew that option was unavailable, as the booster engine status lights were also blinking red, and he was nowhere near the altitude he needed for an orbital insertion burn. He calculated they had less than two minutes of flight time.

Stanley twisted a large panel knob to EMERGENCY. A beacon began transmitting a locator beam on a reserved channel. Every lighter in range and the fleet above would know he was having critical problems. His only communication to the crew and passengers was, "Prepare for crash landing!"

He left his flight engineer to deal with all damaged or non-functional equipment while he looked for a place to set down. The lighter shuddered as it descended. Stanley scanned the terrain around him. In every direction were rolling hills and lots of trees. He knew that the nearest safe-landing zone was the firebase seventy kilometers to the north, and that was not possible given the condition of the craft.

Major Stanley moved his attention to the cockpit instruments. A navigation screen was brought up on the largest monitor. Stanley brought up a terrain map with an overlay for all units in the area. The closest friendly unit occupied the top of a hilltop. Stanley saw the SF designator telling him it was a Special Forces unit. However, his choice was severely limited. Land near the SF unit or try for the more distant plains outside the town where the troops had landed earlier. Those lighters were long gone, but the smoke from the lighter destroyed earlier in the day was still quite visible. His altitude was dropping quickly, the town was behind him, and he would lose a lot of altitude turning; too much. He made up his mind instantly. It would have to be the hill, as that was almost straight ahead and required minimal maneuvering.

Stanley still had forward momentum, but the rear of the craft was starting to droop badly. The small airfoils on the rear of the lighter were getting less and less effective as the speed bled off. In truth, their effectiveness at any speed was low. He could apply more power, but that would increase speed and therefore do more damage on impact. The major rode a knife's edge between stalling and controllability as he tried to compromise his way down out of the sky. He began to make minor corrections in course. He had no time to try to contact the unit on the ground to find out exactly where they were located. Stanley nudged the nose down slightly, the hill came into view, and he could see the two low peaks. One was slightly higher than the other, with a slight depression that had a rough saddle shape between them. Stanley instinctively aimed for the saddle, but recognized he would probably not make it that far. He hoped if anyone was there, they had time to get out of the way.

Within seconds, the belly of the lighter was scraping the trees. As soon as he felt the first branches strike his craft, Stanley cut fuel to the front engines to minimize the fire hazard, and the vessel dropped like a stone into a thick grove of trees. Branches broke like matchsticks under the weight of the lighter. The rear of the craft struck the ground, jarring the occupants, then a moment later, the front smacked into the hill. Brush and small trees were scraped from the ground as the lighter bulldozed its way along. The occupants screamed incoherently as the severe forces rippled through them. A large granite boulder hit the right side of the lighter. The flight engineer was crushed in his seat and killed instantly, while Major Stanley's legs were pinned, then partially severed by parts of the center instrument panel. The lighter spun to the left slightly and then stopped, its momentum finally checked. It ended up resting only a few degrees off level. Major J.P. Stanley had the satisfaction of knowing he had gotten his passengers down safely before he went unconscious from the shock.

* * *

Lieutenant Pratt's first thought was that a medevac flight was finally coming to take Mendez off his hands. That impression lasted less than a second when he recognized the steep angle of approach and saw black smoke coming from the hind end of the craft. He could see the lighter would strike the hill just below his position. Someone shouted a warning, and everyone in the unit scrambled for cover. Pratt watched the lighter glide down out of sight of his position, then felt the impact vibrate the ground. It had landed no more than ten meters from the edge of the hill before sliding and then striking the granite. Thankfully, he saw no explosion or visible flame.

The lieutenant's shouting got everyone's attention. "Smith, Popov, Jacobs! Get down there, and see if the crew is OK. I'll be right behind you. Bennet, take over in LP2." Grabbing their packs, Sergeant Smith and his two companions ran down the hill toward the crash.

"Williams, get Fleet on the dish, and let them know we have a Fallen Angel. Make sure to tell them it is down in our lines. The rest of you, stand to and keep watch. We just had our location broadcast to the world, and we might be getting company."

* * *

General Carstairs tried to stand up several times and was thoroughly confused why he couldn't before realizing he was still strapped into his chair. Sense seemed to return all at once, and he realized where he was. While the rear compartment had not been breached in either the missile explosion or crash, the back end of the lighter was a mess. Only dim red emergency lighting was on, giving an eerie illumination. A coffee canister had cracked, throwing a huge stain along a wall. It looked to him like blood in the red glow. Several monitors that had been loosened from their mounts for easy positioning had been thrown clear of their supports. Glass and plastic shards from one of the screens were scattered throughout the compartment. Communication cords and headsets were haphazardly tossed around. One keyboard panel was bent upwards at a severe angle, with a technician's arm jammed in the metal.

A quick look around showed the general that his staff was alive, at least. Some were making noises from pain and discomfort and others were quiet, but they were all moving.

Carstairs released his harness restraints and stood. He was near the front of the aircraft, and with two steps, he was able to look to the cockpit. The flight engineer was obviously beyond hope. His body was wedged between a chunk of granite and the back wall of the flight deck. Carstairs could not fit a hand width between them.

On the left side of the cockpit, the pilot lay unconscious, covered in blood from the waist down. Carstairs felt for a pulse with the tips of two fingers against Stanley's neck and thought he felt a weak one. He didn't pause to double check, as time was the pilot's enemy right now. The general could not get to the pilot due to the twisted debris, so he went back into the cargo area. He grabbed a first aid kit, looping the handle over his shoulder. Then he grabbed the locking handle of the loading hatch and opened it. The hatch pulled in and slid smoothly back. Carstairs went outside into the torn up earth and surviving grass.

Shattered tree branches lay around him, and he could see the craft rested in a deep gouge in the mud. The belly of the lighter was bent and distorted, but he could see remarkably little damage. Carstairs moved around to the pilot's side of the lighter. Below the window was a yellow banner that read 'EMERGENCY ACCESS HERE,' with an arrow pointing to a small panel. Carstairs opened the panel that had alternating yellow and black ribbon markings around it. An oversized metal handle was inside, resting in two metal clips with a cable attached. The general put his hand through the handle and pulled it free. He walked away from the craft, pulling the cable with him. When three meters of cable was exposed, the line went taught. He gave the wire a sharp pull, and explosive bolts on the pilot's hatch fired with a dull WHUMP. The pilot door hatch separated and fell to the ground, exposing the pilot. Carstairs ran to the wounded man.

The general reached in to undo the pilot's harness when a stranger appeared beside him in camouflage uniform and a rifle. "We saw you come down. I am Smith of the 154th. I have a medic with me. Damn—"

Carstairs saw the sergeant blanch visibly when he looked inside the cockpit. The crushed man on the opposite side of the cockpit and the condition of the pilot took away all words for a moment. Smith keyed his radio. "Jacobs, I need you here! How many on board?"

Carstairs did not even turn to look at the newcomer. With the leg wounds, every second resulted in lower blood pressure. It would not be long before the pilot's body began to shut down. "There are eleven all together. One dead. I have a man with a trapped arm inside, but he can wait. I need this pilot looked after. J.P. saved all of us. Grab the first aid kit."

"Right," was all Smith could say before a medic unceremoniously pushed the general and Smith out of the way. He had a handful of aero-gel combat bandages and surgical tubing in hand.

* * *

Smith stepped back to give Jacobs room, but also to get away from the grisly scene. He watched as Jacobs worked, efficiently staunching the blood flow on the legs. Jacobs had been a combat medic for several years, and Smith trusted him implicitly. Jacobs gave sharp, short, and direct instructions to the older man holding the pilot, and the man followed directions unquestioningly.

Smith realized Corporal Popov was standing behind them. "Popov, get inside and help where you can. If they're wounded, leave them where they are; otherwise, get the crew out. Let me know if you need a hand." Popov disappeared through the hatch.

* * *

Lieutenant Pratt appeared behind the group with his weapon held loosely. "Sergeant, what do we have?"

Smith replied quickly, "Sir, we have eleven people on the lighter. One dead and the pilot is busted up badly. One man with a trapped arm inside. Popov is in there now."

The older man working with Jacobs looked over his shoulder at the officer; Pratt could see the man scanning his rank insignia before he turned back to help Jacobs. "Lieutenant, I need you to contact fleet and get a medevac lighter here ASAP. Use channel 4700 with call sign Olympus. I also want a couple of kilos of plastic explosive rigged in the back end. At the first sign of enemy activity, I want the equipment in this lighter destroyed. How many troops do you have here?"

Pratt was taken aback by the stream of orders. He was unable to see the collar or rank insignia of the man, as he was assisting Jacobs and had his back to him. Not knowing with whom he was dealing, he decided to be polite for the time-being. "Ten, all ranks. We've been waiting all day for a medevac flight for one of our men. What makes you think they'll give you one?"

"Just use that call sign, son. They can take your man up, as well."

"Forgive me, but you are?"

"General Carstairs, Second Marine Division. Oh, and tell them I'll need a new command lighter, too."

* * *

The cool mud of the relaxation pit was getting uncomfortable. Drawwl's body temperature had been reduced significantly as he lounged in the mire. Drawwl began to move from the pit and slid into the swirling rinse tank. Clouds of dirt appeared around him as the water rinsed his body clear of the wet earth. Drawwl slid from the rinse water quickly. He planned on lying in the sun for a while to let his body warm up in the rays.

The door opened, and before Drawwl could shriek at whoever had disturbed him, he saw Kek, prone with his chin against the ground.

Drawwl took his time. He used the scale scraper, even though he typically didn't. He wanted Kek to know who was in command. Keeping him on the ground was a valuable object lesson for the subjugated commander.

Drawwl slid up to the doorway and spoke. "Why do you disturb my rest? Speak, worm."

Kek did not move from his subservient position as he replied, "My Lord, the Great Swamp Master Borrk commands your troops engage the warm bloods assaulting the growth facilities. You are to take your forces and strike from the east, then secure the town and production areas as soon as possible."

Drawwl was taken aback by this news. No radio of his was even turned on, and a swimmer could not have made it to his position from Borrk this quickly. "How did the orders arrive, pond scum?"

"Lord, Swamp Master Borrk radioed the orders to my command post. He also commands you to acknowledge his orders immediately."

"Get out!" roared Drawwl with fury.

Kek left quickly, retreating backwards down the short corridor as the door closed of its own accord. Drawwl had commanded *his* unit's radios be shut down, but he had neglected to tell Kek to do the same. A stupid error that would now cost him. He had few options. Even killing Kek would not stop the order. It had been witnessed by several of his staff, no doubt, and recorded in their logs. No, he had no choice but to obey.

Drawwl left the pit area screaming for his troop commanders. The decision to take the majority of Kek's troops with him was already made. If he was going to attack, he would use overwhelming force and Kek's troops would be suitable fodder for his own soldiers' follow-on assault.

Drawwl didn't need maps, as he knew the terrain well and had excellent guides. Before he threw any troops into a battle, he needed to find out what was going on around the town and where the warm bloods were. He needed a piece of high ground to get that info. Only one piece of suitable terrain existed between him and the growth facilities. Drawwl began to plan the steps in his mind. First, he had to acknowledge the orders. Drawwl would do that only after he had left the compound. If his radio signal caused a violent reaction from the orbiting enemy, then it would strike an empty field. Then, he had to take his combined force to the crest of Skull Ridge to oversee the plains and town below.

* * *

Several repetitions of the signal from the Gecko probe finally touched the receiving antennas of several orbiting Federation ships. The radio transmissions were sent to a decryption mainframe in the communications center of the *Aristotle,* where each fragment was compared to the rest and errant bits discarded. The first layer of encryption was then removed, and a message header was read. The header held the message priority, destination, and the time-date that the signal was sent. The remainder of the message was still coded, but the message header told the computer to not care about that. It simply directed the message onto the recipient without further processing.

The message was then sent through a series of network connections. After being received on the command deck, it went through a second decryption process, where the rest of the message was revealed. Marshal Kosnov was in his command chair when the two-tone alert for a priority incoming message was heard. Kosnov punched in his personal decryption code, and the message text displayed on the screen built into his armrest. The display was angled so that only he could see the text.

%%%%%%%%%%%xx291-HHER-262887-EDDx
%%%xxfrom: FCC - 217
%%%xxto: OIC-F9
%%%xxpriority: 5/5
%%%xx**message follows**

newpara forward supply base at allens rift attacked by fourteen plus medium and heavy warships stop facilities and orbiting docks struck by several nuclear warheads stop heavy casualties comma heavy damage stop enemy ships pressing attack with troop landing stop

newpara f6 comma f7 comma f12 comma cs-omega diverted to interdict assault stop no support for f9 on withdrawal from mindon space stop

newpara mindon-2 raid to continue with withdrawal as scheduled stop f9 to withdraw to wolf 359 for repair and reassignment stop elimination of mindon-2 as enemy base of operations priority stop nuclear option at your discretion stop updated threat assessment attached stop

newpara give them hell andrei stop

newpara signoff adm winston s11466723

%%%xx**message ends**xx

%%%xxdata attached 4127245 units

The marshal read the message twice. *Damn,* was all he could think. Fleet Nine was based out of Allen's Rift. The population was two hundred thousand colonists, plus the military personnel who ran the base and orbiting dockyards. The Rift was one of only three places where orbiting ships could get large-scale maintenance work done on their hulls. While things were weightless in space, they still had mass. Replacing a sheet of dense cruiser armor plating required special facilities and many trained people. Fleet Nine would have gone there for refit after retreating from the Mindon star system. The attack on the Rift would hurt the war effort badly.

The marshal shook his head and concentrated. He had his orders from Admiral Winston. The raid was to continue, and he was to do as much damage as possible. Kosnov could not keep this news to himself. He needed to talk to the senior commanders to let them know of the change in plans. Kosnov began issuing orders to assemble his senior staff.

* * *

Kaaw was satisfied at the report of one of his soldiers destroying a warm blood craft. The shoulder-fired anti-air missiles were crude, but proving somewhat effective against warm blood technology. They were just starting to be used in the field, having been distributed from central stores in the last few hours. It was good news in a day that had little. The report of the destroyed craft arrived just as his anti-air battery reported they were operational. *Finally,* thought the commander. *Now they would start to pay, and even their vaunted technology could not help them now.*

* * *

Pratt walked up to General Carstairs, who sat beside the wounded pilot. Stanley lay unconscious on a folding stretcher that someone had produced from the inside of the crashed lighter. His legs, or specifically the stumps of his thighs, were heavily bandaged. Jacobs had been forced to amputate both legs above the knee. He had used surgical tubing as tourniquets temporarily. After sewing up the ends of the exposed veins and arteries, large sponges laced with throblin and tannic acid were put in place to stop the minor bleeding that remained. When they had taken effect, the surgical tubing was removed. Stanley's lower legs still remained jammed inside the cockpit.

Two units of plasma hung on a nearby branch stub. They delivered much-needed liquid volume into the wounded pilot's bloodstream. His blood pressure had dropped to a dangerously low level, and the plasma would replenish the fluid in his cardiovascular system. Several blankets were wrapped around him, providing him with warmth. His skin was pale, and a series of small bruises could be seen on the left side of his jaw where his face had hit the side window during the crash. His flight helmet had been carefully cut away, and a brace was wrapped around his neck as a precaution. He was unconscious and not moving.

Many of the divisional staff were spread out around the lighter in between the nearby trees. They were, for the most part, in good condition, considering their unexpected descent. Some had small arms close to hand just in case, but none were in a mood to fight. Many of them dozed in the shade of the trees and left the guard duties up to the Special Forces section.

Pratt spoke to Carstairs. "General, Fleet reports a medevac lighter is on the way. ETA is twelve minutes. No word on a replacement command lighter. I have a couple of my people clearing off a landing zone further down the hill. If you hear explosions, it is them clearing out some trees. I told my radioman to monitor the frequency for more news." Pratt looked down at the pilot and saw the concern on the general's face. "Jacobs, my medic, says the pilot has lost a lot of blood. He has been given plasma and is stable for the moment, but he is not sure if he will make it into orbit."

"Sit down, Lieutenant." Carstairs waited until Pratt had done so before continuing. He pointed at the wounded pilot. "Would you believe J.P. here redid flight school twice? During his first solo flight, he crashed a trainer right into the base headquarters on Sigil Prime. He did it purposely, too. His engine died from a faulty seal just after take-off. Now, he could have taken the safe path and ejected, but he decided to stay in control and minimize the damage. Looking around, he saw he had a choice of two places to set down. The base HQ or the preschool right next door. He went straight in the orderly room, through the BSM's office, then a bathroom, and ended up upside down in a stairwell two floors down on the opposite side of the building. One hundred fifty people were in there at the time. Not one was killed. J.P. walked away with half the people in the building shaking his hand for not risking their kids' lives next door. However, the base commander didn't appreciate the redecorating bill and had him busted back to basic. He wanted to kick him out, but they proved engine trouble had forced the crash. With no one hurt, kicking him out was hard to justify.

"J.P. went through all the classes, tests, and qualifications again and got his wings. That set him back nine months, but instead of complaining, he set to improving himself and got top marks on every test they gave him. He passed his solo, but again due to interference by the same base commander, they assigned him to Jovian transport shuttles. He spent two years in low gravity orbits around Io, Europa, and Callisto. During that time, he learned to fly in every condition with underpowered garbage scows. He didn't complain, he just did the job he was given. They assigned him to lighters when the war began, as they needed every warm body they could find.

"His first combat mission was on Cyrix. A platoon got cut off in the lowlands and was besieged by overwhelming opposition. The enemy had the place surrounded with all kinds of weaponry. That valley was a death trap. The unit suffered seventy-five percent casualties within two hours. Three lighters with trained CSAR crews had gone down trying to get the wounded off the moon. J.P. came along in his transport lighter without gunners or countermeasures. He had to circle the field twice before they could clear a spot big enough for him to land. Flak, shells, and bullets hit his ship continuously. Every square meter on that ship had a hole in it. If you go to the Smithsonian Air and Space Museum, you can still see that lighter on display. After landing, he went out into the battlefield and helped retrieve several bodies from their positions. He was wounded three times. He didn't give up, and he got them all out to a nearby firebase— every man and woman, alive or dead. He earned the Medal of Honor that day.

"My point, Lieutenant, is that J.P. does not quit easily. All we have to do is get him back up there, and he'll be just fine. You hear me, son?" The last sentence was said quietly, but carried such force, it could not be argued.

"Yes, sir. Sorry, sir. I'll go and see how the landing area is coming." Pratt retreated from the general quickly.

* * *

Carstairs watched him go. J.P. had indeed done all those things. However, what the general had not told him was that a young officer was in charge of the stranded platoon. They were taking withering fire from several directions, and losses were high. The young officer was covering the withdrawal and had been hit in the back during the evacuation. J.P. had seen him fall within meters of the hatch as he was throttling up to leave. He had aborted the take-off, resulting in the panicked majority in the back end screaming at him. Weapons were pointed and threats made unless he took off immediately. J.P. ignored them. No one fired, as he was the only pilot, and Stanley retrieved the fallen officer into the lighter.

On the hospital landing pad, the lighter was met by the wounded officer's father, who, coincidentally, was the commander of the firebase. Lieutenant Stephen Carstairs was three days short of his twenty-fourth birthday on the day he died in his father's arms.

The general later heard that the military wanted to put J.P. into early retirement due to his wounds. He had pulled strings and had him assigned as his personal pilot. That decision had saved his own life only minutes before, he was sure. Any pilot other than J.P. would not have landed so well. He owed J.P. multiple debts.

A loud noise penetrated the peace of the glade. The general started to grab his pistol in reflex as a loud whine began near the lighter. He relaxed when he realized that the sound was a generator being turned on inside the lighter itself. A higher pitched whine started soon after, as air conditioning pumps turned on.

After a few minutes, a smiling technician named Brubaker appeared from the side hatch holding a piece of portable electronic test equipment in his hand. He saw the general and walked over quickly. "General, the forward electric wiring is shattered, but that only affects the flight deck. I was able to reset the circuit breakers on the secondary panel in the back end and get a backup generator on line. The COMM system is fine, and the internal computers are booting up. I just did a quick radio check back to Fleet, and we are good to go."

The general was confused at the man's exuberance. "Staff Sergeant Brubaker, that lighter does not have a flight deck and is not going anywhere."

Brubaker smiled even wider and spoke with more confidence. "Well, sir, we don't actually have to fly to do our jobs. The HQ staff are all on their feet. We have fleet and field COMMs, and computers are up, so the command post can carry on its work." The general still looked sideways at the crumpled lighter. "Sir, we don't need to actually fly; the back end is operational."

At the last sentence was the briefest of pauses. Carstairs then realized what the man was saying and grabbed the startled chief's hand. The general shook it vigorously with a huge grin on his face. "Chief, maybe it's the after-effects of the crash, but there are days when I am addlebrained. Thank God for men like you." *Brubaker just made gunnery sergeant because of what he accomplished.*

Carstairs released Brubaker's hand and then turned to the officers and men who had been roused by the noise of the lighter. "Right. Duty stations everyone. We have a battle to coordinate."

CHAPTER 19 – MEDEVAC

Second Lieutenant Wicks was glad to see that all of the huts in his area had been searched, cleared, and secured. He had talked to the engineers who had come in behind his position and made sure they had a decent defensive position within a small circle of huts. He wanted them out of the way in case of trouble. They were happy to cooperate, as they carried huge packs filled with high explosives. Each pack weighed a considerable amount, and a rest was welcome. On his way back to his section, Wicks instinctively made a visual count of his people. He saw all of them in various positions. They were spread out and prepared, he was glad to see. He was lucky to have a veteran like Blake, as their training showed. Wicks didn't have to see Perkins to know he was there. The lieutenant could clearly hear his radioman shuffling along on the rubble behind him.

* * *

Sergeant Blake met with his lieutenant in the doorway of a Drakk'Har hut. LCPL Belliveau stood just beside them to the right of the hut doorway with his weapon raised. Belliveau swept his weapon left to right slowly with his right index finger

300

off the trigger and resting on the trigger guard. His magazine was full and the weapon cocked, but the safety was on. His right thumb rested on the knurled surface of the safety catch. Blake thought he looked like a recruiting poster.

Calm and professional, Belliveau followed the prescribed drill for maintaining perimeter security. One always kept one's weapon raised and ready when expecting trouble in a combat zone. Most of his body was behind a stone wall, and he was mindful to keep the hut close as well. A surprise mortar attack would necessitate his taking cover inside that building very quickly. On the left side of the hut, PFC Perkins stood with his weapon raised, covering the opposite side of the hut. He looked obviously uncomfortable under the extra weight of the radio pack. Perkins kept shifting the pack weight back and forth across his shoulders, trying to get it comfortable. Blake saw him and knew all he had to do was tighten the shoulder straps, but he said nothing. A little chafed skin and sore back muscles would teach Perkins far better than a chewing out.

Wicks spoke, and the Sergeant made eye contact with his officer. Wicks had a map in hand.

"Sergeant, the engineers were early, so I tucked them in behind us just over there. We need to move up that road and cover the crossroads here. I want Sanchez and Johnston on point, with Messina and Tyler covering. Arrange the rest as you see fit to form two assault teams to clear the houses on each side of the street. If either team gets into trouble, you and Belliveau will reinforce. Make everyone aware that there are friendly forces in the area. They may transit that crossroads. Make sure everyone knows to employ positive target identification before firing."

"Yes, si—" was all Blake could utter before Belliveau's head was thrown back forcefully, and the howl of a rail gun shattered the peace. Chunks of the hut wall flew high into the air as hyper-velocity projectiles impacted on it. Everyone dropped for cover immediately. Blake saw the officer drop the transparent cover on his helmet and hit the imaging stud on his weapon. He shoved the weapon over the wall and moved it, searching for a target.

Blake crawled on knees and elbows over to Belliveau. The young man's helmet was gone, torn off by the impact of a Drakk'Har round. The lance corporal was moaning, holding his head in his hands. His head was slashed open, and a lot of blood oozed between his fingers. Blake looked over at Perkins, who as radioman also carried a field first aid kit. "Perkins, get over here!"

* * *

Wicks had to yell to be heard over the rail gun fire. "Two crocs! Two o'clock. Twenty meters and closing! They are moving up the side street, using the rubble for cover!" Wicks let go of the weapon, leaving it on top of the wall, freeing up his hands, and also keeping the video camera on the enemy. Wicks wasted no time and pulled the pin on a grenade. "Frag out!" he yelled just as it left his hand. He lobbed it with a straight-arm motion that carried the grenade in a high arc in the same direction as the line of his weapon barrel.

* * *

Perkins arrived at the sergeant's side, struggling to get the first aid kit out of his pack. Blake roughly grabbed the radioman's combat bandage that was strapped to the back of his helmet. He ripped off the cover and exposed the thick, sterile aero-gel beneath. He opened it up and pressed the length onto Belliveau's head. He had to move the wounded man's hand to get the bandage in place and then put Belliveau's hand back on top of the bandage. "Hold that in place. Keep pressure on it." Perkins finally had the first aid kit out. "Right, Perkins, take care of him." The sergeant grabbed his weapon and began to make his way to his officer. He stayed low as rail gun projectiles still flew over his head.

* * *

The grenade landed on the wrong side of the rubble. It bounced once before rolling to a stop. The explosion did no damage to the enemy, but it did cause them to drop for cover, and that was enough. The rail guns stopped firing for a moment. Wicks bounced up and grabbed his weapon. He jumped over the wall with Blake beside him, screaming for cover fire. The pair advanced quickly while squeezing controlled bursts into the area where the two prone Drakk'Har lay. Several others in the section began firing at the enemy position as well. Bullets struck all around the two prone Drakk'Har. They took cover as the humans advanced. A scaly head appeared, taking a quick look. Wicks put a three round burst into its face. A second Drakk'Har appeared and tried to get up, abandoning its weapon in its fury to charge. That one was shot in the throat by Blake and then again in the back as it tried to get up. Wicks kept running and firing until he could see they were both down and not moving. He shot them in the head once more each, just to be sure. Blake came up immediately on his left, his weapon raised and ready, covering the ground behind, ready for any more enemy action.

"Search them, sergeant. Get those bloody weapons." More marines came up, covering their leaders and the surrounding area. The whole action had taken less than twenty seconds. Wicks pointed down the road, looking in the direction of LCPL Reid and PFC Johnston. "Right, you two. Go down that street fifteen to twenty meters and make sure there are no follow-on forces. Watch out for friendlies going through the cross-roads. Fall back here and report if you see anything." The two enlisted men strode down the pathway with weapons raised to their shoulders as they scanned for more enemies.

Blake walked quickly back to the wounded man. Perkins had Belliveau's head heavily bandaged by the time the sergeant got back. The radioman had put a neck brace on him, also. This restricted the movement of Belliveau's head. With an impact of such magnitude, the head had been snapped back, and a broken neck was not out of the question.

Corporal Sanchez stood over the pair. She had Belliveau's helmet in her hand. Wordlessly, she handed it to the sergeant as he approached. Where the round had struck, it looked like a small crater on one edge of the helmet. The camouflage fabric cover and the combat bandage tucked under the fabric were gone, ripped away by the force of the blow. Luckily, it had been an oblique hit, off to one side. If it had struck any closer to the center, the projectile would have taken off the side of his head. Blake held the helmet closer and could see the individual layers of composite materials that had been torn apart. He knew how tough that material was.

Perkins looked up at Blake and spoke hurriedly as he continued to tie off the ends of the bandages. "Sarge, with the blood, it looks much worse than it actually is. He has a bad gash on his temple, but he's conscious and stable. He might need some stitches at worst."

"We'll let the corpsman take a look at him to make sure. Corporal Sanchez, go and fetch a couple of those engineers to take Belliveau back to the aid area. I saw they have a stretcher with them. They can take care of him while we finish our sweep. Make sure their corpsmen keeps him under observation." Potential concussions posed high risks, and head wounds were never considered minor. He needed to be examined and cleared by a doctor.

"Right, Sarge," she said before jogging down the path to their rear.

Wicks arrived, pointing at Belliveau. "Good show patching him up, Perkins. Strip off his ammo and redistribute it to the rest of the section. Then get on the radio to command and give them a two-thirty-five contact report."

"Yes, sir," Perkins said as he followed the orders.

* * *

Wicks nodded and turned away from his people. He walked away a few paces and busied himself with his webbing, wanting to look normal even though he felt the complete opposite. The officer was shaking now as the adrenaline in his blood was absorbed back into his system. To cover up the involuntary motion, he fussed and adjusted his webbing straps and pouches. He didn't want anyone to see him like this. He had been afraid when the incoming fire arrived. He had dropped to the ground instinctively when it started. Seeing Belliveau fly through the air and the banshee wail of the rail guns made him mad enough that fear was irrelevant. He felt it now, though. Training had let him survive the combat, but they had never taught them how to deal with the intense emotions of post-combat. The rock in the pit of his stomach made him feel nauseous. It would pass. It always did. That did not make the experience any more tolerable.

* * *

Perkins was shocked that Belliveau had been shot, but he found his training had kicked in and assessing the fallen man's wounds came automatically. The blood had caused Perkins to recoil initially, but he saw in seconds that it simply looked worse that it actually was, and he realized the wound was well within his first aid training. Perkins had taken the officer's praise to heart. He had done a good job and felt a little pride as a result.

Perkins finished taking the last of the wounded man's ammunition. Belliveau stirred, trying to get comfortable on the uneven ground. Perkins placed a hand firmly on his chest and spoke quietly so the officer behind him could not hear. "Hey, man, stay still. A badly wounded guy like you had better take it easy!" Belliveau stopped moving when he heard the words "badly wounded." Perkins continued, "That's right. With a shaving cut that bad, the doctor may not give you your waa-wee-pop."

Belliveau didn't laugh, but he did visibly relax at the joke. He looked up into Perkins's sardonic expression and automatically knew he would be fine.

* * *

Long-term operations allowed portable field hospitals to be set up in secure areas of the planet. These facilities had every resource for dealing with combat wounds. Replete with specialists in all medical disciplines, the quality of treatment they could give was excellent. It had been proven many times over that the faster a wounded person was treated, the better their chance of recovery. Lighters would transport the wounded from combat areas directly to these hospitals in very short periods of time. This enabled casualties to be treated in minutes. However, raids typically took place in much shorter time spans with no time to set up that kind of medical facility in a timely manner. As this operation was only a day long raid, all serious casualties had to be brought from the surface to the orbiting fleet for treatment.

Mantis Three was designated as a medical evacuation flight or medevac in military parlance. The lighter crew had reconfigured the back end of the craft to accommodate stretchers, and they had several medical kits available. Two marine corpsmen had been assigned to supplement the crew to monitor the wounded during the flight. Medevac flights always received priority clearances. It helped troop morale knowing that if you were ever in the back of a medevac flight, you would get help in the quickest time possible. As a result, Mantis Three had waited a minimal amount of time in its holding orbit before receiving permission to descend. Mantis Three dropped through the atmosphere surrounded by a barrage of countermeasures and jamming missiles. The flight had been tasked with retrieving several seriously wounded marines from the surface. The inertial navigation system had been programmed with the coordinates, and the lighter descended in a corkscrew pattern to confuse any enemy sensors—standard operating procedure for lighter landings.

* * *

Lord Kaaw had been alerted to the presence of the countermeasures as soon as they had been detected. The active jammers were easily detected on the Drakk'Har passive sensors, and the pattern was close to what they had been trained to expect. They could not see the descending craft in the noise, but simple logic told them that they were coming. The warm bloods never used decoys in that volume and pattern unless something needed to be protected. Earlier in the day, just prior to the landings, the same technicians had seen identical patterns above them. Their batteries had been unable to interdict because of the effectiveness of warm blood counter fire. This time, they had a prepared battery sited on a hilltop ready for action.

"Alert the battery to wait for my word of command. Update the firing data continuously. We'll hold fire until they come well into effective range," Kaaw screamed to his staff. He could strike now, but that would give the enemy craft a chance at escape. He wanted to minimize their reaction time and maximize the anti-air weapons effectiveness.

* * *

Mantis Three came out through the bottom of the clouds, and the pilot automatically scanned the terrain below looking for identifiable terrain features. Captain Shauna Gesund had done this type of flight many times in simulations, exercises, and live-fire combats. She knew her job very well and had been decorated several times for retrieving combat wounded from active battlefields. As soon as they cleared the clouds, the town was clearly visible, as was the slow-flowing river. By orienting herself to those features, she knew immediately which one she needed to angle for. Her flight engineer gave her a thumbs-up, and she nodded. That was not part of the procedure, and an unneeded distraction. She didn't want to acknowledge the motion, but did so anyway. It was good for morale, and she recognized the value of that. Gesund flicked glances to the heads-up display on occasion to keep aware of her speed, height, and descent angle.

"Crew, prepare for combat landing for casualty retrieval," she announced formally on the internal COMM system before swinging the lighter into a downward spiral toward the landing zone.

* * *

Lieutenant Pratt and Sergeant Smith stood on a ridgeline near the secondary summit of the hill. Corporal Popov was just in sight near the top of the western slope of the landing zone, while Private Williams was on the eastern portion. Both had their weapons trained down the hill and were watching either side for enemy activity. Pratt stood with his binoculars to his eyes. He was scanning above the plains between him and "Croctown," as they had started to refer to it. The expected medevac flight was due to arrive soon.

Smith saw the lighter first. He tapped the officer on the shoulder and pointed. "There, sir, coming around from the east."

Pratt swiveled and brought his binoculars around to track the craft. "Right, Sergeant, mark the landing zone. Pop green smoke."

Smith unclipped a thick cylindrical container from his vest. The body had a light olive band around the bottom with small black letters across the body describing its function and proper use. Smith did not bother to read it; he had used many Mark VII Color Gas Dispensers. The sergeant held the handle down with his palm, and he tore out the pin on the top that restrained the handle in place. Smith tossed the cylinder to the center of the cleared landing zone while yelling, "Smoke out!" A *twink* noise was heard as the handle flew off, and thick green smoke began to emanate from the body of the device. It hissed as the pressure of the chemical reaction within forced smoke out quickly.

* * *

Captain Gesund saw the smoke and angled Mantis Three's course slightly to land in the proper place. She was only two hundred meters above the ground and descending. Her hands unconsciously grasped the steering yoke a little tighter than usual.

* * *

Kaaw had savored the approach of the warm blood craft. He was disappointed on seeing only one, but he satisfied himself with the knowledge that he was at last on the offense instead of running and hiding. He waited patiently for the craft to come as close as possible. Only when he was certain conditions were perfect did he pick up the microphone and say, "Fire!"

A short distance away, on Brawnik's Hump, the short stocky barrels of the anti-air battery were tracking the flying craft in a slow arc. They were directed by the battery commander, who used a simple rod pointing at the lighter as a means of aiming the weapons. The movement of the rod was translated through a mechanical steering package to each gun. Small motors on the mounts turned the weapons, keeping them aligned with the target. Distance was gauged by a crude laser, and that determined the angle of the barrels. The order was received over a buried landline to a handset in the command post of the battery. The command had been anticipated and was acted on immediately. The battery commander stepped on the firing switch. From their hidden firing pits on Brawnik's Hump, five short-range anti-air weapons fired as one.

* * *

On Mantis Three, the incoming threat was detected immediately by the countermeasures pods mounted under the rear of the lighter. Warning lights and alarms were illuminated, and the pilot had two options: Fly away or land. Captain Gesund knew the wounded were on the ground, and that was where her duty lay. The lighter continued to head for the green smoke.

Flares and chaff were vented out of the lighter belly pods as the countermeasure pods began to send electromagnetic signals toward the incoming threats to confuse or blind them. It was a wasted effort, but they had no way to know that.

* * *

As soon as the projectiles had left their barrels, the Drakk'Har crews began to reload them by hand. Other members of the gun pits adjusted the foliage camouflaging the rims of the firing pits that had been dislodged by the blast of the weapons firing.

The fired shells continued to fly upward, above both the terrain and their intended target. They traveled in a high arc, then gradually slowed as gravity forced them to fall back to the ground.

* * *

On the ground, Lieutenant Pratt saw the Drakk'Har weapons fire. Smoke and explosive flashes appeared on the hill they had occupied the day before. Even before the sound of the firing battery had reached them, he was screaming for his people to take cover. Then he heard the CRUMP noise of the firing weapons and, seconds later, the distinctive low-pitched whine caused by the flight of their projectiles.

* * *

The Drakk'Har weapons were no more than simple mortar bombs, but huge in size. They carried no guidance package or electronics of any type. All of the lighter decoys launched to confuse them were completely ineffective. The shells spread out to cover a wide area that bracketed the lighter on three sides. At the center of each cylindrical shell was a huge amount of explosive with a timer fuse that had activated on leaving the tube. Wrapped around this was a ceramic jacket covering that had hundreds of dense ceramic spheres packed inside. When the timer fuse reached its end, the explosives detonated and sent the small spheres in all directions. The explosions occurred about a hundred meters above the lighter in mid-air.

Just like a shotgun, the Drakk'Har weapon only needed to be pointed in the direction of the enemy to be effective. Seventy projectiles actually struck the lighter, with the majority hitting non-critical systems and armor, causing relatively light damage. However, one hit *the* most critical system on board; the female pilot was hit in the chest and went limp instantly. The lighter twisted drastically and struck the lip of the landing zone before bouncing back up into the sky. Now in uncontrolled flight, the lighter rolled over onto its back and fell out of sight over the edge of the landing zone. Inside, the crew screamed as their bodies were subjected to random and violent motions. The flight engineer grabbed his secondary flight controls and tried to regain control. Even with his limited training, he was able to right the craft to almost level flight. However, the low altitude, basic physics, and gravity all conspired against him, and it impacted on the ground at speed. The craft bounced back up, and it looked like it might be able to stay in the air. The damage sustained was too great for this, and the lighter fell once more. It landed past the base of the hill roughly on its nose, then turned sideways after striking a series of large bushes. The ground caused it to roll over several times, with several pieces of the fuselage and engine components being thrown off until it finally came to a stop. It came to rest on the south side of the plain, lying on its starboard side.

* * *

Pratt had emerged from under a fallen tree the second after he had heard the sharp explosion of the mortar bombs. He heard, but did not see, the lighter strike the rim of the landing zone. Experience told him Drakk'Har batteries fired in volleys, and it took them several minutes to reload an anti-air mortar, so he was in little danger. The lieutenant jogged to the edge of the cleared area and searched frantically for the lighter. He saw several patches of brown earth torn into the green plains where it had rolled past. He spotted the lighter just past the base of the hill, a half kilometer away. It lay near one of the closer bends in the river. He fixed the craft in the sight of his binoculars for a better view and saw no signs of life. One of the loading hatches had been ripped off, and an engine was lying in the field.

Corporal Popov appeared at the officer's elbow. "Sir, are you all right?"

"Fine. Have you seen Williams?" He never took the binoculars down as he spoke.

"Yes, sir. He is OK, too."

"Right." The officer dropped the binoculars from his face. The strap around his neck arrested the fall, and they came to rest against his chest. He pulled a map from his breast pocket, referenced it, and started scribbling notes quickly. "Have him call Fleet, and tell them we have a Fallen Angel at these coordinates." Pratt tore the page out of the pad and handed it over. "Then get up to the command lighter and inform the general. He might be able to get things moving faster at the divisional level."

"Sir," replied Popov as he turned.

Pratt placed a hand on his arm, causing the soldier to pause. "I want Williams down here when he is done, with the COMM gear. Go!"

The officer released his grasp of the arm, and Popov retreated in a flat run.

Pratt returned the binoculars to his eyes and scanned the crash area again. Everything was still with no sign of life from the crash site itself, but he did see movement near the river. Lots of it, and it made his skin crawl.

* * *

Drawwl was several klem from the conquered compound and moving quickly. He had acknowledged the orders via radio once he was well clear of the compound walls. One of Borrk's communication specialists had answered the call, and it was thankfully short as a result. Drawwl did not wait around to see if his radio signal would attract attention. He snapped the transmitter off and did not hesitate to move his force away from the place. Drawwl had left only a handful of guards behind. Kek had volunteered to stay and oversee them, which had only resulted in him being placed in the very front of the Drakk'Har column. One of Drawwl's trusted personal guard had been left in command of the reduced guard force. The last thing Drawwl wanted was Kek left behind.

Drawwl's attack force numbered almost ninety troops. As formidable as that sounded, only fifty of them were combat-seasoned and trustworthy. The rest were Kek's compound guards and untested in battle. Drawwl knew that the compound guards would have an important role to play once the warm bloods were spotted. They would be fodder. Cast first into the battle, many of them would die in the confusion of combat. That was to be expected. Only the strong would survive. The strong, in this case, were his core troops who had taken the compound in the first place. They would observe as the guards were killed to see where the enemy was strong. They would learn how the enemy lines were laid out, and then they would attack, taking tributes for themselves. The death of others among the Drakk'Har was just another tool for advancement.

They moved in three columns, with an advance element commanded by Kek well in front. Drawwl's troops moved in the center rank, while on either side, compound guards flanked them. If they were attacked on route, then only guards would be killed, allowing the others to survive. All of the troops slithered along through the terrain of low grass, bogs, and shallow pools of water. They did not walk upright, as it would be too tiring. Drakk'Har military forces tended to use rivers and streams for long-distance travel. They could swim for long periods effortlessly. However, in this case, no watercourses were available. They traveled a different route on their return from the compound, and as a result, there would be no tasty pool of greppo fish, either.

The foliage kept them under cover from the sun. Being in shade, their cold-blooded bodies did not heat up as much. That was a decided advantage when traveling. The trees and brush also disguised them from satellites and other airborne means of detection. Drawwl knew they had not been detected, as they had not been attacked. When Drakk'Har were spotted in mass formations, they were strafed, bombed, and killed in great numbers. His force was unmolested to this point, so he had not been seen.

Drawwl had no maps of the area with him. He relied on his guides who headed up each column and knew the terrain intimately. They were locals who had lived and hunted these hills for decades. They knew where he wanted to end up, and they took him on the safest approach. They had assured him that they could approach the back slope of Skull Ridge through the valleys formed by the slight hills in that area. The thick vegetation assured a clandestine approach almost to the summit.

Drawwl pulled himself over a slippery hump of earth that had a path worn down by the several bodies ahead of him. He carried no weapons other than his blade, so his burden was light compared to the others. None complained at any point, as having warm blood on their tongues was strong motivation for a Drakk'Har warrior.

* * *

Lieutenant Pratt counted Drakk'Har warriors emerging from the water at the river's edge. More appeared every few seconds. Four, nine, twelve. They pulled themselves over the bank and moved toward the wrecked lighter. Several carried rail guns, while others only carried long bladed knives. Sixteen, twenty. More appeared, and he stopped counting.

Pratt's training kicked in. First, he assessed the situation, which was bad and getting worse. The crew had not emerged from the lighter and was either dead or badly wounded. His was the closest unit to the crash, and he saw no way his people could get there in time to change anything. Besides, he had the responsibility of guarding the divisional command lighter, and he barely had enough people to do that. The fallen angel alert would get a high priority reaction from fleet. However, the heavily armed combat search and rescue troops or CSAR could not get there in less than two minutes, and that was all the time they had before the enemy got to the crash site. Being a Special Forces unit, they had no heavy weapons themselves. Their job was to move quickly and strike lightly, defended targets of opportunity. A battery of artillery, mortars, or an air strike was required here, and he did not have them at his command without the radio which was being used to alert Fleet to the issue.

Movement from the open hatch caught his attention, and Pratt immediately framed it in the center of his binoculars. A figure in green coveralls and a crew bug helmet was emerging from the open hatch. Pratt wedged the binoculars to his eyes and took in the scene. The lone man had a pistol in his hand and was talking to someone unseen, inside and below him. He reached up and undid the helmet strap. Taking it off, he dropped it into the hatch. He turned toward the river and saw the Drakk'Har approaching. The man in the hatch didn't have time to react before several rail guns opened fire in his direction.

The sound reached Pratt quickly. Loud, even at this distance, the distinctive scream of the Drakk'Har rail guns carried easily to the hill. The crew member disappeared back inside the lighter as the small rounds began to impact on the body of the wrecked craft. Pratt didn't know whether the man had been hit or not. More Drakk'Har troops appeared from the river, while the ones who had emerged earlier came closer to the lighter.

"Sir?" was all Williams said before the officer interrupted.

Pratt took the binoculars from his face and pointed at a patch of ground near his feet. "Set the unit up there, and get me a voice link back to Fleet. I need a forward air controller." The serious tone of the officer was unmistakable.

Williams grabbed the lieutenant's accessory COMM cord and plugged it into the satellite transceiver without asking for permission. Williams's cord was already attached, and he began plugging in the override codes for voice communications. Fleet tactical communications were typically data rather than voice. However, in certain circumstances, data simply took too long to be practical. In those cases, voice communications were much faster.

A series of static bursts in the lieutenant's earpiece made him wince. Williams tugged on the officer's pants and gave him a thumbs-up. "You are on the regimental FAC channel, sir."

Pratt flicked his COMM unit microphone to be voice-activated, so he could use his hands to hold the binoculars to his eyes. "Dragon, this is Juniper, over." When the officer stopped speaking, the microphone automatically shut off, and a brief burst of static was heard.

A female voice came back within a half-second. She spoke concisely. No one called on this frequency to chat. "Juniper, this is Dragon. Go."

"Dragon, Juniper. We have a Fallen Angel. Medevac flight is down due west of our position on Hill 170. There are confirmed survivors on board with several dozen crocs in close proximity and closing. Be advised, there is an active anti-air battery situated on Hill 237. What do we have in the area? Over."

"Stand by, Juniper." A burst of static followed, and the next few seconds seemed like hours to the lieutenant.

"Juniper, we have a flight of four taking off from Firebase Foxtrot. Their loadout is cluster. ETA 5.2 minutes." Her voice sounded distant, almost bored.

"The crew on the ground has less than a minute before contact, Dragon. Tell them to expedite!"

"Stand by, Juniper." Another interminable silence followed.

"Juniper, incoming flight has been advised and is approaching at maximum velocity. ETA 4 minutes."

Three minutes too late, thought Pratt.

* * *

Planet Lord Slassh was not having a good day. Reports of heavy damage were trickling in from the various Swamp Masters around the globe. Several did not report in at all. What was even more worrying: one had been cut off in mid-transmission. Large numbers of landing forces were reported in three main areas. Two other areas experienced an orbital bombardment, which usually preceded a landing. However, no troops had landed there. At least, he had received no reports of such activity. Slassh was in a hot fury trying to make sense of the many disparate reports as they arrived. They were often contradictory, and he had no way of confirming anything with eighty percent of his communications networks destroyed. Few radios operated for long with the warm blood fleet above. So, the Drakk'Har forces were reduced to sub-orbital message pods and fixed cables for long-distance communication. Not bad for tactical operations, but when trying to coordinate a planet-wide strategic defense, it was intolerable. He had to look for trends and how to counter them, but for that he needed up-to-date information.

A few reports of casualties being inflicted on the warm bloods had arrived, but as with all Drakk'Har claims, they were always taken with a measure of caution. The claims of damage also reported no tribute taken, which cast huge doubt on their veracity. Drakk'Har resistance to this point was token, in the Planet Lord's opinion. He had screamed at his staff to get better information. He had goaded, bribed, threatened, and cajoled them with little result. His own antenna arrays were being neutralized within minutes of broadcasting. Slassh had eventually ordered transmissions to stop, as he had few spare sets remaining. He fell back on swimmers and landlines, which decreased the information received even more.

The good news, if any, was that the land lines were very hard to neutralize, and while they had to relay the information from post to post, it did eventually get through.

"Lord." An eager voice grabbed Slassh's attention.

"What?" came the angry reply. His head whipped around to face the interruption, sending spittle flying from his mouth.

"We have confirmed reports a warm blood craft has been forced down by the river Skad. Swamp Master Borrk's Third Shock Company approaches now."

A curt head movement simultaneously acknowledged the report and dismissed the underling. *At least damage is being done to them, as well,* he mused.

* * *

Captain Levin pressed his throttles to the edge of safety to generate as much thrust as possible. The instruments before him showed the engines operating just over the red line. Grasshopper Two and Three were flying in a wedge formation with him. Grasshopper Four had aborted back to the firebase with a severe hydraulic leak after lift-off. The airframes of the three remaining lighters shook with the vibration of the engines. He had no need to advise the other pilots what was going on, as they monitored the same frequencies. A medevac lighter had gone down and was being swarmed by enemy troops. Levin knew what would happen if the crocs got there first. He called up a map of the terrain around the crash location. Luckily, Special Forces troops had provided an accurate position of the crash, and he would not need to make a pass to locate it. That helped. The report he had received said the medevac had been shot down by anti-air weapons that were on the side of Hill 237. However, he didn't have an accurate location for them, and the target was a huge hill. He could not cover all of it in one run. That limited his options dramatically, and he only had three minutes to come up with a plan of attack.

* * *

Pratt stood on the hill waiting and watching through his binoculars. Everything he could do had been done, and now he had to wait as events unfolded. Green creatures approached the fallen lighter with weapons raised, and as they got closer, they seemed to speed up. *Anticipation for the kill*, he thought pensively.

A blurred motion caught his attention from the hatch. *Someone waving?* Then, seconds later, several small explosions were seen around the craft. The closest Drakk'Har dropped to the ground—some by choice, others because of wounds.

"Yes!" he said out loud as he realized what happened. They were not waving; someone had lobbed a couple of grenades. The enemy troops around the airframe had all hit the ground and were temporarily frozen in place. It would not delay them for long, but the odds just got a little better than tragic. A hand wielding a pistol appeared from the rim of the hatchway and several rounds were fired blindly. The sound was pitiful, by the time it reached Pratt on the hillside—several rapid and flat pops. The hand disappeared when several Drakk'Har rail guns raked the superstructure in response. That noise carried over the distance with force. A few of the closer warriors started to move in under the cover of the rail guns, when another series of explosions went off around the lighter. They fell prone once more in a classic Mexican stand-off. The warriors could not close on the wrecked hull, and those inside could not venture out because of the incoming fire. However, as a medevac lighter, their supply of grenades would be limited.

The powerful impacts of the rail guns ripped pieces of the lighter off the superstructure. Pratt had no idea if the rounds were penetrating to the interior, and while he knew little about the armor on lighters, he willed what was there to work.

* * *

Levin approached the crash coordinates rapidly. All the plans he came up with fell apart with the location of the anti-air weapons being unknown. Then he realized the position he had gotten for the downed lighter was exact. He didn't know where the enemy battery was located, but there might be someone in that area who did. He keyed his radio and called Dragon for more information.

* * *

Williams didn't have binoculars, but he was watching the scene on the plain below. "Lieutenant, can't we call in a fire mission?"

Pratt's stance didn't change in the slightest as he responded, "Negative. They are on a different channel, and we have to stay on this one for coordinating the rescue. I just hop—"

The female voice of the FAC interrupted him, "Juniper, this is Dragon. Request you illuminate the center of the enemy anti-air battery on Hill 237, frequency 312."

Pratt's' response was immediate. "Roger, illuminate anti-air position on Hill 237 with frequency 312." He swung his binoculars around and lined it up on where the volley had emerged from the trees. He could not see any weapons, but he centered the area where he had seen the earlier smoke in the binocular view finder and pressed a stud on the side of the housing to activate an infra-red laser beam. By rocking the stud with his finger tip, he was able to change the frequency of the beam until a "312" was visible in the top left corner of the binocular display. "Dragon, Juniper. Target illuminated."

"Roger, Juniper. Stand by."

Nothing happened for some time. Multiple exercises had driven home the proper sequence, and he concentrated on his role. The laser beam from his binoculars was invisible to the naked eye, but to infrared sensors it shone like a beacon. The beam hit foliage on Hill 237 and scattered light in all directions. That light showed where the enemy was, and others would use it as a guide.

Off to his left, Pratt could hear more grenades and rail gun fire, but he avoided the urge to look at the scene around the fallen lighter and kept his arms and upper body rigid. He kept the laser as close as possible to the enemy weapons site on Hill 237.

Then a lighter ripped across his viewfinder from right to left. He was expecting it, but even he was surprised at the speed it traveled. The craft was flying very low and very fast. Just before it flew over Hill 237, it released a series of parachute-retarded cluster bombs. These munitions broke apart into sub-munitions that also fell apart further as they descended. They dropped exactly where his laser beam terminated. Hundreds of tennis-ball-sized spheres fell into the trees. Some exploded in the treetops, and others went off when they hit the ground. Shrapnel and blast waves churned up the earth and surrounding forest. Little survived in its wake. A few secondary explosions sounded as mortar ammunition stored outside the protective bunkers cooked off. Pratt saw little of the effects as the foliage masked them, but they were not hard to imagine.

Pratt spoke into the microphone pickup, "Dragon, Juniper. The drop was right on the money."

The response from Dragon was muted by two more lighters appearing directly overhead. Their engines were screaming at full throttle, which drowned out the female voice in his earpiece. Separated only by fifty meters, they raced toward the fallen craft. They too released cluster munitions. Each dropped a path of bomblets on either side of the stricken lighter. This time, Pratt could see them as they fell, and a roiling series of explosions formed two paths of destruction on either side of the downed craft. The area surrounding the lighter was immolated. It sounded like a combination of a freight train and rolling thunder. At least fifty Drakk'Har were hit, and any outside the immediate area of impact were thrown to the ground from the shock waves.

The speed of the lighters carried them out of sight quickly, and when the echoes of the multiple explosions faded, a long surreal silence followed. Then Pratt saw movement on the periphery of the impact area. Drakk'Har troops started moving toward the damaged lighter once more. This time no grenades or pistol shots stopped them. They advanced unchallenged and in silence. Pratt wondered if some of the bomblets had gotten inside the damaged lighter, but he saw no smoke or new damage since the run. Their silence probably meant they were out of ammo.

Nothing stopped the Drakk'Har this time, and they rapidly reached the sides of the lighter in no time at all. Only nine or ten crocs remained, but to a wounded crew, even one Drakk'Har warrior in close proximity was too many. Pratt squinted through the viewfinder and steeled himself, unwilling to look away. He found himself saying, "No, no, no, no…" in a low voice as he watched the unfolding drama. His guts were churning at his inability to change things. The green-skinned warriors started climbing up the sides toward the open hatchway on the top. Then without warning, columns of earth began to jump skyward near the base of the lighter. Pratt pulled his binoculars down and saw a lighter with CSAR markings approaching slowly from his left. Combat Search and Rescue were dedicated to responding to a situation where people needed assistance, usually under fire and regardless of the danger to themselves.

The CSAR lighter engines were throttled back and their approach went undetected until they began firing. The flight engineer controlled two chain guns firing twelve hundred rounds a minute out the front end of the craft, while a gunner on either side with a pair of coaxial machine guns added to the mix. Any remaining warriors were cut down as the craft did a lazy circle around the downed lighter.

Suddenly a Drakk'Har warrior leapt to the edge of the hatchway and then became immediately rigid as several small-caliber shots coming from inside the damaged lighter hit it in the upper body. One of the door gunners on the combat lighter saw this and added a few dozen more bullets into its chest. The now thoroughly dead body fell comically backwards off the craft. That was the last of the visible resistance.

The CSAR lighter did a full circle around the wrecked craft before landing with the chain guns pointing toward the river.

As soon as it touched down, several heavily armed troops with green khaki body armor and shouldered rifles erupted from the interior and fanned out around the fallen lighter. The odd shot was heard as they made sure a Drakk'Har warrior didn't get up again. A couple of them climbed up and shouted to the interior. The response must have been positive, as they rushed to the rim and then a couple of heads poked out of the hatchway and started to look around. One person from inside could be seen waving a pistol around. He had thick black hair, and one side of his face was covered in blood from a vicious gash in his temple. One of the CSAR troopers grabbed the pistol out of his hand and, after clearing it, tucked it away. His next move was to press a combat bandage against the side of the injured man's head. Some CSAR troopers dropped inside out of sight. Others remained on the edge of the hatch and kept an eye out for more enemy activity. They sighted down their weapons, using their scopes to check at longer distances.

More of the CSAR lighter crew emerged with stretchers and headed toward the downed craft. These people were corpsmen by training, although each was trained to fight, as well. They were lightly armed with only sidearms, which remained holstered. The CSAR pilot alighted and directed the rescue operation. He still wore his flight helmet with shaded visor down, and with his green flight suit, he reminded Pratt of a giant insect. A few people were pulled out of the hatchway and lowered to the ground. Those that could walk were escorted by the CSAR crew. Those that could not because of wounds or being unconscious were placed into the stretchers as soon as possible and carried quickly, yet caringly, to the CSAR craft.

A second CSAR lighter arrived from the northwest and landed on the opposite side from the first. It disgorged more troops and corpsmen to assist in the rescue. Events moved as rapidly as the injuries allowed them to. The severe cases had to be treated with care, and this slowed things down.

A lone enemy mortar round landed a few hundred meters to the east, and the pace of the CSAR crews picked up significantly. The last of the severely wounded were bundled into the back of the CSAR lighters. A couple of troopers dropped back inside the damaged lighter and, after a few moments, emerged with a couple of boxes of what looked like electronic gear, which they handed up to their team members. This gear was handed down to the others on the ground and carried off to the waiting craft. Meanwhile, several items were passed back to the pair inside, and they disappeared into the interior once more. Everyone else on the edge of the lighter climbed down, and thirty seconds later, the two last CSAR troopers came back into view. They took one last look around and then also climbed down and walked back to their waiting craft. Once they were in, both CSAR lighters dusted off together and began to climb into the air. Pratt didn't know whether it was a timer or if someone had pressed a button on a remote detonator, but several kilos of strategically placed plastic explosives detonated inside the crashed craft. The onboard fuel tanks ruptured and a fireball erupted from the inside of the downed lighter. The fuel, spread by the force of the explosion, destroyed the interior. As the two CSAR craft departed the area, the flaming hulk spewed thick black smoke into the air as flames consumed everything inside.

On the hillside, Pratt felt like he had woken from a nightmare. He had come remarkably close to watching a crew be massacred. That could easily have been him and his people. The thought of being cornered by large numbers of reptiles disturbed him deeply.

The sound of a rapidly running man behind him made him turn. One of the enlisted men from the command lighter jogged up to him. "General's compliments, sir. He needs to see you ASAP."

"Right, let's go. Williams, keep an eye on things, and call me if anything changes."

"Yes, sir."

* * *

Captain Levin and the other two lighters of Grasshopper flight had re-united after their drop of cluster munitions near the fallen lighter. They flew in formation back toward the fire base for replenishment of fuel and weapons. They were happy in the successful resolution.

A beep from his flight console accompanied with flashing text on a monitor told Levin he had new orders posted on the screen. He read them quickly and began to brief his crew on what to expect when they landed at the firebase.

Levin's lighter slipped through the skies easily on reduced throttle. With no payload of external weapons and reduced fuel load, it moved through the skies effortlessly. However, the earlier maximum power burn and radical maneuvering for the bomb run had increased the size of the cracks in the rear engine mount. Lighter B1285 now had several plainly visible, but they were all hidden under the cowling.

* * *

Sergeant Blake walked back to the engineer's aid station see how Belliveau was doing. He moved along a narrow road between the buildings. His weapon was in his hands, and he walked at a steady relaxed pace. However, he still scanned the surrounding area as he moved. Secured or not, this was still a war zone, and the enemy could appear anywhere. His marines were currently holding position until the units on either side of them accomplished their objectives and came up to their line. Blake had heard reports the others had run into more resistance than his marines had. A lot of the mortar fire had subsided, and only the odd enemy round fell in the small town.

As Blake approached the station, he saw a couple of corpsmen tending to the wounded. Seven men and women were on stretchers. A male corpsman was hovering over one of the stretchers with his medi-glove pressed against the neck of one of the injured. He paused before pulling the blanket up over the face of the victim and walked to another injured man.

The sergeant looked around quickly and was relieved to see Belliveau near the back of the small hut. His eyes were closed, and he looked comfortable.

Blake got the attention of a young female corporal nearest to him. She had the usual green khaki fatigues with a traditional Red Cross / Red Crescent stitched above her engineer badge. As she came into the light, he realized she had old scars on the left side of her face and neck. It looked like she had been in a bad fire or explosion at some point in her past. He didn't react to it; a lot of marines had wounds like hers, and he had seen much worse in this war.

"Yes, Sergeant?" she asked.

Blake nodded toward his squad mate and looked toward the back of the hut momentarily. "Belliveau, in the back on the left with the head wound. How's he doing?"

"Pretty well, considering. He has a deep cut on his temple and some bruising. He had some debris embedded in the skin, but we got most of it out. We were able to put in some temporary stitches, sprayed on a dermal patch, and gave him some pain killers. He was complaining of a bad headache a few minutes ago which might indicate a worsening condition, so we're putting him on the next medevac lighter for a cranial scan. As of right now, he's stable; so as long as we can get him back to fleet soon, I give him a good chance at a full recovery."

"When is the medevac scheduled?"

"Hopefully in the next ten to fifteen minutes. We already had two cancelled on us. They must be busy. Do you need anything else, Sarge? We have to get ready to transport these men."

"No, Corporal. Thank you. Carry on."

Blake decided not to walk over to Belliveau. He looked relaxed and was in good hands. Blake turned and walked back to the rest of his men up the narrow road.

* * *

Due to the proximity of the action, reports of the failure of Borrk's Third Shock Company to grab any warm bloods from the crashed aircraft reached Planet Lord Slassh very quickly. Drakk'Har seldom took failure well, and he screamed for Swamp Master Borrk to report to him immediately. Word was relayed quickly through communication landlines.

* * *

"Lieutenant Pratt reporting as ordered, General," the lieutenant said as he entered the command lighter. He had to speak loudly to be heard over the whine of the equipment, air conditioning, and generators. The command lighter staff had large, padded noise-canceling headphones over their ears.

General Carstairs looked away from his monitors and peered over his shoulder. He indicated Pratt should go outside before quickly turning back to look at the displays and talk into his microphone. Pratt retreated through the hatch and waited just outside the door.

Carstairs came out half a minute later and indicated Pratt should follow him. They walked together away from the noise of the command lighter and stood in the shade of some trees. The General turned and talked without preamble. His expression was serious.

"I hear the CSAR evac went well."

"Yes, sir. Was touch and go for a moment, but air support saved the day. A few more minutes and..." Pratt trailed off with a shrug.

"No doubt. Lieutenant, I want to bring you up to speed on what's going on. The bad news: We've lost a lot more lighters than usual on this op. Some of them were lost in space actions when the tenders were hit, but primarily whoever set up the anti-air defenses on this world knows his job. They're well hidden, integrated, and still seem to be communicating effectively. Losses in this area have been severe, and CSAR is working overtime to respond to all of the downed birds. Only one got hit coming into this area, but several were lost ascending back into orbit for the second and third waves. The standard lighter does not have the same level of protection my command post did, and they were able to bring mine down, as one example. As a result, I've no idea when we can get a medevac in here for our people. I spoke with your medic, Jacobs. J.P. and your man Mendez are stable for the moment. Worst-case scenario is a twelve-hour delay and they will both survive, probably.

"We put a lot of effort into communication interdiction, and we thought we had done a good job. However, it turns out we missed the mark by a wide margin. Some of the sites we hit from orbit were decoys, and our lighters are paying for it now. It looks like they have several mobile anti-air elements that we are now playing cat and mouse with. As a result, a lot of the reserve lighters have already been committed to cover losses. I've decided to stay in this position and run the show from here. That should free up one asset, at the very least. We are fully operational and communicating with the division and Fleet; we're just not as mobile as I would like. I was originally hoping to only be here for an hour at the most, but it looks like we will be staying here until we dust off tomorrow."

Pratt nodded as he listened. The general continued, "So, I'll need you to look at the current defenses and revise them to protect the CP overnight."

Pratt didn't mean to interrupt, but he spoke without even thinking. "Sir, there's no way we can defend this position effectively with just my people alone and—"

The general interrupted, holding up his hand. "I realize that, and I've already put in a call. You can expect a platoon to arrive just before sunset as reinforcements. They'll be coming up the west side of the hill."

"A platoon? Sir, a hill this size will take at least a company to—"

"A platoon is all I can give you, Lieutenant. They were tasked to this position regardless, and other units are tied up elsewhere. Our priorities have to be the destruction of the facilities in our ops areas, and we need as many boots on the ground as possible to do that. Besides, we have a commanding view here, and any assault group of any size will be seen approaching from well off."

The general grabbed a short stick and began drawing in the dirt. He scratched a crude representation of the hill in the loose dirt. "When the platoon arrives, you can turn responsibility for the hilltop defense over to their officer. They can set up their perimeter as they see fit around the high ground, here. I want you to take your people and form an inner perimeter around the command lighter in the lower corner of that position, here. You will be the reserve force and can fill in any holes. I will make it clear to the platoon commander that your people are under my command."

"Yes, sir," was all Pratt could say, forced to play with the cards he was dealt. Pratt looked up at the faint red sun. He judged they had roughly six hours of daylight left. A platoon may not have been enough, but that sounded better than just his people holding the summit.

* * *

Swamp Master Borrk had received the summons to the planet lord's command bunker in short order. He took a few key members of his staff with him, in case he needed any information. The trip was not dangerous, as both bunkers were reasonably close and had interconnecting tunnels between them. However, he was worried, and for several good reasons. First, his growth facilities had been ravaged by aerial and ground-based attack. He doubted any of the ships or supplies would be salvageable. It would take years of effort to rebuild. Second, he had miscalculated in sending Drawwl away with the majority of his most effective troops. That had expanded his holdings, but left the main town defenses a lot weaker than they should have been. Last, he had been summoned to see Planet Lord Slassh and had nothing to offer. His loss of the warm blood tribute on the plain outside the town was fresh in his mind. That was the only thing that could have saved him, and his troops had failed to secure them. Borrk was going to punish the troop commander responsible, but Slassh's summons arrived before the commander could get there. Giving Slassh the head of the commander might mitigate his fury, and he did not even have that.

Borrk's mind raced as he tried to think of what to say. On the positive side, his recently acquired resin facility was still undamaged, by all reports. He still had several hundred Drakk'Har under arms, and they were spread out in the wetlands, relatively safe from attack until needed. Also, Drawwl and his troops were poised to strike the enemy forces from behind. In the end, it all came down to Drawwl. If he could succeed and advance from the summit into the town, then Borrk would be given credit for that victory. That was how he had to present it. There would be the usual groveling, but Slassh needed Borrk and his troops for his own personal survival.

Borrk briefly considered a challenge—a fight to the death with the winner taking all. Borrk dismissed it immediately. Slassh was a full head taller and much heavier than Borrk, and even without that imbalance, Slassh was a capable pit fighter and had a lot more experience. The advantage would clearly be on the planet lord's side and, therefore, not an option.

As Borrk approached the hatch to Slassh's command bunker, he decided he would have to hope for positive future events and do a good job being subservient in the meantime. One of his staff members went ahead of him in the tunnel. He would wait until Borrk signaled before opening the hatch to the planet lord's bunker. Borrk took a few moments to order his thoughts and then signaled to the creature in front.

The hatch opened, and Borrk could see nothing out of place. It looked very much like his own command bunker, except Slassh's was larger, with several extra chambers added on. He did have extra staff and equipment, so he needed more room for them. The staff member entered first, then Borrk followed by the remainder of his followers. Slassh was there, off in a far corner talking to one of his minions. The back of the planet lord was to Borrk, and due to Slassh's large size, he could not see clearly to whom he was speaking. Protocol was clear, and Borrk knew he had to report to Slassh. He left his staff behind and moved toward the far side of the chamber. To get there, he had to go around stacked equipment, which placed an empty wall to his left side.

If a signal was given, Borrk was not aware of it. When he was halfway across the room, Slassh side-stepped and turned to face him. Borrk could see that behind Slassh was a warrior with a rail gun, and *that* was unusual to see in a command bunker. Wordlessly and without warning, the warrior leveled the rail gun and fired a burst directly into Borrk's abdomen. Several of the rounds went directly through him and blasted the wall behind with blood and gore. Borrk fell, first to his knees, then onto his belly. The wound was substantial, but he lived. Borrk's breath came ragged and raspy, echoing pitifully in the room. All of his strength vanished as the shock of being shot many times spread through him. He lay there, helpless.

* * *

Slassh approached slowly. He was in no hurry and savored the moment. As he approached the fallen swamp master, the sound of his ceramic blade sliding slowly out of its sheath was the only noise, except for Borrk's raspy breathing.

Slassh leaned over the body of the wounded Drakk'Har and said the traditional words that had been used for centuries. "For your failure, what was yours is now mine."

He slid the edge of the blade across the exposed throat of Borrk, and blood surged from the severed arteries, pooling on the floor. Borrk thrashed a few times and then lay still.

Slassh dragged both sides of his blade across the chest of his victim, removing most, but not all, of the blood. He returned the blade to its sheath. An unblooded blade was a sign of weakness to Drakk'Har.

Slassh regarded the body for a few moments before indicating with a claw flick that the body should be removed and disposed of. Several Drakk'Har leapt to action. As the bloody corpse was dragged out of the room, Slassh's gaze fell on Borrk's surviving staff. He paused to look at them, his gaze hard and unyielding. They were nervous, as staff members would sometimes be killed with their masters to stop retributive killings later. However, Slassh's blood lust had been slaked for the moment, and he simply commanded the staff members to inform him of Borrk's holdings and where his troops were. By default, they were now the planet lord's to command.

The staff filled him in quickly on all that had been requested, and that was when Slassh learned for the first time of Drawwl and his force heading toward the back side of Skull Ridge.

* * *

Drawwl had no idea Borrk was dead as his columns halted at the base of the hill. His radios were turned off, and he would not try communicating until he had something positive to report. He was on the east side of the hill and could see nothing of the higher elevations because of the trees combined with the natural steep slope of the hill. The vegetation was thick, and Drawwl could only see eight of his warriors as a result. One of them was a guide who pointed to the path he needed to ascend. The path wasn't obvious, and Drawwl could only see it when pointed out. It had not been traveled for some time, and small plants and ferns had already grown over the area. The guide began speaking in hushed tones.

"Lord, this path leads up the hill almost to the top. It ends in a narrow valley before heading up higher. From there, we have many trails to use. I've sent scouts ahead, and the top of the hill has a small warm blood force, but the valley is clear."

Drawwl thought on this a while. "Send up the troops, but do not proceed past the valley. I want the full force in place before we attack. We shall overwhelm them as the sun sets. Bring the columns up, and climb in silence. Anyone who betrays our position will feed the fish with their entrails. Understood?"

"Yes, Lord." The guide bowed and backed up simultaneously.

The scouts motioned to the warriors near Drawwl. They slid past him and ascended quietly. Drawwl would wait until Kek and a few dozen warriors had ascended before he went up himself.

CHAPTER 20 – EXPLORATION

The day before, the firebase on which Captain Levin was standing had been sparse jungle. Nothing of consequence had been there—just another piece of unremarkable jungle, no different than any other.

During the initial planning, this particular piece of land had been designated by an unnamed operations officer reviewing initial satellite photos, contour maps, and intelligence reports. As the sixth such area to be designated from orbit, it was associated with the sixth letter of the alphabet and labeled as area F or, in the military alphabet, Foxtrot.

Three lighters had dropped special fuel-air bombs to clear foliage and brush from the area. The bombs were unofficially called "daisy cutters" by the troops because of their design. Only flat earth was left behind, as everything else was cast out of the blast radius. Other lighters had landed within minutes, disgorging troops, and Firebase Foxtrot was born.

The first lighters to land carried in elements of marine infantry who began to dig into the perimeter of the cleared area. Heavy weapons were emplaced and set with interlocking fields of fire. Forward of those positions, they lay mines and razor wire to secure the outer edge of the Firebase. Sensors were established and wired into portable power generators.

Unmanned and heavily armed aerial surveillance drones were launched and began patrolling well out from the Firebase, feeding back intelligence to the operators. Mortar pits were dug, sandbagged, and crudely camouflaged. A few ranging shots were lobbed to check the lay of the weapons and familiarize the mortar crews with the surrounding terrain.

Within an hour of the daisy cutter blasts, the small base was secure and operational. Refueling, repair, intelligence, command, and basic triage medical facilities were all established to assist operations during the raid. Inflatable buildings had gone up in minutes and been occupied before they were fully filled with gas. A network of hoses radiated out from a series of cargo lighters that carried fuel, lubricants, and spare parts. Once empty, each lighter returned to the orbiting fleet, and a laden lighter took its place to offload the continuing cycle of supply runs. Everyone had practiced their roles many times over in training and knew exactly what needed to be done.

The firebase was less than a day old, but had a heavy mixed aroma of fuel and smoke. Several burned-out lighters lay in various positions around the firebase, showing just how hotly contested this piece of real estate had been over the last few hours. There had been several heavy attacks, but all had been repulsed. An enemy mortar crew had gotten within range and was able to get off three rounds before counter battery fire obliterated them. One round had hit a fuel-laden lighter through blind luck, which caused a lot of damage. Two incoming lighters had since been plucked from the sky with shoulder-fired anti-air missiles.

Captain Levin stood at the side of his craft near the charred remains of the fuel lighter. He could see another pile of blackened metal that Levin assumed was a lighter that had hit the ground at full velocity. Nothing visually identifiable was visible in the crater and the thin smoke carried over to him from the edge of the firebase landing zone. Other unidentifiable scents were there as well, but the smell of burnt fuel overwhelmed everything else. Beyond the wrecks, crude trenches and dugouts had been created to house perimeter security. Marines in those positions looked out over the surrounding terrain with binoculars and monitors showing aerial surveillance footage watching for anything out of place.

Levin stood alone. He had sent his flight crew to get a late lunch from the field mess while the lighters in his flight were fuelled and had their internal configuration changed over. The fuelling crew had just left after signing off the flight log book. He watched as firebase marines started to carry light tubular framing through the hatch and into the back of his lighter. They worked wordlessly, having done this many times in the past. The work crew finished quickly, and he entered the hatch while the ground crew supervisor stood in the door filling in the flight log. Levin went around the tubes and physically checked several connections. Those he didn't touch, he inspected and looked for anything out of place. Nothing seemed to be amiss. He walked over to the ground crew supervisor and took the log from her. He slid a stylus out of a holder on the left bicep of his green flight suit and reviewed the latest entry on the flight log data tablet. The ground crew supervisor had written:

'INTERNAL CONFIGURATION CHANGED TO MEDEVAC STANDARD 1C-A. UP WEIGHT 74K' along with the date / time and her rank and last name. Levin checked a box underneath and signed as having accepted the change. She thanked him and walked away, having two more lighters to modify. Levin changed the log display to the Weight & Balance screen and added seventy-four kilos of miscellaneous weight to the total ship weight to account for the addition of the tubes and webbing. He signed that page as well. As he accepted the change, a copy of the log change was uploaded through the lighter communications system to the orbiting fleet for their records. Once it had been registered there, a receipt message was sent down. A square in the top corner of the screen turned green when the tablet received the acknowledgement, which meant all procedures had been correctly completed. He slid the tablet into a holder by the door so Wallace could review it when he returned, but the change was minor.

Levin didn't read too much into his newly assigned role. Typically, as a raid-type operation wound down, many lighters were configured as medevacs to carry wounded for what was known as the last lift. Even though several hours were still left in the mission, darkness was falling and air-to-ground missions at night were less frequent. It wasn't that they couldn't operate at night. The drawback was target designation and potential friendly fire incidents. The bonus was the flight crew could sleep inside the lighter in relative comfort on the newly installed stretcher surfaces.

Corporal Wallace, the flight engineer, appeared around the side of Grasshopper Three, which was twenty meters away. Levin recognized him immediately from the relaxed gait and long stride. Wallace carried a small white box, which he handed to Levin. "There you go, sir. We missed the hot chow by ten minutes, but I picked up a box lunch for you. Any problems with the changeover?"

Levin took the box. "Thanks. No. Everything looks good, and the records have been updated. Nothing to do for eight hours. We are on enforced crew rest." Wallace entered the hatch and snagged the flight log on the way past. He had a few entries to make himself, and Levin knew the eager flight engineer would double-check the installed racks.

The captain looked at the cover of the box and glanced at the white label. The tightly packed blue writing gave a detailed list of contents, ingredients, calories, and disposal instructions in four languages. He skipped over all that. Above the Mandarin characters, he saw a Star of David symbol indicating the meal was kosher, which satisfied him. Meals that did not satisfy all dietary requirements were rare, but he checked religiously anyway. The expiry date was still a few weeks away as well, which meant it should be reasonably fresh. He opened the box lid and rummaged through the contents. He found a steak sandwich on a bagel sealed in thick clear plastic, a plastic bowl with a small green salad, orange juice, a square piece of carrot cake, and a utensil packet with salt, pepper, and an antiseptic hand towel. He sat down against the side of the vehicle and put the opened box in his lap.

He took a folding pen knife from one of his zippered pockets and slit open the sandwich wrapping. Levin took a bite and was pleasantly surprised to find the meat was real beef and quite tasty. Levin wondered what expenses must have been incurred to bring this food across thirty light years, then bring it down from orbit on a supply run. He looked around him and realized how quiet it was. The fuelling pumps had been shut down, and the only noise he could hear was the odd, muted conversation in the distance. A gentle breeze blew in from the east, but apart from that, the day was calm. He relaxed against the side of his lighter and ate in silence, looking out across the scene in front of him. Moments like this were rare during operations, and he savored the moment, letting his thoughts wander far away.

* * *

Second Lieutenant Wicks emerged from a hut near the edge of the Drakk'Har town, leaving his company commander and several other officers behind. Wicks had been summoned to the company HQ for a quick briefing, which was short and hurried. His platoon commander told him that a marine from another platoon had discovered the collapsed roof of a tunnel. It sloped down several meters and appeared to lead into a substantial network of tunnels further underground. As the tunnels appeared to go through Wicks's designated area of responsibility, he was tasked to investigate it.

PFC Perkins fell in behind the officer. Because he carried the squad radio, he had to be within a certain distance of Wicks at all times. Both of them made their way back to the rest of the squad. Wicks found he agreed with the assessment of Perkins that Blake had given earlier. Perkins was not afraid or fearful. He was, well, "twitchy" was the only word that fit. Every time a distant mortar round exploded, even if all the way across town, Perkins would unconsciously flinch. It had annoyed Wicks to the point where he tried to keep Perkins out of his sight wherever possible. Blake seemed to think this would improve over time, and this *was* Perkins's first actual operation in the field. Perkins had reacted correctly in dealing with Belliveau's injury, so at least he had promise. Given that progress, Wicks let it slide for the moment. He had other, more important, matters to deal with.

As Wicks walked back to his squad, he mentally ran through the limited information he had been given. It could be a service tunnel or used for some communications or military purpose. Perhaps some sort of drain or sewer system. He hoped for the latter, thinking of his marines' welfare, as he would not expect to find Drakk'Har in a sewer.

Fighting in enclosed spaces was not the best situation for a professional soldier due to limited cover and many ambush and booby trap dangers. Options were severely limited underground. Still, his marines had some training in enclosed space combat, but not enough, in his opinion. In those situations, you never had enough.

The lieutenant skipped over a low wall surrounding a partially destroyed hut. One of the walls had fragmented from a mortar burst, and a meter-wide hole was blasted in the back side. He could see the barrel of a weapon protruding from the hole and the side of LCPL Reid's face keeping vigil toward the front line. The roof was still intact, which gave shelter from the weak sun and wind. The marines under Wicks had noted that before occupying it as their temporary quarters.

Wicks walked to the door and saw Blake sitting on his pack, eating some fruit out of a can. Wordlessly, the officer summoned Sergeant Blake with quick eye contact combined with a head gesture. Blake drained the remains of the juice from the can while standing and exited the structure. Together, the pair walked to the edge of the wall. Wicks pulled out an overhead map of the town with the entrance to the tunnel marked with a black V. He pointed to the entrance and spoke. "Sergeant, we have what is suspected to be a tunnel complex inside our area of responsibility. Lieutenant Pfeiffer has ordered we investigate it before we head out to Hill 170. Get your people together with their gear. We will drop the packs at the tunnel entrance and proceed in with combat rig alone. We will head out as soon as Sergeant Donovan and his people from First Squad get here to relieve us. Should only be a few minutes. Questions?"

"No, sir. I will make sure we have lots of frags and marker lights handy. I would like to go talk to the engineers and see if they have anything special we can use."

"Good idea. Thank you, Sergeant. Carry on." Wicks turned to sit on his own backpack, which was leaning against the hut's exterior wall. He could hear Blake inside, motivating his people to get up, grab their gear, and get ready to move. He saw no sign of Sergeant Donovan's squad, so he took a few moments and thought through the orders he would need to present to the squad in a few minutes. The small details took the most time, but consideration of those details saved lives. As far as Wicks was concerned, he had no lives to spare in his squad. He regretted losing Belliveau earlier, but Wicks was sure he would live to fight another day, as long as he could get back to the Fleet. That was out of his hands for the moment. Wicks focused his thoughts on the task at hand and began to think through the possibilities.

* * *

Deputy Planet Lord Tlish was content. He had arrived at the small Drakk'Har town almost on the opposite side of Mindon-2 from Slassh after many hours of travel. His low-flying shuttle had arrived minutes before the initial orbital bombardment had started in this area. He had been receiving an update from the local swamp master when the first attack came. They were able to retreat to their bunker safely and had been holed up there ever since. While reports from other areas were fragmented, he knew warm bloods had landed. However, the facilities Tlish was in had only been struck from above, and no ground troops were present as far as he knew.

Tlish would have played a larger role in the planetary defense if he could. On a world closer to the warm bloods, there would have been nuclear-tipped ballistic missiles waiting to engage orbiting ships. However, Mindon was thought to be far enough behind the lines to not need such a luxury. Slassh had made the decision not to get them. They were expensive to procure and even more expensive to maintain. Slassh assigned the funds elsewhere. Each swamp master and lord had an armed force to protect his own territory. A coordinated planetary army did not exist, and even if it did, Tlish knew Slassh would control it and not him.

So at this point, the locals had to defend themselves. Several of the swamp masters did have nuclear warheads and tactical missiles that could reach several klem. However, the warm bloods had landed very close to critical production facilities. Using nuclear devices that close to their own facilities would be counterproductive, to say the least. Radioactivity caused mutations in the growths, and that would be disastrous in the growth facilities.

His landing area had been attacked almost immediately. The first series of blue bolts descended from the heavens, obliterating the shuttle that had brought Tlish and two others nearby. He was relatively safe in the simple bunker on the outer edge of the town. An odd random blast appeared from orbit on occasion, but it appeared to be simple harassing fire.

With the shuttles destroyed, he had no way of returning, regardless of Slassh's demands. Not that he had heard from the planet lord, and with communications severely disrupted, he was not expecting to. That suited him just fine. He was already reveling in the fact that Slassh would certainly fall after this assault, and Tlish would rise to become the new planet lord of Mindon-2.

Tlish would have to spend a good portion of his personal wealth to rebuild the planet's infrastructure so they could start new growth facilities. A considerable investment would have to be made, and it would take many years to come back to a fraction of full production. The orbital bombardment was remarkably effective and left much of the infrastructure in tatters. However, the massive profit in growing ships for the emperor would pay him back in the long term, and he would then be able to sit back and enjoy the fruits of his labors. Other operations producing resins and growth hormone would be easier to set up and profitable in the short term. They could be exported to other facilities; there was always a demand. If he could get the other worlds' production facilities dependent on his chemicals, the sky would be the limit. The last Drakk'Har to gain a monopoly on all ship-growth facilities was currently sitting on the imperial throne.

This thought made him pause. As the emperor had ascended, he had to choose trusted Drakk'Har to take over the individual growth facilities. Slassh had been one of those chosen, and as far as Tlish could tell, he had been loyal to the emperor. *Would that relationship spare Slassh from execution?* He considered this for a long time and decided that Drakk'Har at that level of power were typically pragmatic. Even the emperor could not allow one of his planet lords to live after such devastation, regardless of whatever loyalty existed previously. Planet lords were charged with the safe keeping and continued operation of the growth facilities. *No*, thought Tlish, *Slassh had to die at the emperor's order to pay for the losses suffered on Mindon-2.* No other option made sense.

He kept following the same logical train of thought, regardless. Even if the emperor did spare Slassh, he would be in a much weaker state politically, and Tlish would lose nothing. If that did happen, a covert communication to another planet lord for assistance might prove mutually advantageous. Options always existed, no matter what the situation.

So Tlish would succeed as planet lord. That was certain as long as he was not killed in the meantime, which was remote at this stage. Then, as he rebuilt the production on Mindon-2, he could think about undermining his rival planet lords holding the other growth facilities. Tlish would have many concerns. The others would try to overthrow him, as he would be in a weak position for many years. Plus, he had the usual problem of power-hungry underlings to monitor. Still, the imperial throne would be within his reach. Dare he think he could rise that high? There were so many problems to overcome first! Tlish could not begin to count the issues in just rebuilding the planet. Still, the challenge was not insurmountable.

Tlish was uncommonly intelligent for a Drakk'Har. He had risen to his position not through direct conflict, although he certainly had few qualms in doing that when necessary. Some Drakk'Har wanted power, but just as many were satisfied being common soldiers, guards, or lower level authorities for whatever reason. Some simply did not want to be looking over their shoulder all the time. Others were satisfied with a full belly and a willing female.

A few, like Tlish, were never satisfied and worked, schemed, and plotted continuously to improve their status, power, and holdings. Tlish always took a more passive approach and let others do his dirty work wherever possible. Vengeful allies were known to take retribution against Drakk'Har who killed off profitable relationships with others. However, his black claws were usually free of blame. In this situation, he was absolutely blameless, as the warm blood fleet had destroyed Slassh's holdings. This was the perfect situation for him to be in: Slassh got the blame, and Tlish got the planet. An evil grin spread across his lips as he celebrated the power, riches, and choice of females that were soon to be his. He enjoyed the thoughts so much, he let them wander and imagined rising much higher. Remote? Perhaps, but certainly possible, nonetheless.

* * *

"How is he?" Lieutenant Pratt asked in a low voice. He was standing over Corporal Jacobs, who was in the middle of changing the bandage on Staff Sergeant Mendez's leg. The old bandage was laying off to the side of the makeshift stretcher, and the wound was exposed. The discarded dressing was covered in dark red blood with green- and brown-colored material mixed in. The wound itself didn't look that bad; Jacobs must have cleaned it up prior to putting on a new bandage. It appeared relatively normal except for the swollen white skin surrounding the bite marks which looked like something on a cadaver.

"Well, suh." Jacobs paused as he located his thoughts. His accent was thicker, as he was quite tired. He looked up into Pratt's eyes, and the officer could see the strain of the last few days on his face. "He's in a bad way. We've kept him unda, but de wound is festerin'. He's delusional from de pain, and I's don't have nuthin' powerful nuff to stop de venom from affecting de wound. Only hope he got is to get him up in de fleet right quick and let de real docs get a crack at him."

"You're better than any doc in my books, Jacobs, and are doing a great job, given the conditions. The general has put in another call for a medevac flight. I'm told they're running short of lighters due to anti-air fire. The ones that are left are heavily tasked. Keep him as comfortable as you can, and we'll get him out of here ASAP. Make sure you get some rest, too. Have someone take over for a few hours, and get some sack time. You earned it." The officer emphasized that with a brief touch of his palm on Jacobs's shoulder.

"Yes, suh. Dank you, suh," Jacobs said gloomily.

* * *

For the first time in the entire operation, PFC Perkins was very glad he had the radio on his back. While it would work underground to some extent, it also relayed data and voice signals from the personal radios the team carried and rebroadcast the signals. No one wanted to lose communications to the outside world, so Perkins was detailed to stay at the entrance of the tunnel and guard it as the rest of the group split into two fire teams and entered the tunnel.

Perkins watched as the last of the group went up and into the tunnel. He was starting to relax a bit. The action they had seen to this point was actually less intense than training. In exercises, they threw multiple things at you for days on end. Here, hours of tension were followed by minutes of explosive action. The big difference was in training if you were "'killed," you were evacuated to a holding area and were back on the line the next day as a simulated replacement. The PFC had been intimidated being this close to an officer, but he had found 2nd Lieutenant Wicks to be a decent officer. Perkins was quietly impressed by the man and the amount of detail he could keep coordinated in his mind at one time. Perkins kept his back to the debris next to the tunnel entrance and scanned the surrounding area for anything amiss.

* * *

Second Lieutenant Wicks was in the tunnel about twenty meters shy of an intersection with a large tunnel. Private First Class Messina and Lance Corporal Reid were in front of him, using the walls as cover with their weapons pointed opposite ways down the adjoining corridor guarding the approaches. Wicks wanted to be on point, but Sergeant Blake had taken Johnston, Tyler, and Corporal Sanchez further along the right-hand tunnel. Blake had the experience and much more training. The officer's job was to lead and coordinate, and in this case, Wicks needed to stay behind.

* * *

Sergeant Blake was in front, his weapon butt on his shoulder. He walked slowly forward, testing the footing and looking all over with every step. Step, look low, look waist high, look at the ceiling, step again, and repeat the process if clear. None of them had night vision or flashlights active. A thin film of bioluminescent algae on the walls gave off a surprising amount of light. You could not read by the light, but when their night vision adjusted, they could see where they were by the dull glow.

The tunnel walls were vertical and slowly transitioned inward to a peaked gothic arch three meters overhead. The tunnel was two meters wide, and Sanchez was off to Blake's left side and slightly behind. He had ordered her to keep that position so she was out of his peripheral vision. If he saw anything move, he didn't want to mistake it for her.

Sanchez and Blake had bayonets fixed. Behind them, Johnston and Tyler followed with their weapons raised in a similar way, but with no bayonets. They walked as quietly as possible. No talking, and radio volumes turned as low as possible.

The tunnel wandered back and forth to the left and right by a meter every fifteen meters or so. The tunnel undulation meant that Blake could never see more than fifteen meters down the tunnel. Bad from a reconnaissance perspective, but no one could shoot more than fifteen meters without hitting a wall. The floor was perfectly level, clean and surprisingly dry, considering it was a fair distance underground. Blake judged it had been professionally built and was quite solid. The tunnel was unremarkable, otherwise. No adornments, decorations, or markings.

The silent group had gone down the tunnel about thirty-five to forty meters. They had encountered a few intersections and there were delays as each branch was explored in turn. All of them were dead ends or obvious traps. Sanchez had barely missed being struck by a hidden viper, but Blake's bayonet had made short work of that. The temperature in the tunnel was noticeably cooler than the surface. However, each of the four in the advancing group didn't feel cold. Fear of unknown encounters, the need to be absolutely silent, and the slow speed of their advance all contributed to the constant tension and kept them drenched in sweat.

They had settled into a fairly regular pattern when Blake spotted something in the distance. His hand shot up, formed a fist, and everyone stopped with weapons raised. It was not something he saw, but rather something he didn't see. In the dim glow of the lights, it looked like the base of the tunnel wall was pressed back. He motioned with his hand for the other three to hold still, and he advanced very slowly. Within a minute, he could see a rough diamond-shaped opening in the floor about a meter and a half wide. Reflections of the glowing algae on the walls of the opening let him realize it was either a pool or flooded side tunnel. The closer he approached, the slower he went. The crocs could move lightning quick in water, and he did not want to be surprised.

The surface had no algae, but nonetheless, he could see the side tunnel large enough for a large croc to slip through. He came within a meter of the surface and stared in with intense concentration. Nothing stirred. A little water pooled to the side of the entrance meant it had been used and quite recently. He motioned for the rest of his team to come forward and waited while they padded up behind him.

Sanchez came up on his left, and Blake gave her a signal to cover him. She aimed her weapon at the water, and Blake dropped his weapon slightly as he reached in a side pocket. He pulled out a flat black cylinder a little larger and twice as thick as a hockey puck with seashell-style grooves cut from the outer edge to the center, where they all met. An oversized pin protruded from the side of the unit. Blake pulled this out with his thumb, and a small red light blinked three times. He lowered himself slightly and placed the device on the surface of the water. He placed it near the center of the opening and let it go carefully. The red light blinked again three times as the device settled on the surface of the calm pool. Blake waited patiently as the motion decreased. Once the bobbing had ceased and the unit was fairly still, a green light blinked three times and then went out.

Blake breathed a sigh of relief and backed away from the hole, then motioned his people to move further down the tunnel past the water. He could not see the device now that the lights had gone out. He had been told by the engineers what it could do, and he wanted to be nowhere near it now that the device was armed.

Blake reformed the order of the group five meters down the tunnel. He began to relax, confident no one could sneak up behind him without his knowing. He motioned for the group to continue on and resumed the step–look–look–look–step routine and advanced down the tunnel.

* * *

Planet Lord Slassh was in a foul mood, which would not have surprised any of his staff as that was his usual countenance. Even killing Borrk had not given him any long-term satisfaction. He pounded his clawed feet on the tough floor and fingered the blade at his side. His bunker under the town had become a prison. A large series of interconnected chambers had five heavy ceramic blast doors leading to several tunnels. The work spaces were generous in size, designed for the staff and to accommodate communications equipment. The arched roof gave it an open feel, even though the chamber was deep underground. The ceiling was not designed to be aesthetic, however. The curves gave it strength, and that had saved all their lives earlier with the near miss. It was practical engineering that had other benefits purely by coincidence.

Slassh moved back and forth through the space, waiting for any one of his staff to do something even the slightest bit objectionable. Setback after setback. Defeat after defeat. Slassh's frustration level soared.

He needed tribute and victory to minimize the emperor's wrath. He had been handpicked by the emperor to replace him on this world. He had been a loyal follower in his youth and followed the stronger Drakk'Har leader as a faithful disciple. Slassh followed orders without objection. He bribed, cajoled, subjugated, and killed at his master's behest, and this had allowed the current emperor to take the throne from the weakling who preceded him. Slassh's reward had been planet lord status and domain over this world, but that was now in danger and that could not stand.

If presented with enough warm bloods, the damage done to his facilities might—just might—be tolerated as an act of war. Slassh had never opposed the emperor, at least not in any provable way, so he felt reasonably secure. Still, he was feeling the effects of enemy troops in the town above this bunker. With his communications degraded, few could report to him, and he had no way of coordinating multiple units. He had lost most of his remote sensors. Satellites and other intelligence-gathering devices had been obliterated in the opening moments of the conflict. The few sensors he did have were passive only and unreliable from the interfering radiations of the enemy fleet above.

The situation on the ground was no better. Drawwl had not reported in, so Slassh had no idea of his progress, if any. Tlish was also silent on the opposite side of Mindon-2. Knowing his nature, Slassh assumed he was either dead or in hiding, waiting for the tide to turn. Kaaw was still sending in swimmers delivering messages, but all they were telling him was how many craft had been blotted from the skies. While that was heartening, it did nothing to improve his standing with the emperor. He needed the warm bloods inside those craft alive, but when shot down, they were invariably killed or rescued.

Rage replaced reason, and yet he knew he could do nothing without more information. His scouts were depleted; most were killed within an arkle of reaching the surface. The flooded tunnels were passable and still used. The swimmers could move very quickly through them, but they only went to the major waterways. Once the swimmers left the water's protection to go overland, they were shot, bombed, and strafed—usually never to return. If they did happen to make it back, the news was always bad and fragmentary. He had no big picture overview of the battle space and was therefore unable to take any decisive action, which was exactly what the enemy wanted.

Slassh had to be patient, and that was not easy for a Drakk'Har. For a planet lord, the situation was intolerable. So his ire rose further, and he looked hard for something to trigger a violent outburst to relieve some of the stress he was feeling. A pang of hunger was that trigger.

"You!" Slassh said harshly to a minor staff member. "Bring me a half dozen Kyber monkeys and some fresh Eulba blood. Now!" The yell echoed in the room's sub-chambers.

The terrified Drakk'Har retreated instantly, bowing and moving toward one of the hatches. The doorway lead to Slassh's personal quarters and food storage area.

Slassh moved toward his communications staff for another disappointing update, he was sure.

* * *

Sergeant Blake saw another T intersection up ahead heading left and right and pointed it out to Sanchez. She nodded that she saw it, too. Blake motioned silently that she and he should go left and the others would go right. Everyone confirmed the order wordlessly, and they moved forward again. Just as Blake and Sanchez were about to turn the corner, a shaft of harsh artificial light blazed from around the left turn, accompanied by a loud bang. The light beam was immediately partially interrupted by something moving within it, and the shadows moved on the walls and floor. Whatever approached him was large, making a lot of noise, and in a hurry.

Blake did not hesitate. He stepped quickly into the intersection facing the left hand corridor with weapon raised. He saw a croc lumbering down a short ramp from an open door. He sighted at the center of mass and fired his weapon in a quick burst. Three full metal jacket rounds struck the Drakk'Har in the chest, destroying its heart, and it collapsed.

* * *

Sanchez turned the corner as Blake moved and could see an illuminated chamber ahead with several scaly creatures inside.

Sanchez pulled out a grenade. Her many hours of practice paid off; in a single fluid motion, she pulled the pin and tossed it deep into the chamber. It passed well over the head of the falling Drakk'Har in the tunnel. The grenade struck the floor of the room just past the hatchway before rolling deeper inside.

"Frag out!" she yelled and ducked back behind the turn of the intersection, her voice echoing along the hard tunnel. She left enough room for Blake, who needed no further encouragement to join her. Both covered their ears, opened their mouths, and waited for the blast wave.

* * *

Slassh was seldom surprised, but the sound of three rapid shots certainly did the trick. He was starting to wonder what was happening, when a dull metallic clunk—clunk noise came to his ears. As he was around the corner from the open door, he could not see the cause, but a second later, a terrible explosion filled the chamber. The sub-chamber was filled with white-hot shrapnel. Two Drakk'Har staff members were killed instantly, several pieces of electronic gear disabled, and many pock marks appeared in the roof and wall. While none of the shrapnel reached Slassh or any of the Drakk'Har near him, the noise of the explosion reverberated off the hard walls of the bunker, causing them all to reel. Slassh stumbled toward the explosion, dazed and confused.

* * *

Blake waited for the explosion and immediately ran around the left-hand corner yelling "Johnston, Tyler, watch our backs!" He heard Sanchez follow instinctively. Blake ran up the short ramp and stopped in the hatchway with weapon raised. He took in the bodies on the floor and quickly assessed the layout of the room. A large Drakk'Har stumbled into sight from his left. In fact, it was the largest croc Blake had ever seen, at least five hundred kilos in weight, some three meters or more high, with a thick tail and torso. Heavily muscled, it had a broad neckband of dull, flat, rectangular green stones around its neck. The foremost stone had a tip made from a small piece of jade. The brilliant green color stood out from the much duller scales. A dirty, large-link chain belt was over his shoulder, with a brown cloth material woven through it. A scabbard holding a ceramic blade was slung from the chain. Their eyes met, and the croc bared multiple long white teeth. Blake squeezed the trigger, sending a three-round burst toward the creature.

* * *

Slassh was struck in the chest and belly. In his dazed condition, he felt no pain, no comprehension of any damage at all. He saw the warm blood in the hatchway and clarity returned. There… there was his salvation! At least one and probably more warm bloods behind, literally delivered to his very doorstep. Then he saw a second figure emerge behind the first. *A breeder female!* His tribute to the emperor had just presented itself on his very doorway. That he would take them personally would give an even greater validation of the prize. Slassh never touched the blade at his side before charging. Claws, teeth, and tail were all he would need. The roar he issued equaled the volume of the earlier grenade blast.

* * *

Blake was momentarily surprised after seeing the rounds strike the creature's flesh with no apparent effect. When the creature started to move forward, a horrible, loud wail came from it. It dropped down to all fours, building up speed quickly. Training overrode his disbelief, and his thumb quickly selected AUTO fire on the side of his rifle. He squeezed the trigger and held it down until the last round was gone.

Time crawled by, and everything evolved in slow motion by Blake's perspective. He could have counted each cycle of the rifle's action. The sound of his weapon combined with the howl of the warrior, and Blake found instinctive fear rising in him. To his credit, every round but one struck home somewhere on the creature's head, neck, shoulders, back, and legs. In the enclosed space, the noise of the weapon fire was unbearable. The round to the neck was his salvation. It severed the spinal column of the huge creature, and it lost all control. It ran headlong into the edge of the door with a heavy, sickening thump, then lay there motionless. A chunk of the doorway fractured and fell away where the large head had hit.

As the last round left Blake's weapon, the action locked open. Training took over instinctively. He yelled "out," took a half step back, and proceeded to change his empty magazine for a full one.

* * *

Sanchez came up from behind and covered the room while he did that. A curious scaly face poked around the corner, and a three-round burst from her weapon took off the top of its head. The rest of the Drakk'Har behind the victim saw this and panicked. They retreated from the bunker through the closest hatches, unwilling to share their leader's demise. Sanchez heard the commotion of several large bodies in motion and pulled a second grenade from her chest harness.

* * *

Blake finished changing his magazine and, when done, looked down at the large creature still breathing at his feet. Its eyes were open, and they were the only thing moving on its entire body. Without a second thought, he flipped the switch on the side of his rifle back to BURST and put three rounds into its brain pan.

Sanchez tossed the armed grenade, yelling "Frag out!" Blake retreated around one side of the doorway for cover, while Sanchez pulled back around the other side. The grenade exploded, spraying shrapnel around the inside of the bunker.

Blake and Sanchez advanced into the chamber. The second grenade appeared to hit nothing but walls, floor, and equipment. The rest of the Drakk'Har had fled. Blake covered the room as Sanchez shot any crocs on the floor in the head. To the sergeant, this was obviously a major command post that had already come close to being destroyed, from the looks of the damage to the walls. When they turned the corner, he could not help but stop and stare at the huge pool of mostly dried blood on the walls and floor. Something violent and graphic had happened there. The body had been removed, but a blood trail went from the pool on the floor to one of the hatches opposite. He forced that from his mind as they finished their sweep. When the room had been pronounced clear and the hatches scouted and secured, Blake made a radio call back to his superior.

* * *

Wicks had heard the explosions, gun fire, and other noises. They were distorted by the echoes caused by the tunnel walls and made for a confused picture. He called for a report on the radio, but a heavy volume of fire drowned out the words. No one else could see anything, and his heart was in his throat until Sergeant Blake's calm voice finally broke the silence. His report was short and concise. He quickly described the action that had taken place, and Wicks felt obvious relief at the words "no casualties" when he heard them. Wicks acknowledged the report over the radio and asked for directions so he could examine the bunker himself. He left the rear guard in place and cautiously went up the tunnel alone.

Wicks had been given exact directions, so he ignored the side passages that went nowhere. He also gave the water tunnel entrance a wide berth. His weapon was pointed at it as long as he could see it. The idea of being attacked and dragged into water by a croc was sobering. He saw the odd device floating on the surface, but Blake had briefed him on it before they went in the tunnel, and he did not even consider trying to touch it.

Wicks took only a few minutes to arrive at the bunker entrance. He nodded at Johnston and Tyler still on guard in the intersection and went up into the bunker, walking around the large body near the door. His initial assessment was that his people had stumbled on a major find. This was a large and important bunker. The Intel weenies would go nuts over this place. He saw Blake and Sanchez doing a rough search, and before going over to them, he used his radio to contact the platoon commander. This had to go up the pipe quickly. His radio signal bounced up the tunnel, went to the unit on Perkins's back, was amplified and rebroadcast to Lieutenant Pfeiffer. Pfeiffer would pass it onto the company commander, and she would pass it off to her intelligence officer for investigation.

Once the radio call had gone out, Wicks walked over to the two soldiers. "Well done, Blake, Sanchez. From the look of this gear and the size of the bugger at the door, it looks like you took out one of their more important command bunkers here. Find anything interesting?"

Blake handed over what looked like a thick ledger with indecipherable writing inside. "There's all sorts of loose papers here with their hen-scratch on it, sir. This was the only bound volume we could find. It looks printed, so I suspect it's important, but I've no idea if it contains information on defenses or is just a cookbook. We've sealed the other doors leading into this room as best we can, but we should get some reinforcements down here if you want us to explore further. It looks like this is the nexus of a fairly large tunnel system."

Wicks smiled as he took the volume. "Let's hope for our sake that it isn't a cookbook, Sergeant. Besides, if this place is as important as it looks, we will be elbowed out of the way in record time so others can take credit for your efforts." Nods were seen all around at that comment. Some things never changed. The officer continued, "Others will be tasked with searching the rest of this place, I am sure. However, I agree with your assessment. We have gone as far as we can with the limited number of people we have. My orders are to hold in place until relieved. We still have several hours of daylight left, and this little foray delayed us considerably. I still intend to make it to Hill 170 before dark, if possible." The officer handed the book back to Blake. "May as well keep that safe as well, Sergeant. Carry on."

Wicks left the two soldiers to their duties and exited the bunker to go outside through the tunnels. Once more, he skirted the water tunnel entrance with his weapon pointed at it on his way out. He chided himself as he did it, as nothing happened, but thoughts of what could lurk beneath made his skin crawl.

* * *

Gar was a soldier with one of Kaaw's anti-air units that had been obliterated earlier in the day. That he had survived was nothing short of remarkable, as everyone else in his unit had been vaporized in the opening moments of the battle. By chance, he was behind a thick wall which had diverted a lot of the blast energy up and away from him. He was blown back several meters, but was otherwise unhurt. With a surplus of warriors and not enough equipment for them to use, Kaaw used the extra bodies as messengers. Unable to use radios without violent retribution and with many land lines cut, messengers were necessary. Gar carried a message with the latest information on the conflict. Casualties, dispositions of units, damage inflicted on the warm bloods, and so on. His orders were to take the information from Kaaw's bunker at the base of Skull Ridge to the bunker of the planet lord, as Borrk was dead. He had made that trip successfully twice before, that same day.

The worst part of Gar's trip had been the first leg. Forced to go overland after leaving the bunker, he stayed under the cover of the trees. He moved slowly, fearing detection and ambush. He encountered a small stream, but the water was only ankle deep. He walked down one of the banks of the stream, again moving slowly. Eventually, the stream joined with several others, and Gar was able to lie down and let the force of the water push him along. He made rapid progress from there. The stream widened, and while the flow slowed a little, he was able to swim with it. It eventually emptied into a long river which skirted the production facility. Now confident he could not be seen, Gar swam under the surface of the water. The water was brown and visibility was almost zero, but he knew this river well. At a deep spot in one of the river's turns, he felt the current slack. Gar felt in the mud on the river bottom until he located a crude chain just under the silty surface. He grabbed it with clawed hands and pulled himself along the bottom. The chain ended at an upside-down U-shaped entrance. Many chains radiated outwards from the tunnel entrance as a guide to swimmers. Before he entered, he considered his air supply. Sure he would have enough in his lungs to last for the long swim, he moved into the tunnel entrance. The visibility improved a little as he pulled himself in deeper, but the darkness would not improve until he got into the walking tunnels near the bunker.

The chain ended just inside the tunnel. From there, Gar swam under his own power. His powerful tail propelled him, and he paced himself in a regular swimming rhythm. It took some time, as the tunnels were long and had many twists, turns, and dead ends. Even Drakk'Har would find it impossible to make it through on a single lungful of air if they did not know the route. Gar knew the entire tunnel system well and stayed on the main path.

As he approached the tunnel exit, he was pleased he had judged his air usage perfectly. He had been submerged for thirty-two arkle, and he was anticipating that initial breath of air. Gar normally used his forward momentum to get him up the sharp slope leading into the air tunnel, so he sped up a little to do just that.

Water, as any hydraulic engineer knows, cannot compress. It is eight hundred times denser than air, and as a result, when you are swimming up a tunnel full of water, a pressure wave is generated in front of you. As Gar sped up, the pressure wave increased, and that wave traveled well ahead of him. When Gar was several meters from the exit, the motion of that pressure wave caused the surface at the exit of the pool to move slightly. Ordinarily this would not matter, but it did today. Sergeant Blake had placed a device on the surface of the water called a Rippler. Once armed, it used an internal air bubble level to check for horizontal alignment. Any deviation of fifteen degrees or more in the water's surface activated it. As Gar moved toward the device, the pressure wave caused the surface to move. The level of the device exceeded fifteen degrees, and it exploded. A shaped charge of plastic explosive directed the majority of the explosive force into the water. That force transmitted much more efficiently through water than air, and Gar's body was pulverized in the shock wave. He died without knowing why, and his message would never be delivered.

* * *

Even though the explosive force was directed primarily into the water, the explosion was still quite loud up in the air tunnels, and it immediately grabbed Sergeant Blake's attention. He ran out of the bunker telling Tyler and Johnston to stay put while Sanchez and he ran up the tunnel to the water exit. This time they did use the flashlight under their barrels, as their night vision had been ruined from being in the illuminated bunker. The water was still roiled and bubbling when they got there, but it calmed down quickly. Nothing emerged from the water, so they simply waited. Once the water surface had calmed, Blake took another Rippler from his pouch. He armed it in the same sequence as the first device he had used and gingerly placed it on the surface. He knew he had been told it would not arm unless the device was horizontal for at least ten seconds, but he still backed away quickly. When the flashing green lights on the device went out as he expected, he motioned for Sanchez to fall back the way they came. He reported in to Wicks about what had happened and told him he had replaced the Rippler. As Blake left the scene, he made a mental note. He now had a definite obligation to buy a certain engineer a stiff drink.

Blake and Sanchez retired down the tunnel corridor. Blake suddenly felt tired and wanted a few moments rest. Once back in the bunker, he slipped off his helmet and took a long drink from his canteen. He wondered if he was getting too old for combat and smiled at his own thought. Perhaps, perhaps not. Only time would tell, he decided. With the immediate area secure, he decided to take advantage of the break.

Blake turned to the corporal. "Sanchez, keep Tyler outside to guard the intersection until the Intel folks show up. Make sure she knows we are expecting a large group to arrive soon. Bring Johnston in, and give him a break. Take five yourself. I'll set up in the corner over there and keep an eye on the other tunnel entrances while we wait. We'll rotate guard outside every thirty minutes until relieved."

"Right, Sarge." Sanchez walked outside to follow orders.

CHAPTER 21 – PROMOTION

Planet Lord Tlish was exuberant. Communications had been disrupted severely, and reliable data had been woefully inadequate since the warm bloods had entered orbit. However, word of the death of Slassh spread across the entire planet like a wildfire. By short range radio, by voice, by messenger, by landline, it disseminated of its own accord. Such a profound change in the power hierarchy of the planet was something all Drakk'Har needed to know. It changed base alliances, allegiances, and contracts in a heartbeat, as several individuals tried to take advantage of the death to claw higher in position.

It had worked, Tlish mused quietly to himself. It had *worked!* The planet, with all of its riches, perks, and industries, was now his. He had many new responsibilities, too, but he didn't let that cloud the moment. He was Planet Lord of Mindon-2. The ultimate authority, answerable only to the emperor, and that was all he considered for the moment.

The news had been brought to him by the local swamp master and owner of the town he was in. Smaller than usual for a Drakk'Har of his rank, Mgarnew had been suitably cowed when he reported the news and even congratulated Tlish on his advancement. Mgarnew delivered the pronouncement like he had always anticipated it, as if it had been fate and long overdue, as if his personal existence hinged on the good news, which in many ways it did, Tlish mused. Even so, Mgarnew had been dismissed curtly so Tlish could revel in the news and think on several problems that faced him. Tlish instructed his personal guard to keep everyone away for the moment so he had time to think and weigh his options.

Tlish was certain that others would be making power plays to better their positions, and he had to consider that along with the more pressing issue of repelling the warm bloods. The title had been handed to him by fate, but holding onto power would be an exercise in personal will, and Tlish knew he could rise to that challenge. His retreat to the far side of the planet meant he was away from many of the potential plotters who tended to be drawn to power.

Tlish made several decisions quickly. First, this would now be his base. Mgarnew would not object. He had no basis to, and as the new headquarters of the planet lord, his town would see several direct benefits. Mgarnew's influence would also grow in Tlish's shadow. By default of his direct access to Tlish, Mgarnew would be first of all swamp masters on the planet and be treated with due respect by the others. Tlish could then watch and see who came to him, knowing that whoever did sought power and probably had designs on his. He would watch those individuals closely and hire spies in their ranks to stay ahead of their plots.

Second, Tlish decided Kaaw should replace him as planetary defense coordinator and his second. Even in the spotty reports Tlish had received, Kaaw was the most effective regional air-defense commander and he had the requisite knowledge to apply that to the entire planet. It probably would not matter in the short term of this raid, but Tlish needed that talent in the long term to completely revamp the defenses. If Tlish were to rebuild a successful imperial growth facility here, it had to be intelligently defended to prevent this type of assault again. No expense would be spared. Tlish would recruit the best engineers and technicians for that task. The cost would be steep, but never again would enemy gunfire crater the surface of *his* world. He needed heavy orbital batteries, skirmish ships, and several layers of space defenses. Mines, lasers, guns, and missiles would slow, stop, and then kill any force of any size that came this way again. This would also position Kaaw as his successor, but Tlish would ensure Kaaw had many projects to fulfill. He would be so busy building effective defenses that he would have no time to plot. Spies on Kaaw's staff would have to be found to ensure that, of course. That forced him to consider for a moment who on his staff was in Slassh's pay, but he dismissed it as irrelevant now.

His last decision was personal, and while somewhat practical, it was also thoroughly selfish. Until Tlish could assemble his own staff and construct his own bunker, he would have to use Mgarnew's facilities, staff, and communications. He may as well make himself familiar with his females, as well, as it looked like he would be here for some time.

* * *

Blake heard them coming long before they got to the bunker. He had lots of time to put on his helmet and get himself together. The others who were on guard or resting also looked more alert. That was the usual reaction from the rank and file; officers were coming.

Wicks entered first, saying, "Right through here, gentlemen," as he stood aside to let the next man in.

The second officer through the door was a marine major in green fatigues, combat boots, and helmet. His only weapon was a pistol that was holstered and attached to a thick web belt on his right side. His uniform was pressed and relatively clean. The cloth nametag on his left breast said "PALMER," and he had an intelligence badge sewn above his name. Blake thought his boots were indecently shiny for a combat zone—even for an officer—but said nothing. He simply braced up into a position of attention when he saw the major, while commanding his marines to do the same.

The major stopped one pace in the bunker and regarded the fallen warrior at the door. Several others were forced to stop behind the major and wait, as he effectively blocked the doorway. Slassh's body had not been moved. Given his size, no one had even considered it to be possible.

"My word, he *is* a large one, Lieutenant. As you were, people." The major then let his gaze wander over the bunker as he continued. "You were right to call this in, Lieutenant. Definitely a command bunker. Biggest we've seen yet on this world."

The major walked deeper into the chamber to see more. He took it all in as he spoke. "Communications, counter-measures, and a few things I don't recognize. Some of it looks operational, too. Wicks, your people have done you proud."

"Thank you, sir," Wicks replied.

The next person through the door was the platoon commander, Lieutenant Pfeiffer. Behind him, several other lightly armed marines, also with intelligence insignia, entered and took in the space. Carrying several bags of gear, they all looked like rear echelon types to Blake. In total, he saw six men and women of various ranks. Two were junior officers. None of them appeared in awe of being underground in a croc command post. Systematically, they started to take pictures, video, and examine the various equipment, while the major kept talking to Wicks. "Huge find, son. Huge. We'll take all this gear back with us, people," he announced to the room in general. "Now, where's the book?"

Blake grabbed the volume from a nearby desk and spoke with courtesy. "Here, sir. We found it under a pile of loose papers over there. We stacked all the loose material in the corner."

The major took the book in his hands with what Blake would have called reverence. He examined it and flipped randomly through it. Unable to make sense of it, he simply called for one of his people. "Sebastian, what do you make of this?"

Blake watched the smallest of the group, a sergeant, come over at the major's call. The pistol on her hip covered half of her upper leg. She was only one and a half meters high; a small sized uniform would have hung off her. She was thin, very thin. If he had seen her on the street out of uniform, Blake would have thought "librarian." Her long, dirty-blond hair was pinned up tightly and securely behind her head. Her face was feminine, but angular, and she wore thick-rimmed glasses.

She took the volume and opened it to several random pages. She did not hurry and took in each character on the page. Her finger traced from the bottom to the top. When done, she turned the page backwards and carried on reading. She did this several times. The major did not hurry her, so no one else said anything to interrupt. The remainder of the intelligence staff carried on around the group, taking pictures and examining the room in detail.

"It would appear," Sebastian said in carefully measured words without looking from the tome, "that this is a collection of phrases defining military and commercial terminology. No codes or ciphers *per se*, but a base derivative communalizing their communications. I would consider it similar to one of our own reference manuals in how we refer to places and things within the same context. This section, for example, presents their units of measure for size, distance, weight, time, et cetera, in great detail. I also see several formulas, as well, in their Base 6 math. This suggests it may be a reference book for engineering, although I also see several biochemical references, as well as metallurgy and genetics. This is potentially a major reference source. That is a preliminary assessment, sir, but I feel confident in making that determination. This should give us considerable insight into their language. I can have a preliminary report for you within a day or so, with a full translation in roughly seventy-two hours, sir."

The major appeared satisfied with her appraisal. "So, not their Imperial Code, but quite usable nonetheless." He turned to Lieutenant Pfeiffer and nodded.

Pfeiffer did not hesitate. He came straight up to Blake and took his hand in a firm handshake. "Congratulations, Staff Sergeant. This was a big find, and you were primarily responsible for it."

Blake was speechless. Did he say *staff sergeant*? Had he just been promoted? "Sir, I—" was all he got out before 2nd Lieutenant Wicks was there, also shaking his hand.

"Well done, Staff Sergeant. The nice part of an armed conflict is battlefield promotion. You didn't think you could take down a major command post almost singlehandedly and remain unrecognized for it, did you? You will have to remain with the unit until we leave the planet; then we will have to lose you to another platoon within the regiment. We shall miss you, but that is life in the military. The talented people always move up. Isn't that right, Sergeant Sanchez?"

Sanchez was half expecting this from the previous conversation and did not hesitate in either her reply or enthusiasm for it. "Yes, sir! Thank you, sir! Sirs," she added as handshakes were offered to her in turn. The smile on her face lit up the room.

"Right," said Wicks. "Time to grab our gear and clear out. We have been relieved and will regroup outside the main tunnel entrance."

His people picked up the last of their gear and began to move to the exit.

Blake took Wicks aside and spoke to him in a low voice. "Sir, thank you, but the others worked just as hard as I did and—"

Second Lieutenant Wicks didn't hesitate to interrupt. "Don't worry, Staff Sergeant. Recognition will not end here. Belliveau will be getting a Purple Heart. We can talk about who else deserves recognition when we get back in the fleet. I will be looking to you and Sanchez to make suitable recommendations. Let us get everyone outside and over to Hill 170. Sunlight is fading, and I want to be secure in the position before night fall. It's only a few kilometers, but we will need to push them a bit to get there in time. At least from what the major was saying, opposition in this area has been effectively suppressed, so the rest of our time on planet should be quiet. Congratulations again."

"Yes, sir. Thank you, sir."

* * *

Lieutenant Pratt was feeling better about things after due consideration. His thoughts were not all within his personal comfort zone, but he was mollified to some degree. What the general had said made sense. They did hold the high ground and had overview of the surrounding territory. Any approaching units had a good chance of being spotted, but only from the north or west, which were flat plains with little vegetation. From the south or especially the eastern approaches, many folds in the terrain held heavy vegetation. Trees had canopies which spread well out from their trunks and covered everything beneath. As a result, one also had to be under the same canopy and be within meters of something to see it.

The basic infantry text book said that the only way to secure such a position was to have multiple heavy weapons, machine guns, grenade launchers, and so on covering the approaches, with artillery and mortars dialed in, ready to drop fire. Listening posts should be set further down the slopes of the hill, along with patrols ranging even further to detect and interdict any incoming enemy. Even a much larger force could be defeated if you knew where they were coming from and their intentions. If you had advance warning, you could reorient your people to face the threat head on.

The issue was that until reinforcements arrived, he did not have the manpower to establish LPs and still maintain a viable defense line. So, he had to encircle the top of the hill and look for threats in all directions. That consequently left them weak in all areas, and a strong surprise attack had a much better chance of success.

More negatives added to the mix. He only had eight people he could rely on until reinforcements arrived. Yes, they were highly trained and equaled a section each in ability. As a force multiplier, they were exceptional. The addition of Staff Sergeant MacPherson certainly helped offset the loss of the unconscious Mendez. However, he still wanted more boots on the ground to feel comfortable.

The worse part of his position was the command lighter. Under normal conditions, if his unit ran into strong opposition, the section would melt into the jungle and simply evade it. Having the lighter to defend meant his position was relatively fixed and had few maneuver options. He could not count on the lighter crew to help in any effective defense, and that included the general. They were technicians, not infantry, and while he was sure they would fight as individuals, he needed the sort of unit cohesion that only trained troops working together could provide.

He trusted his unit because they had earned his trust over many months and dangerous missions. The lighter crew would only have light weapons and limited ammunition. They would actually be a liability, probably shooting at everything that approached in all directions, and that could potentially affect his people trying to come to their rescue. Trained troops used arcs of fire and disciplined tactics gained from weeks of repetitive training and exercises.

Pratt had tried to compensate as best as possible and placed his best people and heavy weapons on the east and south sides, including Jefferson, who had a decent position on a rocky outcropping looking down on the eastern slope. However, that view was severely restricted by the trees, and she could only cover the top twenty meters, or so, of the hill. The few Claymore anti-personnel mines they had were stretched out on the eastern and southwestern approaches. *Given the layout, that's where I would come up*, Pratt thought. Pratt had determined that the terrain to the south was steep and would not be viable as an attack path. That was a gamble, but any force attacking from the south had to contend with a very steep hill. That could be covered easily with enough people, but again, he did not have them.

Pratt had taken a few precautions over the last few hours. Those not on guard duties worked alongside the lighter crew to erect protective earth berms and trees in a defensive pattern. They had taken the felled trees from the cleared landing zone, laid them horizontally, and filled the spaces between with earth. Embrasures had been created where needed through the trunks, giving maximum protection to the defenders. Pratt had spent a lot of time making sure the arcs of fire from each embrasure overlapped with the ones to the left and right. Sticks had been embedded in the earth, angled toward the enemy, and their tips sharpened. Bushes had been pulled up and replanted to camouflage firing positions which had been scraped out of the dirt. Loam and sod had been piled against the earth, as well. It would only hide the positions for a few seconds, but that time would be on the defenders' side. One took every advantage. Pratt would have ordered trenches dug, but they were standing on solid granite with only a few centimeters of loamy earth in scattered places.

Overall, the barricades were crude and rushed, but all worked at it with gusto, knowing that it might ultimately save their own skins. This was literally the last line of defense, and no one complained seriously. When the lighter occupants saw the effort that the special forces troops were putting in, they pitched in without encouragement. The seriousness of the situation was reflected in their countenance. As soon as an attack was detected, everyone was well briefed on what to do to respond, including several alternate plans.

If the lighter had only landed fifty meters further up to the north, there would have been a convenient and easily defended path leading down the hill in behind the craft that could get everyone clear if they had to retreat. Unfortunately, it had landed just beyond the edge of a steep eighty degree slope, and the nimblest of mountain goats would have shied from that. The only option down was rappelling, and under fire, that was nigh on impossible unless a good portion of troops stayed behind to literally sacrifice themselves. Pratt valued the lives of his people too much to consider that option. He had ropes rigged and coiled, ready for use anyway, just as a psychological measure. Plus, he wanted the option to at least get the general clear, if pressed. He suspected Carstairs would refuse on principle, but that was an option he wanted available.

Pratt summarized it in his own mind. Until they were reinforced, they were thin on the ground, and a determined attack would breach their feeble defensive line quickly. They would have to adopt a "collapsing bag" tactic at that point and fall back to the lighter defense line. Once that happened, they had no fall-back plan. They would have to stand and protect the lighter crew. The resulting feeling of dread made Pratt's pulse race.

* * *

Jacobs had already supervised moving Mendez and J.P. behind the barricades. Loose rocks had been piled in a secondary low wall near the lighter, and their stretchers were placed behind that. A couple of firing slits had been created between the rocks, but Jacobs hoped they would not be needed. Jacobs took his usual place at Mendez's side. He kept his mind occupied by cleaning his weapon. He was the reserve, and if anything got past the wall, it would be his job to stop it before it got to the lighter. Jacobs's healing knowledge did not include anything on Drakk'Har physiology except where to shoot if one presented itself. That, for him, was enough. He had no moral ambiguity with his being a life saver and his desire to end the life of an enemy. They showed no mercy and had killed thousands of humans without provocation or restraint. Given half a chance, they would end his life without a second thought, so he had no consideration for them. They were animals, just wild animals.

* * *

Back in the Fleet, the raid was entering the final stages. Kosnov looked over the tactical priorities list and was happy to see that even with the reduced landing forces, the Fleet had achieved eighty-two percent of its objectives by that point in time. His troops had achieved all their pre-planned positions. Some did so easier than anticipated, others at great cost. His lighter losses had been heavy, which decreased his options somewhat. Since the first landings, opposition on the ground had all but vanished. The engineers were free to operate in the disputed areas, systematically destroying all of the facilities and ship hulls they had discovered. The troops were in a relaxed posture and dealt with the odd ambush or counter-attack, but no major conflict occured. It looked like the enemy had melted into the undergrowth of the jungle.

Kosnov's intelligence people had presented the discovery and elimination of several key command bunkers as an underlying factor in the lack of resistance. The marshal accepted this on face value, but would not fully accept the collapse of the Drakk'Har forces until they were well beyond the orbital path of this world and on the way home with everyone safe. Being Russian, Kosnov never counted his proverbial chickens early.

Still, the tempo of operations had changed slightly from assault to the pre-embarkation phase. Under the original plan, the areas under General Chew on the far side of the planet would be the first to be evacuated. However, due to the early losses, those areas only contained special forces teams and never had a ground assault component. The special forces contributed by directing orbital bombardments on their encrypted radio and data links, effectively negating the two areas. Flames were still visible at those locations, as tanks of petrochemicals still burned. The smoke from those fires was actually visible from orbit.

Those teams had long moved to be in close proximity to their pre-determined evacuation points several hours earlier, for a pickup at first light. That would be in three hours from now, the marshal noted. They could do it in the dark, but daylight made things so much safer. A lighter on an orbital insertion burn threw out a lot of heat for a missile to lock onto. Against the night sky, it stood out boldly.

On the other side of the planet, General Carstairs's people were also winding down operations. It would soon be dark over his three areas of responsibility. Fate had forced his command lighter down, but by a stroke of luck, he had fallen on a hilltop with a special forces team in close proximity. At least he was still coordinating his people effectively. Carstairs's marines would hold up in secure positions overnight and retire from the surface sequentially, starting at their respective dawns as the planet rotated. Once everyone was off planet (and accounted for at least twice), the exfiltration out of the Mindon system would start.

And that is when things will get interesting, Kosnov mused, thinking ahead. He had received orders authorizing a nuclear option. It would be terribly simple to drop a dozen nuclear-tipped THOR missiles down on the surface before leaving, but many things had to be considered before making that kind of decision. The longer term issues worried him the most, and he tried to keep them foremost in his mind.

Once they left Mindon-2, Fleet Nine would have to deal with at least one, possibly two, Drakk'Har battle groups near the solar system's edge. Of course, the enemy was currently pounding on Allen's Rift, so that might leave them a little light on ships. The distance from the Rift to here was a long haul. Still, he didn't expect a free ride out. He still had confidence in Fleet Nine. They were seasoned, well trained, and Kosnov knew he could rely on them to perform their duties professionally.

Once they got out and set course, they would end up at the heavy orbital docks near Wolf 359. Nothing bad from a military perspective, as it had comprehensive docking and repair facilities. The problem was the barren system. The red dwarf star had no planets around it. Therefore, it had limited shore leave facilities, and truth be told, the station looked no different from the inside of most of his ships. Almost everything was shiny metal or painted gray / green. Kosnov appreciated green, but in fields and sunshine in the open, as most people did. His troops worked hard, and Kosnov liked to reward them for it. Wolf was not his first choice, but he went where he was sent. Allen's Rift had parks, lakes, and a full sized community with bars, theatre, and shopping. As a developed planet, the fleet could relax there after an operation. Having civilians, it also reinforced what the troops were fighting for.

Kosnov remembered the line from the last fleet message he had received. *"Facilities and orbiting docks struck by several nuclear warheads stop heavy casualties comma heavy damage stop enemy ships pressing attack with troop landing stop,"* and he wondered what shape those facilities were in now. With enemy troops on the ground, it would not be a good place to be for some time.

CHAPTER 22 – SWARM

Drawwl was almost ready. His sub-commanders were assembled around him quietly receiving last minute instructions. They were in a small hidden valley about thirty meters under the lip of the eastern edge of the hill. Most of his troops were in place, and the last were making their way up the well-marked trails. From where the troops assembled in the small valley, three paths led up to the summit. Two were on the eastern edge and the last on the southern. The south path would not be used, as that was thought to be too steep for rushing warriors. At the top of the paths was relatively flat terrain. Drawwl was confident they had not been seen in the thick undergrowth. Advance scouts, his three best, had inched slowly forward and seen warm bloods on the hill. The scouts went naked, without equipment to make noise, get snagged on bushes, or be seen. Their green scales blended into the bushes just as evolution had designed. Not many warm bloods were reported, but that just meant an easier victory. The hill occupants had weapons, but Drawwl had almost one hundred armed warriors and surprise on his side. The scouts could not see any formal defenses, but they were limited by their positions and could not see all the way across the terrain at the top of the hill. The scouts only reported what they saw, and that was very encouraging to the attackers.

Kek was at Drawwl's side looking decidedly nervous throughout the briefing. He had been given the honor of leading the first assault wave with his forty provincial troops. There would be two waves in total. Drawwl wanted the lesser trained troops to go first. Any traps or other waiting surprises should be set off by them, and their losses were of no concern to him. The second wave would advance methodically under his command and mop up any resistance that remained. While a priority was to take and occupy the hill, the capture as many warm bloods as possible was also important, with breeder females taking priority, of course.

The briefing was short and to the point. All sub-commanders knew exactly what was expected of them, and the punishments for failure were quite graphically represented. Drawwl dismissed them and was fully expecting to hear another suggestion from Kek about how he should be maintaining a rear guard. He was surprised when Kek went up the path wordlessly. His head was down, and Kek seemed resigned to his fate.

* * *

At the base of the trail leading up the western side of Hill 170, Staff Sergeant Blake looked up and could no longer see the top rear section of the crashed lighter above him. Blake had seen it as they approached earlier, but the terrain now blocked his view. He didn't see anyone up there, either, but was not expecting to. They would either be heavily camouflaged or keeping their heads down to avoid being seen. He had been briefed that General Carstairs was there, along with some of his staff and a small special forces team who had been there at least a week identifying targets and gathering intel. *A week*, he thought. *A week in this hole?* Completely unsupported, with no one to come and rescue or assist you if things went south (and things usually went south in his book).

Living in a soggy, wet jungle with vipers, giant insects, and Drakk'Har patrols all over the place was hard to imagine. Blake had all of Fleet Nine covering his butt while he was on the ground, and he was still nervous about being here. *Whoever could handle being here a week without that sort of support overhead must be one tough SOB*, he judged. Blake had considered volunteering for the special forces, but was damned glad he hadn't after hearing that.

They had made good time getting across the plains after leaving the town. The terrain was flat, with knee-high grass and no opposition. While his platoon was assigned here, his squad was first of three to arrive. Blake held a quick consult with 2nd Lieutenant Wicks, and they decided to move up the hill immediately after topping up their water supplies from a small stream. As they would be first on the site, they would be able to grab a choice piece of perimeter for their overnight stay, assuming they could find a decent place up there. If they could get the furthest point away from the general as well, that would be a bonus. Blake had nothing against General Carstairs. Indeed, he had a fair amount of respect. However, enlisted ranks liked simple lives, and senior officers tended to complicate them. The closest other squad was at least fifteen minutes away, which gave his lots of time to put their claim on a piece of comfortable, but easily defendable, ground. The platoon officer, Lieutenant Pfeiffer, might move them when he arrived with his radio operator, but that was unlikely with darkness falling and given their recent success in the bunker.

The air was a little cool, but with the exercise of the walk across the plains behind them, everyone was warm enough. Besides, they were marines and all in very good shape. Blake sent newly promoted Sergeant Sanchez with PFC Messina up the hill on point. After giving them several meters lead, the rest fell in behind, with Blake in front. LCPL Cole and PFC Johnston were next. Wicks was near the middle of the column, with Perkins behind him. Behind them was PFC Tyler, and rearguard was LCPL Reid. Every even-numbered person had their weapon pointed to the left of the trail. Each odd person had their weapon pointed to the right. They made their way up the hill at a slow, but steady, pace.

* * *

Everyone on top of Hill 170 had settled into a routine. The majority of the defenses had been emplaced, and with the sun hovering over the far horizon, work was winding down of its own accord. It had been agreed to minimize movement outside of the battlements during darkness, and those who were not on guard retired in behind the low log-and-earth wall surrounding the general's lighter on two sides. They would stand a 2/2 watch tonight unless something happened, and then everyone would be awake. The steady hum of air conditioning and generators still issued from the fallen lighter as members of the command staff worked inside to coordinate the division. However, it had become part of the regular noise at that point, and no one paid any attention to it. There would be no fires tonight that might interfere with the sentries' night vision capabilities. It would be chilly without them, but the additional security was worth it to everyone involved.

Jefferson could see the most territory from her position and was the primary lookout. She occupied the highest ground, which was a rocky outcropping on the north end of the hill. The overlook was not that high overall, only being seven meters above the rest of the plateau. However, every little bit helped. Jefferson concentrated on the area to her south and east. Heavy shadows were falling on the eastern side of the hill as the sun sank behind her. She ignored the north completely. Popov was on the western face of the hill and could see most of the open terrain to the north and west, so that was his responsibility. She could not see Popov because of the lay of the land, but he had a radio and would give her lots of warning if anyone did try to come that way.

No one was directly observing the northern approaches. They were quite steep, but just to be safe, several preparations had been put in place. Trip wires, tear gas grenades that only affected Drakk'Har, and flares were rigged on the north trails, plus a few slightly more lethal surprises further up if anyone disregarded the non-lethal warnings and kept coming. The northern paths were all rock and open—no cover and completely exposed. With warning, even a couple of soldiers could stop a major assault there, so the danger was slight. She would remain in place all night, having caught a few hours sleep in the afternoon. Sleep deprivation was something all elite troops were conditioned to accept and deal with. Snipers were the elite of the elite.

Jefferson could see Sergeant Smith's back as he watched over the southern approaches. He was behind some bushes in a fixed position and fairly well camouflaged in his fatigues, but he moved every now and then to shift position, and she could see that movement clearly. He was sited in the only piece of ground that could overlook the south path. If he moved just a few feet back, elephants could cross below him without his seeing them. He had the most exposed and uncomfortable position, but did not complain.

Off to the east side of the hill, Private White stood well back from the lip. White had his weapon held across his chest, the handle of the rifle in the crux of his elbow. He walked back and forth on a twenty-meter path that was parallel to the lip. He had the same look of boredom that sentries always develop after hours trying to stay alert with nothing happening. She had watched his regular pattern. He paused every now and then to listen, but evidently heard nothing. Jefferson had heard Lieutenant Pratt deliberately order him to stay well back from the undergrowth to avoid him being too close to the trees. Crocs moved quickly in short bursts, much quicker than a running man. Besides, even if he were near the bushes, he would not be able to see anything of consequence. The vegetation was simply too thick down the slope.

Movement from the western part of the clearing took Jefferson's attention from Private White. Lieutenant Pratt came into view to make another inspection of the defense line. His weapon sling was over his right shoulder, and the rifle stock was against his chest, muzzle down. Pratt walked through all of the observation points every thirty minutes or so and was currently walking over to Sergeant Smith. In a half hour, they would change sentries for the start of the night watch.

With everything looking routine, Jefferson was relaxed. A light breeze was blowing from west to east, and only the odd chirp of insects was heard. The promise of a peaceful night fluttered against her imagination. She realized she was thirsty. Jefferson was reaching for her canteen when a bush down the eastern ridge shook visibly and then immediately went still. She caught the movement in her peripheral vision and directed her full attention to it. She froze, watching intently, but it didn't reoccur. Several seconds passed, and just as she was about to convince herself it had been her imagination, she saw more movement, but these were not bushes.

Jefferson did not preface her radio call with the usual call signs. Her unit was the only one on this frequency, so there could be no doubt who the message was intended for. She was the only female in the section, so there could be no doubt who was sending it. "Alpha section, Stand-to. Action east, multiple crocs on paths Bravo and Charlie."

Pratt, White, and MacPherson all turned toward her reflexively for a heartbeat before gazing eastward. The lip of the ridge blocked their view down the hill, and none of them could see what she could with her elevation. The jungle was coming alive, and they were coming up both of the eastern hill paths.

Jefferson continued, "Twenty plus advancing rapidly. Fall back, White." White had actually taken a step closer to the ridge to get a better view. His weapon was up, but he obviously could not see what was coming. He stopped in place and hesitated for just a moment.

* * *

MacPherson turned and double-checked the south path, designated Alpha. He saw nothing and turned back to face east. His weapon was also up, with the butt in his shoulder. Pratt was about ten meters away from MacPherson.

* * *

Jefferson lobbed a WP grenade in a high overhand lob to mark the position of the advance. She yelled, "WP out!"

The low sound of the burning fuse hissed in flight. White started walking back instinctively from the grenade. He kept his weapon to the east as trained. As she threw the grenade, Jefferson saw more crocs coming through the bushes. She could see the danger, and White was too damned close for her comfort. When she spoke, her voice possessed a force that came to the edge of incomprehensibility over the digital radio. "WHITE, FALL BACK, NOW!" The grenade disappeared over the lip, landing at the feet of several Drakk'Har warriors on the Bravo path, the one furthest from her.

* * *

Private White took the loud warning to heart and started to back-pedal. His weapon was wandering back and forth left to right as he went backwards, then he saw the tops of several heads. At least thirty, and more coming. *Too damned many.* White began firing his CKP-12 in three-round bursts as he went back.

* * *

The WP grenade bursting charge cracked the case and blew the phosphorus outwards. Pressurized argon gas was used inside the grenade to keep the contents inert. That dissipated quickly and was replaced by air. Being pyrophoric, each piece of phosphorus reacted with the oxygen in the atmosphere instantly and began to burn at a temperature of 2,760° Celsius, half the temperature of the sun. The now white-hot pieces ranging in size from a piece of rice to a pea flew out in all directions. The official range of the grenade was seventeen meters, but that was on a flat range under optimal conditions. The angled approach to the ridge top and lip ensured the effects were blown back onto the Drakk'Har and not the upper part where the humans were.

The WP grenade had several immediate effects, none of them pleasant. The Drakk'Har in the immediate blast suffered most. Each was instantly hit by pieces of various sizes that penetrated its flesh easily. The material continued to burn inside them, albeit at a reduced rate, consuming the oxygen in their tissues, creating painful wounds that caused them to fall and thrash about in agony. The screams of the victims were dreadful.

Many pieces that did not strike anyone embedded themselves in trees, other vegetation, and the dirt of the path itself. The wet vegetation smoldered, causing lots of white smoke. Other pieces were carried up into the air and fell in a fountain arc on the Drakk'Har warriors' heads and shoulder. The pieces burned with such intensity that they stuck to their flesh. Trying to knock them off with their claws only caused burns to their hands, as well. The last effect was the reaction of the phosphorus and oxygen which coalesced into a noxious white smoke. The cloud formed quickly, causing breathing spasms and coughing to those nearby. As a secondary effect, it also reduced visibility within its radius dramatically. The Drakk'Har below the lip of the ridge suffered dreadfully.

Several Drakk'Har further down the ridge made it over the lip before the explosion and were uninjured. As they crested the eastern slope, the sun struck them directly in the eyes. They hesitated a moment, as they were blinded by the oblique rays of the sun coming from the western sky, but when they saw White, they rushed him in a swarm.

* * *

In his peripheral vision, White could see MacPherson and Pratt each drop to one knee to give themselves a stable firing stance. This is where many hours on the firing range and exercise training paid off. Their fire lanced in from the side as the warriors advanced on him. White himself slowed his rearward advance to give himself a more stable aim and tried to shoot as many of the creatures as he could. He desperately wanted to turn and run from this nightmare, but training and fire discipline suppressed the desire to flee. White had played football in his college days, and the parallel of sacking the quarterback came to him briefly. Several three-round bursts took down warriors easily. The depleted uranium and mercury cores in the bullets did their jobs with merciless efficiency. The few troops in the area added their rounds into the mass of reptilian flesh, but several bursts often struck the same creature, and that allowed the others to advance further than they normally should have. Four warriors made it to White. The first to get within a meter of him was driven violently sideways as a snapshot from Jefferson's RUK sent its brains through its left ear. Both Pratt and White both got a burst into the next warrior. MacPherson could have taken the last two, but Pratt was between him and the last targets; too close to risk firing. The two remaining crocs hurled themselves on top of White, who screamed as he fell backwards. He kept screaming and flailed as he was assaulted. One bit his forearm; the second drove its teeth into his upper thigh. Each creature tore a huge chunk of flesh out of his body, and blood sprayed everywhere.

* * *

Pratt and MacPherson rushed forward, instinctively fighting the horror. One warrior raised its head and upper body to swallow the flesh in its mouth. White's blood flowed freely over the creature's face and jowls. Pratt saw a clear shot and took it, putting three rounds through the creature's chest. It fell backwards, already dead, landing heavily on the ground. The last creature did not hesitate. It turned, grabbed White by the ankle, and started to run back toward the eastern ridge, dragging him behind. In doing this, the creature was no longer obscured by Pratt, and MacPherson drilled three holes into its upper back. The creature fell heavily, not dead, but well along the way.

* * *

Kek was screaming orders and choking on his words as the fluffy white cloud of gas thrown off by the phosphorus surrounded him. He had avoided the pieces of WP, but the choking fumes filled his lungs and interfered with his speech. The attack had stalled. The first wave was not even completely on the ridge yet. The screaming of the grenade victims had stopped Kek's inexperienced troops dead in their tracks. None of the troops could see or, in many cases, even breathe due to the smoke. Kek knew the only thing to do was move forward and get out of the cloud. He considered going backwards, but knew Drawwl had his troops lined up with rail guns in that direction. Instead of yelling, Kek grabbed warriors in front of him and physically pushed them forward. They, in turn, pushed those ahead of themselves forward. If they were wounded, they were flung aside, off the paths. Slowly, they started moving up.

* * *

Pratt did not hesitate and ran to White, with MacPherson close behind. They found him whimpering and trying to get up despite the horrible wounds on his limbs. His camouflaged fatigues were red with blood and ripped badly. His soft field cap was gone, and his weapon had dropped off to his side. One look was enough to know he was going into shock. Each man grabbed one of White's shoulders; MacPherson picked up his fallen weapon. They began pulling White across the grass toward the western side of the hill.

Pratt's voice went out over the COMM link, "Jacobs, man down! Meet me at the western edge of the clearing."

* * *

In her over-watch position, Jefferson could see little. The prevailing light breeze was still going from west to east, and the dense smoke had spread back onto the eastern edge of the hill. She could see fleeting movement coming through the roiling smoke on occasion and hear noise from that area, but saw nothing of consequence. She switched her tactical contact lenses into thermal mode, which allowed her to see through the smoke, but the hot spots were hidden behind the cooler foliage. She returned her contacts to normal vision and pulled a frag grenade from her webbing. She twisted the timing ring to three seconds, pulled the pin, and lobbed it overhand. "Frag out!" This time she threw it further, hoping to catch the follow-on forces she had missed with the WP grenade. It disappeared into the dense smoke.

The grenade landed, unseen, inside a hollowed-out trunk of a long-fallen tree. When it exploded, it did no immediate damage, as the shrapnel was absorbed by the thick, rotting wood. The explosion was behind Kek, and the only result was motivating them to move faster up the hill to get away from the noise. Indeed, it did more to inspire them to move forward than Kek's efforts. Jefferson had inadvertently renewed the assault.

* * *

Jacobs met Pratt and MacPherson at the edge of the clearing. Smith and Bennet both came along soon after from the camp, still buckling up their webbing. The gunfire was a rude awakening, and Smith looked a bit dozy after rolling out of his sleeping bag. Pratt and MacPherson placed White carefully on the ground. MacPherson went through White's pockets and pouches and grabbed all his ammo and grenades. He passed some of it to Smith and the rest to Bennet.

MacPherson reloaded both the rifles he had while casting nervous glances toward the east.

Pratt was curt. "Get him back to the lighter, and take care of him, Jacobs," was all he said before turning back toward the eastern edge of the ridge.

Pratt activated the radio circuit. "Popov, report to the defense line. Western end of the clearing. Williams, help Jacobs evac White, get to the lighter, alert the general, then man the battlements and watch our backs. Smith, over there." The officer sliced his flat hand through the air to show Smith where to go to his left. "Bennet there. MacPherson, behind the rocks to the right, there. Hold the line!" Pratt could see nothing to the east save the thick smoke and the copious blood trail White had left behind on the grass. The resulting anxiety formed a knot in his stomach.

* * *

MacPherson moved to the right and knelt behind some loose boulders. He edged White's recovered weapon over the top of one of the larger rocks to steady it. He left his rifle slung over his chest as an immediate backup. MacPherson placed several grenades on the rock near him for quick use.

* * *

Smith moved off to Pratt's left and lay behind a small earth mound. *Minor cover, but better than nothing,* Pratt thought. The officer stayed in the center. He had no cover, so he dropped down onto his belly. Only his head and weapon were visible in the twenty-centimeter-high grass. Bennet was off to his right by a couple of meters. *No cover for him except grass, either.*

Being special forces, they were essentially light infantry. They often needed to move multiple tens of kilometers a day and, as a result, could not be slowed down by carrying mortars, lots of ammo, or heavy machine guns. They had decent weaponry, training, and could fight effectively, he had no doubt of that. However, they were supposed to be intelligence gatherers primarily. Like ghosts, they were supposed to be silent, unseen, and moving where they needed to quickly. If they did hit a target, it was quick and dirty. In and out, fast. You wanted the odds and surprise on your side, because if you gave the enemy a fair fight, you had not planned it correctly. In this case, they had no surprise, the enemy had the initiative, and they were fixed to the defense of the lighter. Given those facts, the advantage was firmly with the enemy.

On the plus side, Pratt had command of the flat clearing, which was a rough U shape with his people grouped on the bottom side and Jefferson up high to his left. Any attacking enemy would have to come directly from the front and be funneled into a fairly small area. A kill zone. The cover was sparser than he would have liked, but he could only play the cards he was dealt.

Pratt, seeing nothing, keyed the radio. "Jefferson, report."

On the high ground, Jefferson visually scanned the smoke. She could see nothing and reported that. "Nothing since the initial push, sir. Wait, one." She saw movement on the edge coming up the path. The light breeze was starting to dissipate the smoke. "Sir, I have ten—correction, twenty plus—crocs advancing up trails Bravo and Charlie. Half with rail guns, the rest with long knives. Claymores?"

They had rigged two anti-personnel Claymore mines earlier to cover the clearing, and Jefferson had the firing handles nearby. Pratt did not want them to be used this early. "Negative. No Claymores yet. Wait for my call. Popov, get that LMG up here ASAP." Pratt had thought about putting the LMG on the outcrop of terrain where Jefferson was, but had dismissed it just in case an assault came from another direction, like the south path where it would have been devastating. He had wanted to be flexible with his limited armaments and keep his options open; this was the price.

* * *

Corporal Popov was running from LP2, and he had his light machine gun in hand. It had a higher rate of fire than their personal rifles and was perfect for suppressive fire. He had thirty more meters to run from his observation post and answered while going flat out up the trail, "On the way, sir."

* * *

Pratt tried to speak calmly on the radio. "Roger. OK, people, pick your targets. Anything to your direct front is your responsibility. Take your time, and make each shot count. Jefferson, focus on the leaders. Here they come."

The first of the warriors crested the ridgeline.

* * *

Sergeant Smith fired first. He could only see the creature from the belly up as it tried to get over the lip directly in front of him. He fired a single shot that hit the warrior in the chest. The mercury tip exploded deep inside the Drakk'Har. The creature toppled backwards off the ridge. The rail-gun in its hands went off as it fell backwards, adding its demonic howl to the sound of battle.

* * *

Popov made it to the clearing along the path from the fallen lighter. As he ran up, he saw MacPherson, Bennet, and Pratt fire at the same time. Their targets all went down. Popov dropped down prone in the grass a meter from Pratt's left side. Dropping a spare box of ammo to the right of his weapon, he quickly deployed the bipod legs supporting the front of the light machine gun barrel and unwound the already loaded ammo belt, letting it lay flat on the grass. With his right thumb, he moved the safety to AUTO, took the butt into his shoulder, sighted on a group of three crocs coming over the ridge, and squeezed the trigger for a quarter second. The weapon crashed back into his shoulder, and six rounds were sent down the barrel. The bullets hit two of the targets. The third target turned and paused at the sight. The ammunition in the LMG belt was caseless and ordered in groups of five—an armor-piercing round, three full metal jacket rounds, and a tracer. They formed a belt with disintegrating links. As the rounds were fired, the hard plastic links fell to the ground in small pieces. Popov sighted his weapon and fired again at the third still-standing target. It fell to its knees as the rounds struck, then its side and moved no more. Many more targets appeared, coming from the east. Popov reoriented his weapon and kept squeezing the trigger in controlled bursts.

* * *

Pratt slacked his fire slightly. Now that Popov was here, the volume of fire from his LMG let Pratt do his primary job of assessing and coordinating the battle. The troops he was facing had little training. They would fire their rail guns wildly and advanced haphazardly without mutual support. Pratt was not complaining in the slightest, but the professional in him analyzed their capabilities automatically. A rail-gun threw up clods of earth to his front as one of the warriors spotted him in the grass. The sunlight was fading, and they had an easier time seeing west now. Pratt fired a three-round burst at the croc with the weapon and saw it fall. So far, the defenders were doing well. A quick scan showed all his people were uninjured, and the attack had been met forcefully.

* * *

Bennet dropped three warriors with bursts from his CKP rifle, and when Popov opened up, he took the opportunity to toss a frag grenade over the ridge. "Frag out," the Canadian called from habit as he released it in a high arc through the air. With only a three-second delay set on the timing ring, the grenade exploded in the air three meters above the ground, sending out red-hot pieces of shrapnel. Anything within five meters of the blast was killed instantly, and several warriors out to fifteen meters were injured, some horribly.

* * *

Kek was near the rear of the assault wave and clear of the smoke now. He was able to finally yell intelligible orders, but did not stop pushing his troops onward up the hill.

* * *

Jefferson saw this and knew he must be a leader. She used the same techniques that had won her a silver medal in the Olympics years before. Laying prone, she brought her scope up, sighted the crosshairs on the creature's chest, and touched the trigger gently. The infrared laser sent out instantly determined the range to the target as 52.4 meters. The number was displayed by the scope reticule. The mini-computer in the scope took the information and applied various corrections. Air pressure, humidity, temperature, the angle of the barrel, even the local gravity reading was taken into account. When done, a small green dot appeared in her scope. She moved her weapon until the dot was at the junction of the crosshairs. This took a third of a second. Jefferson had a lungful of air. She released half of it, held her breath, and squeezed the trigger slowly. The weapon fired, releasing a round flying at 830 meters per second. The bullet hit dead center in the creature's chest, and it collapsed. She sighted on a second probable leader slightly further away and repeated the process. This time, the terrain blocked her going for center mass and that forced her to go for a head shot. At this distance, the shooting offered her no challenge. It—her targets were always "it"—also went down.

* * *

Kek lay on the ground as if struck by a thunderbolt. The hole in his chest bled profusely. He could not see the much larger hole on his back. With venomous spite, he wished Drawwl would receive the same treatment before the battle was over. He died within seconds, knowing he had failed.

* * *

Further down the hill, Drawwl ordered his own troops to press forward. He wanted to minimize any gap between the first and second attacks. Time was on his side here and not the warm bloods'. The smoke had thinned significantly and was just a nuisance now. Kek's provincial guards had done their job; now came his turn.

* * *

The battle slacked of its own accord over just a few seconds. The last of the assaulting warriors went down, and with nothing to target, the special forces troops held their fire without being ordered to. A couple of the fallen warriors stirred slightly, and they were dispatched with precisely aimed single shots. The humans took the opportunity to reload.

Drakk'Har bodies lay all over the field, with none further than ten meters from the lip. The attack had been contained easily. Jefferson reported, "All clear. No enemy visible, sir." She could see the white smoke spread widely through the eastern slope, its gossamer vapors slowly dissipating.

* * *

Pratt keyed his radio. "Good job, people. Anyone hurt?" Five seconds of silence answered his question. "Jacobs, how is White?"

Jacobs's voice came over the COMM system. "Suh, I's trying to get de bleedin' stopped. He lost lots of blood, but I's have him on plasma. He's under sedation; I's used de last of de oxymorphone on him. He's in rough shape, but stable, and I's would bet real money dat he will pull drough. Suh, de general sent out several people to man de barricade with Williams. Shall I's stand dem down?"

"Negative. Let's keep everyone in place," the officer responded.

* * *

Jefferson saw more movement and called it in. "Sir, we have major movement on the back side of the hill. I can see ten, no, twenty. Thirty. Forty. Sir, I see at least fifty lining up on the back side of the ridge. They are staying low and moving into several assault lines. They are advancing in a coordinated manner. This looks like their varsity."

* * *

Pratt felt the cold fear returning. He pressed it into the back of his mind, but thoughts of fifty or more well-trained warriors was enough to seed fear in any heart. "Right, Jefferson, stand by on the Claymores. Everyone else, grab a frag. Let them go on the back side of the hill in three. Two. One. Frags out!"

* * *

Just as the grenades left their hands, the first wave came over the berm of earth at the top of the ridge. Twenty advanced in the initial wave, and they didn't waste time firing. They simply ran forward over the edge of the ridge as fast as possible. Popov opened up with his LMG, but they advanced in line, and he could only hit one at a time. Only four fell.

* * *

Jefferson saw the large group advance and pressed the firing handles on the Claymores at exactly the wrong moment. The thrown grenades landed on the back side of the hill.

* * *

The running warriors had been trained repeatedly on their assault tactics. After running exactly six paces, they all fell forward as one onto their bellies. The Claymore mines were set back about twenty meters from the ridge and spiked into the ground. When they went off, thousands of small soft metal ball bearings were released from their epoxy bed and flung at high speed in a sixty-degree arc. They normally would have destroyed any enemy, but the Drakk'Har were now prone, and most of the ball bearings went well overhead. The slight deviations in terrain absorbed many of the spheres. Only five of the warriors were struck with minor wounds in the head and upper body; only one died after being hit directly in the forehead. The survivors lined up their rail guns and started firing toward the emplaced enemy.

As the distinctive sound of rail guns filled the clearing, the remainder of the warriors behind the eastern drop-off broke from cover and surged forward. Each group had an objective. As they moved, the grenades went off behind them, catching the slower Drakk'Har in the back. The dying unconsciously shielded those in front from much of the fragments and shrapnel. The odds had been reduced, but the majority of the assaulting force was still viable, and they now had a foothold on the plateau edge.

* * *

Jefferson saw the Claymores had failed, and she responded with a single word starting with the sixth letter of the alphabet. It was not broadcast over the radio and went unheard. Jefferson watched as the assault teams moved in-between the prone warriors and started a professional fire and advance maneuver. They went three paces past their prone comrades and then fell forward themselves before shooting. The back row then got up and started forward themselves, repeating the tactic. She began firing at obvious leaders.

* * *

Unseen by Jefferson, a smaller team of four had split from the extreme left side of the advance. MacPherson did see them and sent a three-round burst their way. One of the creatures was killed and a second wounded in the leg. The three survivors were lost to MacPherson as they disappeared around the base of the rock outcrop where Jefferson had her aerie. He tried to radio a warning to her, but the thundering sound of rail gun fire was simply deafening, and nothing intelligible got through.

MacPherson was exhilarated by the combat. His capture, days of rough treatment in the confining sack, and hearing Willy Tobes killed by these animals drove his need for revenge. MacPherson chose his targets and aimed carefully at the center mass of each. Every creature that dropped from his bullets gave him a satisfied feeling. MacPherson saw the warriors disappearing behind the high ground and knew they were taking the trail up to where Jefferson was located. He was trying to warn Jefferson on the radio and looking in Popov's direction, when two rail-gun rounds struck the Russian in the head. Popov's head snapped back, and his soft bush hat went flying. Even if the rounds had not killed him, his neck was broken instantly by the impact. MacPherson, angry at the loss of his comrade, angled his weapon around the safety of the boulders and shot twice in quick succession. Two bodies fell, which made him feel a little better, but the ledger needed more payment to be balanced properly in his mind. MacPherson grabbed a two-second-delay frag grenade from his cache, fitted the spoon handle to his palm, pulled the pin, and tossed it into the center of the field. He grabbed a second grenade and repeated the procedure, tossing it a little further than the first. He yelled, "Frag out," but no one heard it. Rail-gun fire overwhelmed all other sounds.

* * *

Pratt heard the rapid fire of the LMG stop and cast a look over to his left. His heart sank when he saw Popov's head wound. His skull was open, and half his brain gone. Without hesitation, he fired a burst to his front and rolled left. He landed right beside the body of the corporal. Macpherson's first grenade exploded as he stopped rolling. Several warriors fell in the shrapnel blast. Pratt ignored the body. He would mourn later. He dropped his rifle in the grass and grabbed the LMG, bringing it in front of him. Pratt saw the advancing troops running forward and sent a long burst into them from right to left. Pratt saw several of his targets fall as the second grenade exploded, taking more warriors down. Tactics broke down on the attacker's side as the survivors instinctively dove for cover wherever they could find it. This interrupted the rail-gun fire, and Pratt could talk briefly. "Fall back to the barricade in pairs." Pratt could see how many enemy troops were left. The enemy now had the advantage, and given their numbers on the plateau, they could not hold this position any longer.

* * *

By tradition, six warriors had been assigned to the assault sub-group. Two of them had been peppered in the back with grenade fragments and killed on the ridge. One had been killed by enemy fire on route. The remaining three made their way up a steep eastern path to achieve the high ground. The last of them limped because of a leg wound. They were all accomplished shots, and each had a rail gun. Their job was to fire down on the defenders from on high and either suppress or kill them. In their brief exposure to the battle space, all had looked up at their objective for troops, defenses, or emplacements. No one had seen anything of note. As they ascended up the trail, the lead soldier hit a trip wire, and a hidden cylinder of tear gas exploded, the vapors enveloping the group.

* * *

Jefferson had heard the call to fall back. She had raised herself onto one knee to get up, and that is when she saw the tear gas cloud. Long before she saw them, the sound of labored breathing and loud coughs came to her, and she knew they were close. Her position was at the southeastern corner of the outcrop, which gave the best view. Three paths led away from the area, and she had studied them all carefully. The first was to the east where a steep, but navigable, path existed. That was where the creatures approached from. The second path was straight north over the exposed rocks. Last was a small game trail to the southwest which lead down to a trail junction skirting the edge and eventually meeting back at the barricaded lighter. She made her decision in a heartbeat.

* * *

The three warriors topped the path with weapons held ready and saw nothing through teary eyes—just small shrubs, bushes, and an area of grass that had been flattened by a body lying there for a long time. Whoever had been occupying this position had fled. They rushed to the edge of the outcrop and looked down. They saw Drakk'Har lying in the grass slowly picking themselves up and starting to move forward to the west. One pointed southwest and identified a warm blood near some boulders. All three raised their weapons to fire at him.

* * *

Snipers lived with their weapons. The rifle was their primary weapon, and they practiced endlessly with it, perfecting their philosophy of One Shot, One Kill. Some snipers considered it blasphemous to use any other gun. Jefferson was not one of those; she used whatever was practical. She also practiced equally with all of her weapons to the same level of proficiency, because one just didn't know when they would be needed.

Jefferson rose up onto one knee from her position at the back of the escarpment and brought up her pistol in a two-hand grip. She sighted down the tritium sights. *Blam-blam. Blam-blam. Blam-blam.* The sound of three pairs of rapidly fired shots rang out as Jefferson put two large-caliber mercury-tipped pistol rounds into the exposed back or side center mass of each of the warriors on the crest. The first Drakk'Har struck simply fell over the edge and landed hard on the rocks below. The second collapsed in place, dropping its rail gun over the edge. The last just had time to turn toward the sounds, and as the rounds struck him, she saw the shocked look on the creature's face.

Surprise, sucker! Blam-blam. Two more pistol rounds, this time to the head, sent the last body toppling backwards over the side, its arms and legs flailing for something to hold onto.

Jefferson didn't pause. She reloaded her pistol with a fresh magazine before holstering it. She grabbed her RUK from the ground and stood to head off to the southwest path. At the top of the trail, she froze at the noise of movement. Something—in fact several somethings from the sound—were coming up toward her and fast. With no time for subtlety, Jefferson knelt down at the top of the path and pointed the barrel of the long rifle down the dirt trail. Her elbow was on her knee, which gave her a stable firing stance. She mentally cursed herself for not reloading the RUK. She would have felt better with ten rounds loaded, but hadn't had time to swap out the magazine.

* * *

As soon as Pratt called for a withdrawal, he could see MacPherson moving backward, angling toward the trail to the barricade. Smith rushed over to Popov, grabbed him by the ankle, and unceremoniously dragged the body backwards. MacPherson had his weapon pointed toward the enemy, firing at targets of opportunity. Pratt laid down a heavy cover fire with the LMG to keep the warriors' heads down. He glanced down to see the amount of ammo he had left and knew he would have enough. While firing, he made a mental checklist of the things he needed to do when his turn to move came. After what felt like an eternity, but in reality was only several seconds, he heard Smith's voice on the radio simply say, "Set.

Go!" This meant the retreating pair had stopped and were ready to support the officer's withdrawal. Pratt abandoned his CKP rifle in the grass and took the LMG. They needed the firepower. He took the spare ammo box with his free hand. Pratt got up quickly. Firing the LMG one-handed was unwieldy and terribly inaccurate, but the enemy didn't know that, and the clods of earth it threw up into the air kept their faces in the dirt for the most part. Bennet retired beside his officer, using his rifle in support. MacPherson and Smith added to the volume of fire from the rear, but as they fired from a braced kneeling position, their accuracy was much higher. They took a terrible toll on those foolish enough to stick their heads up.

Pratt back-pedaled until he came up even with the sergeants. He deliberately avoided looking at Popov's body. "Fall back to the lighter. Set. Go!"

* * *

Private Williams was in behind the barricade. He placed as much of the wood of the tree trunk in front of him as possible while sighting with his weapon to the east. To his front, between eight to ten meters of open ground lay before the heavy vegetation started, and past that he could see nothing. Williams could hear the horrible wail of rail guns and sporadic gunfire echoing through the trees. Several members of the lighter crew were also behind the wooden barricade. They only had pistols, but something was better than nothing at this point. One of them—he didn't see who—fired a single round into the bushes. Williams didn't hesitate. "CHECK FIRE!" he screamed. "No one fires without my clearance. NO ONE. We've got people out there!" Williams saw a tactical officer from the lighter, a major from the look of him, look over with a combination of embarrassment and anger on his face. The major pulled his pistol back and said nothing to the much-junior enlisted man.

* * *

Carstairs walked out of the safety of the lighter and saw Jacobs working feverishly to stop the blood flow on White's leg wound. The arm was already heavily bandaged with blood-soaked aero-gel bandages tied tightly to the wound. A bag of clear fluid was intravenously connected to White's forearm and hung on a latch plate on the lighter. The plasma would help keep up his blood volume.

"Can I help?"

Jacobs looked up at the general momentarily. "No, suh. Not a lot left to do. Thank you, suh."

"Right. Look after him, son." The general walked around the short wall before coming up behind Williams, who was kneeling behind the log wall. "What's the situation, Private?"

Williams looked up at him. "Sir, with respect, you might want to take cover." A burst of rail gun fire through the bushes reinforced the private's point as several enemy rounds impacted heavily on the tree trunk in front of them. Pieces of bark flew off the tree as the fire raked its surface. Instinctively, the general dropped behind the cover of the trunk while Williams ducked lower. Damp leaves fell from above and showered the men beneath.

* * *

Williams heard Pratt over the COMM system order, "Fall back to the barricade. Set. Go!"

"They're falling back to this position, General." Then he yelled to everyone behind the line, "We have troops coming in from the east! NO FIRING!" Williams looked at the General and said quietly, "Sir, may I suggest you fall back to the lighter? This may be your last chance."

"Sorry, son, but this is where I make my stand," Carstairs said simply.

"Yes, sir." *Generals...*

* * *

Pratt kept up his volume of fire and spread the bullets in a thirty-degree arc to his front. He didn't specifically aim at anything in particular. He just needed to keep the enemy pinned until his people got behind the barricades. In his peripheral vision, he saw Smith toss a frag grenade before pulling back while it arched through the air. MacPherson retreated a second later, having delayed to take an opportune shot before leaving. Pratt didn't need to look to see if the sergeants had taken Popov. *Never leave anyone behind, because one day it might be you* was the creed they all lived by.

* * *

Jefferson was watching intently down the southwest trail. The first thing she saw was a weapon barrel and her trigger finger tensed. A figure in green marine camouflage fatigues and lance corporal stripes turned the corner and started to run up the trail. A second figure turned the corner quickly after.

"HALT," she yelled loudly, her finger relaxing, but still near the trigger. "Who are you?"

* * *

Sergeant Sanchez stopped suddenly, as she heard a loud human voice challenge her. Then she saw the ghillie suit and the barrel of a weapon poking from it. As she started talking, the figure stood and came down the trail. "Sanchez of—"

"Let's save the intros for later, Lance Corporal. I need to talk to your officer," interrupted Jefferson.

Sanchez didn't pause. "This way."

Jefferson paused and took the opportunity to replace her magazine with a full one. "We need this trail secured. Can we leave him behind to watch our backs?" Jefferson indicated PFC Messina.

"Roger that. Messina, find some cover and stay here. Fall back if pressured. This way," Sanchez said as both women went down the trail.

* * *

Williams saw MacPherson emerge from the jungle first, then Smith, both dragging something. *Oh my God, a body.* He didn't recognize who that was until he saw the blood-soaked nametag as they came through the barricade defenses. Another burst of rail gun fire went well over their heads, sending a shower of leaves and small twigs down on top of them. Williams didn't take cover this time; he was too shocked by the sight of the corpse.

* * *

Once within the barricade defenses, Smith slung his weapon and took Popov by both ankles. "I've got him; cover the retreat," Smith said to MacPherson. MacPherson nodded and activated his radio. "Set. Go!" Then he moved back outside of the barricade to cover the retreat.

* * *

Pratt heard the radio call and moved back while firing almost continuously. When he got to the tree line, he had roughly ten rounds left in the belt. He squeezed those off in two short bursts. When the last round fired, the LMG action stayed back.

"Bennet, fall back!"

Pratt watched him run back toward the defense line before he himself turned and ran down the trail as fast as he could.

* * *

Williams heard Pratt order Bennet to withdraw on his headset. He yelled again to everyone on the line. "Friendlies coming in from the east. HOLD YOUR FIRE."

He turned to the general. "Sir, the last of the defense line is withdrawing now."

* * *

Pratt and Bennet covered the distance in a hurry. Pratt turned a slight corner in the trail and saw MacPherson standing in the open with weapon raised, pointing where they had just come from. "Back, back, back," was all Pratt said on the way past. The three men jumped behind the relative safety of the wooden walls.

Pratt placed the LMG on top of the makeshift barricade and ripped open the spare ammo box. He yelled to everyone behind the line, "Take cover. Attack inbound from the east. Twenty plus!" Pratt took the end of the new ammo belt and tried to feed it into the action. He had not done this in quite some time, and it showed. MacPherson stepped in. "Sir, I used to work an LMG. May I?"

Pratt stepped aside as MacPherson handed him his CKP-12. Pratt looked at the rifle from habit and saw the magazine was three quarters full. *Good enough*, he thought. MacPherson loaded the ammo belt smoothly, and when he released the action, it caught the first round. He was ready for combat.

* * *

Bennet ran down the wall to his prepared firing position. He lay down in the prone position and stuck his rifle muzzle through an embrasure. He could see little except heavy brush and foliage.

* * *

Pratt took his position near Williams at the center. He nodded to the general, who was on Williams's far side. "Everyone make it back?" he asked quickly of Williams.

"Everyone is accounted for except Jefferson, sir. No word from her."

"Right." Pratt was not worried unnecessarily; he keyed his radio. "Jefferson, report."

* * *

Jefferson heard the voice over her ear-piece. She held up her hand to stop 2nd Lieutenant Wicks in mid-sentence. She keyed her radio and simply said, "Stand by," then returned her attention to the officer in front of her.

* * *

Pratt heard the initial terse reply from his sniper, but didn't press for details. Each of his people was intelligent and well trained; as such, he gave them a lot of latitude. She was responsive, but could not talk for the moment for some unknown reason. He trusted her and knew there would be a good reason for the delay. He knew the enemy would soon press home the attack, and he had to prepare for that.

Pratt gave the order reserved throughout history for the soldier about to enter a truly desperate situation. "Fix bayonets!"

The scraping sound of several metal bayonets clearing their metal scabbards and being clicked into place on the muzzle locks was heard. The coming battle would be up close and damned personal.

Pratt looked all around, but could see nothing that was left undone. Smith had put Popov's body near the front of the lighter and had covered his head and chest with a poncho. Only his boots showed. He was well away and out of sight of the injured men. He saw Bennet steal a momentary glance over at the poncho with rage in his eyes. Pratt knew Bennet and Popov were friends. Pratt was at rest, but his heart rate continued to be rapid. The pit in his stomach deepened.

One of their only advantages, the light from the setting sun, disappeared at that moment behind the horizon. Dim shadows replaced the light beyond the defensive wall. Pratt looked upward at the God he had not spoken to in over ten years and thought bitterly, *Nice touch.*

* * *

Drawwl quickly gathered the survivors of the assault group around him on the eastern edge of the clearing. Only twenty-two warriors remained, which meant he had lost sixty percent of his force, not counting Kek and his provincials. Whether the survivors were more skilled or just luckier than the dead and wounded he did not want to judge. Drawwl himself had a minor shrapnel hit in his left arm, but that was a nuisance and nothing more. *A mark of honor when his assault was successful*, he boasted to himself. His plan was to surge forward from this point and overwhelm the remaining survivors. Blood trails in the grass showed they had made an impact, and now they would carry forward to victory.

Drawwl ordered the survivors into a crude line. They would not attack down the convenient path just to be shot down one at a time. They would crawl silently forward into the heavy brush and attack in line together.

* * *

Jefferson had a stick in her hand and was drawing positions in a piece of exposed mud. A crude representation of the downed lighter, cliff edge, defenses, terrain, and line of enemy advance had been composed in seconds using drawn lines, rocks, and twigs, giving the newly arrived marine officer a quick, but informational, briefing on the situation. Several other marines gathered around her, including a man with sergeant stripes and BLAKE on his nametag who looked like he had "been there and done that" a few times.

"Those are the basics, sir." She finished her briefing.

"Right." He took the stick off Jefferson. "Sergeant Sanchez, return to Messina and take position on the high ground Jefferson described. Take out anything that retreats past you. We will push them back, but will not pursue past the edge of the clearing here, so that is the limit on your arc of fire. Staff Sergeant Blake, I want everyone else in an assault line oriented here." He drew a line to the northeast of the defenses. "We will advance to contact and hit the assaulting force on their flank here." Wicks drew an arrow in the mud to emphasize the point. Blake was nodding his head slightly. He agreed fully. "Questions?"

Jefferson spoke. "Sir, I'll cover the high ground, as well."

"Brilliant. Please let your officer commanding know we are on the way."

"Yes, sir," she replied while keying her radio.

* * *

Drawwl advanced slowly through the brush. He had ordered all of the Drakk'Har to proceed slowly until the warm bloods fired. Once they did, that was the signal to surge forward *en masse.*

* * *

The men on the battlement defense line were hunkered behind the protective wall of wood and earth to the best of their abilities. They stayed low just in case a random burst of rail gun fire ripped through. They had heard nothing for a minute or so, but they knew Pratt and his people had not run from the boogeyman. Ironically, the major who had fired at shadows earlier noticed something first. His body was behind the wall, but he had never considered the possibility of being hit in the head. So, ignorant of that, he could see more than the others who *had* considered that possibility. A bush moved near him, and he craned his neck up to see why. There, staring back at him from a prone position, was a large Drakk'Har warrior. He half-stood to put his pistol over the wall and got two shots off before the warrior returned fire with his rail-gun. The major missed. He had not practiced on the range in nine months; the warrior had much better aim.

* * *

Pratt's attention was drawn by the pistol shots, and he saw the major's shredded body flung back as a half dozen shots from the rail gun struck him in the head, chest, and shoulders. The body cart-wheeled backwards as he was sent flying, surrounded by a red misty haze of vaporized flesh, blood, and bone. The major landed heavily and lay still. No one moved to help him. Half the flesh of his back was gone, and nothing could be done for him.

* * *

Bennet and Williams both tossed grenades over the wall before beginning to fire their rifles at selected targets.

* * *

Drawwl saw a warm blood grenade arc through the air. He pressed his body hard into a depression in the ground to avoid it. The explosions took their toll, but the Drakk'Har still surged forward. Some hung back and fired rail guns in support while others charged forward. The defensive wall was a nasty surprise to all of them, but it was easily negated, given their heights.

* * *

MacPherson on the LMG sent a murderous series of well-aimed salvos into the brush. One warrior targeted him with a rail gun, but he saw the movement and ended the creature's life before the trigger could be pulled.

* * *

Soldiers manning embrasures sighted and fired when they had a target. To them, this was a day at the range, but the Drakk'Har advanced in line and were already close to the wall. They could not see them all.

* * *

Drawwl and a dozen Drakk'Har warriors reached the barricade and came up on their hind legs. Many had ceramic blades in their claws, and they had practiced daily with them. They slashed down on the far side of the barricade. Their stubby arms did not give them the same reach as a human. However, they backed it up with more strength. Several blows landed on the defenders before they could react. Some recoiled from the attack, and others returned with weapon fire or bayonet lunges. There was no longer a coordinated assault. A melee of one-on-one, hand-to-hand fighting of the most brutal kind broke out.

* * *

Most of the humans stood their ground. Some because of their nature, some because of their training, others who were after revenge for past deeds. Those that stood all realized running was a short-term solution, and it would only delay their deaths. Others ran away because, at that moment, their panicked mammal brains were forcing them to. As a result, holes appeared in the defense, and Drakk'Har came over the wall in places to take advantage of it.

* * *

Jacobs saw this and picked off the few who came over the wall with his weapon. The rest of his section were fighting for their lives. All of the special forces troops had stood their ground, he was glad to see, although casualties were evident.

* * *

Pratt countered a blow with a blade, barely, with the side of his weapon. He slammed the butt of the CKP-12 across the creature's head, and it half-stepped back, confused. Pratt's radio flared to life, and Jefferson's voice came through the digital COMM link. Pratt fired his weapon three times into the warrior's chest at that moment, and he missed most of what she was saying as a result: "—approaching from the north." A rail gun went off nearby, and he could hear nothing else.

The creature he had shot had fallen back, and Pratt keyed his radio. "Say again, Jefferson." *More of them coming in from the north?* He knew of no way they could hold off more of the enemy; they were already on the edge of collapse. He saw the situation around him deteriorating. Several people were down, a few were running; he could not take the time to see who had been hit. One of the warriors on the far side of the wall further down grabbed a wounded man in a flight suit and pulled him over to his side. The creature disappeared behind the wall with teeth bared, and he didn't need to see to know what was happening. Pratt recalled White's blood-soaked torso, Popov's head wound, and the pistol-wielding major with no back in graphic detail. He was surrounded by carnage, blood, and gore covering almost every surface of the barricade. The smell of gun smoke was everywhere; the sound of human and Drakk'Har weapon fire combined into a continuous din. Everyone on both sides was screaming, some in rage, some in fear, others from wounds received. Despair began to rise in him. He took a half-pace backwards as his fearful animal brain fought with his intellect for control. There was no way they could stop them all. He had to get out of here! Another involuntary backstep. The ropes! He remembered the coiled ropes he had ordered placed by the lighter. That was his way out!

This time he heard her clearly in his earpiece. "Friendlies approaching from the northeast. Squad strength."

"Roger!" Emboldened by the news, instantly feeling deep shame at the fear in him, Pratt screamed out in between the bursts from his weapon, "Friendlies coming in from the northeast." *Blam-blam-blam.* "Friendlies from the northeast." *Blam-blam-blam.*

Pratt was firing at targets down the wall and had his back to the northeast, but he became aware of several weapons firing from that area. He fired one last time and glanced back quickly to see marines advancing slowly in pairs. One advanced while the other used cover fire to engage targets. He turned back toward the enemy and, with remorseful tears forming, kept firing.

* * *

The marines poured a heavy volume of fire into the creatures on the far side of the wall. From their flanking position, they could hit them almost perpendicular to the battlements. The enemy saw them, as well. One of the Drakk'Har faced the newcomers and unleashed his rail gun. A long burst spread over a wide angle was sent out. Small tree trunks disintegrated, foliage and earth flew from the kinetic impact. One of the rounds struck 2nd Lieutenant Wicks in the shoulder and spun him around like a rag doll. Perkins was to his right and saw the officer go down hard. Perkins had spent a lot of time with the L-T and had come to like the officer. He remembered his friend Belliveau, as well, and the way he had been shot up by these things. Perkins's first reaction was to scream profanities at the enemy and fire a long burst toward them. Two warriors near the end of the wall went down. Perkins emptied his magazine, dropped it to the ground, loaded a full one in smoothly, and began running toward the enemy screaming and firing in long automatic bursts.

For whatever reason, the six surviving Drakk'Har chose that moment to flee from the carnage around them. They crashed through the brush to make their way back to the clearing. Perkins never hesitated. He spotted the trail that paralleled the retreating enemy and took it without thinking. Estimating where the warriors were in the bush, he sent several bursts at them as he side-stepped rapidly down the path.

* * *

Blake had intended to go and help Wicks, but saw Perkins moving up the trail. He screamed at the PFC to stop, but Perkins was oblivious. Possessed by some apparent madness, Perkins ejected another empty magazine and reloaded, moving up the trail, then around a bend and out of sight. Blake charged after him, leaving Wicks to the others. Blake could live without Perkins, but the section radio was still on his back!

* * *

Remarkably, Perkins had hit one of the retreating warriors firing blindly, and only five of them emerged into the clearing.

Up on the high ground, Jefferson and Sanchez lined up on their targets. Messina was on the eastern path guarding that route from another surprise visit with his grenade launcher. Sanchez was using the body of a fallen Drakk'Har as cover. The group had agreed, whoever was in front would be targeted by Jefferson, while those in the rear were Sanchez's targets. The signal would be Jefferson's first shot.

Jefferson waited until the first retreating warrior was half way across the field. She led the target perfectly, and her first shot ended its life. Sanchez opened up with automatic fire, and that was when Jefferson saw a marine emerge from the trail. She targeted the retreating creatures as the marine added his bullets to the mix from the rear. He finished off the rest of the bullets in his magazine, hitting at least one more creature, and reloaded once more.

* * *

Drawwl had survived to this point. As he retreated rapidly on the grassy plain, he thought he was clear, but the warrior who died right in front of him demonstrated that was not true. Being hit from both the side and rear unnerved Drawwl even more, and he went for the closest safe spot he could think of: the steep south slope. Already on all fours, he ran as fast as he could.

* * *

Perkins saw only two warriors left. One ran to the eastern ridge while the other, somewhat larger, croc headed to the south. He raised his weapon and sent bullet after bullet to the southbound Drakk'Har, who was running in a random path to throw off his aim. Dirt clods and pieces of grass were thrown up in front of the Drakk'Har, but no bullet connected. The creature threw himself over the edge of the plateau and kept moving down the hill.

Jefferson fired the last bullet in the Battle of Hill 170, as it would come to be known. She took the last retreating Drakk'Har in the back as he was several paces from the safety of the eastern paths.

* * *

Blake heard the sharp report of the sniper's weapon as he got to the clearing. He saw Perkins standing still on the edge of the grass, his back to the sergeant, and his weapon held limply pointing down. Seeing lots of blood in the grass, Blake ran up to his side, very concerned. "Perkins, are you OK?"

"No, Sergeant," he said flatly.

Blake scanned him quickly for wounds, but saw nothing obvious. "What's wrong?"

The frustrated private whined loudly, "I ran out of ammo, Sarge."

Not believing his ears, Blake repeated it, but stopped short. "You ran out of—" The tension of the battle, the firefight, the head-long chase through the jungle, disappeared in an instant. Blake started laughing. "You ran out of ammo?" The sergeant shook his head as laughter wracked his body.

Perkins was oblivious and continued, crestfallen. He pointed half-heartedly to the south with his rifle barrel. "I almost had him, too."

It took Blake a few moments to get control of his laughter. He patted the PFC on the shoulder and gave him a smile. "OK, Perkins, let's go and get you some more ammo."

The pair started walking back to the trail. Blake saw a rifle in the grass and picked it up on his way by without thought.

"You and I are going to sit down tonight and have a discussion on the proper way for a radioman to act," said the staff sergeant as they walked.

"Yes, Sergeant," the private said dejectedly.

Then, just before they disappeared into the trees, Blake pulled a long, shiny, black metal cylinder from one of his chest pockets. Shaped like a test tube and stopped at one end with a thick black plug, he looked at it briefly. On the surface of the tube was a laser engraved logo with "H. Upmann – Habana" beneath. "Here, Perkins, have a cigar."

* * *

Sharp rocks bit into his soft belly as he descended. His legs were beginning to cramp up from the exertion, but he did not stop until he was well down the hill. Sure he was not being pursued, Drawwl headed east. It took him a long time, but he made it to the base of the hill. He proceeded along a seldom-used trail until he happened on a mud pool just large enough for him. There he collapsed as the lactic acid was slowly absorbed back into his aching body.

CHAPTER 23 – INTERRUPTIONS

Blake and Perkins returned to a charnel house, and whatever bonhomie Blake was feeling disappeared instantly. Blood was soaked into the grass, trees, bushes, and wall on both sides. The smell of it mixed with expended gunpowder and grenades. Some sections of the defenses were pushed in or collapsed. Near the far end of the wall, a body in a flight suit was being covered with a poncho. The khaki flight suit was green only on the legs; the torso and arms were a dark red. Numerous bodies lay on the ground outside of the wall. Croc warriors lay in the brush, their weapons spread haphazardly around them. One warrior was missing a thirty-centimeter chunk from his back. Blake saw another with a back leg that would not stop twitching. He turned away and walked past the barricade. The lighter side of the wall was worse. Several of his people were rendering first aid to the wounded defenders.

One man leaning against the wall screamed, pausing only to take a breath to scream once more. PFC Johnston was giving him first aid and trying to reassure him, but the wild look on the man's face was not based in reason. Johnston pressed a gas ampoule of something into the man's neck, and the screams subsided slowly. Somehow, the resulting silence only made the scene worse. Others in his unit were dragging the dead to the front of the lighter. Blake shook his head and wondered how bad it would have been without his unit's assistance.

"Pick yourself up a souvenir, Staff Sergeant." The British accent from behind took him completely by surprise. Blake and Perkins turned and were both open-mouthed from shock when Wicks stepped forward, apparently uninjured, looking at the unusual rifle in Blake's hand.

"Sir, I saw you go down," was all Blake could get out.

"Yes, bloody hard hit, that." The officer raised his weapon to show the butt of his rifle. A deep, three-centimeter, oblong crater showed in the tough composite material. "My lucky day, I think. A little to the right, and it would have taken my arm off. Knocked the wind out of me, certainly. Where did you and Perkins get off to?"

"Sir, we pursued the remainder of the retreating force to a clearing. Sanchez and her group took care of the rest. I found this weapon on the ground on the way back. Looks like one of the special ops rifles. Seems like we arrived just in time. I'm glad you were not hurt, sir."

The officer looked serious. "Thank you, but the cost was steep. Cole took a hit. Must have been in the same burst that got me. Straight through his chest, I am afraid. It killed him instantly."

"Damn. He was a good kid," Blake said.

"They all are, Staff Sergeant. Right, let's get stuck in and organize this mess. Lieutenant Pfeiffer will be along in no time, and we cannot have him seeing this sorry lot. Let's keep Sanchez where she is for the short term. You may as well see if you can find an owner for that rifle. When the other squads arrive, we can push them out to the eastern edges and reform the perimeter. Perkins, let's set up the squad CP over there for now."

The men moved off to help wherever they could.

* * *

General Carstairs and Lieutenant Pratt were together and leaning with their backs to the wall. Carstairs had a bandage around his right forearm, courtesy of Jacobs, that had been tucked into his fatigue shirt as a makeshift sling. One of the swinging blades had hit him during the assault on the wall. Luckily, it had only been a glancing blow, or it would have cut through the bone. Before moving onto the next wounded person, Jacobs had pronounced he would heal in a few weeks.

"There he is— the one with the radio on his back," the general said. "He took out the two warriors in front of me just in the nick of time. Chased the others off, as well. Will have to have a word with his officer later about that."

"Yes, sir," Pratt said flatly. He didn't even look up.

Carstairs saw the look on Pratt's face, a look he had seen in battle before. Not only his face, but his entire body language communicated he had shut down and just didn't care anymore. Pratt was unwounded. Jacobs had given him a once-over as part of his visit. "We lost a lot of people here today, Lieutenant."

"Yes, sir."

The general's voice was flat, but firm. "We would've lost a lot more if you had not done your job. Lieutenant, your preparations, given the time and conditions here, were exemplary. You thought through the issues and addressed them the best you could. You said it yourself; it would take a company to fortify this hill. Yet you did it with what—just over a half dozen troops plus my people—holding off a force of at least a hundred well-trained enemy? I consider that a significant victory, Lieutenant, and my report will reflect that."

"Yes, sir," Pratt said, his eyes still downcast.

The message was not getting through. Time to kick it up a notch.

"OK, Lieutenant, you have a decision to make." The general's voice was low so no one else could hear, but the steel in his voice was clear. "When we get back to the fleet, you can either resign your commission and get assigned as a PFC rifleman to whatever front line unit will take you, or you can realize that as an officer, you made a difference here, and the majority of your people lived to see another day because of it. No battle plan survives contact with the enemy, Lieutenant. This is war; you know this. People die in war, you know that, too. Good officers who care about their people are needed to minimize those losses. I want you to go and talk to each of your people. See how they feel about the way things went."

The general counted mentally to five, and Pratt remained immobile. The general said flatly, "That was not a suggestion, Lieutenant."

Pratt looked like a train had just rolled over him as he stood. "Yes, sir." He walked away.

* * *

Darkness fell completely on the now-quiet Hill 170. The first and second squads, along with the platoon commander, Lieutenant Pfeiffer, arrived just before the last vestiges of light left the blood-red sky. Pfeiffer set the other squads on the outer ridge encompassing from the north to east to south. Pfeiffer set up the first squad machine gun on the high ground where Sanchez and Jefferson were. This was a slightly heavier version than the one special forces troops carried. Sanchez and Jefferson were relieved and fell back to the lighter defenses, which were being repaired slowly. The second squad machine gun went on the western edge of the grass plateau. They dug it into a shallow slit trench and piled earth and wooden logs in front of it, just in case anyone came back looking for another fight.

He left the third squad under Wicks on the western edge and set up his platoon command post near the southern end of the defensive wall. Pfeiffer could reach out and touch the smashed cockpit of the lighter from his CP. The troops planted a half dozen Claymore mines around the perimeter and set up trip wires with flares and tear gas twenty meters down each major path. Blake's green-painted cans were strung out on lengths of field wire. The loose nuts and bolts inside would rattle if anyone tripped the wire, alerting the troops. Sentries were posted on a 2/2 watch and given extra grenades just in case something came a little too close. It had been drilled into all soldiers manning a fixed position that you never fired unnecessarily, as it gave your positions away. The origin of a tossed grenade at night was almost impossible to locate.

As platoon commander, Pfeiffer had one last card to play, as well. He sent up an aerial surveillance drone. It had a long technical name and in military jargon was designated as a CT-5, Field Deployable Unmanned Aerial Drone, IR Capable. Being a little wordy, the troops simply called it The Vulture. The wingspan was only half a meter wide, and it looked like any small aircraft with a larger than normal wing. It had a propeller, ailerons, and rudder and was made out of a lightweight composite. The drone could be put together in less than a minute from three pieces. A camera in the belly looked straight down and could see in the dark almost as well as during the day. A small radio and data link let this video feed be sent down to anyone with the right decryption codes in their COMM unit. Its infrared capability showed hot things like bodies and weapons as white spots. It gave a bird's eye view of the terrain and was an invaluable resource for Pfeiffer.

The Vulture was pre-programmed to go to a thousand meters over the controlling COMM unit and then stay there while turning in a wide radius over that point. If the COMM unit moved, the Vulture's position shifted to keep above it. Solar cells were embedded flush on the top surface of the wing, but at night, it had to run exclusively on the internal batteries. With no solar recharge, the unit could stay aloft eight to twelve hours, depending on how many times it had to use its motor. The motor was designed to be as quiet as possible, and the blades were computer-designed to generate maximum thrust with minimum noise. Even with trees above them, no large force could hope to approach at night without being seen. It circled above, watching over the troops below.

* * *

Drawwl was over a klem away from the hill. The mud pool was warm, and he was exhausted, so he decided to stay there for the night. Then he had to make his way back to the town to find Borrk and report in. Drawwl knew that his life was only going to last until the end of the following day at the latest. He was the sole survivor of a large assault group. Drawwl had nothing to show for his efforts, absolutely nothing. Borrk was not the forgiving type, and Drawwl had nothing to offer to forsake his wrath. Drawwl fell asleep quickly and slumbered fitfully.

* * *

Pratt had talked to a couple of his people as he wandered the area around the battlements. Some of them had minor wounds, but nothing serious, he was glad to see. Bennet had the worst wound, with a slash mark from an enemy blade across his back and left shoulder. However, it would heal in time, and a broad suture dermal patch was already in place. Pratt talked to Jefferson and Smith first, as they were out on sentry duty and he was expected to check in on them regularly. Those conversations were brief and stuck to the present tactical situation. As a result, neither conversation was long or verbose. *Waste of time doing this*, Pratt thought.

On his way back to the lighter to talk to Jacobs, he saw MacPherson sitting with his back against a stump, cleaning the LMG. He was using a flashlight with a red filter to illuminate the parts spread on a small green utility tarp. He had a cleaning kit out and was currently ramming a patch down the barrel, getting rid of any propellant on the inside surface. As Pratt got closer, he saw MacPherson had a thick field dressing pressed onto his neck.

"Good evening, Staff Sergeant, how's your neck?" The officer decided to sit down across from the sergeant. He was damned tired.

"Good, sir, just a scratch. I slipped up, and one of those bastards got too close. I gave him a belly full of lead in return.

However, I survived, so, lesson learned." MacPherson smiled, and the comment was delivered with such positive good humor that the officer smiled inadvertently, as well. "I wanted to thank you again, Lieutenant," the sergeant said while pausing in his cleaning.

"For what?" Pratt was confused.

"For hauling my butt out of that sack, sir. You saved my bacon that day, and I appreciate it. I have to tell you, Lieutenant, I've never felt more alone and scared than that day. I could only hear what they did to Willy the night before, and that will give me nightmares for the rest of my life. After that, I knew I was next to be done in. I had a hollow, dead feeling inside me that grew throughout the day as they carried me. Horror, terror, abandonment. No one word can describe it adequately. You have to experience it to understand it, I guess. Then you and your people came along, and here I am, a day later, back in the world. My great aunt used to say, 'It always gets better,' and she was right. Anyway, sir, I wanted to thank you."

Pratt knew exactly the negative feelings he was describing, but said nothing.

"Lieutenant, one more thing. With Lieutenant Whitelake and my unit gone, they will be bringing in a new officer. You know how it is, sir; you never know what kind of officer you will get. Most are OK, I suppose, but it's luck of the draw. Well, sir, I was speaking with Jacobs earlier, and Mendez won't be able to come back to the unit without a leg and all, so I was wondering if you would look positively on my transferring to your section?"

"You want to come to the 121st?" Pratt asked with obvious disbelief.

"Yes, sir. You run a tight unit, and the troops respect you. You look after your people, and as was shown today, you know your stuff. Your plan and tactics saw us through today, Lieutenant. Sir, it comes down to this. If I have to choose between the unknown and you, sir, I'll take the proven winner every time."

Pratt paused. Some of what the sergeant had said had hit home. "Let me sleep on it, and I'll give you an answer in the morning. You relieve Jefferson in an hour, right?"

"Yes, sir. Williams and I are on the next shift."

"Right." The officer stood. "Have a quiet watch, Staff Sergeant."

"Thank you, sir."

* * *

General Carstairs had wandered around to meet all the people in Wicks's squad. He shook each of their hands, albeit gingerly. The raw nerves in his forearm felt like they were on fire at times, but he forced himself. He thanked each one for their timely rescue. When done, he asked to speak with Wicks and his senior NCO alone. They huddled together in the squad CP, and introductions were made.

"Blake... Blake," the general started. "I remember a Corporal named Blake at the operation on Proxima. He volunteered to go behind enemy lines with a couple of pioneers and blast a small dam. That flooded a series of defense tunnels and wiped out effective resistance in that area. Any relation?"

"That was me, sir. I, uh, I had a good fire team with me." Blake was seldom embarrassed, but he stammered now.

"You saved a lot of people that day, young man. While the Drakk'Har can swim, their weapons cannot fire underwater worth a damn. We were able to free up an entire brigade due to what you accomplished."

A man in a flight suit jogged up to the general, interrupting him. "Excuse me, sir, this just came in from Colonel Bradley." He handed the general a piece of paper from a printer.

The general read the note carefully with a red lens flashlight. He then handed it back to the messenger. "Tell him to maintain position and not to pursue. He can call in a fire mission onto that position if he feels it is a threat, but I don't want any unnecessary night ops. Actually, if it is Bradley, you had best specify *no* night operations. Otherwise, he may feel it necessary to tromp up that hill on his own initiative. Carry on."

"Yes, sir." The man went back to the lighter.

"Where was I? Oh, yes. This young man, Perkins. It seems he saved multiple lives earlier today. Took out the two warriors directly in front of me, broke up the enemy assault, forcing them to retreat, and actively pursued them single-handed. That was an incredibly brave thing I saw, and I wanted your take on him."

Glad that the topic of conversation had turned away from Proxima, Blake said nothing and let his officer speak. "Well, General, this is Perkins's first operation. I must admit, I didn't see what you described, as I was struck to the ground by a rail gun just before. Staff Sergeant Blake was there and can describe the events."

So Blake did. He took his time and told the general the circumstances starting from when they had heard the gunfire from the hillside. He did it in terms as neutral as possible. He presented the facts as he saw them and mentioned that he had warned Perkins not to run off unsupported again. When he told Carstairs the reason Perkins had stopped running, the general chuckled appreciably. "Probably a good thing he did run out of bullets, or you may not have caught him. Very well. Lieutenant, I would appreciate if you put in the paperwork for a suitable decoration for young PFC Perkins. Given the circumstances, 'The Medal' is out of the question, but I am sure you can think of something."

"Yes, General. I am sure he would appreciate a Bronze Star."

"Probably, Lieutenant, but you have to understand he saved the life of a general officer, among others, and I would not have other generals, who shall remain nameless, make comment about my apparent lack of appreciation of my self-worth. I would consider something a little more meritorious."

"Forgive me, sir, I meant Silver Star, of course."

"Excellent. I have arranged for a dedicated medevac just after first light to get the heavily wounded out. Troop lighters will arrive soon after to take us off-planet. Have a good evening, gentlemen." The general stood and left to return to the lighter.

* * *

Blake waited until Carstairs was well out of earshot. When he spoke, he did so *sotto voce* while shaking his head. "We'll have to get Perkins some larger T-shirts, sir."

"Pardon me, Staff Sergeant?"

"When Perkins gets wind of this, he won't be able to fit his swelled head through the ones he has now," Blake said.

"Yes. Quite right, Blake. Quite right indeed."

* * *

As night fully enveloped Hill 170, silence reigned. Sentries stood guard around the perimeter. Those not on duty either slept or otherwise relaxed. With little wind and the brilliant stars above in the now cloudless sky, it felt as peaceful as a normal camping trip. Overhead, the Vulture drone circled silently and kept watch over the small island of humanity occupying the high ground.

CHAPTER 24 – RESCUE

Pratt awoke as the first beams of red light came over the horizon. He had climbed into his sleeping bag just after one a.m., then tossed and turned for the first hour, unable to relax. In the end, sheer exhaustion caught up to him, and he had finally dozed off.

Pratt lay flat on his back, folded his hands over his chest, and closed his eyes. Once again, he ran through the entire operation in his mind. He examined each decision he had made, every order he had given, and the consequences. At each point, he was unable to think of something he could have done better. Hindsight was always clear, but he tried to stay away from that and use only the information he had at the time. After a few minutes, he decided he had done what he could and nothing would have changed.

Pratt unzipped himself, rolled his sleeping bag into his backpack, and opened the valves on his thin, insulated mattress to let the air out. Rolling the mattress took some time, as the air within had to be bled out slowly as he compressed the material. Once done, he tightened the valves to keep the air out. He then slipped the mattress into the carrier on the side of his backpack.

Pratt felt his cheek and throat and decided he needed a shave. He grabbed an insta-razor from his bag and pulled it across his stubble. A small amount of cold lubricant was automatically applied as it traveled across his face, just before the razor cut the hair. The shaver was not a barber-quality shave by any means, but it made him look and feel a little more respectable. Pratt used a khaki-colored towel to wipe off the last of the gel. When done shaving, he ran some water from his canteen through the blades to clean it. The lubricant gel liquefied instantly, and it and the cut hairs fell out onto the ground. He stowed the razor in his backpack and packed away the rest of his personal items, ready for the trip to the fleet.

Private Williams approached just as Pratt was finishing. Williams handed over a metal canteen holder with handles unfolded. The contents were steaming. "Good morning, sir. Thought you might like a coffee. We have a medevac lighter inbound. ETA six minutes."

"Thank you. Please inform Jacobs we need to get the casualties prepped for the move. Then make sure the general is informed. I suspect we'll be sending the dead up, as well. We'll have to get them into sleeping bags for the move," Pratt ordered.

"Already done, sir—the bodies, I mean. MacPherson and I did that just before first light."

"Right. Thanks for the coffee, Williams. Smells good." The officer gestured with the metal cup and managed a weak smile.

"No problem, sir. It is never a good day unless you start with a decent cup of coffee." Williams smiled, turned, and went back to the lighter to talk to Jacobs.

Pratt grabbed a meal bar from a side pocket on his pack and opened the package with his teeth. He walked over to the edge of the cliff and looked over the vista before him. He took a bite of the meal bar and a sip of the coffee. The air was cool with little wind. In a few hours, he would be standing on a metal deck and on his way out of the system. As the coffee warmed his body, Pratt decided that Williams was right, and this would be a good day.

Pratt finished the meal bar and drained the rest of the coffee. He put the mylar wrapper in the cargo side pocket of his fatigue pants and pulled out a small white pill from a package in his chest pocket. He popped this into his mouth, where it foamed upon contact with his saliva. He swished the foam around his teeth for thirty seconds and could feel the cleaning action. When the bubbles stopped forming, he swallowed the remnants, knowing the contents contained a daily dose of vitamins and minerals.

Pratt checked his watch and saw he had two minutes before the lighter was scheduled to appear.

* * *

Captain Levin had his orders and was approaching Hill 170 at a steady pace. His landing coordinates were set on his NAV system, and his threat indicators were blank. His lighter was in a medevac configuration and carried no weapons. He flew in formation with three other lighters, two of which had a series of air-to-ground weapons loaded. Grasshopper Four's faulty hydraulics had been repaired, and it had been rigged in a medevac configuration as a backup in case of issues. Grasshopper Two would make a pre-emptive cluster run over Hill 237 as Levin came into the hill just in case any anti-air gear had been brought in during darkness to threaten them. Intelligence said it didn't think it had, but no one trusted those reports absolutely, and no Intel types were on any of the Grasshopper lighters. Reports and memos were meaningless unless your own butt was on the line. Besides, ordnance was cheap, and using it on Hill 237 meant less to carry back. Grasshopper Three would keep his weapons in reserve in case another threat emerged.

Levin looked at the chrono on his display. *Time to initiate.* He keyed his radio. "Grasshopper Two, this is Grasshopper One. Start your run."

"Grasshopper Two, roger. Thirty seconds."

Grasshopper Two approached the side of Hill 237 from an oblique angle. This time, no one illuminated the target. Its coordinates were preprogrammed into the computer, and all the pilot had to do was fly to the proper NAV point at the right speed and altitude. When the lighter got to the release point, Levin watched the weapons fall spaced a few hundred milliseconds apart. Once in free fall, the bombs armed and split apart, releasing their contents. Small bomblets fell and spread over a large area. Each exploded on impact with trees or the ground and filled the side of Hill 237 with copious amounts of shrapnel, smoke, and deafening noise. If any surviving Drakk'Har were on the hill, the attack would keep them well down in their protective holes.

Levin saw the impact from twelve hundred meters away as he approached Hill 170. He hit the stud for internal communications and said, "Crew, prepare for combat landing. Prepare to receive casualties."

* * *

Pratt arrived at the landing zone at the same time as the general. The sound of the air strike echoed around them both for a few seconds. The general spoke first, after taking a hard look at the younger officer. Carstairs could see Pratt had shaved and looked in decent shape. "Feeling better, I see."

"Yes, sir," Pratt replied.

"Sleep any?"

"A few hours, sir." Pratt wanted to change the subject as he was very uncomfortable under the general's gaze. "I have the wounded organized, sir. We will just be sending up the serious cases and the dead. The walking wounded can go in the regular dust-off."

"Very well, Lieutenant. Coordinate with 2nd Lieutenant Wicks if you need more manpower. Carry on." The general turned to talk to one of his people arriving with yet another message form.

"Sir." Pratt turned to return to the wounded.

"Lieutenant, one moment please!" the general yelled after him. Pratt walked back over to the general. "It appears I've been recalled by the marshal. He wants me in orbit ASAP to coordinate the exfiltration, so I'll go up with the medevac. When I'm gone, Lieutenant Pfeiffer will take over as overall commander to coordinate the dust-off. Can you make sure the lighter command staff are looked after? Your people will be last off, as planned."

"Roger, sir. Good luck." Pratt did not salute. One never did in the field.

Carstairs stuck out his wounded forearm and shook the younger man's hand as best he could. "I'll see you again, Lieutenant, I am sure."

* * *

Second Lieutenant Wicks had ordered Lance Corporal Cole bundled up in his sleeping bag so it would be easier to carry him. He would be put into a proper rubber-coated bag when he got to the fleet before being turned over to the "ghouls." They were marines who would care for the corpse, clean him up, sew up any wounds, and remove any personal items that would be bagged and tagged for loved ones. They would also decide if the casket should be kept sealed or not. The last thing the marines wanted was for a family to see a loved one with no face. Given Cole had a chest wound, he would probably get an open casket funeral. The family would be informed of his death fairly quickly. However, it would be some time until the body itself would be returned. The distances of interstellar travel were still a huge barrier to overcome—something grieving families had to endure.

Each marine had indicated how his body was to be disposed of. Many chose the sun burial option. Their casket was ejected with a path that would eventually lead to the sun, where they would become a part of the star illuminating their military base. Others chose cremation and having their ashes either spread at a favorite place or returned to their families. A few still preferred traditional burial, and Cole had chosen that for himself.

Wicks had already organized a small group to help load the four badly injured men the special forces medic had been caring for. He had perimeter security out and made sure nothing obstructed the landing zone.

After the wounded were away, he expected to be off this planet within a few hours. He was looking forward to a hot shower and decent food before having to deal with the usual mountain of paperwork that followed an operation.

* * *

Levin's lighter came into the landing zone from the east facing west. A moderate head wind was developing, but otherwise the approach was smooth. An updraft caused by the sun's rays warming the air at the side of the hill hit the lighter and forced it upward. Levin reduced power, and the lighter dropped. As the lighter came completely over the plateau, it left the updraft behind and landed roughly as a result. The four landing struts easily absorbed the impact of landing, but the frame flexed as the weight redistributed itself.

The four engine mounts bobbed slightly as the strain was absorbed. Three of them had no issue, but the starboard rear mount cracked almost all the way through. Under the cowling, one could now place a thumb through one of the fissures.

As soon as the lighter touched down, Levin throttled back the engines to idle, but did not shut them down. He looked back to watch Sergeant Allan open the side hatch with a single pull. Immediately, the marines brought the wounded through the hatch. After the wounded were aboard, Allan indicated the dead should be loaded. They were placed at the rear of the lighter, and a cargo strap was zigzagged across them and cinched down to hard points in the wall and floor. This was not disrespectful; no one wanted floating corpses when they hit zero gee.

General Carstairs entered the cargo bay while this was going on and tapped Levin on the shoulder through the opening to the flight deck. Levin pulled his helmet up so his ear was uncovered. "Captain Levin, good to see you again. I'll be catching a ride up with the wounded. After we get them off, we need to get over to the *Aristotle*. Is that a problem?"

Levin thought about this for a moment while turning and checking the displays for information. He was due to return to the planet at least once more to pick up troops. He double-checked his timings and saw he had enough reserve time to accommodate the general without involving flight operations to reschedule. "No problem, sir. Welcome aboard."

Carstairs patted the pilot on the shoulder and went to sit on the passenger bench. Levin called Sergeant Allan on the intercom and told him of the extra passenger. The general's *aide-de-camp* would normally sit beside the general, but he had a vicious leg wound and occupied a stretcher.

* * *

Sergeant Allan intercepted the general before he got to his seat. In addition to the O_2 mask, he had the general put on a parachute harness identical to the one Allan wore. Allan gave a quick briefing on the parachute rig that the general had heard many times before, but Carstairs said nothing and listened politely.

After making sure the general was secure in his seat, Allan turned and double-checked that the wounded were all strapped in. Each had three broad straps across their chest, hips, and upper legs to hold them securely in place. Seeing nothing out of place, Allan gave a marine officer standing outside a thumbs up and closed the hatch. The hatch had been open less than four minutes. He could see the officer moving away from the lighter. Allan looked out the port and starboard windows and saw no one near the vehicle. "Pilot, LZ clear port and starboard for dust-off."

* * *

"Roger. Crew, begin lift-off checklist," Levin said, and the crew proceeded through the brief list of things to check. Levin inserted no jokes this time. The cargo and wounded in the back of the lighter made that inappropriate.

After the checklist was successfully completed, Levin advanced the throttles, and the lighter took off vertically. He kept the lighter facing east before vectoring the engine thrust to send the lighter forward. As forward momentum built, the stubby wings began to generate a little lift, and this let Levin transition to traditional flight mode. The landing pads were retracted to smooth airflow across the airframe.

"Crew, prepare for orbital insertion burn."

A quick check of the flight deck instrumentation showed no threats detected. Levin advanced the throttles to full military power, and as soon as the engines responded, he pulled back on the yoke, and the lighter began to climb. The orbital booster on the back of the lighter would only work if the lighter was higher than twelve thousand meters in altitude. If fired any lower, it would have insufficient fuel to make it to orbit. Once the booster was fired, it could not be shut down, and it only worked once.

The lighter shook with the strain of the engines at military power. Levin tried to maintain a thirty-seven-degree nose-up flight angle, which gave him the most efficient climb. Corporal Wallace kept monitoring the engine, power, fuel, oil, and temperature gauges. Everything was nominal, with gauges registering in the yellow band and just under the red.

"FE, deploy countermeasures," Levin said at twenty-five hundred meters altitude. This was part of the ascent protocol.

Wallace punched a button to launch a series of RADAR decoys and flares behind the lighter. If anyone fired a weapon at them during the ascent, the countermeasures would ensure a better chance of survival. A series of dull *whump* sounds came from the rear of the lighter.

"Countermeasures away, sir." Wallace returned his attention to the lighter engine gauges.

Levin concentrated on keeping the thirty-seven-degree angle of attack. At nine thousand meters, he would incline the nose up to fifty-three degrees, and at twelve thousand meters, he would activate the orbital insertion engine. The lighter speed was increasing slowly and steadily. Everything looked like a normal flight profile, and while alert, the crew was relaxed.

At 3,123 meters altitude, the crack in the main starboard rear engine caused the mount to fracture. The stress was too much for the secondary mounts, and they sheared, severing wiring and fuel lines. The now unsecured engine flew forward, driven by the fuel left in the lines. It struck the forward right-hand engine in the rear before dropping toward the planet. That impact cracked the forward manifold, but also crimped the main fuel line to the forward engine. It stalled almost instantly, and the resulting thrust from that engine went to zero.

Levin was checking his threat indicator just as the incident occurred and had seen nothing. The lighter was violently shaking, and Levin had no idea why he had just lost all power to both engines on his right side. Several alarms screamed and lights flashed. Both right-hand engines indicated zero on the thrust gauges. "Wallace, check your door mirror. What do you see behind you?"

Wallace reported in an excited voice, "Sir, number four engine is missing! It's gone, sir! No thrust from number two engine."

Levin commanded a restart of the number two engine. This took twenty seconds and failed to re-ignite the engine.

"Sir, fuel flow to the number two engine is zero."

With the loss of power, forward speed started to bleed off, and the nose began to come down of its own accord. The lighter also began to dip to the right, turning back the way it had come, and Levin had to use the maneuvering thrusters normally used in space to maintain level flight. In a heartbeat, the pilot knew a controlled landing would be impossible. Thrusters would not work effectively enough at low speeds.

He didn't hesitate to give everyone the news. "Crew, abandon aircraft."

As soon as he said those words, Levin knew the wounded men in the back were dead. He had no way of rigging them with parachutes, and even if he could, they were unconscious and incapable of pulling the ripcord. Levin turned a console switch to Emergency, which broadcast an automated signal the fleet could track. Levin also keyed the radio and broadcast on a reserved channel to everyone in the area. "Mayday, Mayday, Mayday. This is Grasshopper One. We've lost both right engines, and we're going down. The crew is abandoning the aircraft."

Levin knew he had to remain at the controls to keep stable flight so the others could live. If he left the controls, the lighter would roll hard to the right, spinning until it impacted the planet below. He turned to his flight engineer who was still sitting there. "Wallace, get out!"

Wallace looked like he was about to argue, but he slipped out of his restraints and went through the flight deck doorway to the cargo bay.

* * *

Sergeant Allan had heard the order and followed procedures to the letter. He opened a clear protective cover at the side of the starboard hatch and grabbed a yellow and black handle marked "Access Hatch (Right Side) – Explosive Bolts – DANGER." He pulled it sharply, and the side hatch blew away from the lighter with a loud and hard *thump*. Air rushed into the cabin, and anything loose was stirred up by the incoming rush of air.

* * *

The rushing wind in the cargo area roused Mendez from his unconscious state on one of the suspended stretchers. He found himself assailed by the air around him. In his delusional state, he imagined himself to be on top of a stormy outcrop of rock. Surrounded by Drakk'Har, nowhere to go, his weapon jammed, abandoned by his section, he stood alone in a violent storm. Mendez flailed against the restraints, and his palm brushed the hard sphere in his side cargo pocket. His hand dove under the blanket, and Mendez reached into his pocket and grabbed it, feeling the familiar cool, spherical shape. He pulled it out of his side pocket and held it in both hands.

* * *

Wallace saw the movement on the stretcher as he left the flight deck and recognized one of the wounded was conscious. He grabbed a spare parachute harness and moved to the wounded man, intending to save him as well. Wallace had to keep hold of the metal rigging as he moved slowly back into the cargo bay.

* * *

Sergeant Allan was right beside the general. He leaned forward and yelled, "We have to get you out, sir."

Carstairs undid his restraints and grabbed the sergeant by both arms to steady himself. His wounded arm caused him to wince in pain. He had to yell over the cacophony of rushing air to be heard. "What about the wounded?"

"You first, sir!"

"I will help you with them!" Carstairs yelled.

Allan knew full well nothing could be done for the unconscious wounded. He grabbed the general forcefully and turned him so that his back was to the door. He had intended to push him out. Carstairs resisted, selflessly wanting to help the men on the stretchers.

* * *

Mendez looked around wildly, the Drakk'Har venom in his blood causing him to hallucinate. He could see a single Drakk'Har making its way toward him. Behind that one, two other warriors fought between themselves. Their teeth were long, white, and threatening. He imagined they were fighting over who would get to eat him. Mendez had seen unedited footage from the *Cherubs Song* and knew how Drakk'Har fed. The other warrior was getting closer, and Mendez could see the green scales and wild, cruel yellow eyes. Mendez was terrified at the thought of being eaten alive. *No. No. Not again. No,* his tormented mind screamed. He pulled the pin from the grenade, waited until the warrior was within biting distance, and released the handle. The timing ring was set at zero seconds and exploded immediately.

* * *

The grenade went off with Wallace less than half a meter away. Under the blanket, it went unseen to the flight engineer. Wallace, Mendez, and the two closest men on suspended stretchers died instantly in the blast. Shrapnel ploughed into the deck, roof, and Sergeant Allan's back and legs. As Allan was standing directly between the blast and the general, Carstairs suffered no damage from it. However, the shock of the blast wave pushed Allan forward. Both men stumbled out the open hatchway and fell, with Carstairs grabbing Allan in his hands instinctively.

* * *

The grenade shrapnel also severed several main flight control data lines in the ceiling, and the lighter toppled in all three axes. Levin stayed in his seat and tried to regain control to give his people in the back end the best chance to get out. Everything he tried failed to have any impact. By the time he recognized his lighter was too far gone, he looked over his shoulder into the cargo bay and saw no one else moving. Knowing he could do nothing more, he reached for the lever controlling the explosive bolts on his door, but powerful centrifugal forces fought him at every step. He began to pass out from the building gee forces imparted by the spinning and forced his hand forward for one last desperate attempt.

* * *

Carstairs and Allan tumbled as they fell. The general had no idea how high they were, and he could see Allan was unconscious. Purely on instinct, he pulled Allan's rip cord. The small pilot chute ran out on the bridle and caught the rushing air. The main chute was dragged out, and Allan was torn away from Carstairs as the latter continued to fall. Carstairs twisted over so he could see the ground and pulled his own rip cord. His parachute also deployed, and Carstairs found himself at one thousand meters altitude, being pushed back toward Hill 170 to his east by the light wind.

* * *

Jefferson's keen sight saw the bright parachutes first. Her RUK scope was up within a second, and she zoomed the scope in to its limit. Instantly, she could see they were human in shape. At this distance, recognizing a face was impossible, but she saw the bandaged right forearm on the man in the lower parachute, and she only knew one man who had that wound. She wasted no time in bringing attention to it. She sent it out on the shared COMM frequency they were using with the marines. "Herd, this is Owl. I have two parachutes off to the east drifting toward us. Approximately two kilometers away. One appears to be General Carstairs."

* * *

Pratt just happened to be in the Platoon Command Post talking to Lieutenant Pfeiffer when the call came in. A thunderbolt would not have gotten their attention faster. Both officers shared a look, and Pfeiffer simply said, "Go! I'll call in the Fallen Angel." Pratt ran out of the CP area and keyed his radio on the channel for his special forces soldiers only. "Alpha section, this is Six. Everyone, report immediately to the top of trail Bravo with light weapons only. Jefferson, stay where you are and direct us onto the LZ."

* * *

Drawwl spotted the parachutes at the same time. He could see two of them and recognized them instantly as warm bloods. Drawwl could also see they would land quite close to him. He moved from his mud hole with a purpose. Salvation had just been delivered, and he now had a chance of surviving the day if only he could take at least one live tribute back with him.

* * *

Carstairs twisted around and saw the lighter impact on the jungle floor about a kilometer away. The fireball was huge. Even at that distance, he felt the heat of the blast. He looked for more parachutes in the air, but only saw Allan's just above him. The realization that J.P. and everyone else on board were gone hit him hard. The parachute was a simple, non-steerable round version, and the general had no input into where he landed. He grabbed the risers and prepared himself for the landing as the ground came closer and closer. He now struggled to remember his many briefings, before putting his knees slightly bent with feet together. It looked like he would be landing in an open area with no trees to worry about.

* * *

Pratt was running flat out down the eastern trail, followed by his people. He had to jump over the several trip wires they had set out earlier, plus a few natural obstacles on the trail itself further down. The slope of the trail was steep in places, as well. He heard Jefferson on the radio.

"Six, this is Owl. I have a fireball at my ten o'clock. Looks like the lighter. I only see the two parachutes. No enemy activity visible."

Pratt was leaping over fallen trees, navigating down an unfamiliar trail and ducking to avoid the undergrowth. "Roger, Owl, as soon as they... land give me a... bearing and distance to... their position. Get a grid reference for Lieutenant Pfeiffer."

Behind Pratt, his section was trying to keep up. They ran flat out, weapons in their hands, knowing they had a couple of kilometers to cover. Pratt could hear the odd curse as someone tripped, fell, or hit a low-hanging branch. He didn't stop to check behind him; those two men in parachutes were deep in croc country and unprotected.

* * *

Carstairs landed hard. He was expecting grass and landed in a wet, muddy bog. His left ankle twisted on landing, and he fell face-first into the muck, screaming in pain. He never saw Allan land.

* * *

"Six, this is Owl. Target's down, bearing one zero seven degrees at one four five zero meters. Second chute at one one one degrees, one three nine zero meters. Suggest you use one one zero degrees as your bearing."

"Owl, this is Six. Roger." Pratt paused only long enough to set a one hundred ten degree bearing on his gyro-compass. The vertical navigation bar came up displayed on his tactical contact, and he was off running again.

* * *

Jefferson was startled by Lieutenant Pfeiffer and 2nd Lieutenant Wicks coming up from behind. Pfeiffer had binoculars and held them to his face. Wicks only had his 4X rifle scope, which revealed little at this distance. They didn't talk to her, and she concentrated on her job.

* * *

Carstairs pushed himself out of the mud with a loud outburst caused by his twisted ankle embedded in the mud. He rolled on his side and turned, looking for Allan. He saw the canopy of the load master's chute collapsing a short distance away. He had landed in the same field. Carstairs released the chest straps on the harness, and his risers came loose. The general reached down and, using his good hand, pulled his sprained foot out of the mud, screaming at the agony of it. Once free, he started crawling to Allan on his elbows, trying to ignore the pain as best he could to get to the other man.

* * *

Drawwl ran a lot faster than he should have, but gaining a pair of warm bloods was too much incentive to ignore. He had lost sight of the parachutes, but knew roughly where they were. Drawwl was elated. He was back in the trees for the moment, but knew that would change to open bog soon, and his progress would be much faster.

* * *

Carstairs dragged his lame foot behind him as he made his way through the mud. Every time his lower leg hit a clump of grass or uneven ground, he groaned loudly. His breathing was rapid and ragged from the exertion. He eventually came up to Allan's body, which was lying facedown. Carstairs could finally see the multiple grievous wounds on Allan's back and knew he could do little. The general observed the rear of Allan's helmet, which had three small holes with blood running out. Too much blood had been lost, and he had far too many wounds. Allan had probably died in the original blast. Still, he pulled the sergeant's face out of the mud and rolled him onto his side. That caused Carstairs to scream with the effort as his ankle rolled. The general cleared Allan's face of mud and checked the man's pulse, but felt nothing. He opened the prone man's eyelids; his pupils were fixed and unresponsive. Having no first aid supplies, he had done all he could do.

Carstairs pulled on the sergeant's parachute risers and pulled in the white parachute nylon. He covered the body with it and then leaned against the sergeant's legs and examined his own ankle. He could see the thick swelling. He knew enough not to remove the boot, so he tried to relax it as much as possible. Looking over at the dead man, he said, "I'm sorry, sergeant," before he broke down in tears from a combination of frustration, pain, and adrenaline.

* * *

Drawwl exited the woods. He could not see anything, but he did spot a rise in the earth further away where he could get a better view. He made his way there and stood to his full height to see the field.

* * *

Jefferson saw the creature as it climbed the back side of the rise. "Six, this is Owl. Single croc in sight fifty meters to the southeast of the parachutes."

"Roger." Pratt was still several minutes away. He pushed himself forward as rapidly as he could.

* * *

Through teary eyes, Carstairs saw the warrior as it came up the rise to the south. He pulled his sidearm from the mud-covered holster on his thigh and dropped it onto his leg. The general realized that, due to his arm injury, he could not hold the weapon steady in his right hand. If he wanted to shoot, he would have to use his left, which he had never done before. The creature was too far away for a pistol shot. Carstairs willed himself to be patient.

* * *

Drawwl saw the flapping white material and the two prone humans. One was motionless, but the other was alive. It held an insignificant weapon, but was not firing. Drawwl paused, letting his body recover a little. He had exerted himself a little too much getting there, and he fought off cramps. He knew he would have to overcome the two warm bloods with a fast attack. This was a moment to savor.

* * *

Up on the high ground, Jefferson lightly pressed her trigger, gently sending out a beam of laser light into the croc's back. Her scope said 1347, which was forty-seven meters over the stated maximum range of the weapon. The scope did its job and compensated for all of the variables, but the light at the center of the reticule kept blinking red, which was its programmed way of saying *you are nuts to try this*. She ignored it and, instead, used her skills to assess the shot. The only advantage she had was the additional height of the hill she lay on. That would let the bullet fly just a little farther. A piece of blowing parachute nylon near Carstairs told her how hard the wind was blowing and in what direction. She had spent countless times on the range, and her experience told her where to place the cross hairs to compensate for the motion of the target, the long distance, and time of the bullet travel.

Jefferson forced her body to relax. She took in a lungful of air, released half, and held it. She could hear her heartbeat in her ears and timed the shot between beats to minimize any hydraulic deflection caused by blood-flow through her system. Such was her concentration that when the weapon fired, it took even her by surprise.

* * *

Leaving the barrel at eight hundred thirty meters per second, the bullet took almost two seconds to reach the target. It lost a lot of energy on the way and only hit the target due to an unexpected updraft coming up the east side of Hill 170. The bullet struck Drawwl on the top of the skull. A human skull would have shattered, but Drakk'Har skulls have much thicker and denser bone. Instead of penetrating, the bullet bounced off the top of his head, causing a gash and serious concussion, but not death. Drawwl tumbled forward on the earth rise, momentarily stunned.

* * *

Pratt heard the rifle-shot from behind as he ran. He heard Jefferson's voice on the COMM. "Target down. Far side of the earth berm, fifty meters southeast of the chutes." Pratt didn't respond. He was too busy running.

* * *

Carstairs saw the creature fall and had no idea why until the sound of the rifle shot finally made it to his ears several seconds later. Someone had fired from an extreme distance away and scored a miraculous hit! Then the general saw the creature move, and he knew he was not out of the woods yet. Carstairs quickly checked Sergeant Allan's body for additional weapons or a radio, but found neither. When he turned back, the creature was stirring.

* * *

Drawwl tried to raise his arms, but could not. His head rang with a strange sound. His body refused to follow his brain's commands. He concentrated on his right hand and willed his claws to move. They eventually did. He did the same to the left and felt movement there, as well. His back legs started to respond, and he lifted his head to see his quarry. They were still there, wrapped in white material and not moving. Drawwl took a half step forward on all fours. He was in the bog now, and the terrain made it impossible to stand straight up. His claws dug into the muck, and he pulled his body forward. The slippery bog would make his progress much quicker. Drawwl moved ahead, gaining speed with each muscular pull.

* * *

Pratt reached the top of the earth berm and saw both the creature in the boggy grass and the general further back. He knelt and sent a three-round burst toward the creature. Pratt's rapid breathing and adrenaline from the fast run caused the first shots to miss. He forced a deep breath and took careful aim, leading his target. The second group of bullets struck home, lancing into the croc's side. It howled, whipped around to face the new danger with teeth bared menacingly, and charged him. Pratt fired again and hit the creature in the shoulder and chest. The Drakk'Har flailed wildly as it died.

MacPherson was the next to arrive, and he rushed over to the general, skirting the dying warrior. The others arrived quickly thereafter. Pratt turned to the closest man. "Williams, stay on top of this rise, stand watch, and guard the area."

"Yes, sir."

The rest went over to assist the fallen pair. Jacobs scanned Allan with his medi-glove and pronounced him dead before turning his attention back to Carstairs. The general's only new injury was his ankle and a few additional minor scrapes. They helped the general onto his good foot, and Jacobs and MacPherson each took an arm. Carstairs turned to Pratt and asked quietly, "Did anyone else get out?"

"Not that we saw, sir. We only saw two parachutes, and the lighter crashed a kilometer northeast of here. I'm sure Lieutenant Pfeiffer has a CSAR lighter on the way."

Pratt could tell he hadn't convinced the general with his words. The general lowered his head and simply nodded as Jacobs and MacPherson assisted him across the bog.

Pratt and Williams cut away the white shroud of the parachute, gathered it up, and carried Allan's body out in it. At the edge of the trees, they solemnly wrapped Allan's body in the white parachute fabric. They did this in silence. Each was busy working through his own thoughts. Blood soaked through the white nylon in many places. When they were finished, the group began making their way back to Hill 170.

* * *

A CSAR lighter landed unopposed by the still smoking ruin of lighter B1285. The rough position had been determined from the last automatic transmission sent out on the emergency frequency. On the way, the CSAR lighter had seen black smoke rising from the site and had no problems locating it.

B1285 had landed upside down, with the nose dug into the earth. The air frame was tilted nose down at a thirty-degree angle and horribly twisted. Smoke was still issuing from the open hatch, and the harsh smell of burned fuel and plastics filled the air. The CSAR corpsmen rushed into the cargo bay through the hatch with hand-held fire extinguishers, while other marines spread out around the crash site looking for survivors or some signs of life. There were none.

The corpsmen worked quickly and recovered the bodies from the wreck. Even though they had done the same job many times before, they never got used to the smell of burned human flesh. They zipped the recovered corpses into proper rubberized body bags and carried them the short distance to their waiting craft. The body of Captain Levin was the last one extracted.

Once all the remains were aboard the CSAR lighter, a last check was made inside the fallen craft. The corpsmen pulled the B1285 flight recorder out of the instrument rack for later analysis of the crash and what had happened. The case was charred and warped by the internal fire. Nothing else of consequence was found. The corpsmen took bricks of plastic explosive into the flight deck and secured them to the instrument cluster and main flight computer. The last man aboard flipped the toggle engaging the remote detonator circuit, then left B1285 to retreat to the CSAR lighter.

As soon as the last man was aboard, the CSAR lighter dusted off and pulled away from the crash site. Once well clear, the corpsman thumbed the firing switch, and the plastic explosives obliterated the flight deck controls, equipment, and instrumentation. The CSAR pilot set course for Firebase Foxtrot to deliver his grim cargo.

CHAPTER 25 – ASCENT

The return of the special forces section to Hill 170 was greeted in silence. Lieutenant Pfeiffer had sent a small group of marines to the base of the hill with some makeshift stretchers, and the extra manpower made the process of getting Allan and Carstairs up the hill much easier.

Carstairs was placed in the same spot that Mendez had occupied only an hour before, and Jacobs set to removing his boot and binding the ankle. He had a bad sprain, but that was all. No breaks or ligament damage that Jacobs's medi-glove could detect.

Pratt made his way to the platoon CP and reported to Lieutenant Pfeiffer. Pfeiffer was alone and spoke first. "Just heard back from Fleet. No survivors at the crash site, and everyone has been accounted for. I'm sorry."

Pratt nodded once, accepting the bad news. Mendez and White were gone. He never thought of the other crash victims. Those two were his men and his responsibility.

Pfeiffer continued, "You did well getting the general back. The shot your sniper made was unbelievable. She told me the shot was forty-seven meters past the maximum-rated distance of her weapon. You have some damn good people, and I have to admit, I am a little jealous."

This caused Pratt to look up. "Jealous? Why?"

"The way your people just ran after you blindly. I saw them react; they grabbed their gear and ran down into croc territory without hesitation. They trust you implicitly, and I am not sure my marines would have done the same. You have done a tremendous job being here for a week gathering intel, holding this hill against all odds, and finally rescuing the general. I suspect you will need a week on some sunny beach."

Pratt was pensive as he responded, "I suspect a month would be better."

Pfeiffer continued, "We do have some good news. We're getting out of here sooner than expected. We're expecting a trio of troop lighters coming in thirty-five minutes. Your people and the lighter command staff will be coming with us when we dust off—everyone in one go."

Pratt nodded once more, this time with more energy. "Great. I know the troops will enjoy hearing that. We'll provide cover on the LZ and be last aboard."

Pfeiffer nodded back. "Sounds good."

Pratt stood and left the CP area. He stopped a few meters away and drained half the remaining water from his canteen. Then he continued on his way. He had things to organize and, as usual, would mourn later.

* * *

Marshal Kosnov was standing on the observation deck, looking down at Mindon-2. The battle for the planet was winding down, and he had taken some time to shower and change uniforms. Now he regarded the planet's surface, lost in thought. Reports had come in, and damage to the growth facilities was complete. The engineers had systematically crippled key areas of the facility, and all of the major structures had been destroyed or rendered unusable. He did not need to drop nukes on the surface.

Kosnov was sure seeing mushroom clouds from orbit would make a positive impact on crew morale, especially given the nukes the enemy had used at Allen's Rift. However, he tried to look at things objectively wherever possible. Adding a nuclear warhead would accomplish nothing extra from a strategic point of view. At some point, they would be coming back, and how to deal with lingering hard radiation was something human science had yet to accomplish.

Reports of General Carstairs's lighter going down had been hard on Kosnov. They were not friends, but the loss of his only remaining divisional commander was not good news. The follow-up report of his survival and rescue was most welcome. The marshal had already alerted his staff that he wanted to see the related after-action reports personally. The people of the colony worlds needed heroes, and stories of a dramatic rescue always went down well in the press. Public support for the war had never wavered, but Kosnov knew that support was always balanced on a very sharp edge. Heavy casualties and setbacks in the field eroded the most ardent support over time.

The marshal already had his battle staff looking ahead to the battle they would encounter at the edge of the system. Mainframes were running simulations and trying to come up with alternatives that did not involve a toe-to-toe slugfest with a Drakk'Har battle fleet. However, experience had taught Kosnov that was exactly what would happen.

"Sir?" a polite voice interrupted, approaching from behind. His staff intelligence officer stopped a few paces away.

"Commander Tran."

"Sir, one of our deep space probes has detected a single vessel, dreadnought class, entering the system at the far side of the solar system. Course is set for Mindon-2. We estimate they will be well behind us as we withdraw. It is possible they just want to scare us away from the planet."

"Thank you, Commander. It is a good thing we don't scare easily. Detail a drone to keep it under surveillance, and advise me if there are any changes to its course or speed."

"Yes, sir." The commander withdrew, heading back to the elevator.

A dreadnought was the largest vessel the Drakk'Har had, according to all sources. It was certainly the biggest enemy ship seen to that point in combat operations. If they had anything larger, no one wanted to encounter it. It would be comparable to a human cruiser in firepower, but not as maneuverable, thankfully. Being on the far side of the system gave Kosnov a warm and fuzzy feeling. He doubted that the dreadnought would be a concern to him, as the fleet would be leaving on a diametrically different course.

Kosnov put the dreadnought out of his mind and returned to the mission. The withdrawal from operation area Alpha had been successfully completed, and the last of the lighters from that area had just docked. Once the Alpha troops were unloaded, the lighters would have their orbital engines refueled, and they would return to the planet's surface to exfiltrate another set of Marines. The area Bravo dust-off had just started, and, finally, Echo would begin soon. They would only be in orbit for another four hours at most, and then they would be on their way out of the system.

The marshal considered that aspect of their withdrawal. The initial plan was to meet the intercepting force with support from other Federation units. That part of the plan had vanished with the attack at Allen's Rift. Instead, they were heading for an encounter with several Drakk'Har warships unsupported. They would make it through; he had no doubt of that. However, it would not be without losses, and Kosnov had lost enough people on this raid. He needed an alternative.

Kosnov turned to the elevator. His ever-present marine guard was to the right of the elevator door, standing at attention for the commander as he waited. The elevator doors were just cracking open. "Commander Tran."

Tran paused in the open doorway. The optical sensors sensed someone in the doorway and kept the doors open. "Yes, sir."

"Would you ask Commander Collins to join me for a moment please? We need to discuss the exfiltration."

"Certainly, sir." Tran stepped into the elevator, and Kosnov returned to looking out the window.

* * *

Sshaq stood on the bridge of the *Vengeance,* a Krall Class Heavy Destroyer that was the flagship of the imperial fleet. None of the crew remained near Sshaq longer than necessary, including the lord of the vessel. Even by Drakk'Har standards, he looked malevolent. He stood three and a half meters high and bore the healed scars of many violent encounters. The most obvious was an old cut above and below his right eye, where a blade had almost taken his sight. His limbs were twice the thickness of an average Drakk'Har's. Sshaq had been a pit fighter in his youth and rose to become the pre-eminent combatant of his time. His matches would draw Drakk'Har from twenty worlds to witness. However, over time, age had become his most bitter opponent, and in his last matches, the younger fighters had the edge. Pit fighting held a limited future for its participants. They fought until they died or were too seriously injured to continue.

An unexpected offer of employment from a powerful planet lord had given Sshaq an out. He was offered the position of personal bodyguard with many incentives. Deciding that dying in a pit was the lesser of the choices, he accepted. When he withdrew from the sport, he retired undefeated. His planet lord continued to rise in influence and power with Sshaq at his side. Many plots rose to usurp him, but none succeeded. Sshaq would take bribes from the planet lord's enemies, then report the approach to his master and what they wanted. Counterplots were initiated, and Sshaq continued to leave bodies behind him. His master rewarded the loyalty, as it enabled his own power base to grow. When the planet lord ascended to higher office, Sshaq was given a sliver of jade to wear on a neckband. Today, Sshaq was a personal bodyguard to the Emperor of the Drakk'Har Alliance. When he spoke, he did so with the words of his master, and anyone who opposed him never did so a second time.

* * *

Preparations for departure were going smoothly, Wicks thought as he looked around the hilltop. Third squad would be the first aboard the lighters, where they should be the last. Technically, as the LZ was within their squad area of responsibility, they would secure the area until everyone else was aboard. However, Lieutenant Pratt and his SpecOps people were handling that, so once the lighter showed up, they were clear to board. The rest of the squads would fold back from their positions on the ridge. This maintained an ever-shrinking perimeter or collapsing bag defense until the special forces troops themselves were the only ones left. They would then board the transports, dust off, and leave the hilltop to whoever wanted it.

Wicks thought that was unfortunate, as he felt a bond to the special forces section. Having fought side by side with them, it was hard not to. However, niceties were the first thing to be sacrificed in battle, and he knew the surviving divisional command staff and the special forces section were heading to the same troop transport, so it only made sense they had their own lighter. General Carstairs would also be on that lighter so he could get back to the fleet ASAP.

"Has the general talked to you about Perkins, sir?"

"No, nothing. Is there a problem?" Lieutenant Pfeiffer turned to face him.

"No, sir, but the general would like him fast tracked for a Silver Star on return to Fleet. General Carstairs said I should let you know of his personal interest."

"Thank you. I'll pass that on. Oh, by the way. Your man Belliveau made it up to Fleet and the reports are positive for his recovery."

"That's good news, sir. I'll pass that on."

The sound of an approaching lighter cut off any further conversation. Pfeiffer dismissed Wicks, and the 2nd lieutenant headed off to join his squad.

* * *

Blake had third squad ready to go by the time Wicks arrived. Wicks quickly informed Blake about Belliveau and got a grin and satisfied nod in return. The conversation was short-lived as blowing debris from the downdraft of the landing lighter forced them to turn their backs on the landing zone.

The troop lighter landed in the cleared area on the secondary hilltop, and the side hatch opened instantly. The load master tossed out parachute harnesses, and Blake distributed them to his people. No one wasted time getting into them. Once they were ready, the load master gave an OK signal, and third squad entered. The first pair of marines carried General Carstairs under their arms as he hopped aboard. They gave him the seat closest to the hatch and moved into their own seats. The load master gave the general a parachute pack and harness and carefully assisted him into it while giving him the standard briefing.

The second squad officer and his people arrived shortly afterwards, having just pulled back from their defensive lines. Harnesses were also issued to them. Second squad took the opposite half of the lighter. As soon as those troops were belted in, the engine noise increased dramatically, and the lighter rose off the ground, taking both squads skyward.

The load master handed Wicks and General Carstairs a headset so they could communicate on the internal COMMs. They were the only spares aboard, so the second squad officer had to go without one. Wicks could hear the flight crew completing their checklists as vertical flight slowly transitioned to forward motion.

Wicks could hear the pilot speaking as more power was applied to the engines. "Lift-off checklist complete. Crew, prepare for orbital insertion burn."

The increasing engine power caused a violent shaking in the lighter. Wicks looked over his people. They all looked calm; the vibration meant they were going home.

"Deploy countermeasures," the pilot said. More minor bumps were felt as flares and RADAR jammers were ejected. Wicks could see Carstairs looking uncomfortable and attributed it to his injuries.

"Countermeasures away, sir," the female flight engineer replied flatly in a Scottish brogue.

The lighter continued upwards steadily. Wicks could feel the lighter's acceleration. After several minutes, the nose rose even more sharply, and everyone grabbed hold of whatever they could, as they knew from many flights what was coming next.

The pilot's voice came over the COMM unit. "Orbital insertion burn in three. Two. One. Ignition."

Everyone was jerked in their seat as the motor on the back of the lighter kicked in. Raw power surged out the back end of the orbital booster engine as the pilot pulled the lighter nose even higher to gain altitude.

"Cut aero-engines," the pilot said as soon as the rocket motor had ignited.

It took eight minutes and forty-five seconds before the engine consumed the last of the solid fuel and died of its own accord. The craft fell silent, the vibration went to almost nothing and everyone applauded. No one knew the origin of the tradition, but no one cared. They had survived, and that was all that mattered. Everyone on board could feel they were in zero gee, but no one was even tempted to undo their restraints with a general on board. The lighter was now in a low orbit, and the pilot used its maneuvering thrusters to move higher to rendezvous with the fleet.

* * *

Back on Hill 170, Pratt had watched the second lighter disappear skyward, carrying Lieutenant Pfeiffer and the last of his platoon. His people were getting on the last lighter, along with the divisional command staff. The sound of the wrecked command lighter being destroyed in a controlled explosion reached him, and the vibrations tickled the soles of his feet. He checked his timepiece and saw that was right on schedule.

The parachute harness he wore was uncomfortable, but after today's experience, he would never question its need again. Pratt stood outside the hatch entrance and visually verified that each of his people boarded the lighter. No one would be left behind in this wet hell.

Pratt would remember Mindon-2 for a long time. This planet was a place where he had lost good people and discovered that his courage was not unlimited. He had been forced to face his own limitations and had emerged changed by the experience. Whether that change was for the better or worse, he could not state objectively. That would only become obvious with the passage of time. He would not resign his commission, he had already decided. While he might be flawed, he had been forced to recognize he was still an effective officer and leader. His people's loyalty showed that, and after a fashion, he was grateful that the general had forced him to reflect.

MacPherson was about to pass Pratt, and he realized he had not given him an answer about him joining his unit. Unable to speak over the roar of the engines, he tapped the staff sergeant on the shoulder. MacPherson stopped, turned, and looked at him. Pratt reached up and grabbed a small cloth patch on the upper right arm of his fatigue shirt with the fingers of his left hand and pulled on it sharply, tearing away the stitching.

Pratt looked down at the cloth badge in his hand. The fabric had various shades of embroidered green thread and showed a symbol of two daggers crossed at mid blade with the tips pointing up. The daggers rested on the outline of a shield. Under the symbol it said, '121 SPECFOR,' with the banner underneath stating *Fortes Fortuna Juvat*. Pratt handed it to MacPherson with his left hand and took his right in a handshake. The newest member of his unit looked down on the cloth patch, smiled, nodded with satisfaction, and boarded the lighter.

Jefferson was second to last to board, clearing the live round from her weapon at the last possible second. Pratt knew she had earned her sergeant's stripes and a decoration from this operation, but gave no outward indication of that.

With all of his people accounted for, Pratt looked out on the surrounding jungle and made sure he had not forgotten anything. If nothing else, this fight against the Drakk'Har had just shown he was a normal human being, and that was not such a bad thing, he decided. Pratt took one last disdainful look at the pink sky and jungle around him, then boarded the lighter.

His was the last human boot to touch Mindon-2.

The hatch closed, and the lighter dusted off. Twelve minutes later, they were all applauding in orbit.

CHAPTER 26 – EXFILTRATION

As soon as the last lighter had sealed its airlock to their troop transport, the fleet fired its main engines and started to move away from Mindon-2. Several ships deployed OID mines and intelligence stealth satellites in their wake.

The ships rendezvoused as they came up from their various orbits and reformed into a defensive wedge formation. This took time, even though the various captains were well-versed in the maneuver. No one wanted a collision. Ship captains tended to be removed from their positions after ramming another vessel, however inadvertently.

The cruisers formed the front of the formation with the transports and tenders falling in behind. A reconnaissance ship flanked each side of the formation, and the third flew beside the command ship at the rear of the formation in reserve.

The transit away from Mindon-2 was unremarkable. Kosnov ordered an active scan on all bands as they proceeded through the system. No opposition was detected, except for the dreadnought-class ship which was well behind them, decelerating and not a viable threat.

"Commander Collins, secure LADAR and maintain full EM sweeps on all other frequencies."

"Yes, sir." The Australian's hands flew over displays and menu prompts to follow the order.

Kosnov knew the electromagnetic radiations would give a better chance to detect incoming ships and drones than a passive mode. The down side was the enemy could use those same radiations to track them. That was fine with him, as he *wanted* them to know where he was, at least in the short term.

"Set course for exfiltration coordinates. All ships to accelerate to standard cruising speed," Kosnov ordered.

* * *

Staff Sergeant Blake had everyone strip and clean their weapons as soon as they were in their assigned living quarters. Blake collected all unexpended ammunition, grenades, and anything else dangerous and detailed Perkins to sort it into the proper containers. The only weapon each soldier kept was their bayonet, which they were expected to take care of.

Blake handed out new field dressings to those in the squad that had used them. He also made a list of all broken, lost, and damaged gear. Everything from weapon slings to boot laces that needed to be replaced were his responsibility. Blake would go to stores later that day and replace those items. The staff sergeant would also have a case of fresh batteries for all radios and flashlights, but those would be kept in his care until just before the next operation.

It had been the usual post-operation atmosphere. Little talk and lots of activity to keep people busy. Once the weapons were accepted into the weapons locker and secured, the marines had one last responsibility. Each person on the squad made a verbal declaration to the sergeant that they had no weapons, explosives, or ammunition in their possession, and they were dismissed from their duty.

Several of them grabbed showers while the rest went straight to their bunks, stripped off the dirty uniforms, pulled the privacy curtains closed, and went to sleep. Those that took showers also headed to their bunks, and within fifteen minutes, snores resounded through the room.

* * *

Second Lieutenant Wicks had spent his first hour and forty-five minutes on board the transport supervising the proper accounting and storage of the squad's weapons and equipment.

Wicks had cleaned his weapons efficiently and checked them into the weapons locker himself. The marine corporal in charge of the locker double-checked both weapons were unloaded and clean before accepting them. The rifle was placed into a wall rack and the pistol placed into a cut foam drawer with several others. The barcodes embedded in the gun metal were scanned. The serial numbers of the weapons, the time code, and name of the duty corporal were all entered into electronic logs.

"That's the last of your squad weapons, sir. All accounted for."

Wicks nodded in return. He was relieved. A missing weapon necessitated an investigation, followed by at least two hours of filling in endless paperwork, affidavits, and forms. Satisfied that all the weapons had been accounted for, Wicks entered a stairwell and walked two decks down. This area of the transport had been designated as medical quarters, and he spoke with the duty nurse, who gave him directions.

Wicks walked through three hatchways and turned left as instructed by the painted markings on the bulkheads. The only sound he could hear was the hum of air conditioning and the odd heartbeat monitor.

Wicks found the right compartment and entered. This room had housed a couple of combat squads on the way to Mindon-2. Now it held lightly wounded men. Each bunk had panels removed on the sides and back of the bunks to reveal oxygen, vacuum pumps, and other medical instruments. This room was reserved for male patients, and each had a heart monitor attached to his chest, but that was the only thing they had in common. Some had plasma, blood, or other medicinal IVs inserted in their arms. A few had casts, bandages, or some exotic device attached to them, depending on the severity of their wounds. Many were sleeping or resting. A few looked at him as he entered.

Wicks spotted Belliveau immediately. The lance corporal had a thick white bandage wrapped around his head. He was a lot cleaner than the last time the officer had seen him. The patient was on the lowest bunk.

Belliveau saw Wicks approach and tried to sit up. Wicks held up his hand and said immediately, "As you were, Belliveau. How are you feeling?" Wicks went down on one knee so their faces were level.

Belliveau relaxed back onto his pillow. He was smiling at seeing his officer. "Good morning, L-T. I'm doing fine. The doc says I'll be up in a few days. They're keeping me here as a precaution only because of the head wound. Apart from a pounding headache, I feel fine."

"Excellent. Until then, lay back and rest. I'm sure the others will be down to see you as soon as they get squared away. Can I get you anything?" A corpsman entered the compartment behind Wicks as he was talking.

"No, sir, they're taking good care of me. They have someone come through twice a day with books and vids. Plus, as a bonus, the nurses are cute," Belliveau said with a smile while pointing to the side.

Wicks looked over and saw a marine in fatigues, with a stethoscope over his shoulders, checking a screen. The corpsman looked like he could bench-press a hundred fifty kilos. Wicks laughed and turned back to Belliveau.

"Sir, how's everyone else? Did everyone else make it?" Belliveau asked seriously.

Wicks paused. The amusement of the joke faded from his face quickly. He never knew how to say things like this. "Cole was killed yesterday during an assault on Hill 170."

"Oh," was all Belliveau responded. A cloud appeared on his face.

"Look, Belliveau, you get better, and I'll see you in a few days. If you need anything, make sure you let me know." Wicks briefly touched the wounded man's shoulder.

"Yes, sir. Thank you, sir. Say hi to everyone for me, will you?"

"Of course," Wicks said while standing. "See you soon."

Wicks left the room quickly, as he was starting to feel the loss of LCPL Cole. The officer knew he needed to sleep for a while, but he had one more duty to fulfill before he could even think about it. Wicks went back up two levels and walked past his compartment. He went down the corridor to the Regimental Orderly Room and spoke with the master sergeant on duty. The NCO directed him to a cubicle off to the right of the room. It had a data terminal and basic office supplies. Wicks sat down in front of the keyboard and waited. The master sergeant brought Wicks a single-page printout soon afterwards. Contact information for Lance Corporal Cole's next of kin was on it.

"Here you are, sir. There are some prepared form letters in the public folders under 'Casualty.'"

"Thank you, Master Sergeant. I'll let you know when I am done."

"Yes, sir," he said, bracing to attention before withdrawing.

Wicks keyed his access number and password into the keyboard. Then he opened up a word processor. A blank page opened, and the cursor blinked regularly. He knew the family would be officially notified long before his letter arrived, and as a result, he did not even think of using a form letter. He glanced over the information he had been given:

Name: Richard Albert Cole (LCPL)
Service Number T72006529
Father: Morgan David Cole
Location: Deceased
Mother: Cynthia Doris Cole (née Paulson)
Location: Mars – Syria Planum Colony, 217 Bradley Prospect, Camerontown 007-99843

Wicks stared at the screen for a long time. Not knowing what to say, he simply started typing and the words came forth of their own accord.

Dear Mrs. Cole,

Richard was one of the finest young men in my unit. He was dependable, responsible, and never failed to support his squad mates. I cannot think of a single bad thing that anyone ever said about him. As I think back, I remember his smile and sense of humor which never failed to ease tensions on our operations.

I had the honor of presenting him with his promotion to Lance Corporal last July. He earned the rank because of hard work and dedication. When I handed him his stripes, he mentioned how proud you would be. I was honored to serve with him. Richard was a valued member of my team and will be both missed and remembered.

I know that these words are insufficient consolation for your loss. I cannot tell you of the circumstances we were involved in, but I hope you can take heart in knowing that he was a good soldier who died bravely assisting those in desperate need.

Please accept my condolences for your loss.

Sincerely,
2nd Lieutenant Carleton Wicks
Third Squad – Officer Commanding

Wicks saved the document, logged off the terminal, and checked out with the master sergeant. He headed back to his quarters feeling drained and desperately needing many hours of sleep.

* * *

Sshaq received news that sensors had detected the warm blood fleet departing the orbit of Mindon-2. Sensors on the *Vengeance* had detected their powerful signals and tracked them easily. They were reported to be heading away from the

Drakk'Har world and toward the edge of the system. Sshaq spoke to the lord of the vessel, "Send a message pod to Kraasis. Give him the position, speed, and heading of the warm blood cowards. They are not to escape after defiling one of our worlds."

"Immediately, Lord Sshaq." The ship lord retreated.

Sshaq did not concern himself with the warm bloods. They were the responsibility of others. His destination was Mindon-2. The lord of the *Vengeance* would have fought through the warm bloods and even sacrificed himself and his ship to get Sshaq and his small entourage onto the surface of the world, for such was the wish of the emperor. The *Vengeance* proceeded on its course to Mindon-2.

* * *

Over many hours, Fleet Nine accelerated slowly. It continued to maintain its course to the edge of the Mindon system. Once the fleet was well past the asteroid belt, a series of Ferret Hunter/Killer drones were released into space; one for each ship in the formation. All were in passive mode and controlled by technicians on several ships. They took position in front of the fleet and established a crude wedge formation that closely mimicked the present layout of the fleet.

The timetable had been worked out to the second in advance. One of the cruisers, the *Stalingrad,* shut down its active sensors on schedule, and one of the Ferret drones turned its sensors on, actively searching for targets. Minutes later, the *J. Michael Straczynski* shut down its electronics, and another Ferret began transmitting soon after. This process continued until all of the ships' sensors were turned off and all of the drones were actively broadcasting detection beams. *Aristotle* was the last vessel to turn off active sensors. To anyone monitoring the signals, they saw the same number of active sensors as before.

"Sir, all Ferrets are actively broadcasting, and all fleet ships are now under EMCON. Drone course set to edge of solar system as ordered. Fleet will be commencing turn to new course on radial 1-9-4-7 in one minute on my mark," Collins at the Tactics (Space) board reported. "Standby and... Mark."

"Very good, Commander," Kosnov replied.

Fleet Nine was well past any surviving sensors in the asteroid belt and could now start their deception. The enemy knew the position of the fleet from the active scanning it had been doing. Their course had been consistent since they had left Mindon-2. Now those signals were being duplicated by the Ferret drones still on the original course. Meanwhile, the fleet began to make a hard right-hand turn without advertising its location. *We are letting the enemy see exactly what they expect to see*, thought the marshal, smiling inwardly.

* * *

A day later, Lord Krassis and his battle fleet of twelve warships dropped into reality on the edge of the Mindon system. Luckily, the message pod from the lord of the *Vengeance* containing the last known location and course of the warm blood fleet had arrived only moments before their departure. Krassis was able to use that information to adjust his destination slightly. None of his ships used active sensors. Krassis wanted surprise on his side.

"Report!" Krassis demanded of his detection specialist.

"Lord, the warm blood fleet approaches us directly. Speed consistent at 3.2 of 6. They are outside of active detection range, and their position is within parameters."

Krassis felt the surge of battle approaching. "Prepare for battle. Proceed into the system, direct intercept course. No active detection without my express order."

"Yes, Lord."

* * *

The *Vengeance* entered high orbit over Mindon-2. The lord of the emperor's flagship was no fool and knew there would be traps left behind. He sent a messenger to request Sshaq come to the bridge. The emperor's bodyguard arrived soon after, ignoring the lord of the vessel.

"What is the location of the planet lord?" Sshaq asked of the senior communications technician.

"Lord, he was expected to be within the holdings of Borrk, but we've just received a transmission from Mgarnew's holding that the planet lord is there. He bids you welcome to his world and inquires how he may serve."

"Inform him he's to be at the landing field to greet us," Sshaq demanded. He turned to another crew member. "Prepare the shuttle for immediate launch, and command the rest of the Touched to meet me there."

"Yes, lord, immediately!"

* * *

When the active sensors of the Ferret drones detected the incoming Drakk'Har fleet, internal timers activated. The delay was simple. The Federation did not want the enemy to know just how sensitive their detection beams were. After a preset time, the sensors locked onto the enemy fleet. They then simulated a weapons lock, which gave them exact speed and direction of the enemy vessels. As soon as they had that information, they accelerated as fast as possible, adjusting their course slightly to intercept. They also started jamming on all known Drakk'Har frequencies.

* * *

"Lord, incoming warm blood fleet has locked onto us! They're accelerating and on intercept headings. Heavy jamming. I now show multiple targets inbound."

Krassis considered this for a moment and decided he had no reason to stay hidden any longer. "Engage countermeasures. Start active scans, all sensors, maximum power! Target their lead ships, and fire!"

The Drakk'Har fired their weapons at the phantoms on their screens and hit nothing. As the drones got closer, their jamming was somewhat more effective, but the raw power the Drakk'Har fleet was emitting started to cut through the noise, and several of the fake targets disappeared off the sensor screens. The weapons of the Drakk'Har were reoriented, and they fired again. This time, a few of the drones were hit and vanished in clouds of metal and fuel vapor. The majority continued on. Krassis continued to fire, thinking he was engaging capital ships.

"Lord, sensors show warm blood vessels on collision courses with our ships. Optical sensors show no vessels approaching."

"What?" Then Krassis realized what was happening and broadcast to the fleet. "Enemy missiles approaching. All vessels, defensive fire!"

The Drakk'Har fleet sent up a wall of intense fire to greet the drones. Many of the drones were hit, but the deception worked long enough to gain rewards. Eleven drones made it through, and nine of those made direct hits on Drakk'Har warships. The drones carried no warheads, but moving at a high percentage of the speed of light gave them considerable kinetic energy. They lanced through armor and decking, causing terrible damage. Krassis's vessel took no damage; five others did. One unlucky warship was hit by three drones, and it tumbled, on fire, into the vacuum of space. It exploded brilliantly several minutes later. Three of the struck vessels lost most of their atmosphere and crews to vacuum.

As reports of the damage came in, Krassis was livid and wanted revenge. "Full sensor sweep. I want the ships that fired those missiles destroyed!"

Several seconds passed before the detection specialist reported, "Lord, we have no targets in sensor range."

Krassis was left alone with his fury in the vacuum of space.

* * *

Planet Lord Tlish stood dutifully at the base of the ramp of the recently landed shuttle. The noxious fumes of spent fuel from the engines had dissipated quickly. The group was assembled on one of the few places on the landing field that did not have a crater. Mgarnew stood with a dozen surviving troops carrying ceremonial pikes and forming a crude Guard of Honor. Tlish was heartened to hear an emissary of the emperor was arriving. Now, his plans could proceed.

Sshaq descended the ramp flanked by three other large Drakk'Har. Each of them had a sliver of jade on his neckband along with the usual ceramic blade. Tlish noted they also had Imperial tattoos on their left shoulders designating their position. They were "Touched" of the emperor's claw and his personal soldiers and bodyguards. All were larger than average, which spoke of their age and experience, and all had some form of battle scarring, though none more than the leader. Tlish recognized Sshaq, but felt no apprehension. On this world, Tlish now outranked him.

* * *

Sshaq could see the larger Drakk'Har was clearly in charge, but he had met Slassh on several occasions, and this was obviously not him. None of the Drakk'Har before him wore jade. "Who are you?"

Tlish spoke. "Lord, I am Tlish, Planet Lord of this world. I welco—"

Sshaq interrupted, "Where is Slassh?"

"Lord, Slassh died in the battle with the warm bloods. His cowardice and indecision failed to keep this world safe, and as you can see, the damage was extensive. He paid for his many crimes with his life, just as we suffered for his incompetence. As his second, I rule here now as planet lord."

Sshaq considered this for a moment and decided his orders could still be carried out. He nodded to the Touched, and they moved around Tlish.

As the Touched surrounded Tlish, his voice had shifted from confident to confused. "What are you doing?"

The three Touched grabbed Tlish simultaneously. They pressed him down onto his knees and held him there forcefully, his arms held straight out to his sides. They had done this many times before. Mgarnew backed away quickly to a respectable distance and watched.

"I command you to release me! I'm the planet lord of this system, and you will release me NOW!" Tlish was on the edge of hysterics and looking around wildly.

"You say you're the planet lord of this world?" Sshaq queried quietly.

"Yes! I rule here; this is *my* domain!" Tlish screamed.

"I was given one order by the emperor." Sshaq quoted directly, "'Deliver the head of the Mindon-2 Planet Lord to me.'"

The expression on Tlish's face contorted in disbelief. "He meant Slassh! He was planet lord when the order was given! It's Slassh's head you want. Not mine! He was the planet lord that destroyed this world! He's the one who should be punished! I am destined to rebuild this world greater than it ever was! Take his head, and release me. I can make you richer than you can imagine!"

Sshaq slowly pulled the razor edged ceramic blade from his belt. He considered it intently, turning it in front of his scarred eye, looking at the freshly sharpened edge and feeling the weight as if for the first time. He looked at Tlish without mercy and simply said, "The emperor's order was quite clear." Sshaq advanced on the helpless Drakk'Har slowly.

"*No!*" Tlish howled for the last time.

* * *

Kaaw had traveled back to Borrk's former holdings alone from his bunker, leaving his staff to deal with rebuilding the planet's defenses. His recent promotion to Planetary Defense Commander under Tlish gave each of them a boost in importance as well. Kaaw was staggered by the volume of work to do. It would take many sun rotations, maybe ten or more of effort. Not only did he need to rebuild, he had to make it considerably better than before.

The defenses were just one of his concerns. Kaaw wanted much more robust communications established, as well. A weapon without the knowledge of where to fire it was useless in his opinion. One of the lessons learned in this conflict was that they needed more hidden landlines for secure communication—at least three backups per run, all going by different routes. Radio communications were interrupted, intercepted, targeted, or jammed too easily. The landlines were the best option, although several intermediate communication posts would have to be established as well, to route messages efficiently on a planetary scale.

Kaaw had already decided to build his main operations center in new bunkers on Brawnik's Hump. Keeping away from the main holdings was only one of his ideas. Engineers were already starting to survey the ground and outline the positions of tunnels. The distance was too far to link with tunnels in the main town directly, but he could create swimming tunnels to the river Skad which would lead to the complex indirectly. Kaaw would have to visit each production facility and make similar arrangements. The amount of work ahead of him was almost unimaginable.

Off in the distance, Kaaw observed a shuttle land just outside of Borrk's former holdings. He ignored it; he had far too much work to do, and he did not have time to speculate about who it carried. Soon after, a messenger came to get him. He had obviously traveled quickly and was cramping badly from the over-exertion. He fell to Kaaw's feet in the position of submission.

"Lord, the Touched have arrived to speak with you at the landing pad. They command you to appear before them immediately." His voice shook with fear.

Without knowing the reason why an imperial emissary would want to see him, Kaaw was understandably nervous. He made his way through the town heading to the landing pad, but took his time. If this was going to be his last walk, he wanted to enjoy it. He could see the smoke rising around him from the destroyed facilities. Kaaw thought it was ludicrously simple to figure out why the Touched were here. He had been in charge of protecting the growth facilities, and he had failed. The destruction of the imperial shipbuilding facilities had been total, and he was being called to pay the price for that failure. Borrk had already died for that reason, and as his anti-air commander, he was just as culpable. He looked over the devastation and the several bodies left rotting in the street as he moved past. He passed several workers who had emerged from their hiding places and were beginning to clear roads and repair damage. In the end, he decided he regretted nothing. He had done his best, and damn the barbarian animals for having such efficient weaponry.

In the latter part of his walk, the landed shuttle came into view. The ramp was down, and three large Drakk'Har wearing jade slivers were speaking amongst themselves at the bottom of it. Kaaw knew the rarity of jade. It indicated imperial authority, and those who wore it were both feared and respected. As Kaaw came up to the shuttle, he had accepted his demise as inevitable. He was a Drakk'Har warrior, and this was the price that he knew he might have to pay one day. He decided he would not run, he would not beg, and he would not grovel. They could take his life, but not his pride. It started to rain lightly as he made his way to the small group. They quieted at his approach and turned to face him.

The obvious leader of the Touched spoke without preamble as he stopped before them. "You are Kaaw?"

"Yes, Lord." He bowed respectfully with his palms out, but never took his sight off the larger Drakk'Har.

"I am Sshaq, Touched of the emperor's claw. You will take me to Slassh," He commanded flatly.

Confused, Kaaw said nothing. The small group went into the town and wordlessly went below ground via a hidden portal. A series of cross-connected tunnels eventually led to the command bunker of the planet lord. Slassh's body still lay where it fell. His blade and scabbard were missing, but the neckband was still in place. Sshaq bent down and carefully removed it. Kaaw waited patiently and hoped the Touched had what they wanted. Being in the presence of the Touched was nervewracking.

"Lead us back to our shuttle, Kaaw. We are done here," Sshaq said.

The group made their way back by the reciprocal route and emerged in the town. On their way to the landing field, they passed several destroyed buildings, many of which were still smoking. The chaotic smell of burned petrochemicals and seared growths was almost too much to bear. Kaaw's trepidation rose the longer he was near the Touched. He had already accepted his failure, but this second exposure to the destruction shook his resolve to remain brave.

When they reached the shuttle, Sshaq turned and faced Kaaw. Sshaq stared at him silently for some time. "By order of the Imperium, Tlish is no more. As his second, this world and all who dwell upon it are now under your claw. This world needs to be rebuilt and producing warships and material in minimal time. Any more warm blood damage shall be your responsibility from this point forward. The emperor expects regular reports and tribute. You are to take and wear this piece of jade touched by the claw of the emperor himself as a symbol of your rule. Hail, Planet Lord Kaaw."

Sshaq handed the neckband to Kaaw.

Kaaw opened his mouth and tried to form words, but nothing emerged. What could he say? The gravity of the moment completely overwhelmed him. *How? Why? Could this be true?*

Before climbing up the ramp of their shuttle, Sshaq and the rest of the Touched all bowed slightly to Kaaw with their palms open and facing him as a show of respect. On this world, he was now, effectively, their superior. The shuttle access hatch slid closed slowly, and after a few moments, the engines wound up. The shuttle departed the landing field and made its way up into space for a rendezvous with the *Vengeance* and a return trip back to the imperial court.

The engine exhaust forced Kaaw to backpedal several steps to get away from the searing temperatures. After it had gone, he absorbed what had just happened. In one planet rotation, he had risen from being a regional air defense commander to planetary defense commander to planet lord. No plots, no plans, no conspiracies; he had done nothing for this to happen. Expecting death, he had instead been given a gift beyond words.

Planet Lord Kaaw was left standing alone on the shattered landing field. He stared at the jade necklace held loosely in his claws. Droplets of rain water fell from the tip as the shock of the moment pinned him in place.

* * *

"Marshal, all ships report they are clear of the Hawking zone. Passive sensors are clear. No enemy ships within detection range. We may transition into hyperspace at any time," Commander Collins reported from his Tactics (Space) position.

"Very well, Mr. Collins. Target coordinates are Wolf 359. Jump the fleet at your discretion," Kosnov replied.

"Yes, sir." Collins's hands flew over his console.

Kosnov knew there would be a week-long medical quarantine before anyone would be allowed onto the station. That was in case something picked up on Mindon-2 proved unhealthy to the human species. Fortunately, most of that time would be spent in transit back to Wolf 359. Kosnov would compensate for the rest of the time by transiting through the Wolf system slowly and arrive with the week well behind them, so everyone could do their shore leave immediately.

"Hyperspace coordinates set fleet wide. All ships reporting green status for jump. Gravity meters are clear. Jumping in three. Two. One. Mark."

Command Space Fleet Nine vanished from real space.

AUTHOR'S AFTERWORD

Predation was the first novel I wrote and shall always be my favorite. The novel was written during traumatic times in my life, when negative emotions and thoughts were frequent. Using that negativity to drive the actions of the Drakk'Har was a productive way to keep them from interfering with my day. I never consciously intended this novel to be cathartic, but that is exactly what it turned out to be. In hindsight, writing was the best way to deal with things at that time. It is not the destination; it is the journey.

I doubt I could write *Predation* today. My life has evolved, and I find myself in much better circumstances. Should that ever change, I might sit down and write another Drakk'Har story, but don't hold your breath waiting for it. Vegas wouldn't touch those odds.

Don't worry. I have many other stories to tell.

I would like to thank Lynn McNamee and her staff at Red Adept Publishing for their professional support, advice, and welcoming nature. Working with them, on this and other projects, has been educational, interesting, and above all, fun. True professionals always make your life easier. Thank you everyone.

http://redadeptpublishing.com

Thank you for supporting my work! Please feel free to leave a review where you purchased the book to let other readers know what you think.

My website and the latest news on my other projects can be found here:

http://sjparkinson.com